SANDRA BROWN

Three Complete Novels in One Volume

HEAVEN'S PRICE
BREAKFAST IN BED
SEND NO FLOWERS

WINGS BOOKS
NEW YORK

Originally published in three separate volumes by Bantam Books under the titles:

Heaven's Price copyright © 1983 by Sandra Brown
Breakfast in Bed copyright © 1983 by Sandra Brown
Send No Flowers copyright © 1984 by Sandra Brown

This edition contains the complete and unabridged texts of the original editions.

This 2007 edition is published by Wings Books, an imprint of Random House Value Publishing, by arrangement with Bantam Books, divisions of Random House, Inc., New York.

Wings Books is a registered trademark and the colophon is a trademark of Random House, Inc.

Random House
New York • Toronto • London • Sydney • Auckland
www.valuebooks.com

Printed and bound in the United States of America.

A catalog record for this title is available from the Library of Congress.

ISBN: 978-0-517-22953-8

10 9 8 7 6 5 4

CONTENTS

HEAVEN'S PRICE

Chapter 1

Blair carted the last box up the top three stairs. *Squeezing* herself between it and the jamb, she maneuvered it through the door and dropped it down on top of two others piled just inside the door. Her arms quivered from the exertion. Her legs ached.

"Thank heaven that's the last one," she said to herself on an exhalation that escaped her lips slowly and leisurely. With rigid arms she braced herself over the top of the box and tried to catch her breath. When she straightened, she noticed the tightness of the muscles in her lower back and groaned. Was there any part of her body that didn't ache?

Glancing down at her wristwatch, her lips thinned

with irritation. She had called the YMCA over two hours ago and asked them to send over a masseur. Not having changed residences in more than eight years, she had forgotten how physically exhausting moving could be. A massage was the most relaxing thing she could think of. Since her telephone hadn't been installed yet, she had driven to the nearest service station and used the pay phone. The receptionist who answered the Y's telephone had assured her that someone would be sent over within an hour.

"So much for efficiency," she muttered to herself, whisking off the bandana-print scarf she had tied around her long dark hair. It tumbled to the middle of her back like a bolt of satin being unrolled. If the staff of the YMCA typified the pace of life in this provincial backwater town, she'd be a raving maniac in a week.

She gazed around the three-room apartment that would be her home for the next six months. It didn't look like much now with boxes and bundles heaped on its hardwood floors, but with a little imagination, she hoped she could make it at least livable. Pam had assured her that it was the best and most private place in town, ". . . unless you want to live in one of those sterile apartment complexes, which I'm sure you don't," she had added.

Upon arrival from the city to the small town on the Atlantic side of Long Island where her friend Pam Delgado had moved several years ago, Blair had to admit that living in a garage apartment behind a

Victorian house on a quiet, tree-shaded street had more appeal than living in a concrete cracker box.

She skirted the maze of boxes as she made her way to the small kitchen on the other side of the large room that served as both living and sleeping area. She had been pleased to see that the refrigerator was no more than two decades old and had a bucket inside the freezing compartment in which to empty ice trays. Taking out a few cubes, she plunked them into a tall glass she'd managed to find earlier and popped off the top of a diet soda can. Just as it was foaming over the ice, someone knocked on the door.

"Wouldn't you know it," she grumbled. Taking a sip of the not yet cold drink, she weaved her way through the boxes again and pulled open the door.

"It's about time," she said querulously.

"I beg your pardon," the man on the doorstep said.

Blair's green eyes were level with a massive chest and she had to lift them a considerable distance to greet the most intriguing pair of eyes she'd ever encountered. Startlingly blue, they were surrounded by thick, curling lashes, dark at the lashline and gilded at the tips. A network of weblike lines, white against darkly tanned skin, extended from the outer corners of his eyes to fade into his temples. Brows well defined, but thick, arched over the eyes that were examining her as closely as she was him.

To avoid that careful scrutiny, she quickly lowered her eyes, mistakenly thinking that would be the safest thing to do. She wasn't prepared for them coming to rest on a golden-brown mustache, the exact color of the brows that framed his eyes. The mustache curved over a wide, sensuous mouth. Beneath sculptured lips was a strong, firm chin with a vertical dent carved into its center. She avoided analyzing that too, and lifted her eyes to take in a well-designed nose, slightly concave cheeks, and assertive cheekbones, which brought her back to those eyes. They hadn't wavered from her face.

All in all, it was the most marvelous assembly of masculine features Blair had ever seen. She felt like stammering, but somehow managed not to when she demanded, "Didn't anyone tell you how to get here?"

He shook the head that was capped with blond wavy hair, slightly silvered at the temples. "No."

"Well, it's no wonder you're over an hour late. None of the streets in this town are marked with signs," she said crossly. Stepping aside, she said, "Come on in. I need you more now than I did when I called."

He stepped through the door and she closed it behind him to conserve the air that flowed from the one-window air-conditioning unit that cooled the entire apartment. He hadn't brought any equipment in with him, only a body that would intimidate the most fearsome professional football lineman.

Clad in white shorts and a navy-blue T-shirt, the man looked marvelous. Blair could see that the tan that bronzed his face covered the rest of him, as did that fine curly golden hair. His legs were long and lean, but muscles rippled in his calves and thighs as he made slow progress around the first boxes blocking his path. Blair excused her interest in those muscles as purely professional. She was well acquainted with every muscle of the human body, its use, and how to treat it.

"Didn't you bring a portable bed or table or anything with you?" she asked.

He stopped suddenly and turned around to face her. "No."

She sighed. "It's just as well. I don't know where we would have put it. I've already padded the kitchen table with a quilt. Will that be all right?" He turned his head to eye the table dubiously. "I haven't made up the bed in the sofa yet and didn't want to plow through all these boxes looking for linens. I need you right now. Do you mind doing it on the kitchen table?"

His eyes crinkled at the corners, but there wasn't even the slightest smiling twitch of his mustache when he answered levelly, "Not at all."

His laconic answers annoyed her. She felt like a babbling moron while he remained aloof, watching her with indulgent amusement. He hadn't even apologized for being late. But then he didn't look like a man to whom apologies would come easily. He was looking at her steadily with a curiosity he couldn't disguise. She strongly suspected that lying just beneath his placid features was a booming laugh dying to be freed. Why, she couldn't fathom.

She tracked the path his eyes took down the

length of her petite body. Never having known a moment's modesty in her life, the sudden impulse to cover herself was foreign, but there nonetheless. His eyes seemed to wash over her, leaving behind a blushing stain everywhere they touched. There was certainly nothing alluring in her attire, yet his slow, silent appraisal made her feel that the denim cutoffs and white eyelet halter-top were the flimsiest of negligees.

Had he made some lascivious remark like the ones that were often thrown to her on the streets of New York, she would have flung back a scathing insult. Or had he commented clinically on her good muscle tone, the length and formation of her legs, her graceful carriage, she would have thanked him and never given it a thought. Those kinds of comments she could handle. The ones eloquently transmitted by his eyes, she had no comebacks for.

"Well, shall we get started?" The corners of his mouth lifted in the suggestion of a smile.

His voice sent a shiver up her spine. It seemed to caress her ears with its deep rumbling timbre. How else could it sound since it originated in that chest? "Don't you want me to undress first?"

One brow leaped into a quizzical arch over his eye. "I guess so. Yes."

"I'll be just a minute then." She hurried into the bathroom, where earlier she had brought out an old sheet from one of the boxes. Her fingers fumbled with the fastening on her shorts. What was wrong with her? Why was she so nervous? She'd had massages before, many in the privacy of her apartment in Manhattan. Never had she been anxious about it. She hadn't been anxious about this one until she'd seen the masseur. Maybe if the guy bothered her so much, she shouldn't go through with it.

One shooting pain from her legs told her she would be foolhardy to pass up this opportunity. Her abused muscles needed soothing, and the doctor had recommended this sort of therapy. She was being silly. In her nearly thirty years, she'd never been fainthearted about anything. Wrapping the sheet around her naked body, she boldly opened the bathroom door and stepped out.

"I take it you didn't bring any lotion either," she said, brushing past him disdainfully.

"No, I didn't bring any lotion."

"I should be glad. Sometimes the lotions masseurs use smell medicinal. You can use this." She handed him the plastic bottle of lotion she'd brought from the bathroom. It was scented with her favorite fragrance. "And here are some towels for when you . . . for when you need them," she finished self-consciously, extending him the folded terrycloth towels.

She wished he wouldn't look at her as though he were about to devour her. She had shared matchbox-sized dressing rooms with men and women all racing to get into the next costume change. Often she'd been forced to forgo a trip to the dressing room and change just offstage with no screening whatsoever.

Why now was she seized by a maidenly awareness of her nakedness beneath the sheet?

In hopes of distracting him from his absorption with her bare shoulders, she said, "I . . . I was drinking a soda when you arrived. Would you care for one?"

"No thank you. Maybe when we're done."

She looked away from him and moved to the rectangular table in the kitchen that was barely long enough for her to lie on. She had draped it with an old quilt she'd found in the top of one of the apartment's two closets.

"That looks comfortable," he said.

"The table?"

"The quilt."

"Oh," she looked down at the faded spread. "I guess so. It isn't mine. It came with the apartment."

"I take it you're just moving in."

"Yes."

She turned her back to him and lay face down on the table, stretching out and adjusting herself as comfortably as she could. The quilt didn't do much in the way of padding the hard surface. Raising herself up, she unfolded the sheet and spread it out on either side of her until her front was lying directly on the laundered-soft quilt. Folding her hands one on top of the other, she lay her cheek on the back of the top one and turned her face away from him.

"Do you like the apartment?"

"It's okay for someplace temporary. I'll be here six months at the most."

"Are you from the city?"

"Not originally," she answered. She held her breath for a moment when she felt him raise the sheet and slide a towel over her hips, covering them.

"Originally where are you from?"

"Minnesota." The word came out in a gush of air as his palm held the towel over her hips in place while he tossed the sheet aside. Naked but for the towel, which felt about as large as a Band-Aid across her derriere, she could all but feel his scorching blue eyes as they surveyed the expanse of bare skin.

Long moments passed. He didn't speak. She didn't breathe. Neither moved. Finally, unable to bear the suspense, she turned her head toward him. "Is something wrong?"

He cleared his throat. "No. Nothing. I was just flexing my fingers."

"Oh."

She felt rather than saw his movements as he poured some lotion onto his palm and spread it to the other one by rubbing his hands together. Then his hands settled on her shoulders. Moving slowly at first, he bore down gently on the tense muscles and smoothed the scented lotion over them. Increasing the pressure slightly, his hands began to work a magic and Blair felt her tension dissolving.

"Have you worked for the Y long?"

"The Y?"

"Yes, have you worked there long?"

"Uh . . . no. Actually I don't work there. I sort of free-lance."

"I see. Do you have enough clients to keep you busy in a town this size?"

"You'd be surprised."

Both hands were on one shoulder now, squeezing the ever-relaxing muscles. "Your hands don't feel like most masseurs'. They have calluses."

"I'm sorry."

"I wasn't complaining. It was only an observation."

"I work out with weights fairly often. They leave calluses."

"So you're into all kinds of physical fitness."

"I guess you could say that."

"I thought so. You seem very fit."

"So do you." He chose that moment to slide his hands from her shoulders to just beneath her raised arms where his fingers curved into the tender, sensitive skin. The heels of his hands were planted in the groove of her spine and Blair realized how large and strong they were. With only the merest pressure, they could crack her ribs. She breathed easier when they began a gradual descent and his fingers were no longer touching that particular spot underneath her arms.

"I'm a dancer. I have to stay in shape."

"What kind of dancer? A ballerina?"

"I attend ballet class every day to work out, but I dance mostly in musical comedies."

"Hey! What shows have you been in?"

She laughed lightly. "At one time or another

nearly all of them, both on and off Broadway. Sometimes with a road company for months at a time."

"You've been at it for a long time then."

"Yes. Since graduating from high school. Much to my parents' dismay, I came to New York when everyone else was going off to state college."

"They didn't want you to?"

"That's an understatement. Even getting my degree by going to night classes didn't convince them that I wasn't on the road to destruction. I had told them for years that I was going to New York to study and dance and they humored me, thinking I'd outgrow the notion, or that I'd meet some nice hometown boy and replace hopeless dreams with marriage."

"But you didn't."

"No."

"Surely they're proud of you now."

"Yes, but it's a qualified pride," she replied slowly. Reminders of the heartache she had brought her parents always made her sad. For so many years she had sought their approval of her way of life. It was an impossible dream that she would never attain, for they would never understand her compulsion to dance. "They won't consider me successful until I marry and present them with a passel of grandchildren."

His thumbs were melting each vertebra with a revolving, mesmerizing motion. When they met at the base of her spine, his palms settled over the top curve of her hips. The towel slipped a few inches. Without sacrificing pressure, his hands massaged, taking skin, muscles, and weariness with them. Blair's eyes closed with a sigh of pure physical pleasure.

"You must be their one and only."

"That's just it," she mumbled sleepily against the back of her hand, "I have two brothers and a sister who have provided them with more grandchildren than they can afford to keep in birthday presents."

He chuckled and she liked the sound. It was as soothing as his hands, which were raising her hips slightly with each gentle squeeze only to press them back onto the soft quilt with the next downward stroke. "I guess that's the way parents are. They're not happy until their children conform to their idea of success."

"Maybe there's hope for the next generation of parents. My friend Pam has five children and she treats each one as an individual. You may know her. She lives here in Tidelands and is responsible for my being here. Pam Delgado."

"I know the Delgados. He's a policeman, isn't he?"

"Yes." Blair laughed, barely noticing that his hands were once again spanning her ribs. "If you'd known Pam ten years ago, you'd never believe her now. She gave up dance to marry Joe and live in the suburbs. I still can't quite believe that my friend who suffered through starvation diets and rigorous classes with me is now the happy mother of five little Delgados."

"You don't approve of her decision?"

Blair shrugged her shoulders. "It wasn't for me to approve or disapprove. It's just that I can't understand anyone giving up dance who isn't absolutely forced."

His fingers were trailing up and down her sides over her ribs while the heels of his hands made lazy progress up her spine. Blair was jolted to the soles of her feet when his fingers brushed the sides of her breasts, plumped out against the quilt. She shifted her weight and he got the less-than-subtle message. His hands left her long enough to get more lotion. When next he began, they were on the backs of her knees.

"If you're so dedicated to dance, what are you doing here? It doesn't seem convenient to move out here to Long Island when you've lived in the city for so many years."

He was kneading the muscles of one calf with both hands. The rhythmic motion brought on a delicious lassitude and Blair relaxed again. She didn't want to admit, even to herself, how it had alarmed her when she'd felt the feathery touch of his fingers at the sides of her breasts. Her heart had thudded against the hard surface of the table and the blood in her veins had seemed to concentrate in her earlobes, making them throb. Now that his movements had returned to those of the detached masseur, she could only think that what had happened had been an accident or that she had been unaccountably touchy.

After all, every part of her body had been handled by men for years. When one danced with a partner, the execution of a step often depended on the hold. Such holds left no room for timidity or modesty. But though she had been handled with much more intimacy, she didn't recall when a touch had made her throat constrict or when it had made her stomach feel like it would sink to the top of her thighs only to explode in a shower of tickling sensations.

"Did I miss your answer?"

The sound of his voice as he leaned close to her ear roused her from the momentary lethargy. Even though she could have done without his breath fanning her ear, she was glad he had pulled her from her musings that were becoming increasingly disturbing. She stirred restlessly as his hands moved up to the backs of her thighs. "I'm sorry. I . . . I have to stop dancing for awhile under doctor's orders."

Both hands stroking her thighs came to a standstill. "Why?"

"My knees mostly. I have some tendon and cartilage damage that needs time to knit."

"How long before you can dance again?"

"Six months," she said quietly, remembering again the anguish that had pierced through her when she heard the doctor say those fatal words. He was the third specialist she had consulted, not accepting the diagnoses of the first two, but passing them off as charlatans who didn't give as much thought to her knees as they did her checkbook.

The hands began massaging again. "That sounds serious."

"Well it's not," she snapped. She closed her eyes,

squeezing out the facts she didn't want to accept. "It's not," she said more softly, but with just as much conviction. "Things like this happen to professional dancers all the time—tendinitis, muscle sprain, shin splints. A few months' rest and I'll be fine."

"You can't dance at all?"

"I can do minimal workouts to retain muscle tone. Nothing strenuous."

They were quiet for a moment as she tried to block two things from her consciousness. First, the agony of having to give up her career for even six months. Second, the riotous sensations plaguing the erogenous parts of her body with each touch of his callused fingers on the backs of her thighs.

"Did you carry all those boxes up by yourself?" he asked at last, breaking the heavy silence.

"Yes. Pam lent me her station wagon for a few days. I drove it from the city this morning and didn't want to wait for anyone to help me unload it."

"Carrying all that weight up the stairs couldn't have been good for your knees."

"It didn't hurt them." Actually they had been hurting by the time the last of the boxes had been carried to the second story, but she wanted to deny that just as she wanted to deny that there was anything wrong with them in the first place. She was playing a childish game with herself and she knew it. Ignoring the problem wouldn't make it go away. But she wasn't ready to admit that she might have to give up dancing forever. That was as good as admitting that she would have to give up breathing, for to her one was as essential to life as the other.

"Surely you could have asked for someone to help you."

"Pam's children had planned to go to the beach today and I told her not to disappoint them. She said she and Joe would come over later to help me, but I didn't want to wait that late, much less impose on them. There's a man who lives in the house across from me. I'm leasing the apartment from him. Pam said to ask him for anything I needed, but I haven't seen him. He had given Pam a key for me and I picked it up from her this morning."

"You haven't met him then?"

"No, he's a friend of Pam's and she handled the leasing for me. He's a carpenter or something like that."

"I'm sure he wouldn't have minded helping a dainty thing like you lug all those boxes up here."

"Probably not," Blair said, dismissing the possibility, "but I don't want to be obligated to my neighbors."

"I see. You're independent."

"Totally. And I like it that way."

She heard a chair scrape across the floor as he pulled it to the end of the table. A glance over her shoulder showed him sitting down. She felt uncannily relieved that he was no longer touching her thighs.

Taking one of her slender feet in his palm, he began stroking the sole with his thumb. "What in the world did you do to these feet?"

She laughed. "Ugly, aren't they? Toe shoes, blisters worn into calluses, bigger blisters, more calluses—after years of dancing, a dancer's feet look like hooves."

He laved lotion over the bumps and knobs. She wouldn't have let him smooth them away if she were going to be dancing. It took a while to build up calluses hard enough to withstand the brutality heaped on them. Instead she gave in to the luxury of having his fingers stroke and press. Each of her toes was squeezed through a wringer made by his strong fingers.

He lifted her feet one at a time and rotated the ankle. "No, no, relax," he said quietly when she began to do his work for him. "Let me move it." When he was finished with her feet, he stood and bent her knee back, rotating it in the same way, but gently enough not to hurt her. She relinquished what small control she stubbornly maintained and let him work the kinks out of the tired muscles until her joints seemed to move as they hadn't for weeks.

After giving the second leg the same treatment, he lay it back down on the quilt. A weighty languor blanketed her until she felt like every bone in her body had gone as limp as a noodle. Her eyelids refused to remain open. She never wanted this hour with the man with the gifted hands to end. He had given her the relaxation she'd thought she'd never know again after leaving the doctor's plush Park Avenue office and limping home with tears of angry frustration rolling down her cheeks.

"You can turn over now," a low, compelling voice instructed her. She gave no thought to disobeying, but rolled over with one supple motion, her eyes still closed. She heard what could have been a soft gasp of surprise before she felt the cool towels being spread across her breasts and lower abdomen. Something about that gasp should have bothered her, she knew, but was too sleepy to concentrate on it.

He moved to the other end of the table to stand behind her head. She knew he was pouring more lotion into his palm by the heady fragrance that suffused her nostrils. When he leaned forward to return the bottle to the table, she felt the pressure of his thighs against the top of her head. She heard the lotion squishing in his hands before he lay them gently on the front of her shoulders. With long, measured strokes, he smoothed the emulsion along her upper arms. His breath fell like a mist on her face.

His fingers curved around her shoulders while his thumbs explored her collarbone. His touch was light, tentative, and unnecessary to a therapeutic massage, but Blair didn't see any value in pointing that out. It was too sublime to lie beneath those marvelous hands and wonder what whimsical mood would strike them next.

Her idle curiosity was soon satisfied, as his hands slowly descended to graze the upper portion of her chest. Her skin experienced a rebirth beneath his touch. A seed of desire burst open deep inside her breasts and blossomed outward until her nipples tautened with awakening. She yearned to be caressed by the hands that could bring about such wonders. Had she not been so drugged by his fingers drifting ever closer to what begged to be touched, she would have taken his hands under her own and dragged them down, pressing them to her aching breasts and swollen nipples. When his hands reluctantly withdrew to safer terrain, she didn't identify that strange garbled sound as her own whimpering protest.

He lifted one of her lifeless arms by the hand and, stretching it up to its full length, rested it against his chest. Applying minimal pressure, he squeezed the fragile muscles. His fingers could encircle each part of her arm as they inched upward from her armpit to her hand that lay like a wilted flower against his massive chest. Her fingertips knew the airy caress of his breath as he bowed his head to observe his effectiveness.

Blair wondered what he would do should she reach up to touch the cleft in his chin or drag her index finger across the brush of his mustache. She lacked the energy to carry out such a notion even if she had had the temerity, which she didn't. But thinking about it made her insides feel warm and heavy, as though a thick, sweet syrup were flowing through her veins.

The fingers of the massaging hand finally reached her wrist. They gripped it lightly while the thumb of the other hand impressed concentric circles into her palm. He rocked her hand back and forth on the pivotal bones of her wrist, persuading her to surrender all control to him. Methodically he massaged each of her fingers, beginning at the base and working his way up to the tip. The fleshy pad of each finger was caressed by the corresponding part of his thumb. It might well have been his tongue for the thorough, thrusting, darting, erotic seduction it performed on each finger-tip.

Blair, with what mental capacity she had left, ordered her eyes to open and make sure that such was not the case. Her eyes slammed into the stunning blue ones that were staring down at her. He lifted her other arm and lay it against his chest like its partner. He secured them there by moving his arms in front of them and placing his elbows in the undersides of hers.

"Have I ever seen you dance?" he asked in the tone of a hypnotist asking, "Are you asleep now?" His hands closed around her jaw, his thumbs massaging just in front of her ears.

Grateful she still had the wherewithal to understand her native language she said gruffly, "I don't know. Have you?"

"Tell me something I might have seen you in."

Her eyes gave up the fight to remain open when his hands closed around the base of her neck and his thumbs lightly measured its graceful length. "I . . . I was in an orange juice commercial for television," she said breathily.

"Yes?" He was pressing her temples now, rolling her head from side to side. The muscles of his thighs were rock hard against the crown of her head.

"I was a figure on a pinball machine. A giant silver ball rolled toward me and I did a leapfrog over it."

"I've seen that, but—"

"You wouldn't recognize me. I had on a silverfoil wig and huge daisy-shaped sunglasses with bright yellow lenses."

He rested his thumbs at the center of her hairline before following its heart-shaped course around her forehead to her ear. "I can't imagine you in a silver wig. I can't imagine you as having anything but glossy black hair. Daisy-shaped sunglasses with yellow lenses?" he asked softly. "No. Nothing but green eyes as fathomless as the sea." As on command, they opened to give him their full attention. His index finger traced the smooth, perfect arch of her dark brow.

Blair knew she shouldn't be allowing this. He might be a degenerate, a—but she could think of no reason she wanted to stop the inevitable. He trapped her hands against his chest as he bent over her. She could see each facet in his diamond blue eyes and they paralyzed rational thought with their brilliance.

"I can't imagine you as being any way except exactly as you are. I wouldn't change a thing." The fingers that had been caressing her cheeks were replaced by the silky touch of his mustache. Imperceptibly but inexorably he moved closer to her mouth until he hovered above it. She breathed in the intoxicating bouquet of his breath. Just as she was expecting the pressure of his lips on hers, someone knocked on the door.

She stifled her murmur of regret. He sighed and

brought himself upright, releasing her hands and lowering them beside her gently. Hastily she sat up and groped for the sheet, hot color rising to her cheeks as she watched him wade through the boxes to casually open her front door.

"Hi." The voice was masculine, but lacking in maturity. "Sorry to be so late, but someone at the desk got their wires crossed." The tall blond man didn't seem inclined to respond. The younger man, wearing white trousers and a white T-shirt with YMCA printed in red letters on the left breast pocket, said with a questioning inflection, "I'm the masseur."

Chapter 2

The young man's words hit Blair with the impact of a blow from a baseball bat. She sat on the edge of the table, clutching the twisted sheet to her, her hair a tangled dark cloud cloaking her shoulders. Her face, so flushed only moments ago, now drained to a chalky white.

"We won't be needing you now," the blond man said casually.

The young man's eyes swept past the broad shoulders to see the disarrayed Blair on the table and he assessed the situation immediately. When his eyes swung back to the larger man, they were glittering with insinuation. "I see what you mean," he said slyly. A playful elbow-in-the-stomach jab was implied by his smirking tone.

"Go ahead and bill Miss Simpson for your time."

"Yeah. Sure. Thanks." He winked at the blond man before picking up his leather bag of supplies and clumping down the stairs.

Blair watched as the blond man closed the door, but she was off the table before the latch clicked. No longer rendered senseless by her initial shock, she was now bristling with fury. "Who the hell are you? How dare you take advantage of me like this? Get out of here or I'm calling the police."

"On what? You've no telephone yet," he said reasonably. A broad grin split his mouth and showed her a beautiful set of gleaming white teeth. "The telephone company called today. An installer will be out the day after tomorrow."

"Who—"

"Sean Garrett. I'm your landlord. The carpenter and neighbor you don't want to be obligated to." He raked her disheveled appearance as she stood still, haphazardly wrapped in the sheet. "All you owe me is one thorough massage."

"You tricked me!" she shouted. Lightning flashed from her green eyes as she glared at him.

"No I didn't. I never said I was a masseur. You didn't give me a chance." He walked toward her and she found herself backing up instinctively. His size diminished the room which she had previously thought to be spacious. "Indeed, up to a point, I wasn't sure what service I was expected to perform."

The golden mustache quivered above the smiling mouth.

"You—"

"Let's see, you said you needed me now more than ever. You asked if I minded doing it on the kitchen table since the bed hadn't been made up. And you offered to undress. Now, what *is* a man supposed to think hearing words like those?"

He had continued to close in with that predatory gait as he spoke. She had backed up until she was against the kitchen countertop. Then he hitched a hip over the corner of the quilt-covered table, blocking off any route of escape. Feeling trapped, but knowing better than to concede any advantage, she stood as tall as she could and, despite her ridiculous costume, straightened her shoulders and raised her chin.

"You know good and well I mistook you for someone else. The decent thing to do would have been to identify yourself. I don't see how I can live here now knowing what kind of man my landlord is. As soon as you leave,"—she stressed that—"I'll carry my things back down to the car."

Whatever she expected of him, it wasn't the laughter that thundered out of his chest. His smile widened and he threw back his blond head in pure enjoyment. "So the heavenly body and innocent eyes are deceptive. Beneath them lurks the soul of a tigress. I like you, Blair Simpson."

"Well I don't like you," she shouted. "You're a liar and a sneak. Get out!"

"I never lied," he said with maddening calm while she thought she would burst with the anger roiling inside her.

"What would you call it?"

"I told you honestly that I didn't work for the Y. I said I was a free-lancer, which I am. I'm a contractor. You asked if I had enough clients and I said that you'd be surprised. I *do* have many clients. I buy old houses, restore them structurally, then sell them to wealthy city-dwellers who want a vacation home near the beach. So you see, everything I told you is the truth."

"But misleading."

He shrugged, his mouth tilting at the corners into a mischievous grin. "As I said, what's a man to do under such circumstances? When a beautiful woman offers to take off her clothes and lie down on the kitchen table, do you know any real man who would politely turn and leave?"

Thinking she'd shock him, she thrust out her chin and said defiantly, "As a matter of fact I do."

He wasn't impressed, as his nonchalant shrug testified. "I don't criticize anyone for his lifestyle. I only know what *my* sexual preferences are. And a beautiful woman wearing only a bedsheet, lying docile and pliant and begging for my touch appeals to me greatly."

"Begging! I didn't . . . the only reason I was letting you touch me is because I thought you were a professional masseur. Had I known—"

"Don't try to tell me you weren't enjoying it because I know better. You were practically purring. You weren't even aware of turning over and treating me to a look at all of you." He spoke the last words softly as he got off the table and took what few steps were necessary to stand directly in front of her. "From the back, you look like little more than a child. But from the front, for all your daintiness of figure, Blair Simpson, you are undeniably a mature woman."

His hands came up to cradle her jaw. She couldn't ward him off with her hands. They were occupied with holding up the sheet. "Don't," she said, trying uselessly to twist her head aside. She was ignored. His mouth was only a breath away from hers.

"I'll tell you something else. I'll blister your fanny if you ever again open your door to a strange man and let him come in. Don't you know what can happen to ladies when they act so carelessly?" The mustache made a brushing pass across her lips. "All kinds of perverts are walking the streets. If you had let one of them in instead of me, something terrible might have happened to you."

His lips pressed against hers and what little will she had remaining sifted through the barriers of her mind like the last grains of sand in an hourglass. His hands, cupping the back of her head, were as gentle as they had been while giving her the massage. His thumbs rotated hypnotically against her temples. She felt herself gravitating toward his body as though pulled by a magnet.

He dropped a few light kisses on her mouth before stepping away. Blair couldn't focus on him clearly, so dizzy was she made by the embrace and his untimely and cruel withdrawal. When her senses finally returned, the first thing that registered on her desire-clouded mind was his victorious grin. Any lingering passion she felt was immediately swapped for rage.

She shoved him away from her with one hand risking her hold on the sheet. "Get out!" she screamed. "You're the only pervert I've ever had the misfortune of meeting."

"I'll leave now," he said, turning away from her and navigating his way around the boxes to the front door. "But I'll have dinner ready at eight. Just come to the back door of the house and knock."

"Dinner! Are you suggesting that I have dinner with you after this?"

"I see no reason why not. Now that we know each other so well." The meaning behind his smile left nothing to the imagination.

"Good-bye, Mr. Garrett. You'll see me on the first of next month when my rent is due."

"I'll see you at my back door at eight or I'll come get you." Before she could respond he added quietly, "Pam told me about your knee injuries. I'm truly sorry you won't be able to dance for awhile."

Then he was gone and Blair was staring at the wooden door he'd quietly closed behind him.

"You mean you were lying there n-a-k-e-d with Sean Garrett's hands sliding all over your body?" Blair

watched sadly as Pam Delgado popped another chocolate chip cookie into her mouth and chewed it lustily
while her eyes were staring with wide incredulity at
her friend.

"Yes. It was awful."

Pam laughed, nearly choking on the cookie. "Oh,
the pits to be sure," she scoffed. "Who do you think
you're fooling, ol' friend? Much as I love and adore my
Joe, I'd probably be tempted to submit should Sean
offer to give me a massage on the kitchen table and so
would ninety-nine percent of the women in town."

Pam and her brood of five had descended on Blair
an hour after Sean had left. Pam had assigned jobs to
her four oldest children. Two were emptying boxes of
books and records into the built-in bookshelves in the
main room. One was folding towels and linens into
the closet in the bathroom. The other was unpacking
pots and pans into a kitchen cabinet. Pam and Blair
were sitting at the table, talking over the clatter. The
youngest Delgado, a boy a few months past his first
birthday, was on his mother's lap, smearing himself
with a soggy cookie.

"Well then, I'm one of that one percent who
wouldn't. Pam, why didn't you tell me this man, who
is my nearest neighbor and landlord, is a . . . a perverted—"

"He did something perverse?" Pam asked eagerly, dodging at the same time the bite of cookie the
baby was foisting on her. "What?"

"No, he didn't do anything perverse," Blair said
in vexation, standing to go to the countertop to pour

more soda into Pam's near-empty glass. "The whole thing was perverted. He took advantage of me," she cried. "I was mortified."

Pam's eyes softened a bit. "Well I can see how you might be upset. But you've got to admit being taken advantage of by Sean isn't exactly a fate worse than death. I know women who'd—"

"Would you stop saying that please?" Blair asked, slightly irritated. "As you know I'm not like other women. They can have the macho types. I'm not impressed by Sean Garrett as being anything other than a scheming womanizer."

"But he's not," Pam came to his defense quickly. "Blair, he's one of the pillars of the community. He's successful in business, he's on the city council, a member of the school board—"

"My God! You mean he's got children?"

"No, no. He's never been married, but he's interested in all aspects of the community. In addition he's charming, and damned good to look at. Don't tell Joe, but I nearly ran the Volvo off in a ditch one day when I saw him working on a roof wearing nothing but a pair of shorts. Without a shirt he's—"

"Okay," Blair said, throwing up her hands in a gesture of surrender. "He's absolutely wonderful and I'm weird for not realizing how lucky I am that he made a complete fool out of me."

Pam's smile drooped. Reaching across the table, she covered Blair's hand with her own. "I'm sorry. Knowing how . . . well, how headstrong you are, I can see how you'd be angry that he duped you so easily. But, Blair, you have to admit that it's funny. Some of the things you said . . ." She couldn't hold back the laughter any longer and it bubbled out of her throat.

"Thanks a lot," Blair said, with a wry smile. "Traitor. Are you sure you aren't descended from Benedict Arnold?"

"Does his machismo make you nervous?"

"Whose? Benedict's?" Blair said in an attempt to avoid Pam's perceptive question.

"Sean's."

Blair laughed. "Of course not."

"I just wondered," Pam said with obvious off-handedness. She crimped the curls on the baby's head. "I mean, you haven't really been involved with a man since Cole."

Blair looked away. "No I haven't." Neither Pam nor anyone else knew the whole story of her relationship with Cole Slater and no one ever would. By tacit agreement, they'd never discussed it. If Pam harbored any curiosity about that segment of Blair's past, she was friend enough not to pry. For that Blair was grateful. Pam wasn't prying now. She was only providing a key should Blair want to open a closed door. She didn't. "Sean Garrett just isn't my type, that's all."

Pam laughed. "If you're a woman, he's your type."

Blair studied her friend who had gained too much weight with each successive child until the accumulation had carried her far beyond being pleasantly plump. "If you're so enchanted with Sean Garrett, why didn't you go after him instead of Joe?" Blair teased.

Pam spread her arms wide. "Because Joe loves me just the way I am." Her eyes sparkled happily. "And can he ever love!" she added with an exaggerated sigh. Her skin, which she had sense enough to protect from too many sunny days on the beach, was clear and smooth. Her hair, piled up on top of her head in a careless knot, was a summation of her philosophy of life. She looked happy and totally fulfilled, and Blair knew a pang of envy.

"I know you think I've let myself go to pot," Pam said with characteristic honesty. "I know I look like a blimp and no longer resemble the svelte dancer who fought every ounce. Don't think I don't look at you and get pea green with envy for your tiny figure. I do. Firm thighs, a flat stomach, and breasts that don't sag are history for me. But I'm happy, Blair. I've got Joe and the kids and I love them. I wouldn't trade places with anyone. I wouldn't trade places with you, glamorous career or no glamorous career."

Strident voices from the living room indicated that Andrew didn't approve of the way Mandy was doing her job. Mandy said she was going to tell Mama if Andrew didn't leave her alone. Andrew yelled, "Tattletale, tattletale."

The two women scarcely heard them. Blair was staring down at her hands and Pam was watching helplessly as she read the heartache on her friend's enviably youthful face.

"I wouldn't blame you for not wanting to trade

places with a thirty-year-old gypsy with banged up knees," Blair said forlornly.

"Your knees will heal and you'll be back dancing in no time."

"And if they don't heal? What then?"

"Then you'll do something else."

"I don't know anything else, Pam."

"Well, you'll learn something else. My Lord, Blair, you're beautiful and talented and the fact that you're thirty may be threatening if you want to be a professional dancer, but there are other things you can do that haven't even occurred to you yet. I know you're not stupid enough to think that your life is going to end now that you're thirty and may not be able to dance anymore."

"The life I *want* will be over."

"How do you know what you want? You've never known any other life but dance. Something wonderful may be in store for you that you couldn't even guess at. Do you think I thought, God let me be mugged that day in the park so I'd have to file a report with a cop named Delgado who had beautiful brown eyes and a wonderful laugh? That your knees are giving out may be the best thing that's ever happened to you."

Blair saw that arguing was useless, so she patted Pam's plump hand and said, "Maybe so," knowing full well that such was not the case.

With Pam helping and the children causing a minimum of chaos, they managed to unpack most of the boxes in the next hour. Pam sent the older chil-

dren down the stairs with the empty boxes with instructions to put them into Sean's trash barrels.

"Can we go see Sean?" Mandy, the oldest girl,
asked Pam.

"No. He's probably out working somewhere."

"His truck's here. So is his car," Andrew said. He
was the oldest of Pam's children, just approaching
nine.

Pam sighed. "Just for a minute then." Despite
her warnings that they be careful on the stairs with
the boxes, they raced down them.

"Andrew's got a terrible crush on you," Pam said.
"He asked me the other day if I thought you were
pretty. Usually he scorns females of any kind."

"I thought boys had their first crushes on their
teachers."

"It's summertime," Pam said and they laughed.

When the two came bounding back upstairs they
were slurping on Popsicles. "Sean gave them to us.
He sent these to the others," Andrew explained,
handing the other three Popsicles to his mother.

"Oh, let's hurry out of here or we'll drip all over
Blair's floor," Pam said, quickly grabbing up the baby,
her purse and car keys.

"Oh, yeah, I almost forgot," Andrew said to Blair
just as his mother was shooing him out the door.
"Sean said for you to dress casual tonight."

Pam stopped her frantic efforts to herd her children down the stairs and looked over her shoulder.
"Tonight?" she asked on a high note.

"He has the mistaken idea that I'm going to eat dinner with him," Blair mumbled.

"You're not?"

"No!"

"Wanna bet?" Pam asked, winking before she turned to assist three-year-old Paul down the steps.

When Pam had first told her about the garage apartment, Blair had asked if it had a bathtub. One of the things the doctor said would help her knees was frequent soaking in hot baths. Pam had assured her it had one. Now, Blair was taking her first relaxing bath in the old-fashioned, deep, claw-footed tub and it felt wonderful. The tension that had been building since she first saw Sean Garrett standing on her threshold began to dissolve in the steamy water.

When the water finally began to cool, she stood up, reeling slightly. The hot water had weakened her and she realized that she hadn't eaten anything all day. She dried, noticing that her skin was smooth and fragrant with the residue of the lotion that Sean had massaged into it. Starting to pull on her oldest and most comfortable robe, she paused to reconsider. What if he carried out his threat to come get her when she didn't show up at his back door at the appointed time? Cursing him and her own culpability, she sacrificed the robe for a pair of jeans and a tank-top T-shirt, both old and well-worn if not as comfortable as the robe she'd intended to wear.

The package of chocolate chip cookies had been

virtually demolished, but the rest of the groceries Pam had brought by way of a housewarming gift lined the shelves of the cupboard and refrigerator. Blair was inspecting them when she heard the first footfall on the stairs.

"It can't be," she whispered. Her eyes flew to the clock and the digital readout told her it was 8:01. The heavy footsteps on the stairs grew ominously louder as they neared the top. "He won't bully me," she swore to herself as she marched across the living room with a militant stride. As soon as he knocked on the door, she flung it open, ready to do battle if necessary.

Her scathing refusal to join him for dinner died on her lips. He was anything but menacing. Instead he looked like a boy calling for his first date. He was dressed in a pair of jeans and a sport shirt. It was opened to the middle of his chest, revealing a carpet of curling golden hair over coppery skin. His hair was well brushed and picked up the glow from the soft porch light Blair had switched on earlier. His cheeks shone with a recent shave. His cologne was elusive but potent and did nothing to alleviate Blair's light-headedness due to hunger and the hot bath. In his hand he carried a green paper-wrapped bouquet of daisies.

"Hi."

"Hi." Her voice didn't sound like her own. The word was forced out of a throat swallowing convulsively.

"This is a peace offering for what I did this afternoon. Will you forgive me?" he asked penitently. She didn't answer, only stared at the flowers he was extending to her. "They really should be put in water," he said gently. He stepped forward and, like someone in a trance, she moved aside and allowed him to enter the room. His arm lightly grazed her breast. "Do you have a vase?"

"In . . . In the kitchen . . . I think," she stammered and went to the cabinet where she had put incidentals. There she found a slender, clear glass vase, filled it with water, and carried it into the living room to set on the coffee table.

He unwrapped the flowers and carefully arranged them in the vase with hands that looked too large to undertake such a delicate enterprise. But then Blair knew just how tender those hands could be.

"There. That looks terrific," he said, wadding up the green paper. He casually went to the pantry in the kitchen, opened the door, and dropped the ball of paper into the garbage can he'd correctly guessed would be there. "Everything's shaping up," he said as his eyes surveyed the room. The lamp's soft glow camouflaged some of the areas that hadn't come under her attention yet, and Blair had to agree that the room had a certain ambiance.

The walls were painted a soft beige, while the woodwork of the window frames, door frames, baseboards, and moldings around the ceiling were painted white. The windows were tall and wide and shuttered with white louvers.

"Have you tried the bed yet?" Sean asked, indicating the sofa.

"No," Blair said, shaking her head. "I made it up this afternoon, but I haven't uh, I . . . lain down on it."

"I hope it's comfortable," he said, ignoring the bed and studying her mouth. "When I bought furniture for this apartment, I wanted things that were simple and comfortable."

"Everything's fine."

"Good."

They stared at each other for an endless moment, then both looked away awkwardly. "I really am sorry about this afternoon," he said after a while. Only when Blair lifted her eyes to meet his gaze again did he continue. "I want you to understand that I'm not sorry it happened, or that I saw you that way, or that I touched you." His voice had the stirring bass vibrations of a fine cello. "I'm only sorry that you were embarrassed. It was a low trick I played on you and you had every right to be angry."

She tried to banish the words about his seeing and touching her and concentrate on his deception and her anger. Why had he approached her this way? She had built up an arsenal of rebukes, of condemnations, but she couldn't use them now that he was so meekly apologetic. He had robbed her of the one weapon she had—anger. That was another low trick.

"You're right. I was furious."

"I promise the next time I give you a massage, it will be with your full consent."

"I—" She was never allowed to tell him there wouldn't be a next time.

"That's a strange print," he said, looking over her shoulder.

She turned to see that he was looking at Harvey Edwards's *Hands.* "You're looking at it from the wrong angle," she said. She went to the brass-framed print that was leaning vertically against the wall and turned it horizontally. "It goes this way. I haven't had time to hang it yet."

"Oh, I see," he said, nodding. "Interesting, isn't it?"

"I love it, as I do most of his work." They studied the photograph that captured the arched torso of a ballerina being supported by a pair of masculine hands that defined strength, yet intimated sensitivity. "He photographs dancers. That's one of his, too." She indicated another print of a pair of well-worn faded pink toe shoes against a solid background of black. "It's called *Shoes.*"

"Big on titles, isn't he?" Blair was intrigued by the way the lines around his eyes crinkled when he smiled. "Do you have a pair of shoes like that?"

She laughed. "Several hundred."

"How do you ever learn to wind those ribbons around your ankles and make them stay?"

"Practice. And the ribbons have to be sewn on just right."

"The shoes don't come with them already on?"

"No, you have to do it yourself. And it's bad luck for anyone but the ballerina to sew on her ribbons."

"I didn't know that."

During this whole inconsequential exchange

there was an important battle being waged. Their eyes competed against one another to see whose could take in and register the most information about the other in a given amount of time.

Her eyes noted the way his hair molded so nicely, yet disobediently, to his head; the way his mustache curved over his upper lip; the way the cleft in his chin punctuated the total masculinity of his face like a small exclamation point.

His eyes recorded the number of times her tongue nervously wet her lips; the way her hands moved in their own special ballet when she gestured; and how long her dark lashes were when she lowered them in an unconsciously seductive manner.

"Hungry?"

The question was so abrupt that Blair was ripped from her dazed inspection of him and brought back to the subject at hand. As though she'd been shot from a cannon, it took her a moment to orient herself, to gather her wits about her enough to say, "Mr. Garrett, I don't think it's a good idea for me to have dinner at your house. I appreciate your invitation but I—"

"Don't want to be obligated to your neighbors," he finished for her.

"Well, yes. That and—"

"You're afraid that I'll do something underhanded like I did this afternoon and put the make on you."

"No—"

"You're afraid I *won't* put the make on you?"

"No!" she fairly shouted in exasperation. His

piercing blue eyes were unnerving her. They kept wandering in the vicinity of her breasts. Why hadn't she put on a bra, or another top? "I'm not afraid of anything," she stressed, "but—"

"Gossip? Are you afraid that our having dinner together would jeopardize our reputations? You're right that in a town this size everyone knows everyone else's business, but I assure you I have more to lose than you. I'm known here. You're not. If I'm not concerned about gossip you shouldn't be."

"I'm not," she said, finally losing the tenuous grip on her temper. "I'm a grown woman, Mr. Garrett, who has lived alone for many years in New York City. I can take care of myself and I don't give a damn what the busybodies in this town think of me or what I do." She paused to heave in a breath.

"Then there's no reason for you not to have dinner with me. Are you ready?"

"Haven't you heard one word I've said?"

"I've heard them all and they're so much hot air. Are you ready?"

She threw up her hands in defeat. "All right," she shouted. "I'll go eat your dinner."

"Now see how easy that was?" he said with an amiable smile. "Come on." He ushered her toward the door.

"Just a minute. I need to comb my hair."

"No you don't. It looks good just like that."

"Well at least let me put some shoes on."

"Feet that have worn out that many pairs of toe shoes deserve one night off. Go barefoot."

"Very well," she said, giving in. "Come on."

"Just a minute. There is one other thing," he said as she turned toward him, a questioning frown on her face. "You forgot the light. I'm paying the utility bills, remember?"

He switched off the lamp on the table at the end of the sofa, plunging the room into darkness except for the glow of the porch light filtering through the shutters. Blair's hand was on the doorknob when she felt his hands settle lightly on her shoulders and turn her around. Her heart began beating in an irregular tattoo that affected her breathing as well.

"We have some unfinished business, Blair."

"I don't know what you mean, Mr. Gar—"

"Dammit! If you call me Mr. Garrett one more time, I'm going to remind you just how familiar we are," he warned in a low growl. The darkness didn't obscure the fire burning in his blue eyes. Each emphatic word caused a warm puff of breath to strike her face. The fingers wrapped around her upper arms were like velvet bonds, possessive and strong but warm and soft.

She swallowed. "What business, Mr. G . . . Sean?"

"This." His hands dropped from her shoulders to slide under her arms and close around her back. Spreading his fingers wide, he pulled her to him, pressing her against the rigidity of his large frame. "God, you're so tiny I feel like a child molester holding you this way," he murmured into her hair. He moved against her in a way that demonstrated a shocking insight into how to arouse her. "But I know that every inch of you is woman. I could almost encircle your waist with my hands, but it curves into the most feminine of hips." His large hands slid down the slender mounds, appreciating their firmness. "Your breasts are small but beautifully round and full. They respond to me. I've seen their response and now I can feel it against my chest." He peered down into her face.

She knew that her eyes were wide and unblinking. She knew that her lips were softly parted in disbelief. She knew that her expression showed how mystified she was that this was happening, that she was being held in the arms of a fiercely virile man. Most perplexing of all was that she wanted to be held.

"You're so small you make me feel like a bungling giant. I'll never hurt you, Blair. I promise. You'll tell me, won't you, if I ever hurt you?"

She could only nod dumbly. His mouth was teasing hers with feather-light kisses that barely qualified as such. She'd never been kissed by a man with a mustache and the masculine feel of it against her mouth was like an aphrodisiac that injected her with desire.

As his mouth grew more demanding and his tongue boldly glided along her lips, she resisted.

"Blair," he whispered urgently against her lips, "let me taste you. Open your mouth."

"No," she cried.

"Yes," he said adamantly and this time brooked no arguments. His mouth slanted over hers as he pulled her ever closer into him. Her back arched to mold her femininity against what it had been created to complement. Harmonizing sighs of gratification spiraled above them. Hands that had made futile attempts at extrication, now linked behind his neck. Softness conformed to hardness.

He conquered with tenderness and she yielded. He tickled the corners of her mouth with the tip of his tongue until her lips involuntarily relaxed. When he pushed it between her lips, his tongue didn't plunder, but persuaded. It flicked over her lips, her teeth, then gently pushed past that last barricade to explore the interior. He caressed with loving strokes each delicious discovery. He flirted with the tip of her tongue, then delved deeply. More than a kiss, it was an act of love.

When at last he pulled away, she leaned against him weakly. His hand smoothed over her hair and she thought it might be trembling slightly. Their breathing was that of two people who had climbed to a high altitude.

"I think we're doing things in reverse," he said. She felt his smile against her cheek. "We're having dessert before dinner."

Chapter 3

Engulfed by embarrassment over her unrestrained response to him, Blair avoided Sean's eyes as he escorted her down the outdoor stairs. She dreaded having to face him in full light once they reached his house across the brief expanse of lawn. The moment she entered the back door he held for her, though, her self-consciousness was swept away by enthrallment. His house was exquisite.

"Sean," she exclaimed, "this is beautiful."

"Do you like it?" he asked, obviously pleased by her reaction.

"Like it," she said, "what an understatement." He had led her into a screened back porch that was filled with wicker furniture, potted plants, and plump cushions piled onto the quarry tiled floor. Two ceiling fans with cane blades rotated overhead. The cushions on the natural wicker seats and on the floor were in a bold blue and brown print.

"When I bought the house, the porch was here, but it wasn't enclosed. I thought it would make a nice garden room. In the winter, I can weather secure it by sliding panes of glass into those frames."

"It's wonderful."

"Come see the rest."

His evident pride in the house was justifiable. As he walked Blair into the kitchen she caught her breath. Never having had more than a one- or two-room apartment in the city, she was aghast at the spaciousness of the room.

"I converted that old wood-burning stove so it could use gas."

The freestanding appliance was black iron and trimmed with brass. It matched a huge baker's rack of the same materials that covered another wall. Its shelves were loaded with brass and copper utensils, cookbooks, and plants.

"Did you decorate this yourself?" she asked.

"No. I only do the structural work. Then I turn the houses over to clients and they hire their own decorators. A friend helped me with this one."

Blair wondered about the identity of the "friend" with the impeccable taste as Sean led her through the rest of the lower floor. The dining room with its four-faceted bay window had been furnished with a round table worthy of the room. The living room boasted an antique European marble fireplace. Blair could see now why Sean would notice and appreciate her prints. The high ceilinged walls of the living room were splashed with prints of varying shapes, sizes and styles, yet all blended with the colors and textures found in the furniture, which was a congenial mixture of old and new.

A tiny powder room had been squeezed in under the polished oak staircase. One wall of the landing was stained glass, and Blair could only imagine how breathtaking it would be with sunlight behind it. Area rugs served to accent the aged patina of the parquet floors.

"Upstairs there are three bedrooms and three baths. We'll see them later. Right now I'm starving," he said, taking her arm and propelling her back toward the kitchen.

She was still mulling over what he'd said about seeing the bedrooms later, when they entered the bright kitchen and he said, "I hope you like chicken and wild rice."

"Yes. Can I help?"

"It's all done, but you can get the salad and dress it while I pour the wine."

"Okay."

She found a huge bowl of salad in the refrigerator and, selecting a vinegar and oil dressing out of the shelves in the door, poured a liberal amount onto the greens. She carried the bowl into the dining room where the table had already been set with informal china, linen napkins, and candles.

"Did you do all this yourself?" she asked Sean when he brought in the casserole and set it on a silver trivet.

He shrugged. "Yeah. I don't go to this much effort every night, you understand. I usually eat a bologna sandwich and drink a bottle of beer on the porch, but this is a special occasion."

She was standing beside her chair nervously. "Special?"

"I think so." He held her chair and she sat down, thankful that she had an excuse to let her knees collapse beneath her. Rather than moving to his chair immediately, he wrapped his arms around her shoulders and leaned down to place his mouth directly over her ear. "I could get accustomed to sharing meals with you." His mouth slid from her ear to the side of her neck, taking small love bites as it went. At the juncture with her collarbone, he kissed her, bathing the tender spot with his tongue. When he straightened at last, he slipped his finger beneath the shoulder of her tank-top and caressed her skin briefly before sitting down.

Blair, trying to restore some order to a world suddenly gone haywire, fumbled with her napkin as she placed it on her lap. "I feel like I'm underdressed," she said, tucking her bare feet under her chair.

"You're not. I'm only trying to impress you."

"I'm impressed. Where did you learn to entertain so graciously?"

He heaped her plate high with the seasoned rice
and a boned chicken breast. "I guess I absorbed it by
osmosis. My parents entertain quite a bit. Whatever I
learned, I learned from my mother."

"Where do your parents live?"

"In New Jersey."

She passed him a basket of hot buttered bread
after tearing off a generous hunk for herself. "What
business is your father in?"

"He's retired." He changed the subject quickly
by asking about her own family and they finished the
meal over idle, chatty conversation.

When Pam had first told her about him, she had
envisioned a near illiterate who made his living doing
handiwork with a saw and hammer. Meeting him had
altered that opinion considerably. Seeing the quality
of the restoration on his house had elevated her as-
sessment of his career, and through their dinner conversation, she learned that his interests were varied
and many. He was intelligent, well-read, witty.

All the while she was enjoying his entertaining
company, she searched for a flaw, something in him
that repulsed her, some secret sin for which he could
be despised. There was none. In every aspect, he was
the most attractive man she had ever met. His very
appeal shook the foundations on which her life was
built. His smile made her want to flee, but at the
same time she longed to bask in its golden warmth.

She declined his offer of dessert. "I'm not working out six hours a day," she said. "I'll have to start
watching my calories."

She did accept a cup of coffee laced with Kahlúa and topped with thick whipped cream. He suggested they drink it on the porch and she quickly agreed. No lights were turned on as they settled themselves against the deep cushions of the furniture. A breeze off the ocean only a few blocks away filtered through the screened wall. Crickets chirped in the oak trees, and the fans overhead provided a steady humming lullaby.

Blair curled up in the corner of a small settee and tucked her feet beneath her. She sipped the foamy hot drink.

"You like?" he asked.

She smiled, licking whipped cream from the corner of her mouth. "I like."

He watched her in silence for a moment, then asked softly, "When did you start dancing?"

"When I was four."

"Four!"

She laughed. "That was when my mother enrolled me in my first ballet class. For my first recital, I was a pink and white cupcake."

"Yum-yum."

How he could fill such an innocent expression with such sexual implication amazed her. It disturbed her that in the darkness of the room and the flickering shadows caused by the circling fans, she couldn't tell the direction of his eyes. She quickly picked up her story.

"I've danced ever since. It's more than a career. It's a way of life that no one except another dancer can understand. We all eat, sleep, and breathe dance. We go without lodging and food to pay for classes. When we're not working in a show, we wait tables, do anything, to support ourselves. But we never sacrifice our classes. If someone's broke, he moves in with someone else until better times come along. It's a campy way of life. I guess that's why we're called gypsies. We carry our livelihoods around in canvas bags—smelly leotards, mended tights, worn-out shoes, leg warmers, ointments."

"But you've been successful. Pam's touted the many shows to your credit."

"I've been lucky, yes."

"Lucky, hell. You're good."

She smiled at him. "I'm good, but always striving to be better."

"Didn't you ever want to pull out of the chorus and be the star?" he asked.

"If you could hear my singing voice you'd know that would be a pipe dream. I couldn't even fake it. After years of voice and acting lessons, I recognized the hopelessness of playing a lead. And strangely enough I wasn't really interested. Love of applause wasn't my driving force, but rather love of dance. I was content to be the first dancer behind Liza Minnelli saying, 'Gee, that's super,' and other profound lines of dialogue like that."

"That should have won you a Tony," he laughed. But his eyes were serious, staring into the bottom of his cup at the dregs of the coffee he whirled round and round in a miniature whirlpool. Almost too casually he asked, "In all this moving in and out with people, was there ever anyone you lived with for an extended period of time?"

A year—would he consider that an extended period of time? A heartbreaking year, but one with rare moments of joy and sharing that made it worthwhile. She knew what he was asking—Had she ever lived with a man? Had there been a man in her life? "Yes." She answered him truthfully. "I lived with a man named Cole Slater for awhile. That was several years ago."

"And?" he asked when she didn't expand on that.

"And since then I've lived alone."

"I see."

He didn't, but she wasn't going to enlighten him. "I'll help you with the dishes," she said briskly. She unfolded from her relaxed position and picked up the cup and saucer she'd set on a glass-topped wicker table.

"I'll let you," he said jovially, following her into the kitchen.

They decided it would be expedient if she rinsed the dishes and stacked them in the dishwasher and let him put things away as only he would know where to put them. She was neatly folding a dish towel when he came up behind her and closed his arms around her waist, hugging her to him. The back of her neck knew the sweet nuzzling of his mustache and mouth.

"If our reputations are shot to hell already, we've

nothing to lose by really giving them something to talk about." He nibbled at her earlobe gently, his tongue batting against it playfully.

Softly, she gasped his name, "Sean . . ."

"Hm?" His hands scooted up her ribs to coast over her breasts. He took her indistinguishable murmur as consent and held her breasts gently in his palms. "Oh, God, Blair, you feel better than I imagined. So soft and full, so . . ." His mouth opened over her neck for a kiss that involved all of his mouth. His inquisitive fingers stroked and the cotton knit of her top couldn't contain the firm contraction of her nipples. "Yes, yes," he whispered harshly.

Only then did she realize that she was grinding her hips against his middle and that he needed no further encouragement. His arousal was firmly apparent against the cushion of her hips. Shocked at her own abandon, she tried to pry herself away from him, but was stayed by a hand stroking downward to insinuate itself under her top. The snap on her jeans was no deterrent and was deftly opened. Then that boldest of hands was flattened over her navel, exploring its perimeter with audacious fingers, fingers that were brazen enough to move ever lower, to toy with the elastic top of her bikini panties. When one slipped beneath that demarcating line, alarm bells pealed loud and clear through the fog of passion that swamped her and Blair broke free, whirling away from him. Her eyes were wide and her lips trembled uncontrollably as she faced him like a frightened doe.

"No, Sean." Her hair rippled around her as she shook her head emphatically.

"Why?" His chest heaved in an effort to still his rapid breathing. The pupils of his eyes were dilated, almost obscuring the blue irises.

"Why?" she repeated on a shuddering expulsion of air. "Because we only met today for one reason."

"What does that have to do with anything? I knew from the moment I saw you I wanted you. And admit it or not, you want me just as much."

"I don't," she shouted, hurriedly resnapping her jeans and pulling her tank-top down over the waistband. She was tempted to cover her breasts with her hands to hide their pointed agitation from his avid eyes. She willed them to relax. They refused. Her whole body, which had been trained to obey each command of her brain, had rebelled. It betrayed her with throbbing reminders of his touch, with aching pleas that it craved what he could provide.

Summoning what strength she could she said heatedly, "I made it clear from the first that I'm here temporarily. I don't have the time or the inclination to become involved."

"Oh . . ." His expletive was strained through his teeth. For long moments he stood with hands on his hips, glaring at her from across the narrow space that separated them. For all his gentleness, Blair knew then that Sean Garrett had a temper that could flare to life when properly provoked. The fire in his eyes now wasn't so much lust as it was anger.

His ire only increased hers. Wasn't she permitted

to say no? Did he think she was only so much putty in his hands, waiting to be molded however he saw fit? A spineless female panting for his attention? After hearing a happily married woman like Pam expound on his sex appeal, she shouldn't be surprised by his arrogance. He couldn't be completely oblivious to his virile attraction. Well for once it would be rejected.

Raising her chin stubbornly, she said, "It all boils down to this. I don't want to go to bed with you, Mr. Garrett." With that inspired exit line, she turned on her heel and stalked through the kitchen. He caught her at the back door.

Before she had time to react, he scooped her up in his arms. "What do you think you're doing?" she asked haughtily as he pushed through the screened door and started across the grassy lawn.

"As long as I'm here there's no reason for you to climb those stairs. You may not *think* you need anybody, and I know you'd never ask for help, but I can at least save your knees that much effort."

He carried her up the stairs without any exertion and deposited her on the top step. With as much dignity as she could muster she said, "Thank you for dinner."

Before the last word had completely left her mouth, it was being kissed by hot, fervent lips. Bands of steel in the form of arms wrapped around her and pressed her into a body that radiated carnal energy. Her mouth wasn't prepared for the onslaught of his and could find no strength to resist when his tongue plunged inside.

Then just as suddenly as the storm broke, it subsided. The arms relaxed, holding her no less firmly, but more tenderly. His tongue made slow dipping forays into her mouth that left her breathless.

Sensing her acquiescence, his hand moved from her back to lightly cup her breast. His thumb skated along the undercurve and she heard her own moan of rising passion. As he coaxed her tongue into his mouth and sucked it gently, his thumb brought her nipple to a hard pebble of need. This torment went on and on until Blair was inundated with blind desire, moving against his hard body mindlessly, seeking fulfillment for the emptiness deep inside her.

She swayed drunkenly as he pulled away. Were it not for his hands on her upper arms, she would have toppled down the stairs. There was no smile on his face now, only set lines of stubborn resolution. "Like hell you don't want to go to bed with me, *Miss Simpson.*"

Two mornings after she'd heard those words, she was still seething over them. She had avoided leaving the apartment the day after having dinner with Sean because of the fear of meeting him in the yard. Pam had loaned her the family's extra car indefinitely, but she really had nowhere to go. After she finished arranging the apartment to her satisfaction, she had spent the day as the doctor had advised her to spend most of her days—reclining with her legs elevated. She'd read, watched two old movies on the portable television set she'd brought with her from the city, ate when she was hungry, and napped.

She knew when Sean's battered truck lumbered into the driveway between her apartment and his house, but she refused to even look out the window to catch a glimpse of him. Yet when he left in his Mercedes in the early evening, she couldn't help but wonder where he was going and with whom. That he hadn't yet returned by the time she fell asleep made her unaccountably angry—both at him and at herself for caring.

The second morning, she had awakened cross with herself for letting a man like Sean Garrett bother her. She'd be here six months. Despite her threats to move out and find another place, she knew she wouldn't do it. Apartments like this were too hard to come by. And why should she let problems with her landlord force her to live somewhere she'd loathe? Nor was she going to live like a phantom, sneaking in and out at times when she was unlikely to run into him. She'd live like a sane, mature adult, which she'd seemed to have forgotten she was since meeting Sean Garrett. *That* was subject to change starting today.

She restored her bed into a sofa, then walked into the kitchen and bent down to take the teakettle out of the lower cabinet. With no more movement than required to do these two small chores, she knew that her muscles had become soft and her joints stiff with just one day's inactivity.

Donning a pair of pink tights, ballet shoes, a black leotard, and a pair of blue leg warmers, she went to the area in the large room near the windows. She'd purposefully left this space empty. Slowly and methodically she began to do her stretching exercises. She was into the second set of *pliés* when she heard someone on the stairs. A moment later he knocked on the door.

When she opened it, she was braced to face Sean, but breathed a sigh of relief when she saw it was the man from the telephone company.

"Miss Simpson?"

"Yes, come in."

She moved aside and he entered the room carrying a roll of cable and a rectangular box. "One desk slimline, ivory, push-button," he said, consulting an order he held in his hand. He was a young man in his early twenties with long hair and bright smiling eyes.

"Yes."

"Where do you want it?"

She indicated a low table at the end of the sofa. "I thought here."

He surveyed the area clinically. "That should do it. I can attach it to that baseboard under the window and run the cord under the rug. That way you won't be tripping on it. How's that?"

"That's fine."

He went about his work, making several trips back and forth to his truck. "Why don't you leave the door open?" Blair called to him. "That way you can come in and out even with your hands full."

"Thanks."

Unself-conscious of her attire but knowing she

shouldn't cool down too quickly, she pulled on a shirt and tied the tail in a knot at her waist. She left it unbuttoned and rolled the sleeves to her elbows. She went into the kitchen to brew a pot of tea while the telephone company man told her that he was a student at NYU who was only working as an installer during the summer. He was majoring in marketing.

He was finished with the installation by the time the tea was brewed. "Would you care for some tea?" she asked hospitably.

He hedged. "Got a Coke?"

She laughed. "Coming up." She filled a glass with ice and Coke and handed it to him. He drained it before taking a breath.

"Are you some kind of dancer?" he asked, looking down at her shoes.

"Yes. I dance professionally."

"No kiddin'! How about showing me a few steps?"

"How about you clearing out?"

Two surprised victims came under Sean's baleful gaze as they whipped their heads toward the deadly voice. The young man standing beside Blair swallowed a lump of fear.

"I . . . I was just about to go," he stuttered.

"Don't let us keep you."

The young man set the glass on the tabletop, but it fell over to send ice cubes scuttling across the varnished surface. Hastily he uprighted the glass, chunked the ice cubes back in it, and nervously dried his hand on his denim-clad thigh. He backed away to gather up his equipment.

Too angry to speak until now, Blair said to him, "Thank you for the telephone."

"You bet. If you have any trouble call m . . ." He darted a cautious look in Sean's direction. "Call us," he amended. He squeezed past Sean's looming bulk and scampered down the stairs as though grateful to escape with his life. Sean slammed the door shut behind him.

Fists digging into her hips, Blair faced him down when he turned around. "Well I hope you're happy with yourself. You succeeded in bullying a perfectly harmless boy."

"Boy my ass. And how do you know he was harmless? Didn't I warn you about letting strange men into this place while no one else is around?"

"My mother has warned me about that since I was six years old. I don't need you to keep harping on it. Besides he wasn't a 'strange man.' I knew he was from the telephone company. All I had to do was look at his big truck with the bright blue and yellow stripes down its side." She was shouting at full voice, letting off some of the steam that had been collecting inside since he had insulted her with that torrid kiss the night before last.

His volume was no more monitored than hers. "If he were a sterling character, he could be tempted to fall from grace after seeing you. Have you looked in a mirror? Or are you so used to prancing around like that, that you didn't realize what a come on it is?"

Truly perplexed, she glanced down at herself. Raising her eyes back to his she said loftily, "These happen to be my work clothes. And I wasn't *prancing*. I was doing some exercises when he arrived, and yes, I am accustomed to wearing leotards and tights."

"Of course you have no idea what those woolly things—"

"Leg warmers."

". . . what those leg warmers do for your body," he finished sarcastically. "It's pure coincidence that they come to just above your knees and draw attention to the top of your thighs. Not to mention that the legs of that leotard are cut up so high you might as well not have anything at all over your tight little rear. Oh, I'm sure our sweet boy didn't notice any of that when you opened your door to him dressed like that." As he talked, he made slow progress into the room until he stood within an arm's reach of her.

"As a matter of fact," she ground out, "I wasn't dressed like this when he came in." With frustrated fingers she worked at the knot at her waist until it fell free. "I didn't have this shirt on." She peeled off the shirt and flung it aside, baring to his livid eyes the deeply scooped neck and thin shoulder straps of her leotard.

His eyes riveted on her impertinent breasts that strained against the black cloth stretched over them like a second skin. His breath was vacuumed in sharply. Then his arm shot out and he clamped a hand around the base of her neck. He hauled her against him with a movement so swift and sudden that it drove the breath out of her body on impact.

Ineffectually she pummeled him with her fist as his mouth cemented with hers. His other arm went around her waist and he lifted her against him to carry her squirming, struggling form to the sofa. His knee sank into the cushions as he lay her down and followed with his own body. One heavy leg lay across hers, pinning them down while his hands trapped her head and held it still for his kiss.

During it all, even while she writhed against him and fought with all her strength, he kept his promise. He didn't hurt her.

When she began to weaken, the pressure of his mouth decreased until he was sipping at her lips, laving them with his tongue. She whimpered her last protest and surrendered to her thirst. He didn't delay in spearing his tongue into her mouth and claiming it as his own. He cradled her cheek in one of his large palms while the other hand went undetained to her breast and fondled it reverently.

"I've become a jealous maniac, Blair," he said into her mouth. "I don't want any other man looking at you." His hand slid between her flesh and the elasticized leotard, pulling it down until her breast was free of its confinement.

"No," she groaned at his misplaced possessiveness. "You have no . . . say . . . over who . . ." Then she groaned for a different reason. He'd be so disappointed. Dancers were characteristically flat chested and—

"My God," he whispered.

The awesome tone of his voice forced her eyes to open. He was studying her with careful attention to detail. "What a gorgeous color you are, Blair. Delicate." His blond head rested against her chest. For a moment she thought she imagined the light caresses, until she felt the air cooling against the damp skin. Then all too keenly she felt the finessing of his tongue. "Delicate and so sweet," he murmured against her.

"No, no, Sean. Please . . ."

"Why? Tell me why." His tongue caressed elusively until she was surrounded by the hot, honeyed trap of his mouth.

Her fingers plowed through the thick mane of his hair and held his head secure. He drew on her with a sweetness that made her want to weep. "Because . . . because . . . there's no room in my . . . life for this. I don't . . ."

He levered himself above her to pierce her with his laser-beam eyes. "You don't want anything or anybody to interfere with your career, is that it?"

"Yes," she said fiercely and didn't know if her desperation stemmed from her wanting him to accept that fact or from the withdrawal of his mouth from her breast.

"When your legs heal, you'll go back and nothing will stop you."

"Yes."

"You don't want to build a life here."

"No."

"And you don't want anyone in your life. You don't want this?" He moved against her in a way that blatantly stated his meaning. The thin leotard and tights were no protection from his aroused sex.

"No."

"You don't need it." He pressed himself against her more firmly.

"No," she sobbed.

"And you're a liar. You need me right now so badly that you're in pain."

His knee gently prized her legs apart and he lay atop her, gathering her under him as though to harbor her from any and all harm. "You're aching, Blair. Let me heal you," he whispered passionately. Contrary to her protestations, her body adjusted to his with a silent entreaty and they clung together.

It was then they heard the rapid knocking on the door.

"Shhh," Sean hissed into her ear. "Please don't answer." He squeezed his eyes shut as though to block out the intrusion. His expression was agonized.

"Aunt Blair, it's me, Andrew," a high, piping voice called. "Aunt Blair, are you here?"

Chapter 4

Sean's head dropped to his chest as though a hinge at his neck had let go. Breath filtered through his teeth in a long, low sigh. Slowly he eased away from her.

"Aunt Bl—"

"Coming, Andrew," she called shakily as she fumbled to raise the strap of her leotard. Her eyes refused to meet Sean's as she swung her legs off the couch and hurried to the door. "Hi!" she said with a false gaiety as she pulled open the door.

"Were you in the bathroom or something?" Andrew asked with childlike candor.

"Uh, no. S . . . Sean and I were trying out my

new telephone. Remind me to give you the number to give your mom."

At mention of his hero's name, Andrew's dark eyes swept the room. "Hi, Sean," he said brightly and skirted past Blair into the room.

"Hi, there." Sean extended his palm and Andrew slapped it with his fingers.

"How did you get over here?" Blair asked.

"I walked," Andrew said proudly. "I know a shortcut. Mom sent me to tell both of you that she's having a party tonight. Well, it's not really a party, just some people coming over for steaks, ya know? Anyway you're both supposed to come at eight o'clock. She said you could drive over together and save gas."

"Great," Sean said.

"I don't know," Blair said at the same time.

She could hug the boy in gratitude that he had prevented something disastrous from happening. Whatever had possessed her to let things go so far? Sean's hands, his lips, had seduced her into a realm where she didn't even recognize herself. His touch was lethal and yet she responded to it each time, though vowing she would not. Her lack of control whenever he was around was frightening.

The first time he had kissed her, she had been shocked by the potency of his kiss and the overwhelming effect it had on her. The tantalizing power of his lips, the intrusion of his tongue into her mouth, had all been new to her. She had been kissed many times, yes, but never with such dominance. Always before she had remained detached, barely tolerant of the man who was slaking a desire she couldn't understand. She understood now. For what had been inconceivable only a few days ago was now familiar. The nuances of Sean's mouth had become like an addiction to her. Knowing it was dangerous, even deadly, she craved more in increasing amounts and frequent doses. Each time he kissed her, he created a gnawing need that could well destroy her life's blueprint.

More alarming than her own physical susceptibility was his possessive attitude toward her. Who had given him the right to watch over her, to say who she could and couldn't invite into her own apartment, what she should or shouldn't wear? She had lived thirty years without his protection and she didn't think she'd need it for at least thirty more.

After the debacle of a few moments ago, spending the evening with him was out of the question. "I'm awfully tired, Andrew, my legs have been hurting this morning, and I'm sure I won't be missed."

Andrew turned to her, his eyes peering out from bangs in need of a trim. "You gotta come, Aunt Blair. Mom said she was giving the party to introduce you to people."

"Yeah, Blair, you gotta go," Sean added tauntingly.

She read the challenge in his eyes. His grin was salacious, daring. If she backed out of the invitation, he would see it as cowardice and he would be absolutely right. She blessed him with a withering look. "Okay, Andrew," she said through tight lips. "Tell your mom I'll be there."

"Super. She said Mandy and me could stay up until eight-thirty if we promised not to get in the way."

"Mandy and I," Sean corrected him. "Say, I could use a helper today. I'm working on a house on the beach. Would you be interested in earning a dollar or two?"

"Gee, Sean, that'd be great!"

Sean smiled. "Go call your mom and tell her where you'll be. The back door is open. I'll meet you in the kitchen. We'll need a cooler of water on a hot day like today."

"Okay. See ya tonight, Aunt Blair," Andrew called as he dashed out the door and bounded down the stairs in his excitement.

As soon as the boy was out of earshot, Sean turned to Blair. "Are your legs really hurting?"

Prepared to light into him about his high-handedness with her, Blair was defeated once again by his gentleness. She shrugged indifferently. "A little."

"Maybe you should call your doctor."

"No," she snapped. Then thinking that sounded too defensive, she said, "I didn't do much yesterday. I just need to work some kinks out with exercise."

"I think you should rest them."

"Well I didn't ask to hear what you think, did I? And whatever you do think is of no interest to me."

"Isn't it?"

"No." Her breasts rose and fell with her growing irritation. She was furious with him for always being so damnably right and furious with herself for always being on the defensive. "What happened here," she indicated the sofa with an impatient gesture, "was a mistake and won't be repeated. And it certainly doesn't give you license to pry into my life."

"I wasn't prying. I was only expressing concern."

"Well I don't need your concern."

"Yeah, I know. You don't need anybody."

"I'm glad you finally got the message. Now you can stop pestering me all the time."

"You don't like my company?"

"Not particularly. You're overbearing. I don't like aggressive men."

"You don't like it when I kiss you?"

"No."

"You don't like it when I caress you?"

"No," she cried, hoping the strident sound of her voice would drown out the questions he asked in a soothing tone.

"When I touch and kiss your breasts?"

"No!"

"You're lying again, Blair."

He was right. Even now her body was quivering with remembrance of his embraces. She longed to feel again the silky caress of his mustache on her flesh. But she'd be damned before she'd say that out loud to him. Forcing the sensuous thoughts from her mind she faced him, her whole body crackling with anger. Again he was too quick for her. He turned the tables.

"Relax, Blair. I've never forced myself on any woman. If my caresses are repulsive to you, then I won't touch you as a lover again. However, I see no reason why we can't be friends. I'll pick you up just before eight. In the meantime, *as a friend*, I recommend you rest your legs."

Then he was gone before she was able to utter one word of objection.

The sounds of loud conversation and laughter reached them as they walked up the sidewalk to the Delgados' house. "I guess the party is already in full swing," Sean said.

"I guess so."

He had arrived at her door just as he had said, a few minutes before eight. She was ready except for her jewelry. He waited inside the threshold as she put pearl studs in her ears and misted herself with fragrance.

She couldn't have criticized his manners. They were above reproach. Glancing at him surreptitiously in the mirror, she saw that he wasn't looking at her, but was fiddling with the brass doorknob. "This is loose. Remind me to fix it," and "That's a pretty dress," were spoken with the same degree of emotion.

"Thank you." The white eyelet halter dress fit tightly through the bodice and waist to swing full and loose to just below her knees. With it she wore a pair of strappy gold sandals that wrapped around her ankles. Both the hemline of the skirt and the sandal straps around her ankles accented the perfect formation of her calves.

If his fingers touched her bare back as they descended the stairs, she was certain it was only for courtesy's sake. He ushered her into the Mercedes and then launched into a tale about Andrew racing across the beach with a sack of nails. When he tripped in the deep sand, the nails went flying and it had taken him and Sean a half hour to sift through the sand to see that all were picked up.

"I only hope we didn't miss one and someone finds it for us with his heel," he said.

Blair was laughing when she replied, "So do I. Was he worth the dollar you paid him?"

"I had to pay the little con man two dollars. Inflation."

By the time they pulled in front of Pam's house, she had relaxed her guard. Apparently Sean had taken her at her word. He was behaving as a good friend and not as a would-be lover.

Pam greeted them with warm, effusive hugs. "The guest of honor is here," she called to the other guests who were milling around the hors d'oeuvre trays strategically placed around the cluttered room.

They were swarmed by those wishing to be introduced to Pam's friend whom many of them considered a celebrity. Blair gave Pam an I-don't-believe-this look when she realized her friend had colored her successful career to sound more grandiose than it was. She was aware, too, of Sean being greeted just as enthusiastically as she. The women simpered; the men spoke deferentially.

Amidst all the confusion, Blair stooped to kiss each little pajamaed Delgado before he or she was aimed in the direction of the bedrooms with a stern command to go to bed.

"Those kids!" Pam exclaimed when the last was seen disappearing into the hallway. "They're enough to make me want to abstain."

Just then Joe Delgado, wearing his perpetual grin and a chef's apron with "This Cook Knows How to Sizzle" printed on it, came up to them and encircled his wife with his arms just below her breasts. "Well, not completely *abstain* . . ." Pam said suggestively to Blair and winked lewdly. The two women laughed.

"Did I miss something?" Joe asked good-naturedly and greeted Blair with a kiss on the cheek and Sean with a hearty handshake. He was as lean and wiry as his wife was plump and soft. "The room is coming along great, Sean. We can't wait."

"What room?" Blair asked, now feeling that she'd missed something.

"Sean's adding a playroom onto the back of the house. Did I forget to tell you?" Pam asked.

"Yes," Blair said, stealing a glance up at Sean who stood as close as he could without actually touching her.

"Oh, we can't wait for it to be finished. I'll show you later. First there are a dozen people wanting to meet you."

For the next few minutes Blair fielded the myriad

questions hurled at her. Had she ever danced with Baryshnikov? Was a ten-year-old too young to start *pointe*? Did she adhere to any special diet to stay so thin? How much did she weigh anyway? Was it true she and Pam had once taken classes with Juliet Prowse? Were her nails real or were they sculptured? Would she even consider auditioning the players for the PTA benefit talent show?

Over that question, she stammered a polite promise to think about it. She almost jumped when large hands cupped her shoulders. "What would you like to drink?" Subconsciously, only for a precious moment, she leaned against the tall, strong frame behind her. The bare skin on her back met the texture of his navy summer weight sportscoat and the smooth coolness of his pale blue cotton shirt. She wasn't even aware that she tilted her head to the side to better feel the mustachioed lips against her ear.

"White wine on the rocks," she whispered, trying unsuccessfully to listen to the lady from the PTA expounding on the value of their talent show. Blair's shoulders were squeezed lightly before Sean moved away.

Minutes later he was back with an icy glass of sparkling wine. The woman's incessant chatter hadn't flagged for one moment.

"Blair, I think Pam's looking for you. She's in the kitchen."

"Excuse me," Blair said graciously before letting Sean steer her away from the woman.

"Thanks," she said out of the corner of her mouth.

"That broad would bore a statue," he said, leaning down to whisper in her ear. "She pulled the same thing with me a few years ago. Since I was Irish she thought it would be so nice if I'd sing 'Danny Boy' in their talent show."

Blair nearly choked on her sip of wine. Tears of mirth filled her eyes. "You're kidding," she said on a laugh.

"I wish I were."

"And did you sing 'Danny Boy'?"

He scowled darkly, lowering the thick brows over his brilliant eyes. "I bought her off with a hundred-dollar check."

They were laughing when they entered the chaos of the kitchen. Pam was taking bowls of potato salad and cole slaw from the refrigerator. "Oh, I'm glad you two wandered in. Sean, go show Blair the new room."

"Don't you need any help?" Blair asked.

"Not this minute. Go on. Have a good time."

They exited through the sliding glass door leading off to the patio. The aroma of charcoaled meat wafted toward them. Joe was flipping large slabs of steak on the grill.

"You *look* like you know what you're doing," Sean said teasingly.

"Rare, medium rare, well done," Joe enumerated, pointing out each section of the grill with his long-pronged fork, then taking a large gulp of beer.

"Lay off the beer until my steak's cooked," Sean

said. Joe saluted him with the fork. They laughed and strolled to the other end of the patio. "Watch your step."

Sean guided her through the skeletal wooden framework of the new room. "This is going to be a playroom?" Blair asked, her eyes scanning the bare concrete foundation.

"Yes. Over there will be a fireplace. Here, bookshelves and a built-in desk, should any of the children ever feel inclined to study," he said, smiling. "We're even going to install a small refrigerator along with a television set."

"Sounds terrific."

"I'm going to skylight it," Sean said, gazing up at the uncovered rafters overhead. "That'll save electricity, because I don't think the kids will be conscientious about turning off lights. I'm going to use—" He broke off and turned to her suddenly. "You really aren't interested in this, are you?"

"Yes I am." She was. She discovered that she liked the enthusiasm in his voice when he spoke about his work. His hands, gesturing descriptively, were eloquent. They had felt so warm on the bare skin of her shoulders. Reassuring. Comforting. "The kids are going to love it."

"I think Pam and Joe will too. Theoretically with all the kids in here, it will give them some privacy."

"I can imagine that their moments of privacy are few and far between."

He chuckled. "They couldn't be too hard to come by or there wouldn't be so many kids."

She joined his laughter as she looked up at him, and then suddenly, at the same time, their laughter broke off. The moment had become intensely intimate. Moonlight streamed in through the rafters overhead, casting his face in deep shadows as he looked down at her. She couldn't discern his expression, she only knew that he was studying her.

The moonlight that crowned his light colored hair bathed her face with a silvery glow. Sean longed to run his fingers over the glossy strands of her hair sleeked back into a classic ballerina's bun on her neck. His lips were starved for a taste of her mouth, moist and pink in the shimmering light. They longed to roam to her dainty ear with that beguiling pearl that almost matched the luminescence of her skin. His eyes traveled the path of the moonlight until it disappeared into the shadowy cleft between her small breasts. Imagination placed his tongue there and he could all but taste the warmth he knew he would find.

Fantasies filled his head. He could see again the shell-pink crest of her breast. He could feel again its velvet-button texture against his tongue. He could hear again her throaty purrs of pleasure as he had indulged his hunger for her taste.

In years, he didn't remember wanting a woman as he'd wanted Blair from the first time his eyes had encountered hers. Since then he had been single-minded in his daydreams. His body ached for hers. That made no damn sense at all. She wasn't the type he usually preferred. Because of his own size, he had commonly dated taller women, with generous figures.

To him Blair seemed like a doll. But a doll that lived and breathed and moved and was capable of quenching the fire in his loins that constantly mocked him.

It was all wrong and he knew it. Once, he had made grave errors in judgment and they had cost him everything. He had come away with a sounder insight into life's priorities and had managed to re-establish himself. He was now successful in all but one area of his life. He had no one to share it with. So far he'd found no one he'd risk sharing his life with. Love was so often dependent on things going right. When something went wrong . . .

Blair Simpson had her own problems to cope with. She was undergoing a crisis that she would have to confront. He didn't need her in his life. That would only complicate things. And she claimed not to need him.

Yet now, standing here in the moonlight, desire stampeded through his body. He wanted nothing more than to kiss away her insincere protests, to clasp her to him and bury himself deep inside her, begging her to relieve him of his agony.

The fierceness of his musings must have shown in the rugged planes of his face for she said his name tentatively. He shook his head to clear it, then drained the contents of his cocktail glass. "Yeah, I, uh, guess we ought to rejoin the others."

Blair had taken only a few sips of her wine. Her fingers were stiff with cold. She had clenched them around the glass as though it were her last handhold on sanity. Sean stepped aside and ushered her back across the patio. Joe was still at the grill, deep in discussion now with a defense attorney about crime on the streets.

Pandemonium had broken out in the kitchen. Pam was listening to first one offspring and then the other as they offered conflicting accounts of a pillow fight. A third child was wailing, tears rolling down her cheeks. Pam was fishing ears of corn out of a vat of boiling water and placing them on a platter.

Despite the children's obvious disobedience and Pam's anxiety, Sean and Blair burst out laughing. "What's going on?" Sean asked.

"I think they're just too excited to go to bed." She looked down at the children threateningly. "I'm going to call Daddy and he'll be mad."

They gave about as much credence to that warning as they had to the others. "Why don't you let me put them to bed?" Blair offered.

"But you're my guest," Pam protested.

"I'm your friend and you've got your hands full. Come on, kids, enough of this," Blair said firmly enough to get their attention. "Andrew, *march*," she said, pointing an imperious finger in the direction of the bedroom. "Come on, Mandy."

"I'll get this one," Sean said, picking up little Paul and heaving him over his shoulders to straddle his head. Paul whooped in glee and grabbed a handful of Sean's blond hair.

"I didn't volunteer you, too," Blair said as they trooped out of the kitchen, taking the back hallway that led to the two bedrooms the children shared.

"I couldn't let you take on the whole regiment."

As the two bedrooms were connected by a door, Blair and Sean were able to tuck everyone into their respective beds while keeping an eye on those already under the covers. The baby was the only one already asleep. He was still confined to a crib. The two girls slept in a double bed in the room with the baby. The two boys slept in bunk beds in the other. Since Andrew was the older, he had the top bunk.

"Set a good example for your little sister and go to sleep now," Blair whispered to Mandy. "Let your mom and dad enjoy their party. Okay?"

"Okay," she said, yawning. Angela, somewhere around four if Blair remembered correctly, was already drifting off. "Will you leave the lamp on?"

"Mandy is a baby, Mandy is a baby," Andrew chanted from his bunk.

"Cool it, Andrew," Sean said sternly.

"Well she is," Andrew said petulantly. "She has to sleep with Angela. I don't want anybody mashing me while I'm asleep."

"Mommy and Daddy sleep in a bed together," Mandy protested.

"No one else gets to sleep with them and we can't go in their room at night unless it's lightning and thundering," Angela contributed sleepily.

Blair met Sean's laughing eyes across the room and then darted them back to the girls.

"We can't go in their room on Saturday morning either until after *The Lone Ranger* goes off," Paul said, sitting up in his bunk with this important bit of news.

Sean's laugh broke the surface, but he smothered it with a cough as he pushed Paul back down.

"Their bed is real big, Blair," Mandy said conversationally.

"Is it?" she asked on a high note. She gave folding back the counterpane an inordinate amount of attention.

"Sean's got one just as big, don't you, Sean? I've seen it," Andrew said.

"Have you ever seen Sean's bed?" Angela asked Blair.

"N . . . no. Good night now."

"Do you have a big bed like Sean's?" Mandy asked.

"No, stupid," Andrew said. "Didn't you see that sofa she has to sleep on?"

Mandy's face clouded with commiseration. "Maybe if you asked Sean he'd let you sleep with him in his big bed. He doesn't live very far from you."

"Our daddy doesn't mind Mommy sleeping with him," Angela added.

Blair's cheeks flamed scarlet and she didn't remember once in her life blushing before.

"Okay, that's all," Sean said with an intimidating voice. "Good night." He made certain all four pairs of eyes were closed before he turned to leave. After a cursory glance to the sleeping baby, who blessedly hadn't been able to contribute to the conversation, Blair joined him in the hallway. She tried to go past him, but he blocked her path.

"Do you have any favors to ask me?" he asked, his blue eyes dancing.

"No." She could still feel deep stains on her cheeks.

He laughed devilishly. Placing his hand on the back of her neck he said, "Let's go get something to eat."

Pam's dinner, for all her distractions while preparing it, was wonderful, as were Joe's steaks. The guests heaped their plates high from the buffet line and then selected places to sit either in the living room or on the patio.

Blair noticed that she and Sean were the object of many covert, speculative looks. He wasn't openly affectionate, but he was never far from her side either. He joined in the conversations around them, yet was constantly murmuring private asides into her ear. When she was talking to someone else, she felt his eyes on her, ever watchful.

Since he had fetched and carried for her throughout the meal, she insisted on carrying their plates into the kitchen when they were done. She scraped the refuse into the large plastic garbage can standing in the corner and took the plates to the sink to rinse them. She was just drying her hands on a paper towel when one of the guests came in behind her.

"That was quite a feed," he said, rubbing his hands over a potbelly.

He reminded her of "the toucher type," one of those annoying men who didn't think he could carry on a conversation with a woman unless he was pawing her. Men like that had always infuriated Blair. What made such men think she wanted or liked their clammy hands on her? From the moment she'd been introduced to him, she'd avoided him. He had said, "I could have guessed you were a dancer with legs like those." He had considered his remark amusing. She had thought it, like him, repugnant.

"Yes, it was a delicious meal."

He had deliberately placed himself between her and the door. "Get into the city often?"

"I just moved here a few days ago, Mr. . . ."

"Stan Collier. Call me Stan. All my friends do," he said in an oily voice.

"I haven't had an occasion to return to the city."

"Me, I have to commute every day on the damned train. Of course sometimes if business keeps me in the city for a dinner appointment, I stay over in the company's apartment. It's a nice little place. Private."

Blair couldn't believe this. If he weren't so disgusting, he'd be pitiful. Whatever was he doing as a guest of the Delgados? Surely Pam and Joe didn't condone this sleaziness.

"I'm sure it's very nice. Now if you'll excuse—"

"Anyway what I was thinking was maybe if you came into the city and found yourself free for lunch, you could—"

"Sell it somewhere else, Collier. Miss Simpson isn't interested." The hefty Stan whirled around with amazing agility when Sean's words rasped threateningly through the room. Blair sank against the countertop in relief. She hadn't been afraid of this overweight buffoon, she'd only been reluctant to cause a scene at Pam's party.

"Hey, Garrett, relax, relax," Stan Collier said with false bravado. His beefy forehead was perspiring profusely. "I was only funning with her. Can't you take a joke?"

"Yeah, I can take a joke," Sean said, with not the least hint of a smile on his rigid face. "I didn't hear anything funny. Blair?" He extended his hand and she rushed to it, grasping it like it was a safety rope. Sean enfolded her against him, more for the benefit of their observer than for her. Nonetheless, she pressed against him, welcoming the feeling of security his strong body lent hers.

They moved out of the room. "I hope you wanted to be rescued. Maybe you find Stan appealing," he murmured in her ear as his blond head bent over her.

"Oh, please," she said, shivering against him. "Do Pam and Joe know about him?"

"Everyone in Tidelands knows about him and his philandering. Or at least his claims to philandering. I'm not sure the exploits he brags about are more than wishful thinking."

"Why would Pam and Joe invite him here?"

"His wife is a darling woman. Everyone adores her and tolerates Stan because of her. He didn't single you out. He's made that same trite pass to everyone who wears a skirt."

"And here I thought I was special," she said with an exaggerated pout.

He laughed, then became serious as he stared down at her. "You are, but I doubt if anyone with Stan's indiscriminate taste would recognize just how special." He leaned closer and brushed the tip of his index finger over the tiny pearl in her ear. "I'm very discriminating."

She couldn't speak. The muscles of her throat closed around her vocal cords. The quipping reply she knew she should come back with was prohibited from ever being uttered. Instead she stood mute, losing herself in the depths of his blue eyes.

"Would you like some coffee?" Had he said, "Would you like to make love?" it couldn't have sounded more like an invitation to intimacy.

Tell him you can get your own coffee, Blair, her mind screamed. Instead her lips formed the words, "Yes, please. No sugar, a drop of cream." He backed away slowly, his eyes still charting her face.

Dazed, Blair drifted to a chair and sat down. She pretended to listen when one of the ladies started in on how deplorable the dance school in town was, but her mind was in a turmoil. Her heart failed to slow down even though she willed it to. The roaring in her ears drowned out the woman's tirade. Sean had kept his word. He hadn't made one move toward her that could be criticized and that wasn't in keeping with their agreement that they be friends only.

Why then her kamikaze gravitation toward him?

She didn't want to admit how nice it was to be looked after, to be fawned over. Always independent, she now reveled in relinquishing control to his masculine protectiveness. Had someone like Stan approached her months ago, she would have brushed him aside with a lashing insult that would have shocked him speechless and left his ears blistered and his ego crushed. She didn't want to concede how wonderful it had been to let Sean fight that battle for her. Just as seductive as his kisses, was the pleasure she found in being harbored by his virile strength.

"That's a terrific idea," Pam exclaimed, jolting Blair out of her reverie. "What do you think, Blair?"

"Uh, I . . ." she stuttered. Taking the saucer Sean was offering her, she realized that she had been the focal point of the unheard conversation going on around her. "I don't know," she said lamely. *What had they been talking about?*

Pam enlightened her. "The dance school here is terrible. I've wanted to get Mandy started on ballet, but didn't think I'd get my money's worth. And as you know if a child isn't taught properly from the first, there can be irreparable damage done to her muscles. Do you think you'd like to teach some classes while you're here?"

"Well—"

"I know I would love to take ballet," one of the ladies chimed in. "Nothing strenuous you understand, just stretching exercises to shave off some lumps." Several others concurred enthusiastically.

"You want *me* to teach ballet classes?" Blair asked, finally grasping the drift of the conversation.

"Yes! Why not?"

Chapter 5

*B*lair *stared back at the expectant faces surrounding her* and laughed uncomfortably. "Well for one thing, I'm not a teacher."

"But you're a dancer. The best I've ever seen. Now don't be modest," Pam rushed on when she saw Blair was about to object. "You love to dance and since you can't professionally for awhile, this might be the next best thing." The others nodded in agreement.

"Would it hurt your legs?" Blair turned to the quiet, low voice speaking close to her ear and looked into Sean's penetrating eyes.

"I don't think so. The doctor said that a minimum of regular exercise would be good for them and help them retain their strength. That way the climb back after six months' inactivity won't be so difficult."

"Then it's all set!" Pam said, her happy face beaming.

"Wait, wait, Pam. One has to have a studio, you know."

Pam's brow wrinkled in consternation. "Oh, yeah."

"You need a wooden floor, a large room?" Sean inquired.

Blair turned back to Sean. "Yes."

"I bought an old school gymnasium several months ago with the idea of one day converting it into a health club. It has such a room. You could use that. I'll do whatever reconstruction needs to be done."

"Terrific!" Pam clapped her hands.

"But I don't want to go into business," Blair protested. She felt she was being carried along by a current she couldn't fight.

"I won't charge you rent for the building and you won't charge your students. We'll consider it a community project." Sean silently polled the crowd and saw that everyone agreed.

"But I'll need records and something to play them on and . . ."

"I bought a record player at a police auction last month. I'll donate that," Joe said.

"Between us, you and I have got dance records

galore," Pam added. "So you see, Blair, you've got no problems."

She gnawed her bottom lip in contemplation. If living here less than a week had taught her one thing it was that time didn't move as fast in Tidelands as it did in the city. She was going to be here for six long months. If she didn't do something, she'd likely go mad. Was this the answer?

"I could teach basic ballet to students no older than twelve," she said slowly. "For you women I suppose I could conduct exercise classes, but I won't be able to do any strenuous calisthenics."

"We could do those on our own," one of the women contributed.

Pam took both of Blair's hands. "Then you'll say yes? Please, Blair. It'll be good for you, too. If I didn't think so, I wouldn't have suggested it."

Blair's eyes swept up to Sean. He was staring at her in that stirring way, but he neither encouraged nor discouraged her compliance. She looked back at Pam, shrugged, and said, "As you said, why not?"

All the guests had departed except Sean and Blair, who insisted on helping Pam clean up the mess left behind. "Do you do windows?" Pam asked facetiously as Blair stacked the last of the dishes into the dishwasher.

"Only when I can no longer see out them," she said, latching the door and starting the machine that wheezed as though in the throes of dying. "Will this thing make it through the cycle?" Blair asked.

"God, I hope so. Surely it wouldn't go out on me tonight. It couldn't be that cruel. By the way, did I ever thank you and Sean for getting those little heathens of mine to bed?"

"It was our pleasure," Sean said, coming in through the patio door where he and Joe had been enjoying one last cup of coffee. Sean winked at Blair and she struggled to hold back a giggle.

Their amusement was lost on Pam who went to Joe and collapsed into his waiting arms. "Great party, Hon," he said, hugging her tight. "You did yourself proud."

"Thanks, but I'm pooped."

"Then we'll say good night," Sean said, taking Blair's hand and leading her through the living room to the front door.

"I didn't mean to force you out," Pam said as she and Joe followed them to the door.

"I think Blair's had it, too. And now she's got a lot to think about."

"Did I really agree to start teaching ballet classes to kids and housewives?" she asked dismally.

"You sure did," Pam said cheerfully.

"As long as you understand that it's only temporary. Only for as long as I'm here."

Pam's smile drooped. "I'm not going to think about that. I've already become accustomed to your being in town."

All were quiet for a moment, then Sean said,

"She'll be here for six months at least. I don't let tenants out of their leases easily." They laughed then, grateful to him for relieving the momentary tension.

"If I can squeeze my fat body into an old leotard, I'll be the first one there when you start the exercise classes," Pam said.

"Don't work off too much flesh. I've grown so fond of it," Joe said from behind her, as he hugged his wife and nuzzled her neck.

"I think that's our cue," Sean said dryly.

"Good night and thank you for the party," Blair said as Sean steered her away from the door.

"Good night," Pam and Joe called in unison.

"Joe, I need to talk to you about what kind of roofing you want, but as tomorrow's Saturday, I won't call in the morning until after *The Lone Ranger*," Sean teased.

They heard Pam's soft, surprised gasp and Joe's hearty laugh before he closed the door.

Sean and Blair were still laughing when he pulled the Mercedes to a smooth stop in his driveway.

"Coffee? Nightcap?" he asked as he cut the motor.

"No. What you said is true. I've got a million things on my mind. Routines to work out, music to choose." She sighed dramatically. "What have I *done*?"

He chuckled as he opened his door and came around to open hers. No sooner had she stepped onto the ground than she was lifted into his arms. "We've got to take care of these knees now more than ever," he said. "You may be the last great hope for the women of Tidelands on the brink of obesity."

He had taken off his jacket early in the evening and rolled up his shirt sleeves. His arm was like a bar of iron that had been infused with life and warmth as it supported her back. To ward off the desire she felt unfurling inside her she asked, "Do you think anybody will really be interested in coming to the classes?"

"I'm sure they will. They all aspire to look like you. Impossible, of course, but you give them hope." At the top step, he ducked his head briefly to drop a chaste kiss on her forehead. "Good night, friend. Thank you for going to the party with me. I had a wonderful time."

He swung her down, but his kiss, brief and impersonal as it was, had weakened her to the point that she wasn't prepared to support herself. She landed on her knee the wrong way and she felt the abused tendons give way.

"Oh," she cried out when the pain stabbed under her kneecap like a knife.

"What? Oh, my God, what happened, Blair?" Sean fell to his own knees to better inspect hers as she leaned over and massaged the injured joint.

"It's . . . it's nothing," she said unsteadily, trying to block out the wave of dizziness that accompanied the pain. "I landed wrong, that's all. Hurts like hell."

"God, I'm sorry," he said in an anguished voice

before raising her skirt to place his hands around her knee.

"It's not your fault, Sean. It happens all the time. At least this time I was in front of my own door. Last time it gave out, I was shopping in Bloomingdale's on a Saturday no less."

She tried to laugh away his anxiety and her pain, but his face was grim as he stood, propping her against him, and opened the door. He lifted her again and carried her into the darkened apartment, depositing her in a chair. "Sean—"

"Stay right there," he instructed as he left her to switch on the lamp on the end table. "Do you have any medication to take for that?"

She shook her head. "I didn't have the prescription for pain pills filled. I didn't want to get started on anything like that."

"Aspirin?"

"Yes, I'd take a couple of aspirins."

"Where are they?" He had pulled down the sofa and converted it into her bed. There was something disturbingly personal about his handling the linens she had slept on the night before.

"In the bathroom. The cabinet over the sink. But really—"

She was speaking to his shadow as he disappeared into the bathroom. She heard him fumbling in the tiny cabinet, a soft curse, the water running. Then he was back with a glass of water and two aspirins looking like dots in his massive palm.

"Should you rub something on it? An ointment or something?"

She swallowed the aspirins. "No. I'll just elevate it while I'm sleeping. Don't worry about it. By morning it'll be fine."

"What happened?" He knelt in front of her and, before she could stop him, was working at the thin laces wrapped around her ankles and taking off the gold sandals.

"One of those tendons or ligaments or whatever twisted when I came down on it. They're weak and can't take some forms of stress."

He looked up at her from his kneeling position. "Do you have to go to the bathroom before I tuck you in for the night?"

She was struck dumb by the question, then realized how ridiculous that sentiment was. "Uh, I'd probably better," she answered, not quite meeting his eyes.

He scooped her in his arms again and carried her to the door. When he set her down, he made sure she was supporting herself with her better leg. "Hop the rest of the way."

"You're over-reacting."

"Someone has to treat these injuries sensibly, for it's sure as hell you don't."

She glared at him and then shut the door in his face. "Hop!" he called through it.

When she was finished, he was waiting for her on the other side of the door, not having budged from his post. "What do you sleep in?"

"Sean," she said gratingly.

"Okay, if you'd rather sleep in the buff, that's—"

"There are some T-shirts in the top drawer of the bureau," she said with resignation. He was bent on carrying out the Clara Barton routine and she really had no choice but to play along.

He came back carrying a T-shirt with *42nd Street* printed on it.

"Were you in this show?"

"Yes. Did you see it?"

"Yes."

"Then surely you remember me. I was the one in the tap shoes."

"Very funny," he said.

This bantering conversation was designed to distract them from the moment of truth that had just come upon them. She had to get out of her dress.

"Does this go up or down?" he asked in a husky voice.

"I can manage."

"Up or down?" The determination that made his eyes go as hard and incisive as diamonds was unconquerable. She couldn't conjure up enough will to try.

"Down," she whispered, dropping her eyes to stare at the floor.

The bowed position of her head aided him in unfastening the buttons behind her neck holding up her halter. When they were released, he gradually lowered the bodice. She saw his hands moving restlessly, indecisively, as they adjusted the material around her waist.

"There's a button here," Blair mumbled. In what she thought would be an impatient gesture, she fumbled past his hands to find the button at her waist. But by groping through the fabric in her search, the backs of her hands bumped against his in what evolved into a caress. His hands were lifted by the movements of hers, lifted until the tips of his fingers were scarce inches from her breasts. Both regretted when the button was found and undone.

The dress fell to the floor around her feet and she stood before him wearing only the scantiest of panties.

"I'll get it later," Sean said about the dress. His breath was warm against her face, her neck, her chest. So warm. He gathered the T-shirt in his hands and pulled it over her head, helping her poke her arms through the sleeves. He pulled it down to barely cover the band of her panties. "There." He sounded relieved.

He picked her up again and carried her to the bed, lowering her onto it with the care of a mother for her new infant. He turned away quickly as she scrambled to cover herself with the sheet.

"Does this go in the closet?" he asked, keeping his back to her as he picked up the dress.

"Yes. Thank you," she said softly, momentarily closing her eyes against the desire to see him lying down beside her.

He carefully arranged the dress on a hanger and hung it in the closet. "Would you like anything else? Some tea? Wine?"

She shook her head. The hair she had just released from its restricting pins swayed over her shoulders. "No. I'm fine."

He sat down on the edge of the mattress and looked at her for long silent moments. Had he taken her in his arms then, she admitted later that she wouldn't have resisted. She wanted nothing more than to feel the touch of his lips against hers, hard and persistent, banishing her caution. She wanted his soothing hands on her body, coaxing her into responses she knew lay just below the surface of her skin, responses too long denied and dying for the chance to live. She wanted to hear him pouring words into her ear, bold, stimulating love words she'd never allowed any other man to say. Whether he meant them or not, she longed to hear them coming from his beautiful mouth, filtering through that sensuous mustache.

But he didn't take her in his arms. Rather he asked softly, "Don't you need a pillow under that knee?"

"Yes, probably."

He retrieved the second pillow, the one that wasn't blessed with her curtain of dark hair fanning over it, and lifted the sheet. His teeth clamped together to prevent him from groaning at the sight of her naked legs between the smooth sheets. Her breasts lay flat against her chest, with only the pouting of her nipples to inflame him. Her stomach was concave beneath her rib cage and the inch of skin between the hem of her T-shirt and the lacy top of her panties beckoned to him seductively.

Striving for objectivity, he adjusted the pillow under her knee and gently bent it over the cushiony support. He couldn't resist sliding his hand down her shin and then around it to cup the firm muscle of her calf. Her eyes refused to remain open and she sighed as her lashes settled on her cheek.

When next she felt his touch, his finger was gliding over that velvety ribbon of skin on her abdomen that had so intrigued him. "Blair, please look at me."

Slowly she lifted the veil of dark lashes. The lamplight highlighted one side of his face, while the other was cast in deep shadow. The cleft in his chin looked deeper, more masculine and rugged than ever. His hair shone in the golden light.

"I want you," he said with deep intensity. "You know that. I haven't made a secret of it." The backs of his fingers celebrated the softness of her cheek. "When you realize what good friends we are," he smiled slightly, "I'm going to kiss you here." His index finger outlined her lips with a feathery touch that eventually floated down her neck to her chest. "And here." He caressed her nipple through the soft cotton of her shirt and was rewarded with a firm response. "Here," he said, massaging her navel hypnotically with his finger. He lowered his hand farther and touched her again. "Here," he said gruffly. "Everywhere."

Her back and neck arched reflexively and a small cry of helplessness escaped her lips. Her face was captured between his hands, and stroking thumbs adored the bone structure of her cheeks.

"Sean," she sighed.

"Good night." He leaned down to kiss her lightly on the lips, his mustache no more than a whisper against her mouth.

Hurriedly he snapped out the light, crossed the room and let himself out the door. Blair followed his footsteps until they faded into silence. She heard his back door close behind him.

She was left alone in the dark. Alone with the imprints of his fingers burning her skin wherever they had touched. Alone with her imagination branding erotic fantasies on her mind. Alone with that ever-widening chasm deep inside her that ached to be filled.

She was sipping her second cup of tea at the kitchen table and tentatively rotating her knee when she heard him coming up the stairs. He knocked softly.

"Come in," she called. She had put on a pair of shorts and an elasticized strapless tube-top as soon as she had gotten out of bed and tested the strength of her knee. Thankfully she could walk without any discomfort.

He opened the door she had unlocked earlier and came in, his face scowling. "What are you doing out of bed?"

"Drinking tea," she retorted, stating the obvious.

"Smart aleck. Doesn't your knee hurt?"

"I could be cute and say something like, 'Only when I laugh,' or 'Only when I breathe,' but I'd never stoop to such banality."

"Then it does hurt."

She laughed at the deep line of concern that furrowed between his brows. "Will you relax? No, it doesn't hurt. I don't think it's up to a performance of *A Chorus Line* or running the Boston marathon, but I can walk. Would you like some tea?"

"I despise tea."

"Really? I thought all Irishmen loved their tea. How about one chorus of 'Danny Boy'?" she taunted.

"You must be feeling better. You've regained your glib tongue. If you weren't already battered, I'd be tempted to punish your insolence."

"How? By giving me a well-deserved spanking?"

His eyes ran up and down the length of her body, taking in the tightly stretched knit over her breasts. "There are other, more pleasant means of discipline." He didn't need to resort to physical demonstration. Just the suggestion of it and the underlying tension in his voice had caused the tongue he had termed glib to stick to the roof of her mouth. "I came by this morning to see if you wanted to go look at your new studio."

Blair hoped that her act had been played well. Her flippant remarks had been a defense against the fluttering of her heart and the profusion of perspiration that had bathed her palms when she'd heard his footsteps coming up the stairs. Her dreams had revolved around him. All night she had been haunted by memories of past kisses and tormented by fantasies of kisses yet to come.

Repeatedly she had assured herself that her sleeplessness was due to her aching knee and the uncomfortable position of lying on her back, but by dawn she still wasn't convinced. She only hoped that the faint purple circles under her eyes had been successfully covered by make-up.

It frightened her, this preoccupation with a man she barely knew. Things were happening too quickly and she couldn't seem to get a grip on the reins of her own life. When they had slipped through her fingers, she didn't recall, but she thought it was about the time she had opened the door to a masseur and saw Sean Garrett.

She realized, too, that there was no halfway point on which they could meet. They could never be just friends, and saying that they could was only game playing. They both knew that. He had confessed without any apology his desire to become her lover. Toward that culmination, she seemed to fly, knowing all the while it was impossible for her to become involved with any man, especially one she had absolutely nothing in common with.

The only thing to do was to refrain from seeing too much of him. Out of sight, out of mind. Put the temptation off limits—that had been her resolution as she dragged herself from her bed this morning. Now it was being put to the test.

"I can drive myself over if you give me directions. I'm sure you have other work to do." Leaving the table, she went to the sink to rinse out her cup. She didn't care if the cup were rinsed out or not, but it gave her a feasible excuse to turn her back on him. She found him too damned attractive. His jeans were too tight across his loins, his thighs and sex too well defined. The polo shirt conformed to the tapering of his waist from the broad sculptured curves of his shoulders and upper chest.

"Today's Saturday. I usually don't work on Saturday."

"Well then you wouldn't want to take me over there because that would be work for you. I'll go by myself either today or tomorrow."

"But you won't be able to get into the building because . . ." He fished in the front pocket of his jeans, something she wished he wouldn't do because it stretched the cotton even tighter across his masculinity. "Because I have the only key."

Her relief that he had accomplished his task was exchanged for irritation. He was dangling the single key on the brass ring inches in front of her eyes. "I guess it's too much to hope for that you would simply turn the key over to me."

His mustache drooped in parody of a sympathetic expression. "I'm sorry." His sparkling eyes said otherwise.

"Um-huh. I'm sure you're just eaten up with grief."

His mustache then spread wide over a huge white smile. "Come on. Let's go. Have you had breakfast? How about picking up a dozen donuts on the way?"

"Donuts!" she exclaimed. "If I eat breakfast at all, I have a carton of plain yogurt."

He shrugged. "I can tell that enticing you off the straight and narrow into a life of sin and corruption is going to take some work. Come on."

Barely giving her time to grab her purse, he hauled her out of the apartment, carried her down the stairs and put her in the front seat of his ancient pickup truck.

"You don't have to try to impress me," she said sarcastically as she critically eyed the cracked vinyl upholstery with tufts of cotton sprouting from it like blossoms. The bare metal floor was littered with blueprints long used and forgotten and a variety of tools, some of which Blair couldn't identify.

Sean only grinned as he ground the truck into gear and it chugged out of the driveway. "Love me, love my truck."

Negating her protests, he stopped at a bakery to purchase a sack full of donuts. He stowed it on the seat between them, and Blair's stomach growled when the yeasty aroma filled the cab of the truck. Sean roared with laughter. He stopped at a convenience store and bought a quart of milk, then they bounced through the streets in the derelict truck to the vacant building he was donating for her use as a studio.

Leaving their breakfast for later, he came around to lift her down from the truck and carry her to the door of the building. "This isn't necessary, Sean," she said as he followed the sidewalk rather than taking the well-worn path across the dried grass.

"That's debatable since I saw the pain on your face last night, but in any event it allows me to get my hands on you."

She hadn't wanted to admit how she had looked forward to being held in his arms. She loved the feel of his hard chest against her side. Her arms had quite naturally encircled his neck to lock just beneath the strands of hair that brushed his collar. The touch of his bare arm under her bare legs sent electric currents through her body. The hand belonging to the arm that supported her back folded around her side to lightly touch her breast with his fingertips.

"Besides, what's a little familiarity between good friends?" he whispered in her ear.

She immediately lowered her arms and was annoyed when he only laughed. He set her down gently, making sure her leg wasn't going to give way as it had done the night before. He inserted the key in the lock and said by way of warning, "It doesn't look like much, so don't panic. Give me a week or so and I'll have it in tip-top shape."

He was right to warn her. Otherwise her gasp of horror might have been even louder than it was. The place was a disaster. The floor could barely be seen because of the discarded lumber and debris that obscured it. Great chunks of plaster had fallen from the ceiling. The walls were scarred and gouged for reasons Blair could only guess at. The whole room looked as if it had been pillaged by an enraged giant and left to give testimony of his temper.

She turned to look up at Sean helplessly, dismay written on every feature, her green eyes clouded with bewilderment. He placed a reassuring arm around her shoulder. "Chin up. I told you not to panic."

"But this . . . this is impossible."

"Never say impossible. You should see some of the 'before' pictures of houses I've restored. They've had a century or better to deteriorate. This building has only had about forty years." He laughed at her stupefaction. "First thing Monday morning, I'll get a wrecking crew to haul off everything that isn't nailed down. A wall man will come in and do those repairs, a ceiling man will do that, etc. Do the floors look okay?"

He shoved a pile of wormy lumber aside to let her see the floor beneath. She knelt down. "Yes, I think so."

"Someone will sand and revarnish it. The skylight looks intact and weatherproof, but I'll check it."

Now that the initial shock had worn off, she began to recognize a few of the room's merits. She gazed up at the skylight that ran the length of the room. "I like that," she said. "There's nothing worse than a dreary studio."

"What will you need, Blair? I confess to total ignorance as to what a dance studio should look like."

"One wall will need to be mirrored." As she talked, he took mental notes. "A *barre* of course. I think I can give you possibilities of where to find these types of things in the city."

"Okay. What else?"

"I guess there should be some sort of dressing room."

"There's a large one in the back with toilets and showers. I'll see that they're renovated and in working order. There's also a small office you can use. You may want to lock up your record player, records, and whatever else you use in there. I'll fix it up."

"Sean," she said worriedly. "I hate for you to go to any expense on this. And I know it's going to cost you a lot of money. I think I should tell Pam that this isn't going to work. You—"

"Let me worry about the expense. I volunteered the building. It's not doing anyone any good just sitting here rotting. It's an eye sore. It might just as well be a studio for dance classes."

"But it's so temporary," she cried.

"Is it?" His eyes seemed to blaze into her brain.

For a moment she was stunned into silence by his piercing gaze. "Yes. As soon as I can, I'm resuming my career in the city," she said adamantly.

"Then you shouldn't be concerned about what I do in the meantime," he said coldly. "I told you last night I bought this building with the intention of one day converting it into a health club. This will be only the first renovation. I consider it an investment."

Stung by his biting words and hostile attitude, she turned away from him and picked her way through the rubbish on the floor. She had to put distance between them. Space. Air. She couldn't think clearly around him. For a heartbeat, when he had prodded her, she had been uncertain that returning to her work was what she wanted. *Of course it was!* That's all she lived for. But the incident only pointed up to her how his sensuality jeopardized her sound judgment.

The more she explored the room, the more impossible seemed the task to convert it into anything, much less a place in which to teach dance. Sean went on his own expedition, thumping the walls periodically to find beams and locate hollow places.

Blair reached the door to the small office Sean had mentioned and after some hard shoving, it swung open. She had peered through the dusty glass on the top part of the door to see that the room was as littered and filthy as the rest of the building, so she wasn't surprised by the musty smell that assailed her nostrils.

What she didn't expect was the scurrying family of mice that scattered in every direction when the opening door roused them. Only Blair's piercing scream prevented one from running over her sandaled feet. She went on screaming as the terrified mouse changed direction, his tail whipping behind him, to streak under the army green metal filing cabinet in the corner.

"Blair?" Sean shouted in alarm and came hurdling over the piles of debris toward her.

She, in turn, fairly flew over the unsteady floor,

heedless of the danger she was courting for her injuries.

"Be careful, Blair," Sean cautioned. "Don't—
Wait—"

She vaulted into his chest, arms clasping around his neck, legs wrapping around his waist as he caught her to him. She buried her face in his throat. Hurriedly he carried her to the less littered place near the door. He stroked her hair with one hand while supporting her bottom with the other. She was trembling. Her breath hiccuped against the skin of his throat.

"Shhhh. It's okay. I've got you." He murmured into her hair, holding her tight. "What was it? Snake? Spider? Rat?"

She raised a chalky face toward his. Her green eyes were wide with horror. "Rats? God. I thought they were mice. Rats?" She shuddered and, squeezing her eyes shut, lay her face against the strong column of his neck again.

"It may have been only mice and I'll bet they were as frightened of you as you were of them."

She shook her head. "I hate things like that. Little things with beady eyes that scurry furtively. Why anyone would ever want a white rat or a gerbil or anything like that for a pet has always been beyond my comprehension."

"I promise never to give you anything smaller than a St. Bernard for a gift."

She realized then that he was speaking directly into her ear. That his mouth had pushed aside her hair and was leaving a damp vapor on her skin. His mustache was caressing the side of her neck and his teeth were gently scraping her skin.

She lifted her head and pushed away from him as far as she could. "I feel like a fool, acting the way I did, flying at you like that."

"I assure you I didn't mind." His eyes were glinting with teasing lights and his mouth was tilted into a self-satisfied smile.

Blair then became painfully aware of their position. His hands were cupped under her hips as he held her against him. Her ankles were locked behind his back at his waist. She blushed hotly at the implicit juxtaposition of their bodies.

"I . . . I'm fine now. You can let me down."

"It's no trouble. Really," he said sincerely.

"Sean," she said threateningly and he laughed.

"At least let me get you out of here." He carried her that way until they had passed through the door. She tried to avoid his eyes that stared directly into hers. He was enjoying every movement, every jostle, every brush of his body against hers. Once through the door, he regretfully lowered her to the concrete and turned to relock the door. By the time he was finished, she was halfway to the truck.

"I'm supposed to carry you," he called to her.

"I've told you, I'm fine. If I don't exercise these legs, they'll get stiff."

She thought she heard him mumble a vicious curse, but she pulled herself up into the cab of the truck and slammed the screeching door behind her. If he had touched her again she would have exploded and disintegrated, never to be restored to Blair Simpson again. The fragments of her might be assembled into someone else, but if she let him touch her once more the way every cell in her body was clamoring to be touched, she would never belong to herself again. She would be lost.

He started the truck and said conversationally, "Don't worry about the restoration. In a few days, you won't recognize the place."

"I hope not," she said grouchily. How could he be so casual when she was quaking on the inside? Was he accustomed to holding women in his arms, to having them melt against him with no regard to propriety, morality, or decency? Did he go blithely on his way after each embrace as though nothing had happened?

"And the first thing I'll do is set some traps so it will be completely mouse free."

"Thanks," she said curtly.

"Still hungry or did fright take away your appetite as well as your good humor?" he asked, swinging the pickup into the lane leading to the township's small municipal park. She ignored his jibe, sitting stonily at his side as he pulled under the sprawling branches of an oak and cut the choking motor of the truck. "Breakfast is served, Madam," he said in the somber deadpan tones of a stuffy butler.

"Go to hell," she said, but already the corners of her mouth were twitching with the need to laugh.

"Tsk, tsk, no earthy language. I may stop respecting you. And if I ever stop respecting you, look out."

His index finger trailed her inner thigh upward from her knee. She caught his hand just before it reached the leg of her shorts.

She wished her voice held more conviction and wasn't shaking so when she said, "Well, I've never respected you."

She had to put her shoulder to the door before it would open and then she nearly fell out of the truck in a headlong plunge when it came free. He was still laughing when he joined her at the picnic table, bringing the carton of milk and the sack of donuts with him. "That was a graceful step. What do you do for an encore?"

She sputtered searching for a comeback, was chagrined to find that she couldn't form one, and joined in his laughter as she climbed onto the redwood table. He dug into the sack and produced a glazed donut. "For you." When he saw she was about to decline, he glared at her menacingly.

"Maybe just half," she conceded.

"No, no. We've got Bavarian cream filled and chocolate covered when we get through with these," he said, closing his strong white teeth on half of his donut.

She managed to eat two, licking her fingers of the Bavarian cream much to his delight. When they were done, he tossed the crumbs onto the ground. "You don't have an aversion to birds, do you? They have beady eyes."

"But they don't scurry."

"That's true," he said, smiling and brushing his

hands free of crumbs. They watched as a flock of sparrows greedily attacked that unexpected treat. "Ready for some milk?" he asked, opening the carton.

"Just a sip. Do we have cups?"

"Cups!?" he asked in feigned mortification. "What's the fun of eating outside if you use conventional symbols of civilization like cups?" He handed her the carton.

She eyed the V-shaped spout warily. "I don't think this fits my mouth, but here goes." She swallowed a mouthful before she felt twin rivers of milk dribbling down each corner of her mouth to her chin. Lowering the carton, she laughed, trying to wipe up the dripping milk with her hands.

Her wrists were manacled by strong fingers. He hopped off the table to stand in front of her. "Allow me." He watched entranced as the two rivulets of milk funneled into one and rolled down her chest to form a creamy drop on the top curve of her breasts.

He stared at the drop for a long time before he lowered his head and lifted it from her skin with his tongue. He heard her short, soft huff of pleasure and smiled against the skin under his lips. Leisurely, he kissed away all remnants of the milk, using his tongue to bathe away any residue. He worked his way up her chest to her neck, taking an excessive amount of time, devoting far more skill to the chore than it warranted.

Reaching her mouth after long minutes, he licked at her lips lightly with his tongue, torturing her by not doing more. When he pulled back slightly he heard her moan of protest. "All clean," he said, barely making a sound with the words.

Blair felt suspended by tenuous threads over a vat of boiling desire. One by one she had felt those threads snap as Sean's mouth had tantalized each feminine instinct in her body and brought her senses to acute attention. Now she felt it was predestined that she fall into that roiling abyss and be absorbed by it.

"Not quite all," she whispered and leaned forward. One crystal of a donut's sugary glaze was clinging to his mustache. It dissolved against the tip of her tongue. Emboldened by her own daring, she raked her tongue along the underside of his mustache, teasing his upper lip with darting flicks.

The fingers around her wrists flexed and his chest pressed against hers as he moved forward. His voice was serrated as he growled, "Miss Simpson, unless you have a penchant for making love on public picnic tables, I suggest you cease and desist immediately."

Her head snapped up sharply. He winked at her, kissed her surprised mouth soundly and smackingly, and then said, "Besides, we have a lot of work to do."

Chapter 6

They both did have a lot of work to do and the next week sped by. Sean divided his time between the house he was currently working on, the addition to the Delgados' house, and the dance studio. He had contracted specialists in each field to do the work required, but in the afternoons he checked on them to make sure they did everything according to his high standards. When Blair wasn't able to accompany him, he reported the progress to her.

These progress reports were usually given over dinner either at his house or in her apartment or in one of the fine restaurants lining the beach. If Blair felt uneasy about the vast amount of time they were spending in each other's company, she justified it by telling herself it was for the sake of business.

One evening Pam and Joe showed up on her doorstep toting the promised record player. "We thought you might need a few days to get used to operating it," Joe said, carrying it in and setting it on the kitchen table.

"Where are the children?" Blair asked.

"At home with Andrew in charge. He rules like a despot when we're not around, so we need to get back before he's assassinated. Mandy has signed up for your Monday-Wednesday class."

"I think every little girl in town has," Blair said. She went on to tell them how her phone had not stopped ringing since an ad had been placed in the local newspaper. Word of mouth was as responsible as anything for the publicity the dance classes were receiving. "The ladies exercise class is also filling up. I'm going to have to limit the number of registrants or there won't be room to move."

"I knew this idea was inspired," Pam said. "Only three more days and you start. Will the building be finished?"

"Sean swears it will. It's shaping up far better than I dared hope."

"No one but Sean could have pulled it off on such short notice. He's a slave driver, but the men who work for him would march into a wall of fire if he asked them to," Joe said.

"You look fit enough," Pam said, surveying Blair. "How are your knees holding up?"

"Stronger each day." She had been exercising cautiously in the mornings and resting her legs each afternoon by treating them to warm baths and keeping them elevated for several hours. "Do you still want to help me work out those calisthenic routines? If I show you the steps, can you lead the class?"

"I can't wait to get on my dancing shoes again!"

Just then Sean threw open the door and stuck his head inside. "I only have two cheeseburgers, two orders of fries, two malteds—one chocolate and one vanilla, but we're willing to share. *Aren't* we?" he asked Blair mischievously.

She rushed to relieve him of the take-out food and he shook hands with Joe. "We're just leaving and Pam left a pot roast in the oven."

"Pot roast," Sean said, licking his lips.

"I'll trade you one pot roast meal with five children for one cheeseburger eaten in peace," Pam offered. Sean and Blair declined graciously. "Can't say that I blame you."

The Delgados took their leave shortly, but not before Pam winked at Blair conspiratorially. There was no doubt in Blair's mind the message that wink conveyed. She knew she and Sean were raising eyebrows all over town and romantic hearts were pattering with glee.

They would be disappointed if they knew the true state of affairs. Since their picnic breakfast, Sean hadn't touched her except when necessary out of politeness. He made no sexual innuendos, instigated no personal conversations, initiated no romantic scenes.

He treated her like a well-admired friend or a close business partner.

Each night as they parted company, he might or might not kiss her lightly on the cheek with the detachment of a fond relative, but there were no repetitions of the heart-stopping embraces they had shared before. Blair told herself she was glad he had finally heeded her wishes, but she wondered why she found it hard to concentrate on the simplest tasks; why she poured body and soul into her mild workouts as though trying to rid herself of a persistent parasite; why there was inside her a restlessness that couldn't quite be defined.

As promised, Sean had the studio ready in time for classes to open. The night before the big day, he took Blair for one last inspection tour. The mirrored wall reflected her astonished expression that he had brought about such a transformation. The floor had been sanded and treated as necessary for a dance studio; the *barre*, ordered from the city, had been positioned along the wall according to her specifications. The tile showers in the dressing room gleamed; the office was equipped with a small desk, a new filing cabinet, an easy chair, and a telephone.

"One hundred percent mouse free," Sean said as he opened the door to it.

She overcame her bafflement to say, "Sean, this is . . . is too much. I wanted something livable, but this is deluxe. I've never worked in a studio this nice in Manhattan."

"As I told you before it's an investment," he shrugged. "I'm only selfishly planning for the future."

She didn't believe him, but didn't argue with him either. If his goal had been to instill her with enthusiasm for her new project, he had succeeded. She couldn't wait until the next morning for her first class.

By the time the class was over, her enthusiastic outlook had drastically altered and she was almost ready to throw in the towel. She had had to cope with twenty-five excited little girls and twenty-five obnoxious mothers. "You gotta be kiddin'," she said to Pam as she collapsed into the comfortable chair in the office. Silently she thanked Sean for his foresight in installing a chair other than the one behind the desk.

Pam laughed as she stationed Mandy in front of her to rebraid her hair. "Wait until you get thirty-five overweight, out-of-shape housewives who want a body like yours within two or three weeks. They'll dance their pounding hearts out then go home to their secret cache of M&Ms." Pam struggled with the rubber band at the end of the plait. "What are you doing?"

"Making a sign," Blair said, sweeping one last flourish with the Magic Marker on a piece of white cardboard. Then she held her handiwork against her chest for Pam to read.

" 'Mothers are welcome the first class of each month. Otherwise please leave your child at the door. Thank you, Blair,' " Pam said. "You learn quick, kid."

Indeed she learned a lot within the next couple of weeks. She learned that grown women had to be reminded that they couldn't gossip and do strenuous exercises at the same time. She learned that children should never dance with bubble gum in their mouths lest they go home with it enmeshed in their hair. She learned how to mop up accidental puddles when little girls didn't give themselves enough time to run to the bathroom and grapple with leotards and tights. She learned that women can get hostile when told not to bring cups of coffee onto the dance floor please.

Yet each night over their dinner, which they had a silent agreement to share together, she recounted these events to Sean with her eyes shining brightly and her gestures animated. She didn't realize how happy she looked, how seldom she talked about her knees that gave her very little trouble if she were careful in demonstrating steps. When she fell into her sofa bed at night, she slept the sleep of the just, exhausted, but always eager to get up and face the challenges of the next day.

As she was locking the door after her last class late one Friday afternoon, Sean was waiting for her in his Mercedes parked at the curb. She waved to him as she walked conscientiously on the sidewalk and not the grass that, due to Sean's daily watering, was struggling for survival.

"Why are you so late?" he called out the car window. "Everyone left a long time ago."

Blair was sure everyone leaving had taken note that he was waiting for her, too. "I worked out a while and then showered."

"Do you like champagne?"

"Only when chilled to perfection," she yelled back.

"Then you're in luck. It's been on ice all day." He climbed out of his car, detoured her from the borrowed car she was still driving, and propelled her to the passenger side of his Mercedes. "Pam said she'd have Joe bring her by and drive the car back to your apartment. Tonight, we're celebrating with a picnic dinner on the beach."

"To what do I owe this dubious honor?"

"To the fact that you're reasonably sane after two weeks of dance classes with the ladies and girls of Tidelands," he teased, starting the motor and steering out of the parking lot. He had on shorts and a T-shirt. The setting sunlight caught on his legs and burnished the hair that dusted his skin.

"That does call for a celebration, but do you mind your date being dressed like this?" She had slipped on a clean leotard and wrapped a denim skirt around her waist when she'd finished her shower. Her hair was still damp, parted down the middle and left to dry naturally, which meant perfectly straight.

He scanned her out of the corner of his eye. "I guess you'll do." When she looked at him with murder in her eyes, he laughed. "You know I always think you look beautiful." Reaching across the interior of the car, he slipped his hand under her skirt and lay it on her knee. The shock that missiled through both of them went straight to their hearts. It was the first time in weeks that he'd touched her with anything but friendly companionship and it ignited all the pent-up tension and passion that both had been trying desperately to bank.

"How are your legs?" he asked softly.

"Fine," she said in a gravelly voice, then cleared her throat. "I talked to the doctor yesterday. He said to continue doing what I'm doing. He wants to see me in a month."

The fingers around her knee tensed briefly before regretfully sliding away. He pulled into the driveway of a house with a beach front. It was Victorian in design, with a surrounding veranda, cupolas in each corner of the front on the upper story, and filigreed woodwork outlining the porch covering.

"This is one of the houses I restored for a client. They own a stretch of the beach, but I've been given permission to use it when they're not here. I happen to know they're in Europe, so our privacy is guaranteed."

The intensity underlying his words made her heart skip several beats before starting again with a rapid, erratic tempo. The sunset was painting the entire atmosphere indigo. An ocean breeze cooled her cheeks as she opened the car door and stepped out.

"Not so fast," Sean said to her as she pushed open the gate leading onto the property. "I can't carry all this by myself."

"What in the world do you have?"

He took a blanket, a regulation picnic basket, and a Styrofoam cooler out of the backseat. "Can you carry the blanket and basket? This thing's heavy," he said in reference to the cooler.

"Styrofoam?"

"No," he said dryly. "The contents. Two bottles of champagne."

"Two?"

"Yes. I intend to ply you with drink and then take lascivious advantage of you."

She laughed lightly as she sashayed through the gate. They made their way around the house and took the path through tall grass to the beach. Sean spread the blanket and Blair collapsed on it, stretching her legs out in front of her. Situating their cargo within reach, they breathed deeply of the salty air.

"Ah, Mother Nature, there's nothing like her," Sean sighed. His appreciation for nature went even further. He whipped his T-shirt over his head and hopped on alternate feet until he rid himself of his running shoes. Then to Blair's utter dismay, he unsnapped his shorts and they dropped to his ankles rendering him—

Totally naked! She hadn't even the breath to gasp, to scold. Her breath had been suctioned out of her lungs at the sight of his beautiful manhood so nonchalantly displayed.

Paralyzed where she sat, she watched his hand extend down to her. "Join me?"

She shook her head, still dumbfounded. He didn't insist. Instead he turned and headed toward the surf. To his retreating back, she said asthmatically, "Not just now."

He walked into the sparkling water with the arrogant swagger of a nautical god. The lace-edged waves lapped at his ankles and calves as though bestowing on them kisses of worship. He executed a horizontal dive into a wave that embraced him like a lover. When next she saw him, his strong arms were arcing over the surface as he swam away from shore. Coming back, he relaxed and let the tide carry him in.

He stood up and cupped his hands over his mouth to call to her. "Come on in. It feels great."

She shook her head and found enough voice to yell back, "Too cold." Later, she would recall that she hadn't even looked at his face. Her eyes had riveted on the beguiling arrow of hair that pointed down his stomach to what lay just beneath the surface of the water. In the diminishing light that part of him was only revealed at the caprice of waves that sloshed against him with a rhythm deliberately timed to tease her.

When he came running out of the surf, she averted her head and murmured inconsequentially about the spectacular sunset. His breathing was rough from exertion, hers none the less so. But hers became easier as she saw out of her peripheral vision that he was stepping into his shorts. She exhaled gratefully when she heard the top fastener snapping closed.

"Whew," he said, rubbing his hands through his wet hair. "That was great. Now I'm hungry. How about you?"

Hungry? Her insides were churning, but not with the kind of hunger he was speaking of. Never, if she lived to be a thousand years old, would she forget how he looked with the last rays of the evening's sun tinting his body to a deep bronze, highlighting and shadowing in a way that would make artistic spirits soar. Clothed he was breathtaking. Naked he epitomized manhood in its most excellent form.

To cover her uneasiness, she asked cockily, "What's for supper?" She looked just past his shoulder, not quite ready to meet his perceptive blue eyes.

"Lobster salad, deviled eggs, French bread, assorted relishes, and strawberry tarts."

"This is a celebration! Don't tell me you prepared all of it."

"I wish I could take the credit, but no, I had the chef at The Lighthouse pack the basket for me." Taking the first bottle of champagne out of the cooler and scraping off the ice chips that clung to it, he said, "First things first."

Adroitly, he peeled away the foil, unloosed the wire, and popped the cork out of the bottle. The aromatic vapor from the fermenting champagne drifted out of the bottleneck, whetting their thirsts for a taste of the biting, crisp wine. Taking two stemmed glasses out of the basket, he poured each of them a generous amount before returning the bottle to the cooler.

He held his glass aloft and clinked it against hers. "To the most graceful, most beautiful, most . . . sexiest dancing teacher I've ever known."

Blair laughed, but acknowledged the compliments with a regal nod of her head. They both sipped and sighed in delight at the cold pleasure of the wine. Then leaning toward her, he settled his lips against hers. "Congratulations on a job well done."

"Thank you."

The kiss was devoid of passion, but rife with a tenderness that made Blair's breasts ache. Too soon for her, he ended it.

She helped him unload the basket and they attacked the delicious dishes like a pair of ravenous wolves. The first bottle of champagne was polished off within a matter of minutes. They were well into the second when Blair licked the last crumbs of strawberry tart from her fingers and fell back onto the blanket, her appetite fully satisfied.

"I'm going to burst," she said, rubbing her stomach.

"Good," Sean replied quietly. Storing the leftovers in the basket and setting it aside, he stretched out next to her.

She rolled her head to the side to look at him. "That was delicious. Thank you. It's wonderful here."

"You're wonderful," he said thickly. "You look wonderful. Sound wonderful. Taste wonderful." The inches between them lessened until his mouth fastened onto hers in a telling kiss. One appetite may have been satiated, but one was still a gnawing emptiness within them both.

He feasted on her mouth as though it were a delectable piece of fruit fashioned and created for him alone. Her fingers plowed through his wealth of silver-blond hair and held his mouth in place while she sampled it with the thoroughness of a connoisseur.

When they fell apart, both were gulping for air

and trying to focus on each other through passion-bleared eyes. "I've wanted to do that every time I was with you these past weeks. God, it's been hell to keep my hands off you." As he talked, he was nibbling at the tips of her fingers in turn, laving the pads of them with an ardent tongue.

"Why didn't you?"

"To give you space. You weren't ready before."

"Do you think I'm ready now?" Her voice spiraled into nothingness when his tongue seductively delved between two of her fingers at their base.

"If not, have pity, Blair. I'm dying for you."

He kissed her again and the hand that trailed down her side brought a shiver of anticipation over her entire body.

"Cold?" he asked.

"A little."

"Sit up." He pulled her up until she sat between his raised knees, cradled against his bare chest. He draped his discarded T-shirt over her shoulders and slid his hands beneath her arms to meet over her stomach. "You still feel so tiny," he whispered. Erotically symbolic, his tongue probed the small cavern of her ear. "Will you break if I love you?"

"We won't know, will we, until you do?" She took his hand beneath her own and brought it up to cover her breast. "Touch me, Sean."

Where her courage came from she never knew. Where her carefully maintained caution fled to she never knew. Nor did she know when her wall of defense first began to crumble. Her past meant nothing.

The time with Cole could very well not have happened for all the effect it had on this moment with Sean. At this point in time, she didn't want to be reminded of who she was, or who he was, or the opposing directions of their lives. It was suddenly essential that he touch her, that the longing that had plagued her since she first saw him be gratified at last.

His other hand came up to join the first and after closing over her breasts in gentle acceptance of her gift, he fanned them with light strokes. "You're precious. Precious." His thumbs settled on her sides while his fingers cupped the swelling undersides of her breasts. She may as well not have been wearing anything, for the thinness of the leotard masked nothing. He lifted her gently, kissing her neck as he fondled her at leisure.

"I want to see you again," he said as his thumbs came around to circle her nipples with hypnotic repetition. "When I undressed you that night, these were full and erect. Was that because I was there looking at you?" She nodded, then leaned her head against his shoulder, permitting him a better view down her throat.

"I want to watch them grow that way as I touch them. I want to kiss them, taste them, feel them against my tongue, in my mouth, against my face."

She groaned when one hand slipped under the leotard to claim what his evocative words had readied for his possession. The palm of his hand burned against the cool flesh of her breast. The nipple bloomed between his fingers that adored so elegantly.

Moving her chin back farther, she groped for and found his mouth bending toward her, as avid and hot as her own. Tongues skirmished in a passionate battle where all were the victor. And all the while his hand cherished her with a greediness tempered by caring.

As the kiss deepened, he lay back, bringing her with him and turning her over until she was positioned above him. He bartered one pleasure for another. One hand tangled in her hair while the other smoothed up her thigh beneath her skirt. She held her breath when his fingers reached the high leg of her leotard, then sighed with bliss when he didn't let it act as a barrier to his caress. His strong fingers slid beneath the stretched fabric to knead the smooth rounded muscle of her derriere.

Tearing her mouth free of his avaricious lips, she asked, "Sean, why did you take off all your clothes?"

His breathing was sporadic. "To goad you into a reaction. To shock you into some kind of response. To see if I appealed to you at all. Do I?"

She nestled her head on the forest of hair on his chest. His vulnerability was endearing. "Yes, yes," she whispered with her lips against the salty-tasting skin. "You're beautiful. I've always thought that."

"Do you know how much I've wanted you, Blair? Do you know that my body hasn't given me a minute's peace since I first saw you?" He shifted slightly and asked hoarsely, "Do you know how much I want to be inside you right now?" With his hand on her naked buttock, pressing her against him, how could she deny the proof of his desire pulsing against the cradle of her femininity?

She made an adjustment of her own that robbed him of breath. "I think so." Instinct instructed her. She rocked upon him gently.

"Sweet . . ." His head went back and dug a crater into the soft sand beneath the blanket while his eyes squeezed shut and his teeth were bared in what could either be a grimace of intense ecstasy or excruciating pain. "Blair, for godsakes don't do that. I want to make love to you, but not here. Come on."

He rolled her off him and began gathering the remnants of their picnic with quick, jerky movements. She could barely keep up with him as he stalked to the car with his long stride. The wind whipped his hair, the cool evening chilled his bare torso, but he was impervious to the elements as he approached the car with a single-mindedness of purpose.

As soon as the things were stowed in the backseat, he brought the engine of the car to roaring life. Blair sat curled next to him, disdaining the passenger side. Her head lay on his shoulder, her hand on his thigh. The hand alternately squeezed and stroked, growing bolder with each block they traveled.

"You'd better cut that out," he warned when he slammed to a stop at a traffic light.

"Or what?" she dared him on the merest of whispers.

He caught her hand and pressed it to that place that left no doubt as to the unreliability of his control.

"If you want to fondle something, fondle that. It's begging for it."

For a moment she froze, mortified by what he had done. But when the initial shock wore off, she found herself without a convincing reason to remove her hand. Inquisitive fingers threatened his sanity.

"So much for my good ideas," he anguished. "Thank God we're home."

He swung the car into the driveway. The sight that greeted them as he screeched to a stop was totally unexpected and unwanted. Two cars with several passengers each were parked in front of the stairs leading to Blair's apartment. Bodies of each sex were draped in varying poses on the cars. A few were perched on the stairs and bannister. Chatter and laughter punctuated the night air. It looked like a band of gypsies had camped on her doorstep for the night.

And that's exactly what had happened.

Sean's curse seared the roof of the car. "What the hell is this?"

Blair shook off her momentary stunned surprise and scrambled for her own side of the car. "Friends of mine," she said breathlessly, and retreating from his seething eyes, shoved open her door and shouted uproarious greetings that were in direct contrast to her mood.

She was lifted into an adagio hold over one of the young men's heads, then swung from one friend to another to receive a hearty hug. Altogether there must have been twelve to fifteen friends who had driven out to see her, though she never got an accurate head count as they never stood still long enough.

"Where have you been?"

"We've been waiting for hours."

"Is that sand on your toes?"

"Hope we didn't interrupt anything."

Questions and quips were fired at her with the rapidity of machine-gun fire. "Uh," she said, drawing her fingers through her tangled hair, "Sean and I went on a picnic after my classes to celebrate . . . Oh, that is Sean Garrett, my land . . . my friend." She pointed to the tall blond man with the tight, tense expression on his face leaning with deceptive nonchalance against the Mercedes. A dozen or so pairs of eyes were directed at him and greetings were called. He responded with a less than enthusiastic "Hello."

"Well the party you two started on the beach will continue. Lead onward and upward," one of the young men said. He grabbed Blair by the hand, and with one of his hands firmly planted on her bottom, pushed her upstairs. A few weeks ago, she would never have noticed his casual gesture. Now her face flamed with color and she hoped Sean didn't see what the man was doing. At the door she fumbled with her key.

When all had filed in with exclamations of approval of her apartment, she glanced over her shoulder to see that Sean hadn't followed. "Sean, please come on up."

"I wouldn't want to intrude." Why was his voice so chill, when moments ago, he was virtually panting with burning desire?

"You won't be. Please."

"Okay."

Before she could reply or wait for him, she was hauled through the door by someone demanding to know where she kept the drinking glasses. Jugs of wine, already opened and imbibed if the gaiety of the crowd were any indication, were passed around as were slabs of cheese, boxes of crackers, and tins of smoked oysters.

"So what's it like living out here in the boonies?" someone asked over the blare of the stereo which someone else had wasted no time in tuning to an acid rock station.

"It's all right," Blair shouted back, smiling. Where was Sean? Oh, over there glaring derisively at the guy with the punk haircut, tank top, and red bloomer pants. *He's really a terrific dancer*, Blair wanted to inform Sean. "I'm teaching class here."

This produced a howl of disrespectful laughter. "To what? Blimpo housewives and their precious darlings?" The comment brought on another hilarious wave of laughter.

"Well, yes, to housewives and children," Blair said somewhat defensively. "It's really great fun. They all love it. Some—"

"Oh my God!" one of the girls cried, placing her

palms flat against her over-rouged cheeks. "She's turned into a regular schoolmarm." Everyone collapsed in laughter. Blair could feel the smile she had pasted on her face begin to crack.

"No matter what you do, Blair, it can't beat your career in the city, you know," one of the boys said sagely. "It gets in your blood, you know. I'll kill myself when I can't dance anymore, you know."

Blair darted a look at Sean whose shoulder was propped against the windowsill. His smoldering eyes said that he wished the young man who had made that last somber comment would get on with his suicide.

"It shouldn't be much longer," she said, dragging her eyes away from Sean's stony face. "The doctor said—"

"What the hell do they know?"

"Yeah, have they ever danced? Have they ever laid off for six stinking months and then tried to get back in shape?"

"Not to mention a career like Blair's being shot to hell in the meantime," someone else chimed in. "How long a memory do you think those producers have? Six months? Forget it. In six months' time, they'll be saying, 'Blair who?'"

"Now, wait a minute." One of the less loquacious young men stood up and went to embrace Blair. "They're all bloody jealous, Blair. That's all," he said, indicating the others. "You'll be back in a few months' time and dancing better than ever."

Blair reached up and kissed him on the cheek. "Thanks. I hope so."

"I know so."

There was a momentary pause in the chatter, and it was obvious that no one was moved to agree. Blair, swallowing a lump of anxiety, said with forced cheerfulness, "Well, fill me in on all the news."

For the next half hour the subject was less grim as they related current happenings to her and reminisced over shared past experiences. Blair wondered why she no longer felt like one of the insiders. This group that she had been such an integral part of now seemed incredibly young and immature and shallow. They were self-centered to a fault, paranoid, and boring. They talked of one thing only—dance.

Sean was ignored and did his best to remain so. Several times he had to consciously relax his jaw for fear his teeth would crack from the extreme internal pressure he was applying to them. His fists were often clenched at his sides. He wanted to clear the room with one fell swoop; to clear, at the same time, that haunted, terrified, grief-stricken expression off Blair's face.

When at last someone reminded everyone else that they needed to start driving back to the city, the party began to break up. Several hugged Blair, wished her a speedy recovery, and asked her to look them up for lunch or dinner if she came to the city. Others, less sensitive, fled down the stairs, competing for the choicest seats in the cars. They drove out of the driveway trailing blasts of the automobile horns and ribald suggestions that she and Sean could pick up their own party where they left off.

When Blair turned away from the door, she saw that at some undetermined point in time Sean had left, too, leaving her alone. That was fitting. She'd never felt more alone in her life. For a few minutes, she pointlessly roamed the apartment, without conscious thought, without mission, without purpose. Just as her life was.

She had no one. She had nothing. This pseudolife she had been building in Tidelands was just that—a sham. She wasn't a part of life here. Never could be. She had only one thing. Only one thing in her life remained constant.

Suddenly filled with resolve, she yanked up her purse and flew out of the apartment and down the stairs. The car had been returned as Pam had promised Sean. Blair pumped it to life and raced out the driveway and to the studio. She never stopped to think that it might not be wise to go into the deserted building by herself this late at night.

She stumbled to the door and unlocked it. With familiar ease she made her way to the office and plugged in the record player on the small table. She pulled on a pair of tights she kept handy in a drawer and secured the ribbons to a pair of toe shoes around her ankles. Whisking off her skirt, she went to the *barre* and did a preliminary warm-up. Only the light in the office fanned across the vast expanse of empty floor.

Her body was now bathed with a film of perspiration. She selected a record and put it on the turntable. Assuming a position in front of the mirrored wall, she began to move to the haunting strains of the music. At first the tempo was slow and measured, then it gradually increased until Blair was whirling around the room with frenzied abandon.

"What the hell do you think you're doing?" a voice boomed out of the darkness.

Blair didn't stop, nor did her well-practiced movements falter. Without an apology or qualification, she answered Sean's angry question.

"What I was born to do."

Chapter 7

Sean, alarmed to see her dancing so enthusiastically, stamped to the record player and lifted the arm, causing an abrupt cessation of the music. The resultant silence was almost as deafening.

Blair, coming out of a series of spins, wound down like the ballerina on a music box, slowly, slowly, until she came to a complete stop. For a few moments she stood, shoulders slumped, head bowed, abjectly despairing. When she raised her head, Sean saw the tears streaming down her face, twin rivers of silver in the arc of light coming from the office.

"Don't stop me," she begged, all vestiges of pride stripped from her. "I must dance. Now. This moment. Please."

"You'll hurt yourself."

She folded her arms over her stomach and gripped hard. "I'm hurting now," she cried.

Sean looked at her with mixed feelings. He thought she had never looked so beautiful. Her hair was cloaking her head and shoulders like a satin veil. The eyes that rained tears were those of a disillusioned child, and he felt a surge of pity for her. She was trying so desperately to disregard an undeniable fact.

At one moment he was filled with rage that she had let a bunch of idiots spoil the happiness she was so carefully constructing; and he wanted to shake her until she realized that their opinion didn't matter. The next moment he was filled with such love and the need to protect her that he trembled like one palsied. His strength meant nothing if he couldn't be strong for her. He felt frightfully weak.

"What do you want me to do?" he asked in a hoarse whisper.

"Put the needle at the beginning of the third selection and help me."

"Help—"

"Dance with me."

At any other time, he would have bellowed with laughter. For if he looked like anything in the world, it was *not* a dancer. A lumberjack, a longshoreman, a roughneck, a football player, a wrestler, but not a dancer. But the pitiable sound of her voice eliminated any thoughts of laughter. He felt only a tremendous sadness that this was one thing he couldn't do for her.

"Blair, I can't. I wouldn't know the first—"

"I'll talk you through it. Really all you have to do is hold and lift me."

He wiped suddenly damp hands along the sides of his shorts. "I could drop you."

"No," she shook her head. "You wouldn't. I know you wouldn't. Please."

The appeal so soulfully spoken couldn't be denied. "All right," he heard himself say. He turned to put the arm of the record player at the end of the second selection to give him time to walk to her.

She was standing in fifth position when he joined her. "Stand behind me. For the first few minutes, the dance is mine. Just turn in my direction. I'll let you know before you have to lift me."

The haunting strains of Rachmaninoff filled the room and she whirled away. She glided around him, her personality changed into the character she was portraying. She embodied a woman in love—sensuous, provocative, dancing for her lover. Each movement was beautifully timed and executed.

"This time when I come close, put your arm around my waist and let me lean all the way to the ground." He held his breath fearing that he'd do something wrong, but was amazed when his huge hand caught her at her waist and he leaned with her until, her legs straight, her head almost touched the floor. Instinctively he seemed to know when to help her rise. She danced away from him again.

"When I come back, put your hands on my hipbones and lift me over your head," she instructed as she spun away from him. He was almost taken off guard when she came running toward him and all but flew over his head as his hands caught her on the flat plane of her pelvis and lifted her up. "Now walk in a circle slowly," she said, her voice gleeful.

He raised his head to see her back arched, her arms spread wide in the soaring silhouette of a bird. She felt no heavier than one. "Lower me easily," she said, bracing her arms on his shoulders. He was shocked when her knees settled against his chest and she slid sensuously down his body until the pointed toes of her shoes touched the floor.

She talked him through the rest of the dance. As the music built to its crescendo, she whirled toward him. "Kneel down on one knee," she said on a heaving breath. The music ended with trilling notes as she did a daring back bend over his right shoulder, her toes resting high on his thigh. Finale.

For long moments after the music stopped they maintained that position. Then Blair stirred and miraculously lifted herself off his shoulder. His hand went to her stomach to give her better leverage. She stood, keeping her back to him. From his kneeling position on the floor, he slowly turned her toward him.

Her face was wet with tears, but they were no longer tears of pain, but of joy. "Thank you. It was . . . beautiful."

"You're beautiful." His hands skimmed her body to reassure him that she was real flesh and blood and not some fairy creature sent from heaven to enchant him. With his palms flattened at the base of her spine, he brought her closer and rested his head against her stomach.

It was a welcomed heaviness and she weaved her fingers through the blond hair to hold him closer. He turned his head slightly until she could feel the moistness of his breath as it filtered through her leotard to her skin. Then his lips moved over her, brushing random kisses over her stomach, abdomen, and then lower to her thighs.

"Sean," she cried, though no sound was emitted. She collapsed onto him. He cradled her in his lap, bent her over his thigh, and kissed her with wild hunger. His tongue plundered her mouth that was all too willing a victim. His hands moved through her hair against her head, down her neck, clutching at her shoulders and upper arms. The only thing that prevented him from being a ravenous attacker was that she was in total compliance and just as starved for him. Her arms wrapped around his neck, bringing his head down for the unskilled fervor of her mouth.

When he came up for air, he rasped, "Let's get out of here."

Within minutes they were wheeling away from the studio in his car, the Delgados' borrowed station wagon abandoned for the second time. There was no possibility of their going into Blair's apartment. The "party" that had occurred there was still too recent, and Sean didn't want her wounds to reopen.

He carried her into his house, through the screened room she so enjoyed and through the lower floor rooms to the sweeping broad staircase. Her head lay nestled against his chest in absolute trust. When he set her down in the large bedroom, she looked up at him shyly. "I need a shower."

He grinned sweetly. "So do I. Through there." He indicated a door across the room and she walked toward it, still wearing the toe shoes that looked awkward on one's feet when not dancing *pointe*. Sean was right behind her and didn't turn on the bright overhead lights, but only a heat lamp that suffused the room with a warm orange glow.

He opened the shower's glass door and turned on the taps. As the room filled with steam, they undressed slowly, their eyes never leaving the other. His shorts and shirt were easily discarded, as were his shoes. He had the privilege of watching Blair as she peeled the leotard and tights down her slender hips and beautiful legs. She tossed them negligently atop the toe shoes.

Boldly, her earlier shyness gone, she surveyed the splendor of his body. He indulged her, not moving as her eyes traveled the length of him, then came back to study his flagrant masculinity. Maidenly fingers braved the space that separated them. Hovering for a ponderous moment, she at last touched him.

Had she been looking at his face rather than at what she caressed so timidly, she might have been frightened by the sparks of light that flared in his eyes and beamed into infinity like lasers. The iron-hard set of his jaw tensed in reaction, and the hands that knotted into tight, white-knuckled fists might have intimidated her. Instead she felt only the immediate stirrings of arousal and yanked her hand back quickly. Her eyes flew to his.

"I won't hurt you, Blair," he promised with fierce sincerity.

She smiled tremulously. "I know." Bending forward, he caressed her lips with his.

He stepped into the shower and pulled her in after him. He let them both get thoroughly wet under the fine spray before he lathered his hands and began to rub them briskly over her back. He smoothed over her derriere, loving the silky feel of her skin against his work-roughened palms. She moaned with pleasure as he ran his hands down the backs of her thighs and knees.

He turned her around and handed her the soap. She returned the favor of scrubbing his back, standing on tiptoe to wash the tops of his broad shoulders. She watched the water trickle past the indentation of his waist, past the curve at the small of his back, over the firm muscles of his buttocks. She couldn't quite garner the courage to touch him again.

When they faced each other once more, he washed her breasts, squeezing them gently between soapy fingers. He dripped bubbles onto her nipples and laughed in delight as they cascaded over the pink tips. His hands moved down over her ribs, her stomach, her abdomen to the delta that deemed her woman. Most of the dark down had been carefully clipped.

He cocked a questioning eyebrow and she answered bashfully, "Costumes." He nodded in understanding. She closed her eyes, grateful for his easily satisfied curiosity. But her eyes sprang open when she felt his hand cup her. His eyes were startlingly blue even in the strange light.

"Put your arms around my neck, Blair," he said. She did as she was told, and buried her face in the matted hair on his chest. His hand caressed her. She groaned as sensation after sensation rippled through her in time to the alluring movements of his fingers. She sipped at the warm water streaming down his chest.

Then he removed his hand and pressed her to him from chest to knees, positioning himself between her thighs.

"Sean," she breathed, reflexively arching against him when she knew the power of his desire. "Sean."

He broke the embrace and cut off the water. He helped her out of the shower within heartbeats of her speaking his name with such pleading and wrapped her in a fluffy, absorbent towel, then blotted her dry. Haphazardly he dried himself.

Scooping her in his arms, he carried her into the moonlit room and, holding her in one arm, flung the covers of the bed back with the other. He settled her on the cool, soft sheets before following with his own body. He turned on his side to face her. "I'm still afraid of crushing you," he said as he gathered her to him.

His lips fused with hers, melding their mouths together and sealing them with heat. His tongue teased along the inside of her lips. "Do that to me," he said urgently. She did and was rewarded with an animal growl deep in his throat. Praise makes one brave. When next their mouths came together, it was her tongue that darted into his mouth, a fleeting, flirtatious thing that drove him mad. "Blair, Blair, God, you're wonderful."

His lips found her ear and blessed it with ardent attention. Strong white teeth worried her earlobe. When his tongue had soothed it, his mustache dried it.

"Please, Sean," she said, turning her head toward his mouth. He knew what her request was before she asked it. He licked at her lips with slow, leisurely strokes. His mustache was a caress of itself as it oscillated over her shiny mouth, taking up what he had deposited. "That feels so good, so good."

She pressed her breasts against the crinkly carpet on his chest. It tickled and teased her nipples until they ached for a firmer touch. She plumped her breast in her own hand and pushed it against his chest, finding the counterpart of his nipple and rubbing it with her own.

A sharp cry escaped his surprised lips and he crushed her to him. His mouth went on an uncharted trail down her chest to her breasts. His tongue beat against her nipples like the wings of a butterfly. Then one was enveloped in his mouth and suckled. She felt that he was drawing her very soul into himself and she let it go gladly.

The pulsing action of his mouth echoed the throbbing in the lower part of her body. As though on cue, his hand slipped between her thighs. Fingers gentle and knowing caressed, stroked, sought, and found with such accuracy, that Blair heard her own labored breathing as that of one suffocating.

Her hand idled down his side to find his naked hip. Unconsciously, her fingers gripped him and pulled him ever closer to that part of her that beseeched not to be left wanting. "Love me, Sean."

"I am," he whispered as he explored the realm that held all the secrets of her body. "I'm loving all of you. Feel me loving you."

The blissful torture went on and on until she was held in a fine sensual net from which there was no escape. Her body surrendered complete control to him. When she clung to him with silent sobbing, when her body undulated with the need to be fulfilled, he rolled her to her back.

Shifting his weight quickly, he knelt to kiss what he had loved and she called his name plaintively, clasping his hair in frantic hands and pulling him up to cover her.

He cautioned himself to be gentle, as he knew she'd not been with anyone since coming into his life. He introduced himself into her body with a tentative probing. When she had accepted that much of him, he pressed deeper. He was watching her face, so he saw her teeth clamp down over her bottom lip at the same time he realized that he had encountered a membrane of resistance.

"Blair." Her name was an astonished, horrified exclamation. "This isn't possible."

Her eyes opened. "Don't stop."

"But—"

"Please, Sean, if you love me at all."

He searched her face, still incredulous, but eternally tender with emotion. "God, yes, I love you. Didn't you know that's what this was about?"

"Then please." Her hands persuaded him with pressure at the back of his thighs.

The hardest thing he had ever had to do in his life was curb his own raging passions, but he loved her too well to frighten or hurt her. With meticulous care, and unheralded sensitivity, he slowly, painstakingly sank into the chaste vault. Her years of body conditioning made it easier than he had feared, yet he remained still until he felt her muscles relax and her tension ebb.

Lifting his head from where it lay beside hers on the pillow, he kissed her mouth softly. Her eyes fluttered open. "Am I hurting you?"

She shook her head. "No." She mouthed the word rather than spoke it. The heady thought of what was happening between them, the wonder and awe of it, left her too weak to speak.

"You're sure?" She nodded. "Why didn't you tell me, Blair?"

"Do you really want to talk about it now?" she asked unevenly.

She felt his stomach shake with silent laughter. "I'd rather bring this to a mutually satisfying conclusion." He ducked his head to plant a solid kiss at the base of her throat. His tongue delved into the delicate triangle there.

Her back arched off the bed. "Do you think you can?" she sighed as his lips plucked at her nipples.

"*We* can. Together."

"I didn't think that could happen the first time," Blair said, her lips barely moving over the warm skin of his shoulder.

"It's rare I'm sure." His index finger was detailing the fragility of her collarbone. "And only then if the man is lucky enough to initiate a sexpot like you."

She gave him a resounding slap on the bottom. He nipped at her ear with playful teeth and tickled the sensitive skin behind it with his mustache.

"Ah, Sean Garrett, you've turned me into a depraved human being in one evening. Kiss me," she implored, catching his head between her small hands and pulling him down to her mouth.

She was still nibbling at his lips when he pulled back and asked huskily, "Blair, who was Cole?"

Her head thumped back onto the pillow and she stared up at him wide-eyed. After they had regained their strength, Sean walked to the bathroom to bring her a damp cloth to make herself more comfortable. He had switched on the bedside lamp and now it shed a soft light onto their flushed bodies. At his question, her face paled significantly. He could see perfect reproductions of the lamp in each of her wide green eyes.

"I told you he was a man I lived with for awhile."

"Forgive me for pointing out that you didn't live together in the usual context of the word."

Her eyes closed against a painful memory. "No. We didn't."

Suddenly remorseful that he had taken that shining animation his lovemaking had produced from her face, he said, "Don't tell me if it's painful."

"No," she said, taking his hand in a firm grip. "I want you to know."

He gave her time to collect her thoughts. His fingers lightly massaged her forehead as he looked down into her beautiful face.

"Cole arrived in New York after I had been there for a few years. I was older than he was. He was fresh out of sophomore year in college. His coming to New York was really a rebellious move against his father who was an athletic coach at his hometown high school. Coach Slater couldn't imagine anything worse than having a son who was a ballet dancer, even though Cole was as athletic and certainly more dexterous than most of the football players on his father's team."

She sighed, took Sean's large hand and laid it on her stomach, absently smoothing the blond hairs that sprung from his knuckles. "Cole had had all the pressure he could take at home, so he came to New York and virtually starved until he found a waiter's job to support his dance classes. I liked him, felt sorry for him, and asked him to share my apartment until he could get established.

"We became increasingly fond of each other. Affectionate. Everyone began to consider us 'a couple.' He thrilled to calling home and telling his father that he was living with a woman, especially an older woman. You see, the one thing Cole wanted to prove to his father was that, despite the fact that he was a dancer, he was also a man."

"And?" he encouraged when she became quiet.

"And in the year and a half we lived together, he was never able to prove it."

She seemed to be shrinking away from him and Sean drew her close and held her tight as though to keep her from diminishing into nothingness. Now he knew why she had been so unschooled in amorous embraces. He had found her naiveté charming and unique, but puzzling in one her age. He had thought it was an affectation, now he knew it was genuine. "What happened?" he asked, resting his lips against her forehead.

"One day Cole decided that he couldn't live with that kind of conflict in his life and threw himself in front of a subway train."

"Dammit," Sean sighed and squeezed his eyes closed with the same pressure that he held her to him. He knew the shattering pain that would have caused her, and were he able, he would have transferred it to himself. "You loved him?" he asked intuitively after a long silence.

"Yes, though I know now it wasn't a romantic kind of love. I think I pitied him and regretted the misunderstanding between him and his parents. To some degree I suffered that same kind of misunderstanding all my life and could relate to it. He needed me to elevate his self-image. And I needed him to tell me how good I was. Not a very sound basis for any relationship. I never took the chance of loving anyone else again. Dancing was the only love in my life."

Sean's heart did a flip-flop. "Was?"

She looked up at him and caressed his mustache with her fingertip. "Don't rush me into making any commitment yet. Only know that until an hour ago, I thought the ultimate feeling came from dancing as perfectly as I was capable. Now I know there are other levels of emotion that I never knew existed."

"I'm glad I was able to turn you on to them," he said with a solemnity that was belied by the glint in his eyes.

She tilted her head to one side and eyed him suspiciously. "You've never told me how you became so adept in the art of lovemaking. Besides the years of practice, was there someone in your past who tutored you?"

His smile remained, but his eyes clouded momentarily. "At one time I thought there might be a Mrs. Sean Garrett, but things didn't work out."

"Oh." That piece of news crushed her and she wished she hadn't brought up the subject. Maybe she was better off not knowing. She might never measure up to that unknown identity.

He smoothed the wrinkle out of her forehead. "Blair, don't read anything tragic into that statement. It was my decision. I don't carry a torch. I rarely think of her, and then with supreme indifference. And someday I may tell you the whole boring story, but not now. Not while you're lying beside me naked and gorgeous."

"You're gorgeous, too," she said, admiring again the solid length of his body from his shoulders to his well-shaped feet. "And not a half-bad dancer." Mischievously, she pinched at the hair on his chest.

He groaned and covered his face with both his hands. "I'd have died had anyone ventured in there and seen me. I'm sure I looked like a clumsy oaf playing with Tinkerbell."

"You did not," she said indignantly, sitting up. "You move gracefully all the time. And . . ." She averted her eyes.

"What, Blair?" he asked, pulling her down beside him again.

"You were there when I needed you. Thank you." Her eyes were shining again with unshed tears.

He dabbed at her moist eyes. "Don't thank me," he said in an urgent whisper. "You are just what I needed, too."

When she awoke the next morning in the wide bed, she was alone. Sitting up and stretching luxuriously, she took stock of the bedroom that she hadn't even noticed the night before. She liked what she saw. Andrew Delgado had told her Sean's bed was big, and it was a full king size covered with a quilted spread. The room was decorated in russet and navy that contrasted beautifully with the eggshell-colored walls in the rest of the house. Wide slatted shutters covered the windows and allowed only a hint of bright sunlight in through the closed louvers. The room was masculine, but far from austere.

The parquet floor was cool on her feet as she tiptoed from the bed to open the door. Listening for any sounds, she crept down the hall and peered over the gallery. She jumped back in surprise when she heard the back door slamming shut. She was poised on the landing when Sean came through the kitchen door into the living room and saw her.

Both were surprised. She because he looked so wonderful wearing nothing but a faded, ragged pair of jeans that snapped a good two inches below his hair-whorled navel. He because never before had he come into his house to see a beautiful naked woman at the top of the stairs, her hair in seductive disarray, her mouth swollen with a well-kissed pout, her breasts pink and warm and full from sleep. The sun shining through the stained glass window made her naked skin into a living rainbow.

She took two steps down, but the intensity of his eyes burning into hers halted any other movement. With a predatory gait, he started for the stairs, dropping the articles of clothing he carried onto the floor.

He took the stairs one by one never touching the bannister, never looking down to check his steps. He was like a sleepwalker, protected from mishap by her entrancing form that drew him like a magnet.

When he was several steps below her, he stopped. His chest rose and fell as he breathed lightly. His eyes dropped from their absorption with hers to look at her mouth. It looked slightly abraded and he silently chided himself for the ardency of his kisses. His gaze took in the gentle slope of her shoulders—the ingrained posture that was an essential aspect of her art, and the softly swelling breasts with their delicate rosy crowns.

On eye level with them, he adored them with his eyes, loving them so intensely, they reacted and grew firm. The slightest trace of a smile lifted the corner of his mustache before he extended his hand to lovingly fondle first one then the other. He leaned forward to nuzzle her with his nose and mustache before kissing her breasts in turn. He filled his hand with one and brought his mouth over the nipple to love. His tongue circled and stroked and rubbed it until he felt her swaying unsteadily and encircled her with his arms.

Still standing a stair beneath hers, his hands caressed her hips while his mouth kissed an erotic map over her stomach. She knew the sweet touch of his tongue that was warm and wet against her cool skin. He took another step down. His hands slid to the back of her thighs and his fingers flexed around them.

More rapid now, his mouth rained kisses down the tops of her thighs, to her knees, down her shins. He knelt and kissed her feet, the callused toes. Working his way back up, she gripped his hair hard as he kissed the inside of her thighs. Then his mouth went on a quest too intimate to be imagined, but that converted her entire body into a pliable container of warm flowing honey.

When she felt herself weakened to the point of collapse, she stumbled up the two steps to the landing and sat down. Sean took the steps necessary to catch up with her. Their ragged breathing reverberated through the stillness of the house.

Standing before her, he waited. Her eyes scaled his tremendous height and met his blazing eyes. They scorched her lips and she wet them with her tongue. The involuntary action caused his heart to visibly pound in his chest. That was his only motion. He remained still. Hoping. Waiting.

Her trembling fingers fumbled with the snap of his jeans and worked the zipper down. Slipping her hands inside, she smoothed them over his taut hips, pulling the jeans lower. His hands came up to caress her earlobes and stroke her cheeks. She leaned forward and kissed his navel, debauching it with a limber tongue. Her fingertips fanned over the tawny nest that joined his thighs and gloried in the life that was rooted there. She kissed him. He trembled.

Gradually they reclined, heedless of the hard floor beneath them. Without unnecessary preliminaries, his body and hers became one. So profound was their need that the storm raged and was spent within a few fleeting, frenzied moments. When breathing had been restored to an automatic response rather than an exerting exercise, Sean lifted his head, smiled tenderly, and said lovingly, "Good morning."

Chapter 8

If Blair could have relived any days out of her life, she would have chosen the day she opened on Broadway with Lauren Bacall in *Woman of the Year* and the Saturday and Sunday she shared with Sean after their first night together.

After the episode on the stair landing that had left them both dazed, she dressed in the shorts and top Sean had brought from her apartment. "I also cleaned up the mess in there. You've got sloppy friends."

Persuading him not to put on any more than he had on, she dragged him into the kitchen where fifteen minutes later they had produced a six egg omelet. Sean carried the tray bearing the omelet, toast, coffee, and orange juice onto the screened porch and they attacked the food, only now realizing how hungry they were.

Contentedly curled up in a corner of the settee, sipping a cup of creamed coffee, Blair eyed Sean suspiciously when he said casually, "Of course, you're going to have to earn my hospitality. I'm going to make you work for this deluxe breakfast."

"By doing what?" she asked warily.

He laughed at her scowling brows. "Nothing illegal. As a matter of fact you might enjoy it."

Her eyes lit up with green fire. "Oh, if it's *that* kind of work—"

"Whoa! I think I've created a monster," he said to the ceiling. "No, you're going to help me paint a room in one of my houses."

She wrinkled her nose. "Slave labor I assume."

"Absolutely, but you get bedroom privileges."

"Painting, huh? I wondered why you selected my tackiest pair of cut-offs and T-shirt to dress me in today. Don't I get a bra?"

"Nope. But no complaining. I let you wear panties."

"The sheerest, skimpiest pair you could find."

"I never aspired to sainthood," he said, his eyes full of devilry.

They cleaned the kitchen with dispatch and while Sean loaded the truck with the tools of his trade, Blair democratically made the bed. She hadn't gotten over her initial aversion to the truck.

"Don't you ever clean this thing out?" she asked,

slamming the protesting door and nearly wrenching her arm from its socket.

"That would take away its character," Sean replied, unperturbed.

The house he was currently remodeling was beautiful, a graceful, century-old construction on an estate with beach frontage. The structural work had been done, but Sean was completing the clean-up work before his clients took over with their decorator.

"I told them I'd paint this room for them because of the high ceilings. It's already had two coats. Today I'm just touching it up."

He hauled in buckets of paint, a roller on a long pole, and trim brushes for Blair to use. They set about their work after Sean had taken her on a tour of the house. The hours passed swiftly.

Near lunchtime, Sean came to stand behind her where she was perched on a footstool. She was working with a screwdriver to reattach the brass plate around a light switch. Concentration on her task had kept her from realizing he had come up to her until she felt his hands molding over her bottom in an audacious caress.

"You've got the cutest little tush," he said, pinching it lightly through the soft fabric of her old shorts. "Anyone ever tell you that?"

"Lots of people."

"Oh? Who? I'll kill them," he growled, sliding his hands under the T-shirt and covering her breasts.

"I'm not going to get this thing back on straight if you don't cut that out," she warned.

"To hell with that thing. Turn around and kiss me, woman."

Trying to look put out, but not succeeding very well, she turned into his arms. She was on eye level with him. "This is nice," he murmured against her cheek. "For once I can kiss you without breaking my back."

"Well if it's that much trouble, we'll just have to stop kissing."

He pulled back and smiled with what she knew to be a dangerous smile. "You'd be amazed at how inventive I can be." His hands went around her to cup her bottom and lift her off the stool. "Wrap your legs around my waist. Now, see how well that works. Of course if you wanted to you could put your arms around my neck." When she complied he said, "What a fast learner you are."

"You big phony! This wasn't your idea. We were in this position the day I escaped the mouse."

"Well, I adapted it to fit the need. Be quiet and kiss me."

They teased each other with quick, nibbling kisses until their desire was rekindled to the point where that wasn't enough. His mouth closed over hers and agilely explored it with his tongue. Dipping into her mouth repeatedly, it evoked other lovemaking and stirred their memories to the hours of the night when they had loved each other.

He could easily support her with one arm folded under her hips. The other hand slipped around to caress her breast. He massaged it with ever-closing circles until his fingers treated the peaked nipple to his gentle loving. "Let's get naked and do this some more."

"Mmmm." She covered his face with tiny kisses that were like droplets of water striking a hot skillet. Her thighs closed around him tighter, her ankles locked behind his back. She felt his passion growing, throbbing, and moved against it.

"Blair, please," he groaned and buried his face in her neck. For long moments they stood thus, clinging to each other tightly, letting their longing decrease to a level they could handle until a more convenient time and place.

Lifting his head from the fragrant hollow of her neck, he asked kindly, "Are you all right?" Looking up at him with languid eyes, she shook her head. He laughed softly. "Neither am I, but we'll have to tough it out for now. One last kiss?"

He kissed her tenderly, barely breaching her lips to stroke the tip of her tongue with his.

"Mr. . . . uh, Garrett. We're here."

Blair's head snapped up to see two workers standing in the doorway, hats in hand, sappy grins on their faces, staring at Sean and her with acute interest. She scrambled to disengage herself and regain her footing. She needn't have made the effort. Sean wouldn't let her go.

"Hello, Larry, Gil. I'd like you to meet Miss Simpson. Blair, Larry and Gil Morris, brothers and two of my best clean-up men."

Did he truly expect her to respond normally to

this bizarre introduction as though they were at a cocktail party and not standing in a very compromising position? "How . . ." She cleared her throat and tried again. "How do you do?" She glared into Sean's smug face.

"Hello. Hi," the two men greeted her simultaneously.

"Blair and I have finished off this room, so it's all yours. We were going out for a bite of lunch. Can we bring you back anything?"

Blair squirmed against him, trying to get down. He held her fast.

"Uh, no. No, sir. We just ate before we came," one of them answered. Larry, she thought.

"We'll be back in a while then to help you. Bye."

"See ya, Mr. Garrett. Miss Simpson."

Sean carried her as they were past the gaping men and out to the truck. "I'm going to murder you," she said through stiff lips.

"No you're not," he said with breezy confidence. "You're going to kiss me again as soon as we get to the truck and between bites all through lunch and then some more."

He was right. That's exactly what she did.

"This is totally decadent," Blair said, scooping another handful of sea water over Sean's leg.

"Yeah, but a terrific way to wash off paint."

"But I don't have any paint where you're washing."

"See? It works."

Laughing, she leaned forward to kiss him.

By nightfall everyone in town knew that Sean Garrett had taken a woman to one of his houses to "help," something that had never happened before. Indeed, it had always been a bone of contention to avid matchmakers that Sean never mixed business with pleasure.

They had helped the Morris brothers, who were responsible for informing a gossip-hungry townsfolk, with the clean-up after returning from a sandwich lunch. Sean had invented jobs to keep them busy until the brothers finally left at sundown. Then he had rushed her to the private beach. His nude cavorting in the surf was no longer a one-man show.

Now they were sitting in the shallow water, the gentle waves washing over them. Blair sat facing him, her legs draped over his.

He bent his head to taste the flesh of her breast. He took a gentle bite, then raised his head and mimed energetic chewing. "Needs more salt," he said, ladling a handful of water over her breasts just to see the nipples contract.

"You idiot," Blair said, shoving his shoulder.

"I love you, Blair."

The words were spoken with such seriousness and the hands gripping her upper arms were so strong that she didn't doubt he meant what he said. She stared at him a moment, his sudden announcement taking her by surprise, then she dropped her eyes to a point on the middle of his chest.

"You . . . said that last night." Her voice was so low that the ocean breeze nearly ripped the words away before he could hear them.

He lifted her chin with his index finger. "Yes, I did. But I was in the throes of passion. I wanted to tell you now, when we weren't making love, so you'd know that I meant it. I didn't plan on falling in love at the ripe old age of thirty-eight, but I'm head over heels and eaten up with it. I do love you, Blair."

"Sean—"

He placed his finger over her lips to silence her. "You don't have to say anything. I just wanted you to know."

The moon rising over the horizon cast a shimmering beam on the water that pointed to them like a spotlight. Its glowing light shone on Sean's blond hair, touching his eyebrows with gold, and making his eyes sparkle. She outlined his face with her fingertips, touching the bushy brows, tracing the length of his nose, following the strength of his jaw to the vertical cleft of his chin.

"It's not easy for you to believe that I love you, is it?"

"Why do you ask that?" High emotion twisted her throat into a tight knot.

"Will you indulge me in a little amateur analysis?" She nodded. "You didn't fit the mold when you were growing up. Because you weren't accepted by your peers, you separated yourself from them, making yourself even more unapproachable than you already were. Your parents didn't understand your artistic obsession with dance. They wanted you to be 'normal.' You've never gotten over the rejection you felt in your youth. Even now that you're a success, you're still constantly seeking approval, acceptance. That's why your friends upset you so much the other night. Their opinions count."

Tears clouded her eyes. How could he see through her so well? How could he speak aloud the things she'd never been able to admit to herself? How had he known exactly how she felt about herself, her life?

Before she weighed the risks, she heard herself speaking. "I was never one of 'the crowd.' I *was* different. My parents, instead of giving me free rein to pursue my interests, saw my interest in dance and theater as a perversity. Why couldn't I be more like my brothers and sisters? I left for New York with an I'll-show-them attitude."

She tossed her head back defiantly and her harsh laugh was without humor. "I still don't meet with their approval."

"I'm sorry," he said. "I know that hurts you. Parental opinions matter, but no one else's should, Blair. Don't you see that you're seeking approval for accomplishments when what you really want is acceptance for being the person you are?"

He lifted her face between his palms. "You're a worthy human being whether you ever dance again or not. Your talent is a gift, and if God saw fit to bless you with it, why should it matter to you what other people think about it? About you? I love you, Blair, but I know you're terrified of that. You've built a wall around yourself that I'm afraid you'll never let me tear down. Will you? Can you? Can you let me love you? Can you love me back?"

Yes. It was possible, just possible, that she might be falling in love with him. The idea of life without him was desolate and dark. He had filled her days with light, laughter, simplicity. Still she was afraid to make a commitment. Love had been too long in coming. The thought of accepting his love terrified her because he might decide somewhere along the line to throw her back and she'd be alone again.

But he had said he loved her. Could she love him? She would ponder that idea, take it out and examine it when he wasn't so close, so overwhelming, so . . . naked.

She placed her fingertip on his lips. Her eyes penetrated the depths of his in a communication of the spirits. She made him the only promise she could. "If I ever let myself love anyone, it will be you."

"What in the world!" Pam exclaimed, having thrown open the front door to greet her guests for Sunday dinner.

"He insists on carrying me whenever possible," Blair explained. "I can't convince him that my legs are practically well."

"We're not sure after Friday night. You might have hurt them," Sean said to Blair, looking directly into her face, wondering why he hadn't missed her before she came into his life. She was such a part of it now, he couldn't imagine having lived all these years not even knowing her. He had loved waking up the last two mornings with her curled against him, barely making a dent in the mattress she was so small.

He couldn't quite believe how soft her skin was, or how shining and silky her hair felt sliding between his fingers. Watching her apply her make-up in his bathroom mirror, he was amazed as she wielded brushes and wands and pencils that highlighted her complexion and eyes. He drove her to distraction with his questions about the contents of each bottle and jar.

He sampled each of her fragrances on a different part of her body, a research project that had eventually concluded on the wide bed with no definite results documented. He decided that her hair, her breath, her skin all exuded a combination of intoxicating essences that no perfume could champion.

As a collection of toiletries and garments began to litter his bathroom and bedroom, he was made aware of how colorless his life had been without these testimonies of a feminine presence. It was a void he hadn't even known was there. But not just anyone could have filled it. Only this tiny creature who had an iron will, but who, he knew, also was frightened and vulnerable at this point in her life. What she had said as the tide surged around them, he had taken as a vow. She *would* love him. He'd see to it.

Looking down at her now, he saw her face soften at his reminder of that momentous Friday night. "But you were there to help me. I couldn't have done it without you."

His mouth settled on her ear and he whispered, "There are a few other things you've done lately that you couldn't have done without me." She giggled.

"Don't mind me, please," Pam said sarcastically. "The two of you go right ahead with your private conversation and little jokes and when you decide to include me, I'll be standing by."

They laughed at her piqued expression as she moved aside to allow Sean to carry Blair inside. Sean's phone had been ringing when he had stepped out of the shower late that morning, leaving Blair to rinse her hair one more time. The call had been from Pam who extended him an invitation for dinner and cards.

"By the way, I haven't been able to reach Blair. Have you seen her?"

He looked in the doorway where Blair was standing. Only a wispy excuse for panties covered her. She was towel drying her hair. "Yeah," he had drawled. "I've seen her."

"Well, tell her she's invited, too."

"I'll do it." A half hour later, the telephone receiver was still off the hook where he had dropped it.

"As usual this house is bedlam," Pam announced to Blair and Sean as she stepped back from the door. "The baby's taking a nap, but Angela and Mandy have been fighting since they got out of Sunday school and I'm sure they'll wake him at any moment. The boys are the proud owners of a new soccer ball and a few minutes ago it crashed into my new lampshade. They've been banished to the backyard for the time being. Sit down."

Sean and Blair laughed again at her harangue which seemed to have been delivered in one breath. Sean made no apologies for taking a seat on one of the Delgados' well-used sofas. He dragged Blair down beside him and tucked her under his protective arm.

A few minutes later Pam carried in a tray with four glasses, a carafe of wine, and a platter of cheese and crackers. "We can nibble on these while the lasagna is baking," she said.

"I can think of a couple of things I'd rather nibble on," Sean murmured in Blair's ear and looked significantly at her breasts.

Joe, who had overheard Sean, choked on his wine. Pam, who hadn't, demanded, "What's so funny? What did he say? What's going on? Somebody please tell me." To her increasing irritation, none of them would satisfy her frustrated curiosity.

Dinner was a rambunctious circus with five noisy, hungry Delgado children as the featured performers. It was still enjoyable due to Pam's good cooking and the loving atmosphere interspersed with laughter and bantering and scolding. After Blair helped Pam with the dishes, they joined the men in the living room for a game of cards.

"Just think, in a few weeks, we can play cards in the playroom," Pam said, waiting as Joe dealt.

"I thought I was building that playroom for the kids."

"Well, they have to sleep sometime," Joe said dryly.

Two of the card players found their attention wandering. Sean's hand had a habit of finding Blair's thigh under the table and roaming at will, until once she dropped her whole hand of cards on the table. Pam stared at them both with open-mouthed confusion as they simultaneously burst out laughing. When the wine bottle was passed around, they toasted each other and then had to be nudged back into consciousness when they found they couldn't break their eye contact over the tops of their glasses.

Finally, when everyone had waited for several minutes for Blair to bid while she stared transfixed at Sean's hand lying relaxed near her own, Pam said in exasperation, "For goodness sake, would you two like to adjourn to our bedroom for awhile?"

Sean and Blair looked up in surprise. Had they been that transparent? Joe chuckled. "Like hell they will. If anyone adjourns to our bedroom, it'll be us. And I'm not into group sex. Besides, you're taking a lot for granted to even suggest such a naughty thing," he said righteously. "I'm sure the idea of a nice, comfy bed never crossed their minds."

Pam grumbled, "I wouldn't bet next month's supply of birth control pills on it."

"Birth contro . . ." Blair's high squeak dwindled to astonished silence as her wide eyes flew to Sean.

He met her own flabbergasted stare with one of his own. Then he shrugged and smiled guiltily.

"My God, I can't believe it," Pam cried, slapping

her hands over her mouth. "The two of you . . . without any . . . Oh!" Uncontrollable laughter stifled the rest of her words until she was able to sputter, "You'd better be careful or you'll wind up with as many children as we have."

"Sean, we can't. Really. I mean it now." Her hands were spread wide on his chest, staving off his ardent kisses.

"I've told you a thousand times," he said, flopping onto his back on the bed and thumping his fists into the mattress. "Whatever damage could be done has been done. One more time before you see a doctor isn't going to hurt."

"And that's baloney. Every high school boy since Adam has used that line."

"Did Adam go to high school? Garden of Eden High?"

Biting back her laughter she said sternly, "Stop changing the subject and don't . . . ah, Sean, please." She took his hand away from her breast and pushed it away. "I agreed to sleep with you if you would behave. I'll leave if you don't stop."

He had the grace to look contrite. Folding his hands behind his head, he said, "All right. I'll keep my hands to myself if you'll take off that nightshirt."

Her look was one of total disbelief. "If you can't refrain from touching me with my clothes on, how do you expect me to believe you'll refrain with them off?"

"You'll take my word as a trusted friend," he said gravely.

"Oh, sure. Just like I'll take your word that one more time wouldn't matter. I know more biology than that, Mr. Garrett."

"Please, Blair," he whined. "I'm naked and since you're not it's making me self-conscious."

She laughed, propping herself up on one elbow to look at him. "You've never known a self-conscious moment in your brazen life." It was a test of her self-discipline not to reach out and touch him. Ever since Pam had inadvertently reminded her that she was running the risk of pregnancy, she had sworn not to let anything happen between them until she could see a gynecologist. She was only getting used to the idea of loving a man. Motherhood was something else again.

"Please. Truly, all I want to do is look."

She sighed wearily in surrender. "All right. But remember, you gave your word." She peeled the nightshirt over her head. "There. Are you happy now?"

"Immensely," he snarled, lunging toward her and pinning her to the bed with his weight.

"Sean, you—"

"Never take the word of a sex-starved man with a naked lady in his bed. That's lesson number one." In between words, he was scouring her breasts with kisses.

"What's . . . lesson number two?" Blair asked, writhing up to offer him better access to her nipples that were distended with awakened sensations. Her earlier resolve was being defeated by the delicious languor that stole through her body under the dictatorship of his hands, his mouth, his knee between her thighs.

"Lesson number two . . . is that . . . there are other ways we can love . . . each other." His mouth and hands worked together to bring her to a pitch of desire more transporting than she had known before. Her own whimpering pleas thrummed through her head as her fingers dug into the muscles of his back. "Are you . . . willing to . . . learn a . . . few?"

The lessons continued all night.

"This isn't going to work," Sean mumbled out of the side of his mouth.

"It's not going to work if you don't sit still." The tiny silver scissors in her hands clipped away an errant whisker. "If you can sit and bug me while I put on my make-up every morning, the least you can do is let me trim your mustache."

He caught her wrist. "But you might trim off more than I'd like."

"I wouldn't cut off one precious whisker that wasn't absolutely necessary." The last word dissolved against his mouth as she leaned down to kiss it softly. He muttered disagreeably when she straightened and raised the scissors again.

When the telephone in the bedroom rang, he sprang from the small vanity stool supporting him, and chortled, "Saved by the bell." He dashed from the room and left her with a satisfied, happy smile on her face.

"Blair, it's for you," he called.

She could read the puzzlement on his face as he extended her the telephone. To her silent query, he shrugged. "Hello."

"Blair, I've been trying to reach you since sunup. Where are you and who was that?"

"Barney?" she cried incredulously. The last person she would have thought to hear from was her agent. She had sadly told him not to call her until she had notified him that she had been granted a clean bill of health. He had cursed, paced, ranted and raved, and then treated her to a lunch at which they both got methodically sloshed in order to drown their remorse. "How did you—"

"Pam Delgado. After I traced you through directory assistance for new listings and after I spent hours listening to an unanswered ring, I thought to call her. She said you might be at this number. Who's the guy? Never mind. Are you sitting down?"

As usual Barney's subjects changed direction with the speed of a ricocheting bullet. She had grown accustomed to his hyperactivity and hectic pace since he had become her agent seven years ago, but two months out of the city had slowed down her reflexes and she found herself struggling to keep up with him.

"No, I'm not sitting down, what—"

"How would you like to be in the new show Joel Grey's starring in?"

For a moment her brain didn't register a thing. Then it went into overtime, thoughts racing by so fast she couldn't grasp them. "What . . . that show's already been cast."

"Yeah, but five of the dancers got kicked out over union disputes or something . . . hell, I don't know. What difference does it make? The director called this morning, at an ungodly hour by the way, and asked for you."

"He asked for *me*?" Her hand flew up to still the thudding of her heart.

"Well, sort of," Barney hedged in agent fashion. "He said he needed to see my best girls and you're certainly one."

"Yes, but—"

"You're in the big time again, Blair." He gave her the time of the audition and the address of the rehearsal hall where it was to be. "Get your dancing shoes on—soft shoes they said—and get your butt on the next train to the city. By the way, you may have to sing a song, but you can fake it. Just give them volume."

Sean had pulled on a pair of jeans and a work shirt. Now he was sitting on the edge of the bed they had made up together, staring at her like a conscience incarnate. Caught up now in Barney's excitement, she averted her head. "Do you really think I can do it, Barney?"

"Of course. You're the best."

"I'm not too old for the chorus?"

"I'm too old for dumb questions. Call me when

you get to the city." The phone buzzed dead in her ears. She put it back in its cradle, staring at it a moment while she ticked off the things she had to do before boarding the train. She only had an hour or two—

"What's up?"

She jumped when Sean's voice broke into her whirling thoughts. "An audition," she said excitedly. She paraphrased what Barney had told her.

"You're going?" he asked, a trace of disbelief in his voice.

"Of course I'm going," she said defensively. "This is a tremendous break in my career."

"Um-huh. You might also get a tremendous break in one of your legs."

He was saying exactly what she didn't want to hear. Why couldn't he be glad for her? "I won't. I danced the other night. My legs have never felt better."

"You got lucky."

"They're healed!" she shouted.

"Then you shouldn't mind seeing the doctor before you go to that audition. I'll take you."

"I haven't got time," she said, heading for the door and then rushing down the stairs, ignoring the twinge of pain that caused in her knees. "And I don't need you to take me anywhere. I can find my way around the city."

She heard Sean's curse as he tramped down the stairs after her. "Blair, think for godsakes. I know this could be a big opportunity, but if you get in a show, you'll be doing day-long rehearsals and—"

"I know what doing a show involves and I can't wait to get back to it." He was close on her heels as she crossed the yard and climbed the stairs to the garage apartment. When she went through the door, he followed. She turned to bar his progress any farther. "If you'll excuse me," she said coolly.

Undaunted he continued. "If you won't think of your own health, think of your obligations here."

She laughed. "Oh, come on, Sean. No one will remember me a week after I leave," she said, spreading her hands wide. "Those little dancing classes don't mean anything."

His jaw hardened to stone. "Maybe not to you, Miss Simpson, but 'those little classes' mean a helluva lot to the ladies who attend them. They mean even more to the little girls. You yourself said some of them show real promise. Mandy Delgado for instance. How are you going to tell her you won't be around to coach her anymore?"

His arguments struck her harder than she wanted him to know. "Her talent's inherited from Pam. Anyone could coach Mandy."

"But you'd be the best for her and you damn well know it."

"All I damn well know is that you're keeping me from getting ready for my audition."

"And you'll just leave, drop the classes?"

"Everyone knew they were only going to last for six months at the most," she screamed. "What's the matter? Are you sorry now you made such a heavy investment in the building?"

The lines around his mouth went white and two spots of high color rose to his cheeks. His eyes narrowed as he surveyed her scornfully. She thought he might very well hit her with one of the tight fists clenched at his thighs. Without another word, he spun around and slammed out the door, rattling the window panes.

Three hours later found Blair standing outside the door of the rehearsal hall. Through it she could hear the choreographer calling out the steps of the dance he would teach to those auditioning for the five coveted parts. The piano was as out of tune as any in a dance rehearsal hall, though the song being played was familiar to her.

Despite her angry quarrel with Sean, she had managed to pull herself together and drive Pam's car to the train station in time to catch the next train. Still wearing the scarf that hid her hair curlers, she had taken a taxi to the appointed building at Broadway and West 73rd. She had brushed out her hair in the ladies room downstairs where she changed from her summer skirt and blouse into her leotard and tights.

Not wanting to admit how one encouraging word, one good luck wish, one supportive kiss from Sean would have made this much easier after her involuntary sabbatical, she turned the rusty doorknob and went into the hall.

Chapter 9

"*Blair! My God, what's happened?*" Pam asked in a rush of words. She had answered the tapping knock on the front door to see her best friend standing on the threshold, tears pouring down her cheeks from red, swollen eyes, her eye make-up smudged by previous tears. Her shoulders were hunched forward in a self-protective slump.

"Is Sean here? That's his truck."

"Yes, he's here working on the room, but—"

"I don't want him to see me like this, but I have to talk to you."

"Come on in," Pam said quickly. She hustled Blair through the door and then down the narrow hallways of the house to the back bedroom she shared with Joe. "The baby's in his crib. The others are out playing. Andrew's with Sean. Hopefully no one will bother us for awhile." She closed the door behind them and sank onto the bed beside Blair who was already there, bent almost double and sobbing.

For the time being Pam didn't try to stop the tears. Whatever had happened at that audition, Blair would have to tell in her own good time. When Sean had arrived to work on their room addition, his face dark, his eyes stormy, Pam had bravely asked him if Barney had reached Blair. He snarled an affirmative, then went on in the most blasphemous terms Pam had ever heard come out of his mouth about what he thought of Barney, the audition, and a woman who was too stubbornly obsessed to know what was good for her.

"I take it you don't approve of her going back to the city and even auditioning for a part."

"Damn right!" he roared. "She could end up a cripple."

Well, Blair had walked into the house under her own power, so Pam didn't think her trauma was physical, but whatever it was, it was having a devastating effect. She rubbed Blair's back soothingly, as she would do to one of her children. The words she crooned were sympathetic. The wracking sobs finally began to subside.

"Tell me about it, Blair." Her voice was soft, comforting.

Tear-bloated eyes were raised to Pam's. Trembling lips were stilled by being pressed together hard until they turned white. Then, shuddering in her effort to regain self-control, Blair said in a barely discernible croak, "I didn't make it."

Pam masked her sigh of relief. She felt just as Sean did, that the last thing Blair should do was go back to work before her knees were sufficiently knit. She knew the grueling punishment of dancing every day for hours at a time. If Blair were ever to dance professionally again, she had to give her body time to regenerate.

"Did your knees give out?"

Blair shook her head. "No, Pam, that's just it. I warmed up well, I danced better than I ever have. Ever. I put everything I had into that audition, and . . ." She drew in another shuddering breath to ward off an attack of tears. "My limited singing ability didn't count against me. None of the others could sing well either. The choreographer and the producer narrowed it down from about fifty to eight of us. I *knew* I had made it. I couldn't miss. I had more experience, more credits. I danced flawlessly. I was animated. But I was a good five years older than the oldest of the others. When the choreographer named the five who made it, I wasn't among them."

"Oh, Blair, darling, you know that rejection at an audition doesn't mean anything. It just wasn't your show. You've been x-ed from auditions dozens of times. There'll be others."

Blair laughed ruefully. "I wish I could believe that, but I don't. I *had* to make this one to survive.

Don't ask me how I know that, I just do." She squeezed Pam's hands hard. "I danced so well, Pam. I *did*."

"Much as I sympathize, I hope you didn't hurt yourself," Pam said worriedly. "Do your legs hurt?"

Blair shrugged. "A little. No more than usual."

Pam broached the next subject tentatively. "Sean was worried sick about you. He was pawing the ground like a bull, but he was scared silly you'd fall or that you'd hurt yourself and wind up in the hospital."

Blair scoffed. "He was only angry because I didn't heed his unsolicited advice." Her lips began to tremble again. "When I could have used his encouragement the most, he yelled at me. So much for developing relationships. I guess I'll go down as another notch on his belt. I'm sure I meant no more to him than that anyway."

"Don't say such a stupid thing. It makes me angry, Blair. For once will you open your eyes?" Pam shouted. Blair looked up in amazement. She'd never, in all the years they'd been friends, heard such censure in her friend's voice. "The guy's in love with you. Crazy in love with you. And if you were smart, which I seriously doubt, you'd pay attention to him when he tells you he is. He was out of his mind with worry for you, not if you'd make the damned audition, but if you'd survive it. He and I agree that your health is more important whether you think so or not. He was so upset he called George Silverton just to—"

"George Silverton!" Blair interrupted with an ex-

clamation. *"The producer of the show, George Silverton?"*
She came flying off the bed.

Pam was startled by Blair's sudden return to life.
She took a step backward and answered cautiously,
"Yes."

"And how does Sean Garrett know George
Silverton?" Blair demanded.

Pam moistened her lips nervously. Had she
opened a can of worms? She didn't like the icy glaze
that was forming over Blair's green eyes or the ramrod
straightness of her back. "He . . . he, uh, did a
house for him last year. They became fairly good bud-
dies, I think, and—"

"Never mind," Blair said, dashing for the door
and flinging it open. She barreled down the hall with
Pam rapidly stumbling after her.

"Blair, wait. Don't go off half-cocked. He—"

"I know what he did," she shouted over her
shoulder. She cursed the tricky latch on the patio door
before it gave way. Then like a trooper in some
vengeful army, she marched across the patio and
stepped through the framework of the new room.

Sean was standing straddle-legged hammering
long nails into a two-by-four. He swiveled his head
around when he heard her scrambling through the
open wall. Several nails were protruding from his lips.
Andrew, who was assisting his idol, looked up with a
broad grin that dissipated to a frown of apprehension
when he saw that his first true love was bristling with
fury.

"I want to talk to you," Blair announced in a tightly controlled voice.

Without haste, Sean took the nails out of his mouth. "Not now, I'm busy."

"Now!" she shouted, stamping her foot.

Sean's brows lowered dangerously over the glittering eyes. "I'm busy," he repeated in biting tones. "Besides that I don't think this is the time or place for us to air our differences."

"I don't give a damn what you think or who hears us."

"Well, I do." Before she knew what he was about, he dropped the nails which pinged on the concrete slab, dropped the hammer with a loud crash, and plowed toward her, tossing her over his lowered shoulder.

The air was forced out of her body with a whoosh, but when she regained it, she screamed, "Put me down, you oaf." She wiggled, she kicked, she clawed, she pummeled his back with her fists, all to no avail. He swatted her hard on the rump and it hurt so bad tears sprang to her eyes. She dashed them away before he flung her down onto her back on Pam's bed and slammed the door, sealing them alone in the room.

She catapulted off the bed and faced him with both hands grinding into her hips. "I should have known you'd have the instincts of a caveman, a barbarian. They were bound to surface sooner or later."

"I didn't create a scene, you did," he shouted. "I don't apologize for hauling you around like a sack of flour because you have no more sensitivity than one. Even if you didn't mind Pam hearing what we're about to discuss, you should care that Andrew would. He has a worshipful attitude toward you that I frankly think is misplaced."

"Don't lecture me on my behavior," she spat. "I only want to know one thing." Her chest rose and fell with agitation. She could feel the blood boiling in her veins, surging behind her eyelids and making her see red, thundering behind her eardrums and creating a terrible racket. "Did you or did you not call George Silverton this morning?"

"Yes, I did." His expression didn't change. His inflection was calm.

"Are you a friend of his?"

"Yes. We play tennis when he comes out for a weekend."

His succinct, honest answers perversely infuriated her further. "Did you sabotage my chances of getting cast in that show?"

"No."

"Don't lie to me," she screamed.

"I'm not," he yelled back.

"You are! You called Silverton and asked him, as a 'friend,' not to cast a Miss Blair Simpson. What did you tell him? That he'd be risking my falling down one night during a performance? That I was a handicapped dancer? Or was it something just between you guys? That I was your current bed partner and you weren't quite ready for me to go back to work? What did you tell him?"

The words that tumbled out of Sean's mouth as he raked a hand through his hair would only be found on the walls of the vilest public restrooms. He stood in an arrogant pose, hands on hips, one leg supporting his weight, while he eyed her with mingled amazement and disgust.

"You really think that?" he asked finally, when she was beginning to avoid the blue heat of his eyes. "After the past few days we've spent together, you can honestly think that I'd do something like that?"

His voice had gradually risen to a roar. He threw his head back to look at the ceiling while he drew in a deep, restorative, rage-suppressing breath. His eyes closed when he expelled the air in his lungs on one long, sustained sigh as he lowered his head.

"No, Blair, I hate to disappoint you, but I did nothing of the sort. As a matter of fact, your name was never mentioned. I called George, who, yes, *is* a friend of mine. I knew he was producing that show. I asked him about it. Asked him about the type of show it was, trying to learn just how rigorous it would be for you. That's all. Period. Believe me or not. That's the truth."

"Well I don't believe it," she said to his surprise. "I danced too well. I was great. Something kept me from being selected, and it had nothing to do with my performance at that audition."

"And it had nothing to do with me. Why would I do something like that to you?" His voice contained the genuine bafflement he felt. That she could really suspect him of something so devious was incomprehensible.

She laughed mirthlessly. "With your reputation? Are you serious? If for no other reason, to guarantee yourself a live-in playmate-of-the-month."

Livid color flooded his rugged features and he took a threatening step toward her. "I ought to knock the hell out of you for saying that."

"Well that would certainly be in keeping with your style," she flung back at him.

"Or better yet I ought to throw you down on that bed and make love to you until you come to your senses or at least are rendered speechless."

"Conquer with sex. Is that it? Is that what you've been trying to do these past few days?"

"Not conquer. Persuade. Instruct. Convince. Convince you that there's more to life than dancing on a stage."

"Not for me!"

"Oh yes. For you. You've proved it time and again since last Friday night that you can get a high from making love with me that you never knew from dancing."

"No!"

"Yes! I've seen you shine with fulfillment. I've heard you purr with contentment. Radiate happiness like a furnace. Look at you now. Did dancing make you all that happy today? You've been crying your eyes out. And what the hell happened to your hair?"

Stunned momentarily by the question asked so out of context, she reached up to pat her hair, as though to acquaint herself with what could be wrong with it. "I . . . I frizzed it."

"You mean you did that on purpose?" he asked tactlessly.

Her chin went up defensively. "It looks good from the stage this way. It makes me look younger."

"Younger! Yeah, you look like a young guru."

"I don't need to listen to this," she said, stamping past him on her way to the door.

He caught her arm in a fist like a steel trap and whirled her around to face him. "Yes, you do," he said through bared teeth. "You've needed someone to tell it to you like it is for a long time. You, Blair Simpson, are the most self-centered person I've ever known. Your selfishness is so much a part of you that you don't even see it. It's time you did."

She struggled to release herself. It was futile.

"Do you think you're the only person in the world who's ever had a setback? Did life ever make you a guarantee that things were always going to be rosy? What if you never get to dance again? What then? Is that all there'll be to your life? Will you throw yourself in front of a train like your friend Cole?"

"Let me go," she grated, finally managing to jerk her numb arm free. "I won't give up until I'm a success."

"As what? As a dancer? You are. You've had twelve successful years of a dancing career."

"It's not enough."

"It'll never be enough, because there are other

levels of success and only some of them relate to notoriety and affluence. Others have to do with being a warm, caring, loving human being. And as that, Miss Simpson, you're a miserable failure."

The words were like a slap in the face that actually brought tears back to her eyes. "Shut up!"

"No, you shut up and listen to me. No amount of success is ever going to make you happy because you'll never trust it not to fly out the window. You'll still crave acceptance. And it won't matter a damn who else accepts you, because you'll never be able to accept yourself. That's what's wrong with you, Blair. You don't like yourself."

He was too close to the truth and she threw up every shield she had to protect herself. She had to transfer the pain, the guilt. "How dare you lecture me about something you know nothing about. What do you know of disappointments and setbacks? You sit out here in your cushy little nest and hand down sermons on success. Everything you've ever touched turned to gold. Tell me, King Midas, when you ever knew a day of disappointment and rejection."

"Eight years ago when I went bankrupt and lost everything."

The silence was palpable. Sean's unleashed tension rolled over Blair in waves and choked off her oxygen. He had wished her speechless. He had her speechless now as she stared at him vacantly, trying to absorb what he'd just said.

"Bankrupt?" she wheezed.

"Sit down."

She obeyed him without question, walking to the bed and dropping down. He went to the window, staring out it with his back to her.

"I was thirty years old, building crappy houses and condos right and left. Buying up land for more houses and condos. As you said, I couldn't go wrong. But I did. Everything went wrong—unwise investments, a glutted market, high lending rates, tight money. No one bought the houses or condos. Banks called in their loans. I was down to the socks I stood in. I filed Chapter Eleven.

"Country club friends and investors forgot my telephone number and wished they could forget my name. It makes people nervous to be around someone who's going under for the third time, as though they'll catch the contagious disease he's carrying. Anyway I wasn't much fun to be around anymore. I had to sell the sailboat, the XKE, the Cadillac, the six horses, my tennis racquet and golf clubs." He laughed. "I'm not joking. It got that bad.

"Luckily my father had pulled out a few years earlier. He didn't like what I was doing with the high-class construction business it had taken him a lifetime to build. He was right. Anyway his and Mom's financial futures were secured.

"Through the courts I was able to liquify assets and pay back the debts. Slowly. Very slowly. But most creditors got back ninety cents on the dollar. I moved out here and started over. Worked as a carpenter. Found I liked it, working with my hands, building.

"I scraped up enough money to buy my house

and worked on it on the weekends. Then I bought another and sold it, using my house as an example of what could be done with an old house like that. I think you can piece together the rest. I was very lucky. I got a second chance and managed not to blow it."

He turned to look at her now. "You were curious about the woman I planned to marry. She took a walk when the going got rough, panicked at the thought of being chained to a husband who couldn't keep up his country club dues, not to mention her Bonwit's charge account."

"She just left?" All through his tale, Blair had remained silent. Learning that this man who epitomized self-assurance and success had known such failure and vulnerability had drained her of anger and replaced it with a sort of awe.

"Yes, and at the time I was glad to see her go. That was just one less responsibility I had to cope with. But I was mad as hell that she kept the diamond engagement ring. I was planning on selling it." A trace of humor lit his blue eyes.

"You never saw her again?"

"Oh, yes. Several years later, right after a banker from London jilted her for a richer divorcée, she came out here to see me. She ooohed and aaahed over the houses I had restored. I had just bought the Mercedes, which she trailed greedy little fingers over. The *Times* had just done a feature story about me in the Sunday edition. I was back on the way up. She loved my little houses. She loved my little town. She loved me and couldn't imagine why she'd ever thought she didn't."

Blair didn't hide her repugnance. "What did you say to all that?"

"Nothing. I laughed in her face and sent her on her disgruntled way. I wished her happy hunting. As far as I know she's still stalking for a rich husband with both barrels loaded." He wasn't smiling at his own attempted humor when he came to sit beside her on the bed.

Taking her hand, he laid it in the palm of one of his and marveled over its slender fingers and the faint blue veins threading the back of it. "If one lives to middle age, Blair, he has to go through upheavals. Women lose their husbands and have to enter the job market for the first time; men get laid off from a factory job they've had for thirty years and have to find other work; housewives have to cope with idleness when their children leave home.

"I had to start all over. I didn't plan on ever being happy again, yet I'm happier now than I've ever been. This life I'm leading now was totally unpredicted. It just fell out of the blue into my lap like a gift."

Pam had said something like that to her the day she moved into the garage apartment. About something wonderful for her being planned that she couldn't even guess at.

"I love the work I do. I take great pride in it.

There's a tangible satisfaction in watching something taking shape under my hands. I never knew that kind of satisfaction by acquiring a parcel of land that really meant no more to me than the printed deed." He tilted her chin up to peer down into her face. "Do I sound like a complete fool? Maudlin?"

She shook her head. "You sound like a man with both feet on the ground, who knows values by having learned them the hard way. A survivor. A man pleased with his life."

"In all areas save one. My life lacks something vital," he said softly. He lifted the mass of hair covering her ear and brushed his mustache along the fragile rim.

Involuntarily her head fell back and her eyes closed. "What vital something would that be?" She was dimly aware that he was lowering them into a reclining position. Their legs dangled over the edge of the bed.

His mouth maneuvered its way over her cheek to ghost against her lips as he spoke. "A woman to love me. To live with me and share my life. To make laughter and love with." His tongue flicked at the corners of her mouth before gliding along her bottom lip. "Blair, you've been hurt today. If I could, I would have spared you that, but maybe it's better that this happened."

It was hard to think while his tongue was gently probing past her lips and while his hand was playing with the buttons on her blouse, but his conciliatory tone jiggled a nerve that wouldn't let her relax completely. "Why better?" she asked.

"Because now you know you're better off accepting your life here. Now you can forget about ever going back."

She turned her head, dragging her mouth from beneath his. The hand plucking at the buttons on her blouse was caught by hers and removed as she sat up. She twisted at the waist to look back at him.

"I don't *know* anything of the sort, Sean. And I'm not forgetting about anything, especially my career." He came up on one elbow. "You've been telling me for the last half-hour how wonderful and rare second chances are. I've got to make my own second chance. I've got to go back. As soon as I contact Barney—"

"I don't believe this," Sean bellowed, rolling off the bed and driving one fist into his opposite palm. "I've been talking about a second chance with another life, not the same one. Don't be obtuse, Blair. You're only hearing what you want to hear and twisting it to suit you."

"Look at who's accusing me of twisting things. The story you've just told me applies to your life, Sean, not mine."

"They could be one and the same." The simple clarity with which he spoke panicked her more than his earlier forcefulness had done.

"But they're not. Not now, not until—"

"Not until you're too crippled to dance anymore? Maybe even to walk?" He was shouting now.

He turned his back on her and strode to the door,

nearly tearing it from its hinges as he swung it open. "Well, forget that, doll. Forget hobbling back to me. I won't want you by the time you're too battered and beaten to be valuable to anyone else."

The parting words flung over his retreating shoulder were repeated in her head like a satanic chant and held sleep at bay. She tossed on her sofa bed, so uncomfortable and lonely after the nights she had stayed with Sean. They had slept cradled against each other like pieces of a puzzle in his spacious bed. His breath had warmed her ear. His arms had sheltered her. His hands . . .

Pam, laconic and disapproving, had driven Blair home, saying she might be needing her spare car the next few days. They said terse farewells. She hadn't seen Sean as she left Pam's house. She'd only heard the furious cadence of his hammer as he pounded out his wrath on unfortunate nails.

She didn't want to concede, even to herself, how much she was going to miss him. For she had decided on the trip back to her garage apartment that she was moving back to the city immediately. It would be impossible to live within the shadow of his house, seeing him constantly, with this antipathy crackling between them like a spark, threatening to explode into an inferno that would consume them both.

She had begun packing that afternoon as soon as Pam had returned her to the apartment. Tomorrow morning she'd call Pam and explain why she couldn't continue teaching the dance classes. She belonged in the city where she could be on hand should anything break like today's audition. Barney, when she'd notified him tonight, had been ecstatic.

The second thing she didn't want to admit to was the throbbing pain in both her knees. The emotional tumult of the afternoon had kept her from noticing it at first, but once she was alone, the increasing pain couldn't be denied. She had used heating pads and ice packs alternately to no avail. She had taken three aspirins together, then two hours later had been driven to take three more. Cursing and tears of frustration had done no good either. She had danced full force today, holding nothing back. She'd had to dance the lively routine repeatedly. Now she was paying for it. Sean would probably be pleased to know that she was feeling very battered and beaten.

Sean, Sean, Sean. Why did she crave the touch of his hands that soothed and aroused with equal aptitude? Why did she long for the seductive power of his mouth beneath that luxuriant mustache? Why did her hands long to knead the muscles of his back and shoulders, her fingers to lace through the hair on his chest, her lips to taste his own distinct essence, her body to—

"Damn!" she cursed the tears that welled in her eyes. Why was she crying over him more than she was her injured knees? His rebuke had been much harder to take than the rejection at the audition. Why?

There was only one answer and she wasn't ready to acknowledge it.

The telephone jangled loudly near her ear and jarred her out of sleep. She moaned and buried her face in the pillow. It had taken her so long to fall asleep. How dare someone wake her up early after the night she'd had. The telephone rang again.

She pried her eyes open and saw that it was later than she first thought. Her clock indicated a few minutes past ten.

Her arm was tangled in the covers, and she worked with uncoordinated movements to free it in order to answer the telephone that continued to ring stridently. "Hold your horses," she grumbled as she lifted it off the base and pulled the receiver to her ear.

"Blair!"

The voice she wanted most to hear. The voice that had haunted her all night was now speaking to her, but . . .

"*Blair?*" he shouted impatiently.

"Y . . . yes? Sean? What—"

"Is Pam with you?"

Befuddled, she looked around the room, almost thinking she might find Pam there. "No, why? She—"

"Have you seen her? Do you know where she might be?" he demanded rudely.

"I . . ." She wasn't surprised that he was still angry, but this wasn't like him to call and be deliberately rude. "Sean, is something wrong?"

"I've got to locate Pam or Joe. Andrew's had an accident. He's hurt."

Chapter 10

She stared into space, blinking stupidly. "An accident . . . ? What—"

"I was working on their roof. He climbed a ladder to bring me a sack of nails. The damn thing slipped and he fell. Hit his head on the slab. He's unconscious and bleeding all over the place."

A trembling hand was pressed against her lips. Andrew—bright, vivacious Andrew—unconscious and bleeding? *No, no.* "Has . . . has he moved? D . . . did you call an ambulance?"

"No, he hasn't moved and yes, I've called an ambulance. It's on the way. Pam left with the other children about an hour ago. Joe's sergeant is radioing him.

I thought if I could head Pam off she could meet us at the hospital."

Pam! Blair's heart constricted with the thought of what it would do to Pam if Andrew were seriously injured or . . . She clutched at her chest, imagining her friend's pain. Sean said, "I've got to find her."

The telephone went dead in her hand.

God, please no, she silently cried. *Not Andrew. Not Pam. He'll be all right. He has to be. Sean is there. Sean will—Sean! He's alone, desperate. He adores that boy.*

Shoved into action by some invisible, compelling hand, she lunged out of bed, crying out in pain when the hard contact with the floor shimmied up her shin to slam against her kneecaps. She gasped, trying to dodge the rockets of pain that threatened to make her nauseous.

Groping her way to her bureau, she found a pair of shorts and a T-shirt. She shoved her feet into sandals and, disregarding the pain, dashed out the door and down the outside stairs.

"Oh, damn! The truck." Where she had expected to see Sean's Mercedes, the motorized relic was parked instead. She didn't have time to lament.

Reaching the bottom step, she leaped toward the ancient truck and jerked open the door. Sean had told her he always kept a spare key under the seat and, not even thinking about the filth under there as well, her searching fingers located it within a matter of seconds. She crammed it into the ignition and, praying that she would remember how to drive a standard transmission, turned it. Nothing.

"Damn!" she cursed. "Come on and start, you stupid truck." Her feet were working the clutch and accelerator alternately to no avail.

Blair lay her forehead against the steering wheel and gave in to the tears that had been threatening since she had first heard Sean's voice on the telephone. Flinging her head up, she gripped the steering wheel with both hands and shook it. "I've got to go to him. I've got to. Now, damn you, start!" she screamed. All her heartache, frustration, pain and despair poured into that curse. "Start!"

Giving the truck one last useless chance, Blair thrust the door open. She looked around her frantically, hopelessly, wringing her hands impotently. Her eyes swept Sean's backyard, and like a neon sign had pointed it out, her brain registered the alleyway running down the side of the house. "The shortcut," she whispered. Andrew's shortcut. He'd bragged about it, told her how he'd already worn a path through the backyards and alleys to cover the blocks from Pam's house to Sean's.

Driven by some internal force, Blair started off at a run down the alley. She didn't think about the pain shooting up from her knees into her thighs, through her vital organs, along her spine straight to her brain. Indeed, she didn't even feel it.

Precious little Andrew. He loved her. Pam had said so. Pam, her best friend. Pam, whose sound advice and common sense she had often ridiculed, might be facing a crisis. She had always leaned on Pam's strength. It was time she returned the favor.

Had she ever told Pam how much she valued her friendship? And Sean. He loved her. Or had, until she'd rejected his love. *Don't give up on me yet, Sean. Please.*

Through backyards and alleys, she ran. Blair was oblivious to the curious stares of people working in their gardens or pausing in household chores to peer out the window at the woman running at a dead heat. She couldn't be mistaken for a casual jogger.

She didn't see the weeds that slashed at her bare legs or the stones that would leave bruises on her heels and the balls of her feet. She saw only Sean, coming out of the sea, naked and alive and radiating life, exuding a confidence he could share with her.

She didn't hear her labored breathing crashing in her chest. Sean's laughter boomed in her ears to the rhythm of her footfalls; his whispered words of love were the reason behind her thudding heart. Those words had become a salve to her shattered spirit.

The perspiration that ran in myriad uncharted rivulets down her body went unheeded. Instead she felt Sean's caresses, tender and loving, strong and supportive.

How had she thought she could live without all he had to give? She had to get to him, tell him, show him she could be loving and caring. She *did* love, *did* care. This was one time in his life when he might need her. She couldn't—mustn't—let him down. Run! Only one more street.

Her legs pumped faster, working like the pistons of a well-oiled machine. She could see the skeletal framework of the roof Sean had been working on. *Thank you, God. Thank you, God. I'm almost there*, she prayed as she ran the last few yards.

She burst through the hedge of the house that was across the street from the Delgados'. Then everything went into slow motion. Blair saw them—Sean, Pam, and Joe—huddled over Andrew. He was sitting on the step on the front porch, a bloody cloth covering his forehead. He was all right! Wasn't he? He wouldn't be sitting up . . .

Joe looked up. Seemingly from far away, she heard him shout, "Blair!"

Pam and Sean turned to her with the floating maneuvers of characters in a dream. Astonishment and horror twisted their faces into ugly grimaces. They ran toward her, but gained no ground. She saw her name formed on Sean's lips, but didn't hear any sound.

She didn't know that she was running in a crouched position, her knees bent at a hideous angle, barely supporting her. She felt a dull thud as her body struck the sidewalk when she collapsed upon it. She looked down, surprised to find herself on the hot concrete.

Then, for the first time in her life, she fainted.

"Absolutely not!"

"But Pam—"

"Don't 'but Pam' me. I've told you this house is open to you if you want to recuperate here. I'll carry your bedpans. I'll cook your meals, wash your clothes, give you back rubs, anything. But I will not move you out of that apartment."

"Some friend you turned out to be," Blair complained from her sitting position in the bed.

It was four days since Andrew's accident. Andrew was fine, proudly sporting a large bandage on his temple. Blair had progressed to sitting up with a pillow under her knees. This morning she had refused to take the pain pills the doctor had prescribed. Her knees were barely aching and she had celebrated by asking Pam to dress her in a blouse and a pair of slacks.

Pam had put her in a tiny room that was too small for a bedroom but too large to be classified as a closet. It had served as a sewing/storage room. How Joe had squeezed the twin bed in there, Blair never knew. When she had come out of her faint, smothered by pain, she'd been lying on it. For two days, the wracking pain had made her oblivious to her surroundings. Yesterday, she thought she might survive. Today, she was sure of it.

"I *am* your friend. I'd trust you to spend a weekend with my husband and know that nothing would happen, but I'll not do your dirty work for you. If you want to move out of Sean's apartment, out of his life, then you'll be the one to pay off your lease and hand him the key. Not me."

Pam huffed to a chair, the only other piece of furniture in the room, and plopped down, glaring at her friend with exasperation. "The two of you are driving me nuts, did you know that? He's been avoiding this part of the house like we all had the plague or something. He comes to work on the room addition. He leaves. He growls at anyone who gets in his path. He looks like hell—almost as bad as you do."

"Thanks," Blair cut in on the tirade.

"He thinks you despise him."

"Despise—"

"Oh yes. He's thinking about as rationally as you are these days. Since you ruined your knees running to help him with Andrew, he naturally assumes that you'll never forgive him for calling you that morning."

"That's insane."

"Insane the lady says," Pam addressed the ceiling. "Do you see now the kind of whackos I've been dealing with the past four days? And you don't want him to see you this way because he said—in anger—that he didn't want you hobbling back to him crippled. Well, I've had it," Pam said, jumping to her feet. "As I said, my home, my family, *I* am at your service until you get on your feet, but I just resigned as Cupid or Venus or whatever part I've been playing."

Oozing righteous indignation, she stalked to the door. "By the way, your mother called me to ask if you were glossing over what the doctor told you. She'll call you back in a day or two."

Blair extended her hand with a pleading look in her eyes. "Pam?" The other woman crumpled and she returned to the side of the bed to take Blair's outstretched hand. "Thank you for everything."

"What made you pull such a dumb stunt, Blair? You knew that running over here like that would ruin your legs."

Blair shrugged, sniffed back her tears and met Pam's concerned eyes. "I love you."

Pam had tears in her eyes, too. "I love you, too." The next few passing moments were rife with emotion. Then Pam said with soft intensity, "Let me call Sean to come in here to you."

Blair shook her head. "No. It's better this way."

Pam dropped her head. "That's *your* opinion of what's better." With that, she left, obviously still miffed by what she considered to be sheer stupidity on the part of two who should know better.

"Come in," Blair called when someone tapped on her door later that afternoon. She expected to see one of the children with yet another soulful creation of crayon marks on a sheet of manila paper. Her collection of such artistic renderings, the subjects of which were known only to the artist, now numbered eighteen. She was ready with an exclamation of surprise and praise on her lips. It died a sudden death when Sean stepped through the door.

For long moments four ravenous eyes gorged themselves. Looking for signs of suffering, they surveyed each other thoroughly. The diagnosis of each was that physically they were fine, but lines of strain, and pinched eyesockets testified to an emotional malady that refused to heal.

"Pam said you wanted to see me," he said quietly. He barely fit between the foot of the bed and the door.

"She—" Blair bit back her denial. The turbulence in his eyes was painful to see. He needed so badly to be forgiven, to be absolved from the guilt of bringing on her latest setback. For an instant her eyes dropped to the knotted white fingers in her lap. "Yes, I . . . I . . . she said you blamed yourself for this." Her hand swept down to take in her knees. "Sean, you mustn't."

"But I do," he anguished. "If I hadn't asked Andrew for those nails, he wouldn't have stitches in his head and if I hadn't called you looking for Pam, you wouldn't be in here, feeling untold pain and—"

"I'm not in pain. Not anymore. And if I obey the doctor this time, I won't be again. It wasn't just running to Pam's house that brought me to this lowly state," she said with a soft laugh. "It was a combination of things. All of which you warned me against by the way."

She coaxed the slightest smile from him, but he wasn't ready to redeem himself. "Thank God Andrew only had the breath knocked out of him. I thought he was unconscious because of the blow on the head. By the time Joe got here, he was lucid. When Pam arrived, she scolded us for using one of her best towels to stanch the blood. While she and I . . . while she took care of you, Joe drove him to the emergency room for his three stitches."

Blair laughed. "Pam says that bandage will rot off before he'll take it off."

"I wish it were that simple for you," he said quietly. "What does the doctor say?" He knew. He had accosted him as he left the Delgados' house. Pam had called the doctor as soon as she and Sean had undressed Blair and gotten her into bed. She demanded that he come out to Tidelands as Blair wasn't fit to come into the city. He agreed, but at an exorbitant fee.

When the doctor had politely but firmly told Sean that he valued his practice too much to discuss a patient's condition with an outsider, Sean had been all too ready to tell the doctor just how much of an insider he was and that if the doctor valued his life as much as he did his practice, he'd better start talking. Swallowing around the iron fist that had made a garrote out of his Cardin necktie, the doctor had told him what Blair could expect for the next several months.

"I'm not to stand or walk on my own for two weeks, then I can start with short distances and gradually build up. I have to go to the hospital several times a week for ultrasonic treatments. He also recommended taking cortisone shots, but I don't want to. And I refuse to take pain pills," she said adamantly.

She ignored his snort of disagreement and went on. "In a month or so, he'll reassess the situation." Her voice changed. "If everything's healing well, I can start to build back my strength. If not," she said gruffly, "I may have to have surgery. That would entail months of therapy, and I'd more than likely never be able to dance again. At least not professionally."

He was quiet for a moment. Her prognosis matched the doctor's to the letter. He watched her as she picked at a loose thread on the bedspread. "And if you had this surgery and all that it entailed, would you be devastated?"

"Yes." She was still looking down so she didn't see the agonized expression that tore across his already ravaged face.

"I see."

"Because you said you wouldn't want me anymore if I wasn't any good to anybody else. If I was—"

"Blair," he cried, rounding the bed and falling to his knees beside her. "Is *that* why you'd be inconsolable? Because you'd think I didn't want you anymore?"

She nodded. "I would be a physical wreck, Sean. I'd have to be waited on, I'd have scars, I'd have to use a wheelchair until—"

"Blair, Blair," he said, burrowing his face in her lap. "I don't care if you have to crawl on your belly. I'll always want you."

"But you said—"

He raised his head, his agony apparent. "Forgive me. A million times since then, I've cursed my ability to speak for saying such an insensitive thing to you. I was mad, frustrated, loving you so much it was killing me, and dying because my love wasn't enough for you."

She closed her hands around the golden head,

sinking her fingers in the fleecy hair. "It is, it is," she said with a sense of desperation. "I was such a fool, Sean. Spoiled and selfish. Forgive me for not accepting your love, not knowing how to love you back. It had never happened to me before. I was afraid of commitment to anything but dance. *That* I knew. *That* I could cope with. I found a heaven with you I didn't know existed. If having banged-up knees is the only way I could realize it, then it's really a very small price to pay."

His large, roughened fingers smoothed along her temple. "Darling, I hope you dance again. I want you to. Never think I wanted you to stop for any other reason but because it was injurious to you. When I saw you falling, lying there on the concrete, I thought I'd die, Blair."

"I know you'd like to see me dance again," she said, smiling as she traced the groove that adorned his chin. Then her fingertip delighted in the bristly feel of his mustache. "If nothing else, I could be one of the best coaches on the East Coast. And I've got the dancing school here, don't forget. It may have to be suspended for awhile, but as soon as I'm able—"

He placed a finger over her lips. "Don't get too ambitious. I don't want you to ever be disappointed again."

"I won't be, I promise. As long as I have you."

"You do." He kissed her mouth softly, then her neck, her breasts through her blouse, her stomach. He staked small claims, marked his territory, assuring himself that she was real and whole and loving him.

When she tried to speak, her breath came in short spurts, the magic of his mouth having a dramatic effect on her faculties. "My parents will be . . . disappointed."

"Why is that?" He looked up at her.

She lowered her eyes to study the stitching on his collar. "Well, they're old-fashioned. They didn't know about Cole. I don't think they'd approve of my . . . our . . ."

"Living together? I'm old-fashioned that way, too." The quiet words struck her heart with the impetus of lightning. She met his sincere blue eyes with tear-laden green ones. "I've never lived with a woman, Blair. That particular privilege was reserved for my wife. At least I hope you'll think of it as a privilege. Just as I hope you'll consent to being my wife."

She nodded eagerly. "Yes, yes."

He slid one arm beneath her knees and the other behind her back and lifted her off the bed. Trustingly she linked her arms behind his neck. "Where are we going?" she asked, laying her head on his shoulder.

"Home," he said softly.

They passed Pam in the hall. She was slyly smiling.

"That was wonderful. You're getting better and better," the languid voice hummed.

Strong hands rolled her from her stomach to her back and adjusted the pillows behind her. A quick kiss was dropped on the tip of her nose. "I should be. Two massages a day since we got married. Do you think we've set a record?"

"I feel certain we have." Green eyes shone up at him. "But not with massages." She raised her head for a more satisfactory kiss.

It was their fifth night as husband and wife. She was well established in the house, and wondered how she had ever been happy living anywhere else. He carted her from room to room, up and down the stairs, neither complaining nor listening to her constant apologies for the necessary inconvenience. He didn't consider it such. Lying together in the bed, that for so many years had gone unshared, was just one of the many pleasures life was now affording them.

Finally ending the kiss, he eyed her studiously. "Tomorrow I'm taking you outside in the sunshine. You've got a pallor."

"Somewhere private," she said mischievously, dragging the sheet down from her breasts.

"Why?" he asked, his eyes narrowing suspiciously.

"So I can sunbathe in the raw. You don't want me to have unsightly strap marks, do you?" Her eyelids fluttered flirtatiously.

Leaning down and placing his mouth directly over her ear, he drawled, "If I were to do that, you'd end up with no suntan at all, and I'd have sunburned buns." He laughed at her prim expression, which he knew to be fake, and kissed her soundly.

"Did I hear the telephone ringing earlier?" she

asked breathlessly when he freed her mouth. He had taken the extension out of the bedroom so she could rest for an hour each afternoon. Only when he had to be out did he plug it in beside the bed so it was accessible to her in case of an emergency.

"Barney called."

"And?"

"I told him to go to hell."

She laughed. "I'll get back to him in a day or two. His feelings get hurt easily."

He wasn't really worried about her talking to the agent. She'd convinced him that she wasn't bent on dancing again until she was certain her legs could take it, and only then if every other area of her life was being given its priority. It was still a few days until she could begin walking. They weren't rushing anything.

"Andrew called to say that he, Angela, and Mandy colored pictures of the wedding for you. His is the best because in Angela's you're taller than I am and Mandy spilled Kool-Aid on hers." They laughed. Blair loved the sound vibrating against her ear as he held her close.

"Your parents called to say that they had gotten home safely and to check on you." His hand stroked her stomach leisurely, but with tender possessiveness, not passion. "They're very upset about the possibility of your not dancing again. Your mother told me at the wedding how proud they've always been of you. They are, Blair. They just never verbalized it. They're fallible, just like all of us, and couldn't help missing you and wishing you lived closer to them and resenting what had taken you away."

She blotted her eyes against the furred skin of his chest, dampening it with tears. "She really said they were proud of me?" He nodded. With a conscious effort, she pushed the tears aside. She wanted to look forward, not backward. "It was good to see them. They were happy to see me get married at last. And, of course, were most impressed with you." She kissed him under the chin.

"My parents, who can't quite believe I finally talked someone into marrying me, think you're either mentally deficient or a saint. They loved you on sight and told me how beautiful you are. I thought it was a terrific wedding, considering that Pam and I pulled it together within a week."

"It was a strange wedding having the bride sitting down through the whole ceremony."

"And lying down through the whole honeymoon."

She pushed against his shoulder in mock consternation. "Don't you ever think of anything else?"

"Not since you took up residence."

She propped herself up on an elbow to better see him as she combed through his thick hair with loving fingers. "I must say you exercised magnificent self-discipline by sleeping in the other bedroom the week before the wedding."

"I think the least I deserve is the Medal of Honor," he chuckled, but nestled her against his body before he said softly, "I wanted our marriage to be unsullied. I wanted you to know that I love you for many more reasons than what you do to my libido. And, as has been the case since I first met you, I was afraid of hurting you."

He lowered his head to kiss her sweetly on the lips, but after a few moments it grew into something else. He growled against her mouth. "But now that you're my wife, look out, Mrs. Garrett."

"You've got me at a terrible disadvantage. I can't even run from you."

His laugh was a warm blast of air against her cheek as he enclosed her in his arms. "That's good to know. You were long in convincing that I loved you."

Tiny love bites were taken out of his neck by delicate lips and teasing teeth. "My heart and mind were on something else. It took a while to divert my attention from that. And when I really started listening to you, what you said frightened me. It required so much of me. I wasn't sure I was up to it."

"Now?"

"Now loving you and making you happy is the most exciting challenge I've ever faced in my life."

His lips branded an urgent message into her temple. "I love you, Blair."

"I love you, Sean Garrett." She began to giggle and he raised his head to look down at her.

"That's funny?"

"You must know how much I love you if I'm willing to go through life with a name like Blair Garrett."

"I've always had a poetic nature."

She sobered and watched with interest as his

teeth caught her wandering finger. "Sean, are you sure I'm not taking up too much of your time these weeks that I'm an invalid? I don't want you to neglect your work."

"I'm caught up except for the Delgados' room addition and it's being finished by quality craftsmen. I'm overseeing them. The other clients I'm under contract to were understanding about a man wanting to take a few weeks off for his honeymoon. Besides I don't dare leave you alone for too long. You might decide to call that fresh young masseur from the Y. I'm sure he's just itching to get his hands on someone who looks like you."

"I'd never be as threatened by him as I was by you. You had your nerve that day. What made you do it?"

He grinned. "I had to touch you. First to see if you had any substance at all or were just a figment of my lecherous imagination. You looked like such an airy little thing despite the sparks shooting out of your green eyes. Then pure animal lust took over. I wanted to touch you all over." He trailed his mustache along her collarbone. "I'm not over that seizure of lust yet."

He kissed her deeply, his tongue rubbing against hers with increasing ardor. All the sweetness of loving him flooded through her until she was drowning in it. She escaped the fervor of his mouth and dragged his head down to clasp it possessively against her breasts.

"Sean, Sean," she whispered, "I love you so much it frightens me."

He struggled against her frantic hands so he could look at her. His blue eyes pierced through her. "Why? Why, Blair?"

"Because I might lose you."

His expression softened and he stroked her lips with his thumb. "No. Never. Not if I have anything to do with it."

"Love me," she begged.

He needed no second invitation. His eyes navigated each inch of her. She felt their heat on her skin as he looked at her breasts, dwelled on her nipples. His fingers enjoyed the feel of her. Her flesh generously responded. His eyes slid lower over her stomach and navel. The texture of her skin and the white down that sprinkled it were adored by stroking fingers.

"Lovely," he whispered when his eyes encountered the dusky delta that harbored her womanhood.

"Touch me." Her request was a profession of love, as was his intimate, probing caress.

"Here?"

"Yes, yes, yes. Oh, Sean . . ."

"You're so beautiful, so dainty. Sweet." His tongue painted her nipples with dew before he sipped it up with his lips. His mouth sampled morsels of flesh that melted against it until she was consumed with a fever for him.

"Sean, let me . . ."

He gasped as a shudder of pleasure rippled through his body. He recited a litany of love words as she unselfishly loved him. Then he tensed with supreme restraint and rasped, "Blair, now or—" He was welcomed into the tight fluid warmth of her dear body.

"Ahhh, Sean my love, my love." A fervent mouth sought her breasts, kissed them, loved them. Her fingers gripped the hard muscles of his buttocks, entreating him not to withhold any of himself. "Sean . . . I never . . . a gynecologist . . ."

He levered himself up, his eyes burning with passion, but glowing with love and understanding. "My Lord, Blair. I'd forgotten all about that. Do you want me to—"

"No, no," she said, shaking her head, a brilliant smile breaking over her face. "We've got a good choreographer. Let's wait and see what the next steps will be."

BREAKFAST IN BED

One

The moment she saw him, she knew it had been a mistake to grant Alicia's favor.

There he stood on the porch of Fairchild House with his suitcase in one hand, his portable typewriter in the other, his narrow-framed tortoise shell eyeglasses on top of his head, looking a trifle sheepish for obviously having gotten her out of bed.

And there she was, Sloan Fairchild, owner and proprietor of the bed and breakfast establishment, standing just inside the arched front door, clutching her robe to her throat with white-knuckled fingers and shifting from one bare foot to the other.

With her first look into Carter Madison's face, her

stomach lurched, tightened, then stumbled over itself on its rolling descent to the cushiony floor of her torso. She became acutely aware of her nakedness beneath her night-gown and robe. Between her thighs an unspeakably shameful, yet magnificent, tingling was reminding her of her sex.

"Sloan? Ms. Fairchild?" he asked.

Her head bobbed up and down stupidly.

"Carter Madison. I got you out of bed, didn't I?"

Her tousled hair, her attire, and her bare feet, which he had smiled at, were dead giveaways. "Yes. I'm sorry for—" Her hand began a sweeping gesture down her body, thought better of it, and clutched again at the collar of her robe. "I . . . I thought you'd arrive earlier in the day. Come in."

She moved aside, opening the thick oak door wider. He dragged himself and the cases he carried through the passage. "I'd planned to fly up earlier in the day, but David had a soccer game and he pitched a billy fit when he found out I was going to miss it. I called and changed my flight. The game was scheduled for after school, so by the time it was over and we had celebrated the victory with hamburgers and shakes, I barely made it to the airport in time for the last flight. Didn't Alicia call you?"

"No."

"I'm sorry," he sighed. "She was supposed to call and tell you I'd be late." He set his cases on the floor and flexed his shoulders.

"It doesn't matter. Really."

He straightened to his full height and looked down at her. Eyes, so unusual she'd never seen the like before, collided with hers. Even the faint glow shed by the night lights she kept on in the hallways reflected their light brown, sherry color. They were outlined by thick lashes the same rich, mahogany color of his hair, which was streaked with burnished highlights.

"I hate to have inconvenienced you by getting you out of bed. Alicia said you were reluctant to have me staying here in the first place." His lopsided grin was a little too self-confident, a little too cocky, and absolutely captivating.

Sloan self-consciously pushed back a wayward strand of hair and willed that unprecedented disturbance in the lower part of her body to go away. "Not you specifically, Mr. Madison," she replied in a voice she hoped sounded crisply efficient. "Most bed and breakfast houses are managed by a couple. Since I'm a single woman, I've restricted my guests to only couples or women traveling together."

His eyes slid down her body assessingly. "That might not be a bad idea. You have Fairchild House's reputation to think of."

"Exactly," she said, drawing the robe even tighter around her. The tour his eyes had taken hadn't gone unnoticed by her body, over which she suddenly seemed to have no control. Here she had lived comfortably with it for nearly thirty years, and now in the last two minutes it had gone haywire and become a stranger to her.

"You don't think that policy will cost you business?"

She had the grace to smile. "I'm barely breaking even. I need every paying guest I can get."

"I'm a paying guest," he said. Somehow the soft affirmation sounded like an intimate prophecy.

She pulled herself up to a military posture. "I agreed to let you stay here only because you're my best friend's fiancé, and she asked me to house you for a month so you could write the last chapter of your novel before the wedding."

"*Sleeping Mistress.*"

"Pardon?"

"*Sleeping Mistress.* That's the title of the book."

"Oh."

"Have you read my books?"

"Yes."

"Did you like them?"

"Parts of them. I—"

"Which parts?"

"Most parts," she said, laughing at his probing curiosity. Her answer pleased him, but his smile became a little too warm, a little too personal for her already reeling senses. "I think it's wonderful about you and Alicia," she interjected quickly.

"She's a terrific lady."

"Yes she is. I thought . . . never mind."

"Go on. You thought what?"

"Well I thought she'd never recover after Jim got killed. She and the boys took his death so hard. When I talked to her the other day, she sounded very happy.

You're responsible. I know you handled most of the legal ramifications for her after his death."

"I was in China at the time of the accident. As soon as I could, I came home. Jim Russell had been my best friend for years. It wasn't a chore, but an honor to look after his widow for him."

To the point of marrying her? Sloan wanted to ask. This time she kept silent. She'd made the mistake of broaching the subject with Alicia.

"This marriage means so much to me, Sloan," Alicia had said. "Ever since Jim . . . well, you know how lonely I've been and what a handful the boys are for me. Carter's been terrific, patient with them and me, but he's about at the end of his rope, too. I think we need a break from each other before we take that final plunge."

"Alicia," Sloan had said hesitantly, "do you love Carter?"

There was a noticeable pause before Alicia responded in clipped phrases. "Of course I do. I've always adored Carter. He and Jim were best friends. He wants to take care of the boys and me. He loves us and we adore him."

"I know, I know," Sloan had said, impatient with her friend's failure to see the point she was trying to make. "You've told me a hundred times how he and Jim grew up together, went to school together, how like brothers they were. But is that reason enough to marry him? He's not Jim, Alicia."

"That's cruel, Sloan, cruel! I'll never love anyone the way I loved Jim, but I love Carter in a different way. Because of what Jason did to you, you're bitter and skeptical about any relationship between a man and a woman. That's why you've locked yourself away in that old house of yours and haven't looked at a man in the two years since that jerk jilted you."

Since her friend had been painfully correct, Sloan had apologized and let the subject drop. Carter and Alicia seemed to have come to amenable marriage terms. Far be it from her to presume to counsel anyone on matters of the heart.

Shaking herself out of her reverie, she said briskly, "I don't know why I've kept you standing in the hall. I'm sure you're ready to go up to your room."

"I have no complaints about your hospitality. After all, I got you out of bed. Is everyone else asleep?"

"Three of the six bedrooms are occupied, and yes, everyone went up after dinner." That statement seemed to underline the fact that they were alone together in the darkened hallway and that she was in her gown and robe, and barefoot. Nervously, a dainty pink tongue darted out to wet her lips. "Alicia said you'd want a large room with its own bath." She indicated the top of the stairs with a floundering hand. "It's the last door at the end of the hall."

He seemed disinclined to go up just yet. In any event he didn't move. "You weren't afraid to open your door to a man this late at night?"

"Alicia had described you. And I recognized you from the dust jacket picture on the back of your last book."

His eyebrows contributed to an exaggerated scowl.

The brows weren't a matched pair. One arched eloquently while the other remained a straight bar over his eye, with only a jagged crook at its inside end. "God, I hope not. My agent insisted on the Brooks Brothers suit. I think they even combed my hair before the picture was taken."

It wasn't combed now. The San Francisco fog had settled on it like a sparkling veil, drops occasionally beading on the deep russet strands that had fallen casually across his forehead and brushed his collar and the tops of his ears. He was agreeably shaggy. And the army green fatigue jacket had never seen the inside of Brooks Brothers. In fact, it looked like it had survived every war since the one of 1812. Nor had the faded jeans and scarred Adidas running shoes come from an exclusive haberdashery.

The glossy black-and-white picture that had gazed back at Sloan from the cover of *Parisian Escapade* was a two-dimensional parody of the face that was smiling at her now. She had sought out the book on her cluttered shelf yesterday in order to acquaint herself with this expected guest. Alicia could have done a lot worse, she had thought objectively. Once the book was replaced on the shelf, she hadn't given Carter Madison's appearance a thought.

The austere picture couldn't have prepared her for the flesh and blood version of his face. It was a rugged face that had enjoyed his thirty-four years—Alicia had told her how old he was. Laugh lines had been carved down either side of his mouth and there was a network of crinkles at the corners of his eyes. What had been a blandly smiling mouth in the photograph was lazily sensuous in reality, frequently unmasking a brilliant display of white teeth, slightly crooked on the bottom row. The nose that had conveyed a haughty condescension in the picture was in reality long and straight and . . . unpretentious.

His body hadn't seemed all that impressive beneath the Brooks Brothers suit. In the flesh, it made a woman want to touch it. It was hard and lean, intimating both power and grace. It was a tall, rangy physique, but without the slightest hint of clumsiness. It moved as if it knew exactly what it was doing and had been trained not to waste a motion.

"Where to?"

She whipped herself back into the immediacy of the situation. "Oh, your room is ready and I'm sure you're exhausted. Let me get a key." Grateful for an excuse not to look at him any longer, she turned toward her office at the back of the stairs. He halted her.

"I hate to trouble you any more than necessary, but I'm starving. They served peanuts on the flight. Is there a chance that a paying guest could coax a merciful hostess out of a bowl of cornflakes? Something? I'm not particular."

"I served pot roast for dinner. Would a roast beef sandwich suit you?"

"You're talking to a man who would have settled for cornflakes," he said, placing one hand over his heart.

Trying not to notice how adorable he was, Sloan said, "If you'll just have a seat in the dining room," she indicated the room to their left, "I'll bring it right out."

At the flip of a switch, the dining room was instantly bathed with a subtle light from the crystal chandelier. The table had already been set for breakfast, something she always did after the dinner dishes had been cleared away. The crystal reflected the soft light, the silver gleamed against the starched linen cloth, the china plates held napkins standing sentinel in their polished centers. Fresh flowers arranged in an antique soup tureen for a centerpiece added a perky touch of color and homeyness to the formality.

"All by myself?"

Turning around, she found him close behind her as he peered into the elegantly furnished room that was Sloan's pride and joy. He had dropped his eyeglasses onto the bridge of his nose. She liked the way he looked in them. "I don't—"

"Well, you've obviously set the table for breakfast. Wouldn't it be less trouble if I just ate my sandwich in the kitchen? Preferably off a paper plate?"

"No trouble," she breathed. He was so close and so much taller than she that she had to tilt her head back to look up at him. Her hand sneaked up the front of her robe, gathering material as it went until it clamped a damp wad of it at the base of her throat, hopefully to hide the erratic pulse beating there.

His eyes wandered over her face for a long moment, and the slender hand gripping the robe held his attention for an inordinate amount of time before he said softly, "Where's the kitchen?"

"This way." Even as she said it, Sloan knew that what she was doing was highly irregular. No guest had ever been in the kitchen. It was insane to initiate the practice with a single, male guest, yet it would have been ridiculous to stand there in the dark hallway, wearing no more than her bedclothes, insisting that he take a seat at the dining-room table. She shouldn't have given in to his request. She was the owner and manager, wasn't she? When had her authority disappeared?

But irrationally, it seemed the sensible thing to do to lead Carter down the hall. He had left his suitcase and typewriter at the foot of the stairs and was pulling off his jacket by the time they reached the kitchen.

Sloan turned on the light and fairly flew into getting him his snack. It included not only a sandwich, but leftover fruit salad, a piece of chocolate layer cake, and a tall glass of milk, which he said he preferred to coffee. She knew his eyes were following her as she flitted around the kitchen, intent on her chore and cursing her unaccountable nervousness. It was uncalled for. Reminding herself who he was and why he was here, she said, "Alicia didn't tell me David was playing soccer."

There. That was a safe topic. Somehow bringing Alicia's name into the room with them alleviated the intimacy of having him in her kitchen, at her small work table, eating the meal she had fixed exclusively for him in the middle of the night, while she sat across the table wondering if he knew she was naked beneath her gown.

What a stupid thing to worry about, Sloan. Everyone is naked beneath their clothes.

He swallowed a bite and took a long gulp of milk, wiping his mouth with a napkin before he responded. "They start them out young. And some of those little buggers can run."

"I'm sure it meant a lot to David for you to watch him play." She toyed with the sugar bowl in the center of the table. The room was chilly, the heat having economically been turned down when she'd finished working in there for the night. She hoped he didn't notice the tightening of her nipples and mistake the reason for it. To her, their hard distention was excruciatingly apparent. She couldn't have been more aware of them if a red neon arrow were pointing to them as if to say, "Look at me, I'm aroused, I'm aroused."

"Both he and Adam are cute kids, but they need a male influence. Both sets of grandparents are overindulgent. And Alicia finds it difficult to be firm. She's afraid stern discipline on top of Jim's death would damage their psyches or something."

"The accident was so horribly tragic. I'm certain they were traumatized not only by their father's death, but by the news it generated."

"No doubt." He banged his fist on the table. "Dammit, what was in Jim's head to be driving in that race in the first place? Gambling not only his life, but theirs, was foolhardy and selfish. When he proudly showed me that damned car of his, I advised him to get rid of it, begged him not to get serious about racing the thing." Sloan shared his sentiments, but she'd never spoken them aloud. "I know it sounds bad to say this, but I'm still mad as hell at him for doing such an irresponsible, rotten thing to Alicia and the boys."

He took another drink of milk and eyed her over the top of his glass. When he set it down he said, "It's funny that I was Jim's best friend and you're Alicia's and yet we've never met. Why weren't you at their wedding?"

She dragged her eyes from the corner of his mouth, a spot that continued to intrigue her. "Uh . . . I was in Egypt."

"You went all the way to Egypt just to avoid attending the wedding?"

She laughed. "No. My parents are Egyptologists. They coerced me into going on a three-month trip with them. Alicia threatened, cried, and pleaded, but there was no help for it. I'd promised my parents I'd go and it was too expensive to come back for the wedding."

Was he looking at her front? Yes, he was. *Oh, God.* As casually as she could, she crossed her arms over her chest.

"Did . . . did you like Egypt?" He seemed to have something stuck in his throat. His voice had become gravelly.

"It was all right." Actually she'd hated every minute she was there. It had been her parents' trip of a lifetime. Her father, a professor of history at UCLA, and her mother, who had been his research assistant before becoming his wife, had persuaded Sloan to travel with them.

As she'd feared, she'd been to them away from home what she was to them at home, an unpaid servant. She handled their travel arrangements, saw to their packing, their clothes, their appointments. As it had always been, when they weren't totally involved with their work, they were totally involved with each other to the exclusion of everything, even their daughter.

"What did you do before Fairchild House?"

She attributed his prying questions to his writer's curiosity. Her personal history would be boring to him and it was painful for her, so she kept her answers polite and general. "I worked for a company in Burbank that manufactures and markets office supplies."

"And you left all that for this beautiful old house in San Francisco?"

His eyes were teasing, dancing with amber lights.

"Well it *was* a tremendous sacrifice." She drew a sad face, then they laughed together. It felt good.

"How did you acquire the house?"

"It was almost an incidental item in my grandfather's will. My parents had no interest in it. I came up here to see it and knew at once what I wanted to do."

She had returned to Los Angeles, quit her job, notified her parents of the turn her life was going to take, and made the move all within a matter of weeks. "It took every penny of the money Grandfather had left me to have the place restored. It was in deplorable condition."

"But right off Union Street? My God, that was lucky."

"It was in the shadow of a ramshackle warehouse or I'm certain someone would have tried to buy it from us before then. Grandfather had owned it since the thirties, but it had been vacant for years. The warehouse has since been torn down. So I'm sitting on a prime piece of real estate, if the taxes are any indication. But in essence, it didn't cost me anything."

He glanced around the modernized kitchen that Sloan had had to redo from the foundation up. "You've done a remarkable job. The house is great."

"Thank you. Now if I can only keep my head above water until I start making a profit . . ." To complete her sentence, she crossed the fingers of both hands and squeezed her eyes shut. Carter laughed.

"I thought you'd be like Alicia. You're not."

Sloan was dismally aware of that. Alicia had been a campus beauty queen at UCLA when she and Sloan had become friends. Blonde, blue-eyed, rounded and dimpled, Alicia had often made Sloan feel like a diluted washout.

Sloan's hair was dark blond, threaded with lighter streaks in varying shades. Her eyes were the color of the sky seen through smoked glass. Sloan's figure was just as shapely as her friend's, but with all the excess flesh trimmed away.

"I don't think anyone could argue that," she said lightly now, trying to dismiss the thorough way Carter was looking at her as another characteristic of his career. Writers were constantly gathering material, weren't they? "Alicia's beautiful."

"So are you."

She bolted out of her chair and bumped her thighs bruisingly on the table in the process. "Thank you. Would you like something else?" she asked nervously, wishing her hands wouldn't tremble as she reached for his dishes. She didn't own a package of paper plates.

"No thank you. It was delicious."

She carried the dishes to the sink and ran water over them. "I'll take you to your room." She rushed past him, wishing she hadn't noticed how well his shirt fit his torso as he slung his jacket over his shoulder or how his jeans molded to the muscles of his thighs and the bulge of his sex.

God, she was becoming a frustrated old maid with her mind only on one thing.

"I hope your room is satisfactory," Sloan said over her shoulder as she led him back the way they'd come and then to her office under the stairs. Opening a cabinet where labeled keys were neatly hung on cuphooks, she took one down and dropped it into his hand. She dared not touch him.

"Does it have a table I can set my typewriter on?"

"I moved one in there for you . . . and a chair."

"Thank you. I can't tell you how wonderful it's going to be to get in some uninterrupted work."

"I wondered why you couldn't finish your book in L.A. Alicia said that's where the two of you will be living. I assumed you had a place there."

"I do. Right on the beach. Lovely place. It has everything."

"Then—"

"Including a telephone. And everyone has the number. Alicia's mother calls and asks if I know what color dress my mother plans to wear to the wedding. When I suggest she call her she says, 'Oh, but I hate to bother her.' Then Alicia's father calls and asks me to lunch to meet some of his friends and I tell him I'm working and he says, 'But you have to eat sometime.' And then Alicia calls and then David and then Adam and—"

"Little Adam?" Sloan asked, laughing as he verbally painted a truly frustrating picture. "He's only three."

"But he knows how to dial my number." He shook his head. "I can't yell at any of them. They don't realize how distracting those interruptions are to my train of thought."

"What about after you're married and have to work? It won't get any easier."

"Yes, but *then* I can yell."

They laughed softly together for a moment, and when it subsided that sense of intimacy came between them once more, making them each aware of the other.

"Well there aren't any telephones in the rooms here," Sloan said breathlessly.

"It's sounding more ideal by the minute."

"Alicia said you'd be working almost all of the time." She hoped that frantic note in her voice went past him undetected. "I believe you have only the last chapter to go."

They were at the foot of the stairs now, but he made no move to pick up either the suitcase or the typewriter. When he'd been eating, his eyeglasses had remained perched on his head. Now, he flopped them down over his eyes again, but rather than to facilitate his seeing, it was so he could rake a hand through his dry, but no less disheveled hair. "Yeah, but it's a killer."

"Don't you know how the book is going to end?" One hand rested on the oak banister that, after hours of elbow grease had been applied, shone with a warm patina. The other fiddled awkwardly with the tie of her robe at her waist. It was quiet, their voices hushed. She wished she couldn't see the wedge of dark hair beneath his partially unbuttoned shirt. She wished even more that the desire to touch it had never sparked in her mind.

"Yes, but I've got to do the scene where the hero overcomes the villain and the last love scene between the two protagonists."

"That shouldn't be too difficult when you're able to concentrate. You're very good with the suspense scenes, and I'm sure that with a title like *Sleeping Mistress* the love scene will be no problem."

His grin was wide. "But the sleeping mistress isn't a woman."

"It's a *man?*" she asked, aghast.

He hooted a laugh and at her 'Shhhhh,' reduced it to a contrite, silent chuckle. "Not with a Carter Madison hero," he said, trying to look offended. "No, the word mistress refers to his sense of duty. It's his passion, what drives him, what makes him tick. It fades from importance when he meets the heroine and he no longer lets it govern his decisions. It doesn't reassert itself until the final pages."

She didn't realize she had become trapped between him and the wall until she felt it against the back of her head as she looked up at him. "So he'll have to give up the woman?"

He shrugged, his eyes scouring her face in the shadows. She could feel his breath on her skin, warm and fragrant. She wanted to taste it. "I think I'll have to leave it up to the hero to make that decision. And then there's the heroine to consider. Would a woman love a man freely when she knows it's against all odds and that nothing can come of it?"

Just in time, Sloan kept herself from acting on an impulse to cover her breasts which were suddenly full and aching. "Maybe she won't love him freely. Maybe he'll force her."

He shook his head, though his eyes never left hers. "No. He's the hero, remember. Heroes never have to resort to rape. Besides, he knows she feels the same ambiguity that he does."

"Does she?"

"I'm almost sure of it."

"So the ending will be sad?"

"Bittersweet at best."

"I don't think I'll want to read it."

"You may have to help me write it."

By now, he was so close she could feel the heat his body generated. She could see her frightened, inquiring reflection in his eyeglasses as he bent over her. She saw her lips part invitingly, saw her lashes lower until her eyes took on the sultry expression of a woman about to be kissed.

Cruelly, conscience yanked her out of the sensuous web their conversation had spun around them. She squeezed between him and the wall, trying desperately not to touch him, to gain the first stair.

"I'll take you up now," she wheezed.

"Sloan." Had he not closed strong fingers around her wrist to detain her, his speaking her name for the first time would have accomplished it just as effectively. Her name sounded like poetry coming from his lips. She looked first at his fingers locked around her wrist, then up at his face. "I'm perfectly capable of finding the last room at the end of the hall," he said after they had looked at each other for a heart-stopping long while. "No need for you to bother."

"Then I'll see you at breakfast." Could he feel the pulse racing beneath the pad of his thumb? "I serve between seven-thirty and nine-thirty."

"In bed?"

Her throat closed as tightly as the fingers around her wrist, which hadn't modified their hold one bit. She imagined them closing just as firmly over her throbbing breasts and giving them relief. The muscular breakdown in her thighs was a delicious sensation, like having melted butter dripped on them. "What do you mean?"

"Do you serve breakfast in bed?"

"If . . . if a guest prefers not to come down to the dining room, I can bring a tray to his . . . her . . . their room."

"I prefer."

Two

Carter stood in the bay window of his room, watching the morning spread over the fabulous city of San Francisco. From this window, he could see to the corner of Union Street where fashionable boutiques, galleries, and restaurants lined the sidewalks. There was no sun today. Only a lighter wash of pale gray brightened the landscape as the minutes ticked by. The weather didn't match his mood.

He'd never felt sunnier in his life.

And the bubbling wellspring of happiness in his chest made him feel guilty as hell, more despicable than the vilest blackguard to ever grace the pages of the most gruesome fairy tale.

He glanced over his bare shoulder at the bed that still

showed the imprint of his body on its pastel sheets. He'd slept like a rock, like a man who didn't have a guilty conscience. Not that it hadn't taken him a helluva long time to fall asleep. It had. But once he'd faced the fact that the image of her face wasn't going to fade and that there wasn't a damn thing he could do about it, his eyes had closed peacefully and he'd slept like a log. When he'd awakened, he could feel the silly, satisfied grin on his face and was immediately ashamed of it. He hadn't been dreaming of Alicia.

Work. That's what he needed. Hard, frustrating, soul-gripping, mind-wrenching, emotion-draining work. Regretfully leaving the window, he went to the small square table which had been set up in the middle of the room and hauled his typewriter onto it. When it had been uncovered, when he'd meticulously placed a fresh stack of paper beside it, when the box containing the four hundred and some odd pages of his unfinished manuscript had been set at his right hand to receive the pages he intended to rip out with unprecedented ease, when he'd adjusted his glasses on his nose, he sat down in the chair. And stared into space.

God! Had he ever in his thirty-four years been poleaxed by the sight of a woman as he'd been last night? No. He was sure of that. He would have remembered.

She had looked so damned cute standing there with her messed up hair and bare feet. The robe was horrible, pale blue and woolly, something a cold-natured grandmother would wear. Beneath it he could see the hem of a pale yellow nylon nightgown. The ensemble couldn't have enticed a lustful deviate, yet he'd felt the first stirrings in his loins even then.

She had ceased to be "cute" after he'd followed her into the kitchen. When she'd bent down to take a linen napkin out of a drawer and he'd seen no demarcating lines panties would have made on a perfectly wonderful tush, he'd stopped thinking of her as cute and started speculating on the lithe, slender female form beneath that offensive blue shroud.

He'd had a helluva time getting that sandwich past the knot in his throat. Especially when he noticed the twin peaks trying their best to poke through the front of her robe. God, he'd almost choked on the bite he'd just taken. He'd had no illusions as to why her nipples were contracted. It certainly wasn't because of his devastating effect on women. Simply put, it had been cold in the room. That was all. But the effect had been the same and the cause hadn't made it any easier for him to keep his eyes, much less his hands, off her breasts.

Appealing though her body was, it was her eyes that had enchanted him the most. They were beautiful, a subtle shade of blue overlaid with gray. He was sure she wasn't aware of all they revealed about her. There was sadness lurking in those eyes. Pain. Hurt. Wariness. She was like a small animal that had been beaten one too many times and was afraid to venture out again.

That fearful caution had been thrown into high gear just before he'd come upstairs. That frightened look was probably the only thing that had kept him from kissing her.

Kissing, hell. Her expression was the only thing that had kept him from doing anything she was willing to let him get away with.

Because by that time, he'd almost forgotten who Alicia was. Desire, hot and rampant, had filled him, hardened him, until he thought he would burst if he didn't touch her. His heart had been pounding in his ears, drowning out every word of chastisement his conscience was blaring. Conscience, duty, responsibility, morality. To hell with all that. For that moment his whole being had been under carnal rule and it had taken that fear in her eyes to keep him from acting on it.

Now, he pushed out of his chair and circled the table like a caged cat, wiping his hands on the legs of his jeans because even the recollection of how much he'd wanted to touch her had caused them to perspire again.

"You randy bastard," he growled to himself. Because if he didn't know anything else about her, he knew that Sloan Fairchild was a decent woman and would probably die of mortification if she had known what was going through his mind. "You're engaged to her best friend, for God's sake," he reminded himself with disgust. "You're committed, ol' buddy."

He thought he might well be committed in an entirely different manner of speaking if he spent the whole month under Sloan's roof.

The manuscript seemed to call to him from the desk. "Right," he answered as if he'd been sternly castigated. "That's the reason I'm here. To work."

He linked his hands, turned them inside out, and

stretched, then sat back down at the table. He stared at the blank sheet of paper and rested his hands on the keys. Unbidden, a sudden inspiration occurred to him. What would the character in his book have done had he arrived on the doorstep of a beautiful woman in dishabille in the middle of the night?

"Stupid question," Carter said self-derisively. "That's fiction. Anything can happen that you say happens."

He gave his mind free rein. Had he been Gregory, the hero, instead of Carter Madison, a decent enough fellow who usually obeyed his conscience, he'd have followed the winsome Ms. Fairchild into her kitchen. The moment he saw her nipples straining against the front of her robe, he'd have reached across the table and covered one with his palm, massaging it with a slow, measured circular motion until it was as round and hard as a pearl.

This is lunacy, Carter, his conscience warned him. *It doesn't matter. This is fantasy, that's all,* his libido argued back. *Besides you can't be hanged for what you're thinking.*

Gregory would have swept the table clear with one fell swoop of his hand, grabbed her up and—

No, no, no. That's got no finesse. No class.

The floor? Too cold. Again, no class.

Wait, I've got it! He'd have slowly drawn her to her feet. She'd have been shy, reluctant, and put up a temporary show of resistance. But as soon as his lips met hers, she'd have molded against him. His arms would have closed tight around her. Kissing her intimately, sliding his tongue into her mouth like a sword into its sheath, he'd have backed them to the counter, where he'd have lifted her up. She would have murmured a sigh of protest when he untied the robe, but she would have allowed it. Then slowly his hands would part it and he'd see . . . the yellow nightgown that was probably as chaste and ugly as the robe.

"Dammit," Carter said aloud and cursed himself. He dug into his eyesockets with the heels of his hands, determined to concentrate on Gregory and his problems, but Carter's problem was throbbing beneath his tight jeans and wouldn't be ignored.

This is your fantasy, you fool. Pretend there was no nightgown. Pretend she was . . .

Then slowly his hands would part it and he'd see . . . her naked breasts, heaving with longing, tipped with coral nipples that responded to the merest breath of stimulation. He'd touch them as he continued kissing her. Stroke them. Tease them. Then he'd lower his head and take one into his mouth and suck it gently. She'd be virtually wild by now, making low guttural noises in her throat, and curling her legs around him. And when he drew back and outlined the button shape of her nipple with the tip of his tongue, she'd reach for—

"Mr. Madison?"

"*What!?*" he shouted as he cannoned out of his chair, knocking it over along with the stack of papers that flew in every direction when he spun around. He practically broke the stem of his eyeglasses when he whipped them off.

Sloan was standing just inside the door, a large silver

tray covered with a cloth balanced on one hand, her other still gripping the doorknob as though his fierce response had welded it there.

She wet her lips in the nervously reflexive way he was coming to recognize. He tried to blink eyes dilated with passion back into focus, tried to capture lost breath that remained elusive, and tried to pretend that his loins still weren't on fire. He also tried to pretend that he wasn't base enough to bring a lady like Sloan Fairchild into a sordid, lewd fantasy. He succeeded at none of those endeavors.

"I . . . I knocked," she said in a high, timid voice.

"I'm sorry, Sloan. I was . . . uh . . . deep in thought. Here, let me." He took long strides toward the door and a spasm of regret crossed his face when he saw her flinch with precaution. He attempted to lighten the situation. "I guess I scared you to death, yelling like that. I apologize again."

"When you didn't answer my knock, I got worried and . . ."

He relieved her of the tray, but he didn't move away. Instead they stood like statues in the frame of the doorway and stared at each other. That wariness was still in her eyes and his originally sunny mood clouded to become as gloomy as the day.

He could fantasize all he wanted to, but the reality wouldn't go away. He was engaged to a woman and two little boys who needed him. He'd never had passionate fantasies about Alicia, but they shared a different kind of love. Perhaps it was the safest kind. It certainly didn't bring one from the height of bliss to the pits of despair in a matter of seconds.

Love? What the hell was he talking about? He'd been reading too many of his own books. Love didn't happen this quickly. Sometimes it took years to develop between two people. But as he saw the confusion swirling in the smoky depths of Sloan's eyes, he knew she had been poleaxed, too. God only knew what they were going to do about it.

"You'd better eat this while it's hot." She indicated the tray with a nod of her head. When he hadn't answered her knock, why hadn't she gone back downstairs and tried again later? Possibly he would have pulled on a shirt by then. As it was, all he wore now was a pair of jeans. The sight of his naked chest was doing nothing to eliminate the vertigo she'd been subjected to since she first saw him.

He turned away and she let loose the pent-up breath she'd been holding. She was glad she could no longer see that wide chest forested with dark, curly hair. It swirled over the contoured muscles and lay sleek and glossy against the plain of his stomach and then tapered to a fine satiny line down into his pants.

"Join me?"

"No," she said too loudly and too quickly. He was pulling on a shirt, thank God. His back had been smooth, the muscles rippling beneath tanned skin. It had been almost as tempting to touch as his chest. At his surprised look, she tempered her reply. "No, thank you. The other guests are in the dining room. I have to be on hand if they need something."

"And I don't deserve the same attention?"

The arching brow that couldn't seem to keep still no matter what the mood was dancing with mirth. He was teasing her, being deliberately provoking, and her frazzled nerves couldn't handle it. "Yes," she said with a touch of asperity. "But it should be obvious that I can't be two places at once and since they are six and you are one, majority rules. *You* requested the tray in your room. Maybe you should reconsider next time. And, I don't think my other guests would like the idea of their hostess sharing a room with a single male guest. I'll be back later to pick up the tray."

She was convinced that she hadn't slammed the door behind her, but the rattle of the windows said otherwise. "This is all Alicia's fault," she muttered as she smoothed her prim chignon with her hand in the classic gesture of a distressed woman trying to regain her composure. She vowed with each step down the stairs that she'd throttle her friend the next time she saw her.

What was wrong with Alicia? Was she dense? To send a man who looked like Carter to a woman, any woman, was lunacy. Didn't she know he'd attract women like fish to bait? And no matter how good a friend Sloan was, and no matter how dull and dependable and trustworthy she was, she wasn't dead. And that's the only kind of woman who could be immune to Carter Madison's appeal.

Just beyond the archway into the dining room, Sloan paused to draw in several restorative breaths and paint on a gracious hostess smile before she went in. "More orange muffins for everyone?"

"Yes," they chorused.

When she came from the kitchen bearing another basket of muffins, she offered to pack some in a sack for the couple who were leaving that morning. "You can munch on them in the car."

"Why how lovely of you, Miss Fairchild. Thank you." The couple was from Maine and they had driven cross-country to the West Coast. They planned to start the long trek back that day. "Ernest and I have enjoyed our stay with you so much."

Sloan smiled. "Then I hope you'll suggest Fairchild House to your friends who plan to visit San Francisco."

"We certainly will," Ernest said around his mouthful of orange muffin.

The two retired lady schoolteachers were staying until the end of the week. The banker and his wife were leaving the day after tomorrow. Sloan mentally tabulated how much their tabs would add up to and only hoped it would be enough to pay her utility bills. When she had refilled everyone's coffee cup, she went back into the kitchen to sip at her own.

In the nine months Fairchild House had been open, she'd survived only by word of mouth. Just when she'd think she'd be forced to close, someone would call at the recommendation of a previous guest. There were several well-known bed and breakfast houses in San Francisco, but

Sloan's was the newest. By next spring, she hoped to have ads running in travel magazines and the Sunday editions of major city newspapers. In the meantime, she was living on a shoestring, barely breaking even, but she was surviving.

At the time she'd left her boring job and moved to San Francisco, that had been her main objective: to survive. Her engagement to Jason Hubbard had come to a crushing, irrevocable termination. Her parents sadly lamented her disappointment in love and then returned to their dusty books and charts, turning their minds away from their daughter's dismal life to the intriguing one of a pharaoh. She loved her parents with a resigned fondness, and she knew if asked they would say they loved her. But around them she rarely felt like more than a convenient servant when they needed her to see to the rudiments of life, or a nuisance who didn't share their passion for ancient history when she tried to direct the conversation to any other topic. Their affection was sincere when they happened to look up, see her, and remember that she existed.

In short, no one cared what she did with the rest of her life. Not her parents. Not Jason—laughing, handsome Jason—who had stolen her heart, her virginity, then one night blithely told her she was too staid, that he needed someone with more energy, more excitement. Only she had known that if she stayed where she was, doing what she was doing, she'd vegetate.

It hadn't been easy, but with the money her grandfather had willed her, her degree in business from UCLA, her love of cooking, and a wish and a prayer, she'd undertaken to make something of Fairchild House. She'd acquired a knowledge of antiques by poring over books at night. Estate sales became her passion and when she wasn't wielding a paintbrush or papering walls, she was dashing off to one with hopes of finding something both pretty and serviceable. Slowly but surely, the rooms of the house had been furnished.

She took secret pride in what she'd accomplished even if no one else had noticed. Other women had a man, children, to occupy their lives. They could afford to be romantic, impractical, and sometimes irresponsible. Because they knew their man would take care of them.

Sloan had to be pragmatic, frugal, and dependable. Since birth, since she first realized that her parents had relinquished their duty the moment she was brought home from the hospital, she'd learned to fend for herself. It did no good to wish that just once, before she became the dried-up old woman she knew she was destined to be, she could know what it felt like to be cherished. What was the point of dreaming for something that could never be? Why waste precious energy on wondering why she was so unlovable?

This morning her deficiencies where romance was concerned seemed more deficient than usual. Could her despondency have something to do with the weather? Or was its source the man upstairs? But then that was unthinkable. He belonged to her best friend and even if he didn't, a man of his caliber, his world-wide notoriety, would never be attracted to someone like her.

Nevertheless, it took a long time before she built up enough courage to retrieve his breakfast tray.

She tapped softly on the door, halfway hoping that he wouldn't answer or that he'd snarl at her that he was busy and would she please go away. Instead his "Come in" came through the door clearly.

"I'm sorry to bother you while you're working," she said as she entered. "I know you don't like distractions."

He wasn't working. He was standing at the window. His hands had been turned backward and stuffed into the back pockets of his jeans. Tight as they were, she would have thought that impossible. He had finished dressing. His shirt was buttoned—at least *most* of the buttons were fastened. He was wearing the same pair of running shoes as last night. He had showered. The room smelled of masculine soap and a brisk cologne. His jaw looked recently shaved. Though his hair was still damp from washing, it looked like it had been combed by aggravated hands.

"I'm not working," he said scornfully, tilting his head toward the papers he'd scattered earlier. Added to them were numerous balled up sheets. His eyeglasses lay neglected beside the empty typewriter. The chair had been righted but sat askew from the desk. "Are you armed and dangerous this time?" The roguish eyebrow climbed up his forehead.

He was referring to her tart departing speech and she

blushed hotly. "I'm sorry if I sounded cross, but really, Mr. Madison, I'm not—"

"Sloan, please cut the Mr. Madison crap. I'm Carter, okay?" He looked thoroughly agitated. The hands came out of his pockets and he ground one fist into the palm of the other.

Sloan felt the first signals of irritation starting in her chest. "All right then, *Carter*, if you'll allow me to get the tray, which I'm sure is in your way, I'll leave you alone and let you start work again."

Erect and proud, she stamped to the table, covered the now empty plates with the linen cloth, and began lifting it. She saw his arm come from around her and the large, strong hand still hers.

"I'm sorry," was a low, vibrating rumble close to her ear. It sent chills racing up and down her arm, over her whole body, to be followed by an unbearable tide of heat. "I don't expect any special treatment. The breakfast was superb."

His hand had been withdrawn, but still she couldn't move. "Thank you."

"The room is charming."

"Thank you."

"I slept better than I have in weeks."

"I'm glad." *These two word sentences are really terrific, Sloan. Keep it up and he'll soon be nodding off.* It was just that her brain and mouth had lost all contact with each other. She couldn't form a more coherent, loquacious response. Not when he was standing only a hair's breadth away.

"Forgive my foul mood. Not that I don't want you to stop calling me Mr. Madison. I do. But I'm a bear when I'm trying to write and nothing's there. The words just won't come."

In the small space he had allowed her, she turned around and found herself gazing up into the sherry-colored facets of his eyes. "Why not? Is it a rough spot?"

For the sake of his tenuous sanity, he took a step back. It was all he could do to keep from touching her. "Yeah. I've hit a snag. Why did you pin your hair up like that?"

The two sentences were so unrelated that it took a moment for her to grasp his meaning. When she did, her hand flew to the bun on the back of her neck. "Is there something wrong with it?" she asked out of female vanity. Were pins showing? Had she left out a strand?

"No, no. Nothing's wrong. It's just that, well, I liked it better last night. Sort of loose and . . . wild . . . sexy."

She swallowed hard and dragged her eyes away from the magnetic power of his. "Well, wild and sexy isn't the way guests want the hostess of a bed and breakfast house to be."

"I bet you haven't polled the male guests." His eyes were sparkling again with teasing lights. She didn't know which was more dangerous, when they were smoldering, as a moment ago, or like now when they were boyishly mischievous. Both seemed to have a devastating effect on her equilibrium.

She drew herself up straight, turned back to the table, and said hurriedly. "I must get to work—"

"Wait!" he cried sharply and she spun around in surprise. "Maybe you can help me here a minute."

"With what?"

"With my book."

"I don't know anything about writing."

"Not writing. I need a female body to handle."

Probably she'd have been wise to look affronted, rapidly gather up the tray, and huff out. Instead she laughed. "I'm sure you don't mean that the way it sounded."

He looked chagrined and laughed himself. "Perhaps I should rephrase that. Gregory is trying to get information out of the heroine, see?"

"Who is Gregory?"

"The hero. And—"

"What's her name?"

"Lisa. So he gets in a tussle with her and she's struggling. But he loves this girl and he doesn't want to hurt her. I need a woman's body to see how tough a man can get to make his point and still not hurt her. See?"

"Wouldn't that depend on the woman? I mean, if she's a health enthusiast, a lady wrestler, or skilled in martial arts, she's obviously not going to be hurt too easily."

"No. Lisa's soft and feminine. Slender. Like you."

Her hand fluttered to her throat to self-consciously pat at her collar. "What . . ." She cleared her throat. "What do you want me to do?"

He took her hand and pulled her away from the table.

"Let's go over here where we have more room. I don't want to knock over any of your antique china." He faced her and released her hand, shaking his muscles loose like a boxer in the ring waiting for the match to begin. "Okay, I've just called you a tramp—actually a little stronger word than tramp—who would sell your body to both sides if the price were right."

"And you're supposed to love me?" She shook her head, not believing what she'd just said. "I mean, he's supposed to love her?"

"He does, but he's mad as hell because she knows something that will help him get the bad guys, but she's protecting the uncle who has raised her and is being threatened by the bad guys." He took a deep, excited breath. "So, I've called you this terrible name and since you've made love with me on numerous occasions, you're doubly insulted."

Sloan was made uneasy by his putting the story into the first person. She'd have preferred the characters to be referred to as Gregory and Lisa, but she nodded her understanding anyway.

"Come at me intending to slap me."

She glanced down at the floor, deliberately trying to throw him off guard, then lunged at him with her hand raised. The next thing she knew she'd been spun around and slammed into his chest. The hand she'd raised was being held between her shoulder blades in a twisting grip while the other was pinioned between their torsos. His other arm was against her throat while a hand like iron closed over her shoulder. His hard cheek lay along hers as he pressed her head onto his shoulder. The chignon on the back of her head had come down.

"Carter," she gasped in outraged surprise, trying to extricate herself. "Let me go."

"Am I hurting you?"

She drew in great gulps of air. "You don't play fair. You didn't warn me you were going to do this."

"I'm sorry, but that's just how Lisa would have felt. I had to get a realistic physical reaction from you. Am I hurting you?" he repeated.

She analyzed herself. "No," she answered truthfully. He wasn't hurting her, but there was no means of escape that she could see either. She pitied poor Lisa. If Gregory were anything like Carter, his appealing closeness was as deadly as his stranglehold.

"What are you feeling?"

She was feeling that if he didn't stop grinding the fly of his jeans into her derriere, she was going to faint. "Frightened." That was the most honest answer she could give him. The sensations he had engendered inside her were terrifying.

"Even though you know I love you and really don't want to hurt you?"

"Yes," she breathed and closed her eyes. "Don't violence and passion sometimes run hand in hand?"

God, why was he punishing her this way? His legs were as hard and long as tree trunks against the back of hers. His breath in her ear was causing delightful things to happen to her breasts and between her thighs. For a woman as deprived of affection as she, it was like chaining a starving person in sight of a gourmet banquet and denying him the feast. Sloan's chains of conscience and loyalty to a friend were too strong to break easily, but that made her no less hungry.

"If you were Lisa, what would you do?"

If she were Lisa, she'd probably tell him everything he wanted to know and then beg him to take her. But that wasn't what he wanted to hear, so she willed her mind out of sensuous ponderings and tried to concentrate on the strictly physical. "I don't know. I'd probably struggle, if for no other reason than stung pride."

"Okay, struggle."

Her movements were tentative at first, then more earnest. She couldn't budge him, and her efforts only resulted in rubbing their bodies together in a way that was both exquisite and horrifying. Her blouse worked its way out of her waistband. Her skirt became tangled around her legs. Her hair spilled down her neck. And her hand, which was still trapped between them, had accidentally, but indisputably, confirmed that his fly buttoned instead of zipped. "It's no use," she panted, only partially from exertion. "I can't get loose."

"You'll tell me everything I want to know?"

Her head dropped forward in defeat and she nodded meekly. Slowly his arms relaxed and he gradually released her. As soon as she was free, she whirled around and drove her heel down on his instep like a piston.

He cried out in pain and surprise, but recovered before she could run past him. He caught both her shoulders and shoved her down on the bed, following with his own body in a shallow dive. They grappled. Sloan was struggling sincerely now, for he was positioned over her in a way that gratified their sexes. He too, was doing his best to gain the advantage and finally managed to catch both her flailing hands and haul them over her head.

With their labored breathing filling the quiet room, he lay his head next to hers and rested, never letting his fist around her wrists slacken. At last he raised his face only inches above hers.

"Very good," he conceded with a wry smile. "You almost got away."

It felt good, so good, to have his weight pressing her into the mattress. Each time she drew a rattling breath, her breasts rose and flattened against the unyielding wall of his chest. Having thrashed during their struggle, her legs now lay in humbled repose, parted slightly. He was a hard, full pressure between her thighs. Like an electrical connection that wasn't quite complete, sparks shot from that spot and showered them both with pinpricks of delight.

"After you subdue me, do I tell you the information you demanded?"

His eyes rained liquid fire over her features. "Yes," he said gruffly. "Eventually."

"And then what happens?" Her voice was as unsteady and low pitched as his.

His eyes slid down her throat, lower, to the place where the top two buttons of her blouse had come undone in their scuffle. Creamy breasts swelled over the lace-edge cups of her brassiere. He squeezed his eyes shut and tried not to envision his lips pressed into that velvety valley, tried not to imagine his tongue tracing that curved trail of lace or, having passed its boundaries, touching her nipple. When he opened his eyes and lifted his head to hers, he saw that smoky quality in her eyes and knew that her thoughts were the same as his.

"They make love," he whispered.

Their eyes fused in an understanding that would remain unspoken. A sob issued out of her throat, but whether out of anguish, or guilt, or self-denial, neither could have said. He levered himself up and she came off the bed with a bound. She kept her back to him as she straightened her clothes and pulled the dangling pins from her hair, shoving them into her skirt pocket as though she were hiding evidence. The best that could be done to her hair was done with trembling hands. She heard the scrape of the chair as he sat down. Within seconds he was rolling a sheet of paper into the typewriter and then the keys began to tap rhythmically.

If he could act as though nothing had happened, so could she. Going back to the bed, she began to smooth the linens. It cost her dearly to touch the pillow that was still cratered with the imprint of his head. When the bed was made, she cautiously walked toward the table and picked up the tray.

"Thank you for your assistance," he said quietly. He was wearing his glasses again.

"You're welcome. Did it help?"

"I think so. On the other hand it may have hurt."

"How so?"

He shook his head. "Never mind," he said through tense lips.

"I'll be going out for a while. Lunch isn't included with the room, but I can make you—"

"Where are you going?"

"To . . . to the wharf to buy some crab for dinner."

He vaulted out of the chair happily. "I'll go with you."

Three

"*You can't.*" *Her objection was so vehement, they were both* surprised.

"Why not?" he asked, not quite successful in suppressing his amusement.

Her mind groped for a plausible reason. It should have been immediately obvious. "You have to work. That's why you're here, to get in hours of uninterrupted work."

"But even best-selling authors"—he executed a courtly bow—"deserve a day off." His smile was so warm, she could feel her heart melting beneath its glow. "I haven't quite got the feel of the place yet, know what I mean?" he said, glancing around the room. "It's a strange environment. Not that it's not lovely," he rushed to add.

"It is. It's just not home yet, and I'm finding it hard to adjust, to concentrate, to tune out the strange surroundings."

That was all hogwash and she knew it, and he knew she knew it. He pressed on, trying a different tack to see if it sounded more believable. "My legs need stretching. I was in the plane and then in the cab all night last night. At least it seemed that way. I need the brisk bay air to sweep out the cobwebs. Besides, I've always loved the wharf area. It will stimulate me."

Sloan thought that stimulation was the last thing he needed, but she couldn't voice that objection because she would be admitting that she knew he desired her. That was as good as admitting that his desire was reciprocated. Hopefully, if they both ignored it, it would go away.

"Really, Carter, if you want to go, I think you should go by yourself. I have several errands to run and—"

"And an extra pair of hands would come in handy," he finished for her. "Let me get my jacket."

Her usual astuteness failed her, and she couldn't think fast enough to manufacture another reason for him not to go with her. They didn't need another reason when the prevalent one was prohibitive enough. They shouldn't be playing with fire when obviously one ignited every time they were together. It was too late, however. He had already yanked the fatigue jacket from a hanger in the closet and pulled open the door to his room. "Should I lock it?"

"Yes. I have to lock the main door when I leave. I warned everyone this morning that I'd be out for a few hours so they wouldn't plan to return while the door was locked. But it never hurts to take extra precautions."

"You should have an assistant so you don't have to stay here all the time," he remarked as they were trooping down the stairs.

"That would be nice and much more convenient, but unfortunately I can't afford a payroll." At the bottom of the stairs, she said, "I'll be right back."

Gaining her room, she hastily made repairs on her makeup. After raking a brush through her hair and taking the pins from her pocket, she found the thick strands unwilling to be contorted back into their neat bun. "To hell with it," she muttered under her breath, deciding to let it fall freely. The wind on the wharf would wreak havoc with it anyway. At least that's how she justified leaving it down. Her skirt and blouse were a bit rumpled, but would suffice. She pulled on a poplin jacket the color of the blue-gray fog that rolled into the bay from the ocean at dusk, grabbed up her purse, and checked to see that she had her shopping list.

Carter was leaning against the banister with ankles and arms crossed waiting for her. "Ready?" she asked. She didn't miss the appreciative glance he gave her hair before she led him out the door, locking it behind her. The tiny garage attached to the side of the house would hold a car no larger than her compact. "Climb in," she said.

"You gotta be kiddin'," he said dryly. "Squeeze maybe, but not climb."

She couldn't keep from laughing as he sat down on

the passenger side and pulled first one long leg, then the other between his seat and the dashboard.

She was accustomed to the perilously steep streets and the San Franciscan drivers who treated traffic lights as flashing decorations to be disregarded when at all possible. When she pulled into a coveted parking space near Fisherman's Wharf, Carter was a trifle pale, making three freckles on his cheekbone stand out starkly. "Are we here? I hope."

Sloan laughed at him. "Come on. As long as you insisted on tagging along, you can make yourself useful."

He helped her pick out the freshest, whitest crabmeat, sworn to have been brought in with the latest catch. She made her other necessary stops as they walked along the wharf, but she was often distracted.

"Come look at this, Sloan," he would call. Or, "Wait, let's go in here. I've been in this gallery before and it's terrific."

While she tried to make it seem like the outing were for business alone, she had the distinct impression that given half a chance, Carter would have made it into a lark.

When she accused him of that as she guiltily bit into her Ghirardelli chocolate bar, he said, "How often do you get out? I mean for fun and relaxation, not on an errand for Fairchild House." He was unselfconsciously slurping a gooey sundae as they sat at a small round table in the atrium room of the ice cream parlor.

"Not too often," she said dismissively.

"How often?" he persisted.

She fiddled with her candy wrapper. "I'm the sole

owner and manager of Fairchild House. Housekeeper, hostess, accountant, chief cook and bottle washer. That doesn't leave much time for fun and relaxation as you put it."

"You mean you never take a day off? An evening off? Never go to a movie? Nothing?"

"You're depressing me," she said, trying desperately to tease him away from the subject. Her life was far from a carnival, she just didn't want him to know how very dull it was.

"Sloan, that's ridiculous." He lay his spoon aside and studied her with embarrassing intentness.

"It's not ridiculous if there's no help for it."

"Hire some help."

"I can't afford it," she snapped. "I told you that earlier."

"You can't afford to hole up in that house and never come out, either," he flared back. When he saw her stricken expression, he lowered his voice. "I'm sorry. It's none of my business, of course, it's just that I can't understand why a beautiful woman like you would hide herself from the rest of the human race." He tapped his spoon on the tabletop and wouldn't look at her when he asked quietly, "Don't you ever go out with men?"

"Rarely." Liar, she accused herself. "Never" would have been the appropriate answer.

He looked up at her again and she knew with a woman's instinct that he was thinking about what had happened between them that morning on the bed. "Has there ever been a man?"

"Yes," she said softly. Why keep the poor man in suspense? He was apparently dying to know all the gory details of her life. "We worked for the same company in L.A. He was a minor executive in charge of sales. He was very much a salesman, with impeccable taste in clothes, perfect manners, the gift of gab, and lots of shiny white teeth."

She took a drink of ice water. "I had just graduated from UCLA, had just moved into my own apartment, was feeling independent and dedicated to succeeding in my career. I think he must have originally considered me a challenge, me with my dour determination. He made me laugh, relax, have a good time. In turn, I was good for him. I had new insight into what the public wanted. I listened and made suggestions when he was troubled about a particular product. In all modesty I think my ideas proved workable."

"No doubt."

"After a while, he"—she paused to wet her lips—"he had more of his things in my apartment than in his. I saw no reason not to share an apartment since we planned to marry."

She could have told her ardent listener that Jason had grown impatient with her "middle-class hang-ups" as he had called them. What woman came out of UCLA or Po-dunk U, for that matter, still clinging to her virginity like it was some precious treasure? He had made her cry, because archaic as her thinking was, she *did* value her body and hadn't wanted to barter it off. A born salesman, he had finally convinced her that it would be selfish not to grant him what he wanted.

He'd been a frequent and fervent lover, but Sloan had always felt she was missing something. Every time they made love, he would want to know how he'd been, if his performance was up to par. She had smiled and said yes, but apparently her qualified answers weren't enough for his ego and he became more and more impatient for her to give him a rave review. But Sloan couldn't lie and say the sky opened up and heaven fell each time, because it hadn't. Never had. Never did. She knew there must be something desperately wrong with her.

So Jason had moved out. He took his hamster and the diamond ring on her left hand with him. She felt the former had meant much more to him than the latter. She had been devastated. Not so much by the loss of Jason, but by the defeat she was knowing all over again. Why was it so hard for people to love her? Her parents? Jason?

In college she'd dated, but always on a friendly basis, never with any promise of romance hovering on the horizon. As often as not her dates were with men who had asked Alicia out and been turned down because she was already busy. They'd turn to her roommate just to fill the empty night on their calendar. Her virginity hadn't been all that hard to hold on to. Few had bargained for it.

"What happened?"

She jumped slightly when Carter roused her out of her musings. "One day he just left, taking everything with him. He'd found someone better."

"I doubt that," he said tersely. When Sloan quickly looked at him, she was surprised to see that his bared teeth were clenched angrily. "Are you still . . . still . . ."

Soundlessly she laughed and shook her head. "In love with him? No. It would never have worked. He'd have discovered someone more exciting—"

"Why in the hell do you persist in saying things like that?"

He fired the question at her with such impetus, she broke off what she'd been saying. He was truly angry, and that amazed her. He was leaning across the small table like a well-trained hound, ready to pounce on her if she made another wrong move.

"Have you looked in a mirror lately? Don't you know that you have four stunning colors of blond and brown in your hair and possibly a dozen or so more? A man would have to be crazy not to want to catalogue each one. Your eyes are haunting and rare in color, and I'd have to work like hell to find the right words to describe them in a book. They have the darkest, longest lashes surrounding them that any woman could want. And your figure is luscious, though your wardrobe could stand some help. You try to hide that delectable body with frumpy clothes. That's what's wrong with you. You try to hide from yourself and everyone else. Why, dammit? Why?"

Pale and feeling abused by his verbal onslaught, she stared at him wordlessly. When he realized the wounding effect his attack had had on her, his tense posture relaxed and he fell back against the wrought iron chair. A blistering expletive soughed through his lips. After what seemed like a long while, he said softly, "You can kick me in the shins if you want to. Or better yet, step on my foot again. That still hurts like hell."

He succeeded in taking the anguish out of her eyes and bringing a smile to her chalky lips. "You should have lit into me now like you did this morning, Sloan. You don't let yourself go often enough. Give vent to your emotions, for God's sake."

"I'll try harder," she said. "Maybe you can give me temper tantrum lessons during the month you're here."

"Anytime you say." He was grinning, but they'd both been reminded that they were only on the second day into the month he'd be under her roof. Both were wondering how they were going to survive it and what they would tell Alicia if they were forced to call it off in order to retain their loyalty to her.

"You didn't finish your sundae," she observed quietly to break the spell of contemplative silence.

"I guess I got my fill of ice cream a few days ago. I took the boys out while Alicia was shopping. We had hot dogs and Adam got mustard on his shirt. Then the portion of David's ice cream that didn't get in his mouth, ended up on his lap or dripping off his sleeve. When we got home Alicia gave us all hell."

"I can understand why." Sloan joined his laughter, but it rang hollow. "Maybe you'll pick up some hints on keeping them clean after you're married."

"Yeah. Maybe." He was staring bleakly into the milky slush at the bottom of his sundae glass.

Sloan looked out the wide windows next to their table. It had begun to rain.

"Are your books autobiographical, Mr. Madison, or purely fiction?"

Carter set down his wine glass and surreptitiously winked at Sloan. "Miss Lehman, if everything I write about had happened to me, I doubt I'd have lived this long."

The others at the table laughed congenially.

The crab au gratin had turned out to be delicious. With the casserole she served an endive salad, asparagus garnished with lemon slices, and orange sherbet for dessert. She had begun her dinner preparations as soon as she and Carter returned to Fairchild House. He had gone upstairs, but, much as she had listened, Sloan didn't hear the tapping keys of his typewriter all afternoon.

She took time out to shower before serving dinner, dressing in a soft black wool skirt and white georgette blouse with a pleated bodice and pearl buttons on the left shoulder. Repeatedly she told herself that it was no softer and no more feminine a costume than she usually wore. She was proved wrong when two of the guests exclaimed over how pretty she looked when she called them from the parlor, where they had gathered for pre-dinner wine or cocktails, into the candlelit dining room. She blushed at their compliments, thanked them shyly, and refused to meet Carter's eyes.

He had come down to dinner wearing a navy sport

coat over an open throated shirt of ivory silk, and gray slacks. For once it looked as though he'd made an attempt to control his thick mahogany hair, but the effort was just short of having been wasted. As Sloan served the first course, she studied him covertly. His hair wasn't curly, but swerved and dipped and clung to his scalp with a will of its own. It had decided a long time ago which way it wanted to grow around that well-shaped head and would forever defy blow dryers and stiff bristled brushes that tried to change its mind.

It was touchable hair, Sloan thought as she leaned over him to serve his salad. His scent rose from the V of his collar to caress her nostrils. He smelled clean and masculine, in a way that made her think of damp naked skin fresh from a shower. Her hand was trembling when she placed the salad plate in front of him. His eyes followed her slender hand back over his shoulder to meet her eyes. When he said, "Thank you, Ms. Fairchild," he could have been saying, "I've thought of how you look naked, too," and it couldn't have sounded more intimate.

Upon seeing him, one of the retired schoolteachers had splayed a veined hand over her meager breast and cried, "Carter Madison! I saw you on the *Today* show once. Oh, my goodness, I can't believe this. I've read all of your books."

Indeed, she had one in her room which was rapidly fetched for him to autograph. The other guests were equally impressed to have a celebrity in their midst. It was the schoolteacher who had asked Carter about the autobiographical aspects of his writing in a breathy voice much more suited to a girl forty years the lady's junior.

He handled their curiosity and hero worship with aplomb and self-deprecation, which delighted them all. He regaled them with stories about his research, which had taken him virtually all over the world.

Sloan continued to serve the dinner with the same efficient deference she always did. Even though his voice never altered, she knew each time she entered the room from the kitchen, Carter's eyes followed her as she went about her tasks.

"Would everyone like coffee and brandy in the parlor by the fire?" Sloan asked graciously when they were finished eating. Everyone enthusiastically agreed. "I'll bring a tray in there. Make yourselves comfortable."

She went into the kitchen to make certain she hadn't forgotten anything on the tray. The door swung open behind her. Carter was carrying in one of the trays she used for serving dinner, heaped with dirty dishes.

"Carter!" she exclaimed. "What are you doing?"

He set the tray on the countertop. "Helping out a little."

"Well don't."

"Why?"

"*Why?* Because you're a guest. What would everyone think?"

The lines around his mouth tightened and he put his hands on his hips. "I don't give a damn what they think."

"Well I do. I have to."

"Since when is it a crime for a man to carry a heavy tray for a lady? Answer me that."

"You wouldn't bus your own table at a restaurant, would you?"

"Oh for . . ." He muttered an explicit curse his heroes were fond of using. "I'm tired, really tired of this servant scene you play out. It galls the hell out of me and makes me damn near as skittish as you are. It's fine for everyone else," he jerked his head in the general direction of the parlor, "but I don't expect it. They're only customers."

"And so are you," she lashed out. Her breasts were trembling beneath the sheerest, most elegant set of lingerie she owned. She had treated herself to wearing it tonight, and she wished to God now she hadn't. Carter's eyes were searing through her blouse as though to burn it away and find the cause of the agitation so visibly stirring the fabric.

"You have beautiful breasts. They're trembling. Why, Sloan?"

"Oh." Folding her arms across her chest protectively, she groped through the chaos of her mind for the end of the slipping rope of her composure. "Don't say things like that to me. I'll have to ask you to leave Fairchild House just as I would any male guest who said . . ."

"Guest! That's self-defensive crap. What about a *man?* What about a man telling a woman he wants more with each passing hour that she has beautiful—"

"I said stop it or you'll have to leave!" She couldn't meet the fury in his eyes, so she turned her back, keeping her posture rigid. "You're a customer in my place of business. That's all you are, Carter," she said to the floor. "A customer."

He muttered an obscenity more colorful than the last as he shoved through the door on his angry exit.

It was several minutes before Sloan could calm herself enough to heft the heavy tray and carry it into the parlor. She knew what she'd said about asking him to leave had been an empty threat, but she hoped Carter wouldn't think so. They were treading in treacherous water that threatened to drag them both below the surface. This talking at love, their visual insinuations and invitations, were flirting disaster for everyone concerned. For her, for Carter, for Alicia and her boys. It had been necessary to tell Carter exactly where he stood. He had to be made to feel he was nothing special. *He isn't*, she averred as she went down the hallway.

Of one thing she was sure. Tonight, as soon as she took it off, her best set of lingerie was going back in the drawer and it would be a long time before she wore it again. It made her feel far too feminine, far too vulnerable, and too ludicrously close to tears.

He was kneeling in front of the fireplace when she entered, adding logs to the bright fire she'd laid before her shower and lit while the guests were eating dinner. "Mr. Madison," she said with a tight smile, "you shouldn't have bothered." This was for the benefit of the other four guests who were ensconced in the comfortable easy chairs and sofas Sloan had procured and upholstered herself.

"No trouble, Ms. Fairchild. You've made me feel so at

home, I didn't even think about it." His words were dripping with sarcasm that apparently only she was privy to. The others were nodding their heads as though he were an oracle spouting gems of wisdom.

She left them, offering to replenish the china coffee pot if they should need more. In between bites of her own dinner kept warm in the oven, she stacked the dishes in the industrial-sized dishwasher and put the dining room back in order, setting it for breakfast. She squeezed fresh oranges into a sealable plastic container and stored the juice in the refrigerator to be served from a crystal pitcher the next morning. She whipped butter with honey and made the batter for tomorrow's pancakes, again storing it in the refrigerator.

She plastered on a smile before returning to the parlor, but was relieved to find the room empty. Taking up the large tray, she returned it to the kitchen. She checked the fireplace one last time, making sure the firescreen was in place and that the fire was burning down safely. The doors were secured and the lights turned off before she went to her room.

She was down to her slip when she heard the faint tap on her door. That was a first. No one had ever sought her out in her room. A guest, if one should need her, was to press the small button on the light switch in his room, and a buzzer would sound in her room, in the kitchen, and in her office.

"Yes? Who is it?" It was superfluous to ask. She knew who it was.

"Me."

She pressed her fingertips to her lips. "Go away, Carter."

"I have to talk to you."

"You can't come in my room!" she cried softly. "Please go away before someone sees or hears you."

"Then meet me in the parlor." He paused before adding. "I'll come back if you're not there in five minutes."

It took her that long to stop shaking. She knew it was foolhardy to respond to his summons, but she was more than a little afraid that he'd carry out his threat if she didn't. Tightly belting the same dowdy robe she'd had on the night before and slipping into a pair of scuffs, she cautiously opened her door and moved silently through the darkened house toward the parlor. As soon as she entered the room, Carter stepped out of the shadows, walked her backward, and pinned her against the wall with his body.

"Sloan, Sloan," he groaned into her hair, nuzzling it with his mouth and nose.

"No, Carter." The firelight had just enough remnant life to dance on his hair, burnishing the deep russet strands to copper. She longed to plow through the mass and hold his head fast against her neck where his face had burrowed.

She forfeited her chance. His head came up suddenly, fiercely, and it was his hands that threaded through her hair, holding her head still as he peered into the swirling pools of her eyes.

"I've been a good little boy all day. I've done not one

damn thing I have to be ashamed of. I've sat at that bitch of a typewriter all afternoon trying to come up with a sentence that has a subject and verb and makes some kind of sense, and I'll be damned if I could. I've not had one idea that didn't involve you—"

"No—"

"Yes!" he said on a hissing whisper. His breath was fragrant. He'd imbibed more brandy than coffee. Maybe that's why his face was hot and flushed. Or did the brandy have anything to do with it? He ground his hips against her as he moved closer and she closed her eyes and moaned her own sweet agony. "I've thought of nothing but you since you opened the door last night. I've done nothing but imagine having you beneath me, loving me."

"Stop," she begged. "Don't say anymore. Please. For everyone's sake. Carter, *think*. Think of Alicia and David and Adam. They're depending on your love. They need you."

"And I need you," he said, crushing her against him and placing his mouth against her ear where he repeated, "I need *you*."

Her teeth drew blood when they sank into her bottom lip. Tears eked out from underneath eyes squeezed shut. How she overcame the need to surrender to what they both wanted, she didn't know, but somehow she willed herself to push away from him. "You can't have me," she said on heaving breaths, still keeping him at a distance with stiff arms. "You know that. I know it. So please don't do this to me again."

Then she was fleeing down the hallway to the sterile, frigid safety of her room.

He took his meals with the others in the dining room. Otherwise she didn't see him for the next few days. She waited until she knew he had gone out before she changed the linens on his bed and supplied his bathroom with fresh towels. On such visits to the room he occupied, she tried not to look at his personal items, his shaving things on the shelf over the basin in the bathroom, his clothes draped over various pieces of furniture. One day she indulged herself and hung the discarded garments in the closet. Ostensibly she was straightening the room, when all she was really doing was providing herself with an excuse to touch something belonging to him, something he'd touched.

He was polite, but aloof. When the banker and his wife and the two schoolteachers left, they were replaced by two couples traveling together from Iowa. He was immediately recognized and recounted the same entertaining stories for this audience, if not as expansively as before. In the evenings, he either excused himself and went to his room, or left Fairchild House entirely, returning several hours later.

He received a letter from David, if the broadly printed scrawl on the envelope were any indication of the sender. Sloan left it at his place setting at dinner.

"Thank you, Ms. Fairchild," he said, holding up the letter.

"You're welcome, Mr. Madison."

One day a man identifying himself as Carter's agent called and asked to speak to him. Trepidatiously Sloan climbed the stairs and knocked on the door. The pounding typewriter keys stopped abruptly.

"What is it?" His tone would have made the warning hiss of an angry rattler sound convivial.

"Your agent is calling long distance. Do you want to talk to him?"

"No."

The typewriting started again and Sloan politely reported his curt message to the aggravated agent.

"Mr. Madison," she called from the kitchen one afternoon when she heard his heavy tread coming through the front door. He was poised on the stairs looking down at her when she caught up with him. She'd been ironing the mountain of napkins and tablecloths, sheets and pillowcases that accumulated on an exhaustively regular basis. It was too expensive to send them out. The heat from the iron had brought a spot of color to both cheeks. Her hair had been piled on top of her head, but a boiling cauldron of spaghetti to be used in tetrazzini had caused several strands to fall in humid curls around her face and on her neck. She had no idea how domestically fetching she was as she looked up at him. "Alicia called. She wants you to call her back."

He loped down the stairs. "Anything wrong?"

"No," she said breathlessly. This was the first time she had allowed herself to meet his eyes in days. He was windblown and smelled wonderfully of rain. It glistened on his hair and the shoulders of his jacket. Where had he been? she wondered. "I don't think so. You can use the phone in my office."

She led him to the tiny cubicle and then turned away. "You can stay."

"I'm sure you and your fiancée have private things to say to each other." Sloan felt sorry for the telephone as he grabbed the receiver and punched the digits of Alicia's number with a vengeance.

She had carried a stack of fresh sheets upstairs to a linen closet and was on her way down when she met him coming up the stairs. "Did you get through?"

"Yes. She asked me how my book was coming."

"How *is* it coming?"

"It's a pile of garbage," he growled as he proceeded up the stairs without slowing his tread.

Sloan put on a good act, never giving her other guests a hint of the tension and turmoil inside. But every night when she went to her room, she would curl into a tight ball beneath her covers and try to still the fluttering demands of her body. Every inch of flesh seemed to scream for Carter's touch.

She couldn't forget how inescapably he'd held her, yet how gentle his hands were. Too well she remembered how his eyes had toured her the day he held her on the bed. His breath had been hot and urgent on her skin the night he'd whispered, "I need you," in her ear. Speaking it aloud had been unnecessary. She could feel his need, hard and insistent, against her supple, receptive body.

She went through her days mechanically, preparing

the meals with no less competence, but perhaps a little less pleasure. It was with that kind of automation that she was clearing the kitchen late one night a week after the scene in the parlor. All the guests had gone upstairs long ago, so she turned in startled reaction when she heard the noise behind her.

Carter was standing just within the door. "I didn't mean to scare you."

"I . . . I thought you were upstairs." He'd taken off the sport coat he always wore at dinner. The tails of his shirt were hanging around his hips and it was only half-buttoned, as though he'd just put it on out of necessity.

"I was. I have a blasted headache and don't have anything to take for it. I wondered if you might have an aspirin. Something?"

"Yes, yes, of course." She despised the flustered, rushed, breathless sound of her voice. Why couldn't she sound cool, but concerned, and get him the damn aspirin without going to jelly in the process? "In my bathroom."

She was back in less than a minute bearing several bottles of over-the-counter analgesics. "You must get a helluva lot of headaches." The eyebrow she adored arched in humor.

"I didn't know which you'd prefer. Some upset the stomach." God, she sounded like one of those ninnies in the commercials.

"This ought to do." He selected a bottle of plain aspirin and shook two out in his hand. "Water?"

She dashed to the cabinet and took down a glass her

guests never saw. It had Bugs Bunny and Elmer Fudd on it. His brow curved again when she handed it to him, sloshing tap water over her shaky hand in the process. He tossed down the two aspirins and took a long drink.

"Thank you," he said, setting the glass down.

"I hope it works on your headache."

"Aren't you up late?"

"I made a gelatin mold. I had to chop up a lot of . . . stuff."

"Oh. All done?"

"Yes, I was just putting things away."

"Do these go up there?" he asked, referring to two heavy mixing bowls and the third shelf of an opened cabinet.

"Yes." She reached for the bowls, but he stepped around her and picked them up.

"You'll pull a muscle in your back," he said, easily placing the bowls on the high shelf. "You need a step stool or something."

"I guess so."

"Sloan." He spun around to face her and all the placid indifference, the polite inconsequentials, had deserted him. He took her shoulders beneath his hands. "Sloan," he repeated in a more mellow tone as his eyes wandered hungrily over her face, "we've got a serious problem going on here."

"Serious problem?" Her voice was high and airy.

"Yes."

"With your room? Your headache? The—"

"You don't know what our problem is?" The low, velvetly voice stroked the inside of her thighs and made them warm.

Tears clouded her eyes. Her lips began to tremble. She shook her head in remorse. "No."

"Yes, you do," he countered. Then his lips closed firm and warm over hers.

Four

Her only resistance was a momentary tension in her muscles when his arms went around her and anchored her against him. A small cry of astonishment was trapped by his lips as they opened over hers. They were fanatical in their lust to possess, acting solely out of hunger, carnal and beyond control.

Stunned, Sloan gripped his biceps for balance. As his hands scoured her back, she felt the wonder of his hard muscles bunching and stretching. The feel of them moving with sleek precision in her palms was marvelous and she softly moaned her approval.

"Sloan." Her name became his love-chant as he pressed her face into the warm hollow of his neck. His arms enfolded her as securely and warmly as a fur-lined cape. He adjusted his body to hers, instructing her with stroking hands how to mold herself to him in a perfect, breathtaking fit. He held her there for a seemingly endless time, while their hearts pulsed together and chronicled their mounting passion.

Then he lifted her face to his and captured her lips with tethered violence. Their heads rolled from side to side, twisting their lips together, bumping their noses, seeking an outlet for the energy that zephyred through them. Suddenly he was impatient with the fury of it and fused his mouth with hers to still them. A bold thrust of his tongue broke the barrier of her lips and teeth.

A deep growl rumbled in his chest as he swept her mouth with a marauding tongue intent on conquest. He plundered her sweetly, delving deeply into the farthest recess of the honeyed cove, taking up every part of it and making it his. He stroked her mouth, rapidly, slowly, mercilessly, persuasively. The tip of his tongue rubbed against hers in a challenge to join the skirmish. To his delight she did.

Her tongue darted out to bathe his lips with the taste of her. He caught her lower lip between his teeth in a gentle bite. She sipped at his lips, flirtatiously and elusively, until his tongue sank once again into the luscious temptation of her mouth. He made love to it. First with light quick thrusts, then with stronger, slower, deeper ones.

Sloan lost all track of time, of space and distance, of

right and wrong. She had wanted this. From the instant she saw him standing on the doorstep, she had wanted his lips on hers, his hands moving over her body as they were now with an audacious curiosity that wouldn't be denied. His whispered love words and moans of gratification were the music she had wanted to hear falling on her ears. Tentacles of desire ribboned through her, choking off every remnant of conscience.

She was powerless to stop or resist this tidal wave of passion. It had been inevitable and irreversible, gaining momentum since the instant they first saw each other. Impossible to outrun, to withstand, she could only let it wash over her now and flood her with its magic. Her whole body was left renewed, cleansed of loneliness, wealthy with desire.

A shuddering sigh tripped through her lips when his hands slid around from her back to the blades of her hipbones. Each thumb found the crest of one and rotated hypnotically while his fingers curled around her hips to hold her fast. He dipped his knees slightly until he could nestle hard and throbbing in the cradle of her femininity. He rubbed against her in measured circles, moving with a grinding motion that spread a flushing heat from there into her chest. She was melting, flowering, moistening in expectation.

"Carter, Carter," she sobbed, clutching at his hair with frantic hands. In her head a thousand bells were peeling joyously and her heart was bursting with love. Yes, love! She loved him, and the lips that were worshiping her throat with ardent kisses told her he felt the same. "I can't believe this."

"I know, my love, I know. God, it's wonderful. I knew it would be."

He sought the buttons of her blouse and undid them deftly. Then he pulled back to look at her as he parted the garment. Her brassiere was of a sheer, glossy, flesh-colored fabric that encased her like a second skin designed to entice. Virginally pink nipples were pouting seductively, thrusting rebelliously against their confinement. He answered their request and brushed his fingers across them with the softest of caresses.

"Please," she begged in a ragged voice. "Touch me, touch me."

"You're beautiful."

He cupped a breast in each palm and lifted her slightly. He found the ripe peaks daintier and sweeter than in his fantasy, but no less responsive as his thumbs rolled over them repeatedly until they were hard with yearning. He lay his cheek against the plump curve of her and snuggled. His breath touched her first, warm and damp, then his tongue nudged her nipple through the gossamer brassiere cup. Again. Then again, while she was breathing in harsh and rapid pants.

When his lips closed around her and drew her inside his mouth, she arched against him reflexively. She tore at the buttons of his shirt and when they were opened, combed through the thick mat of hair on his chest. His own sighs of unrestrained pleasure harmonized with hers as his mouth continued its sweet foreplay.

Her fingers engaged in an orgy of new sensations, detailing each masculine aspect of his chest. The firm contours of the muscles, the rippling track of ribs, the hard, flat nipples were all examined with hedonistic fingers. The crinkly hair thinned and softened beneath hands that grew braver and moved lower.

He nuzzled the cleavage between her breasts and breathed deeply of her scent. "Sloan," he murmured. He caught one of her hands and, moving slowly, giving her time to object if she should be so cruel, lowered it and pressed it against the fullness in his trousers.

"From wanting you, Sloan. From wanting to be inside you."

His mouth came back to hers and this time the ferocity was replaced with finesse. His tongue swirled inside her mouth until she was dizzy with her need of him. One hand remained on her breast, his fingers squeezing in a gentle milking motion. The other hand glided past the waistband of her skirt, down, down, to close tenderly over the mound of her womanhood.

"May God forgive me," she whimpered. "I want you too."

He moved but slightly, yet she could feel electric currents from each of his fingers shooting into her, igniting a million cells with a burning desire to know all of that which surged with life in her hand. His hand moved again, sliding between her thighs. She convulsed against it and whispered his name in a tormented litany.

He shuddered like one palsied before his hands fell away from the treasures of her body and he took several stumbling steps backward. "Dammit," he cursed before several more colorful expletives were pushed through his teeth. When he saw her ravaged expression, he came to her quickly and took her face between his hands. "I'm sorry, Sloan, to stop like that, but I just can't do it."

She clamped both hands over her mouth to stopper a cry of mortification. She tried to escape him, and when he would have detained her, she fought savagely, whirling away from him. "Don't touch me again," she ground out, when he reached for her. Her outstretched hands staved off his advances. "Leave me alone."

He was dumbfounded by her reaction. "Sloan, I—"

"No need for explanations. If you hadn't stopped us, I would have," she said, grappling with the buttons of her blouse that refused to cooperate. "You're absolutely right. We can't do it. I don't know what happened to me, I . . ." Her voice trailed off and she pressed her fingers into her temples that seemed about to explode with the blood still pounding through them. "You . . . Alicia . . . I should never have kissed you."

"What the hell are you talking about?" he asked in supreme frustration. "My calling a halt to things had nothing to do with Alicia."

Through vague, bewildered, dilated eyes, she stared at him uncomprehendingly.

"I couldn't go through with it because of my fantasy, because of my own warped imagination."

"What? Fantasy?"

"Oh, hell." He dropped into a chair at the table and buried his face in his hands. For several seconds he held that dejected pose while Sloan stood motionless and stared at him. She wished she would petrify there, that she'd never be required to make a decision, that she'd never have to move from that spot, that she would forevermore be emotionally dead.

At last he raised his head and said wearily, "Sit down, Sloan, so we can talk."

"No. I don't—"

"Don't argue with me for once," he barked. "Just sit down and listen." After a short pause he added a terse, "Please."

She took the chair across the table from him and sat with prim rigidity, almost as a punishment for the wanton woman she'd been minutes earlier.

"The morning after I arrived here, I was daydreaming up in my room," he began. "It's silly, I know, but as a writer I spend a great deal of my time daydreaming, envisioning things to happen to my characters. Anyway, *I* was the character this time and I saw us together, in this room, doing what we were just about to do."

She swallowed and continued to stare at her hands that were knotted together, white and cold, on the edge of the table.

He grinned shyly. "It was a terrific daydream, but somehow I couldn't apply it to real life. When I make love to you the first time, I don't want it to be furtive and rushed. I want us to be naked and at leisure and able to enjoy each other. I don't want our loving to be cheapened."

She was shaking her head. "No, Carter. Don't talk

about . . . about that. It must never happen under any conditions."

"Sloan, am I wrong?" he asked in a pained voice. "Don't you love me?"

She raised her head to meet his anxious eyes with hers, which were swimming with tears. Two escaped and trekked down her cheeks as she nodded, at first hesitantly, then more insistently. "Yes, yes, yes."

He seemed vastly, endearingly relieved as he released his breath on a great whoosh and reached for her hand. He examined it as it lay listlessly in his. "Every time I've come near you, I've behaved like a sex maniac. I've backed you into walls, tossed you down on a bed and held you there. I didn't plan on anything happening when I came downstairs tonight. I didn't contrive a headache just to catch you alone and force you against the kitchen countertop. I swear to God I didn't."

"You didn't force me to do anything."

He smiled again and let his eyes range over her face and mussed hair. "I'm a man, Sloan. I've been turned down, as any guy honest enough to admit it has. But I've also had more than my share of women all over the world. I've taken them heartlessly and quickly for my own satisfaction. Rarely did I care if I ever saw them again." He gripped her hand tightly. "That's not what it is this time. This is not only lust. Believe that. I don't want you to think that I consider you a convenient body that's good for a few rolls in the hay while I'm under your roof as if you went with the rent."

She blushed and glanced away. "I didn't think that. How do you know I'm not a landlady who would like that sort of temporary set-up with a virile tenant?"

His eyes wrinkled at the corners when he smiled. "Because you're rare and fine. Because you can still blush when I say something just this side of dirty."

They laughed together and it was a rich sound, filling the corners of the still room and encapsulating them in their private world.

"I've had a helluva time writing this past week," he admitted. "I've been writing about something for years when I didn't know a damn thing about it. And the worst of it is, I didn't even know I didn't know."

He pushed up from the table and went to stand at the sink, staring at the rain that dripped monotonously from the eaves. "In each of my books I had a love interest, sometimes a triangle, but always some form of romance. I convinced myself and tried to convince my readers that my hero was always in love with the girl. Now I know I was writing *at* love without ever having known what it felt like."

He turned back to her. "Now that I know, now that I've met you, I'm dissatisfied with everything I've written because it doesn't convey the total absorption a man has with a woman when he loves her. I want to express that sense of helplessness with this book. Gregory really loves this girl and it's going to kill him to have to . . . to . . ."

"To leave her," she finished numbly.

"I'm not going to think about that," Carter said angrily.

Sloan came to her feet. "We have to, Carter. You're engaged to my best friend, the only person in the world who has ever cared about me. We love each other as friends. I came so close tonight to betraying that friendship and I can't risk it again. She's my *friend*."

"Dammit, she's my friend, too," he shouted, and when she looked nervously toward the ceiling, he repeated it on an emphatic whisper. "She's my friend, too. And that's the way I love her, Sloan."

She covered her ears. "No. You shouldn't tell me this."

He strode toward her and removed her hands. "Maybe not, but you're going to hear it. I think Alicia's a great lady, a little flighty and irresponsible, but charmingly so. She was Jim's wife and she made my best friend happy. That was reason enough to love her.

"But I asked her to marry me because it was convenient to both of us, Sloan. She and the boys need a keeper. I felt duty bound to Jim to take care of them. The time has come in my life when I should have a wife and children. That's the only reason I asked her to marry me. I know she's still in love with Jim, and I've never entertained any romantic notions about her."

She pulled free of his restraining hands and turned away. "But you'll . . . you'll sleep with her once you're married."

He took a long time to answer while the pieces of her breaking heart fell to the bottom of her soul one by one. "I would like at least one child of my own," he said softly at last. "When I do marry, I have every intention of sleeping with my wife every night."

Sloan's eyes slammed shut and she wished she could close off her ears just as effectively. "Yes, of course you will. It was stupid of me to ask."

"But Alicia might not be my wife."

She jerked around quickly. "Of course she'll be your wife."

He stubbornly refused to concede it. "Not necessarily."

"Yes, necessarily."

"How can you say that after what has happened between us, Sloan? How can you even think I could marry Alicia now?"

"And how can you think otherwise?" she demanded heatedly. "Carter, she trusted me enough to send you here. To place you in my keeping."

"That was foolish of her."

She wouldn't accept his compliment. "No it wasn't. She has every reason to trust me with the man she plans to marry. We're friends and neither of us has ever betrayed that friendship. What if the situation were reversed? What if Alicia had died and I was engaged to Jim? Could you take me away from him?"

He broadened her vocabulary with a few words she'd never heard spoken aloud. "It's not the same."

"It's exactly the same. And you know it. Don't you see, Carter? It's only because we're living in the same house. We've been forced together and we've let our imaginations run wild. You naturally have a romantic nature to be able to write the way you do. You're only letting it work overtime. I'm lonely, having lived alone for years. Once you get back to Alicia and the boys—"

"That's crap, Sloan. Now you're the one being less than honest. Don't you think I'm man enough to know what I want? I could have found you in a supermarket as you bumped into my cart or in an elevator or anywhere and I'd have known you with the same familiarity as I did the other night when you opened your door to me."

"Alicia will be a wonderful wife," she said desperately, twisting her hands. She loved the words pouring out of his mouth, but knew she shouldn't be listening to them, much less cherishing each one.

"No doubt she will, but will she be wonderful for me? She doesn't respect my need for solitude when I'm working. If she were here, she'd be running up those stairs knocking on the door every ten minutes—"

"Stop!"

"No. You listen," He gripped her shoulders and shook her slightly until her head wobbled back and she was forced to heed his words. "Would I be good for her? I suffer every writer's paranoia, Sloan. I need to talk. To converse. Often. And to someone who will listen. I mean *really* listen. You do. Like the other night when I arrived, you sat at that table and listened. I had your undivided attention. You weren't bubbling over to relate to me everything that had happened to you during the day. You weren't up and down like a damn jack-in-the-box—"

"Damn you, Carter!" She yanked herself free and backed away from him. "Don't you dare stand there and criticize the woman you're going to marry to me. That's what men do when they pick up a woman in a bar, gain her sympathy so she'll have sex with them. 'My wife doesn't understand me.' Brilliant as you are, can't you come up with something more original than that? I don't want to hear it. It makes me feel dirty.

"If you and Alicia have problems that need ironing out, then iron them out privately. I don't want to know about them or be involved in them."

"Well that's too damn bad because you *are* involved, Sloan." He drew her to him again and, though she struggled, he wouldn't release her. "From the top of your beautiful head to the tips of your ten toes and at all points in between, you're involved." He sealed her mouth to his with a sweet suction. One hand held her jaw imprisoned while a reckless tongue plundered her mouth. The other hand curved over her hip, pressing her close, acquainting her once again with the power of his desire.

With every ounce of depleting moral fiber, she fought the erotic impulses rioting through her. But to no avail. She'd been dead too long. When offered new life, she couldn't refuse the resurrection. He felt her acquiescence, gradually relaxed his hold, and let his hand slip between them to fondle her breasts with a loving caress. Through her restored clothing, his knuckles feathered over the nipples that had already budded with desire.

"If anyone has my child, I want it to be you, Sloan. I

want a baby of mine to nurse on your sweet, sweet breasts."

The verbal picture he painted was right out of her dreams. A man who loved her. A baby their mutual love had created. A sense of belonging. A sense of worth. Being loved in return.

But she knew, as with all her dreams, this one would never come true. His kisses, his caresses were only making her crave something she could never have. Loving him was a masochistic self-flagellation that left her heart lacerated and bleeding. He would come to his senses and return to Alicia, and Sloan would be left alone with her wounds. She wasn't sure she could heal herself again.

He was so wrapped up in their kiss, that he blinked stupidly and incredulously when she pushed him away. "Don't say things like that to me." Her face was a hard, cold mask that if she didn't guard carefully would crumple. "Don't approach me like this again or I'll have to ask you to leave Fairchild House."

Smoldering rage burned away the passion-induced fog in his eyes. They were suddenly brilliant with clarity. "Dammit, Sloan—"

"I mean it. You're going to marry someone else. Kindly remember that."

His sizzling opinion of her reminder was branded into the ceiling and she cringed at the blunt vulgarity. "I know what's wrong with you," he said with a feral curl to his lip. "You've imprisoned yourself in this house, hidden yourself from the world because you're afraid to face it."

"Afraid?" she asked, insulted and not a little in fear of

his uncanny talent to strip her of her defenses and see into her innermost, secret self.

"Yes, afraid. You grew up in a house that sounds about as cheerful as a dusty mausoleum. Your parents, from the bits and pieces I've picked up from you and Alicia, ignored you. In what I think was sheer desperation, you latched onto a jackass of a boyfriend who dumped you."

"Shut up. You don't know anything about it."

"The hell I don't. You may think you're hiding, but you give yourself away, Sloan. You're as transparent as glass. So what if your parents were inept? So what if an egomaniacal bastard went fickle on you? Is that any reason to draw a circle around yourself and not let another human being inside it for the rest of your life?"

"Go to hell," she said, spinning away from him.

Undaunted by her flair of spirit, he lunged after her, catching her just before she could retreat into her room. He braced her against him and held her fast. "You've doomed yourself to a life of loneliness because you're under the misguided notion that that's all you deserve. Hell, Sloan, none of us gets what we deserve or we'd never even be born. Life doesn't depend on merit or we'd all be angels . . . or devils."

"Let me go." Futilely she struggled for release.

"You've thrown yourself upon the sacrificial altar of self-denial and are afraid of letting anyone, especially a man, touch you. This god of martyrdom you've dedicated yourself to is jealous and might not like a sacrifice sullied by happiness and love."

He was so close to the truth that she clawed back like

a wild animal. Tossing back her hair, she glared up at him. "What about you, Carter? You're just the opposite. You've dedicated yourself to a woman and two children who need you, yet you'd toss that promise aside as though it never existed. But it does exist and it is binding and before too long you'll remember that. You'll think about Jim and what you feel is your duty toward him as a friend. You'll go back to Alicia and the boys and give them all the love you so blithely extol to me. No thanks. You'll eventually come to your senses and in the meantime, I won't be your play-mate." Her body was tautly drawn up as she gulped at precious air. "I think it would be best if you left here."

He was fairly bristling with temper and his eyes blazed hotly. He flung his arms wide when he released her, as though touching her an instant longer was loathsome. With lips that barely moved, he strained his parting words out. "Your bed will remain sacrosanct, Ms. Fairchild, but you'll not kick me out of here."

The swinging door oscillated back and forth several times after he shoved his way through it. Finally it came to a standstill. Only then did Sloan realize how exhausted she was. She groped her way into her room and collapsed on her bed, drawing her pillow close and burying her face into it.

His perceptive accusations had left her feeling beaten and battered. Her soul had been his target and each angry outburst a missile aimed at it, striking her where it hurt the most. The truth of his words had been the ammunition in each attack.

Why couldn't Carter understand? *I have no recourse except to protect myself. I will not be hurt by love again!*

But she already did love again and was already hurt by it. No matter the scathing words she'd flung at him, she loved Carter with an intensity close to pain.

She hadn't been prepared for the heartache of Jason's rejection. She had entered into that relationship blindly and without the benefit of experience and warning. This time she would have no excuse for such naïveté. If she followed the path her heart was telling her to, the road would be paved with regret. It had a dead end. Better to turn back now while she still could.

But how was she going to cope with having him in her house? If he worked in his room during the days, she'd probably see him only in the evenings when he came to the dining room for dinner. She would carry no more trays up to him. If he didn't come down to breakfast, he wouldn't get any. Perhaps she'd survive the next few weeks. Perhaps.

It wasn't as though they'd be alone. There would be other people in the house.

The next day newspapers were filled with stories about the unusual amount of rain the Bay Area was having and the consequences of it.

Sloan hadn't really been concentrating on the inclement weather. Her mind had been too occupied elsewhere. On Carter. So she was mildly surprised to read about the mudslides reported in the hills surrounding the city and the local flooding in lower areas. The conditions became disastrous enough to make television network news for the next several days.

"Maybe we should cut our stay short and head for home," one of the women from Iowa said at dinner.

"Naw," her husband drawled. "We planned this trip for months. You won't let a little rain ruin it for us, will you?"

Worriedly, the lady turned to their traveling companions. "What do you think we should do?"

"Stay," the man said, spearing a piece of grilled steak from the platter Sloan held for him.

"I suppose so," the second woman said. "Besides, Dorothy," she teased, "it's not raining in any of the stores."

Both husbands groaned and Sloan sighed with relief. The only other guests she had in the house were an elderly couple who were only staying two more nights. She dared not look at Carter through the entire exchange, though she could feel his sardonic gaze on her.

"No question of my leaving," he said, taking a sip of burgundy wine. "I'm making terrific headway on my book. Oh, Ms. Fairchild, another helping of those potatoes, please," he said with a dazzling smile that only she knew was false.

"Certainly, Mr. Madison," she said with equally insincere graciousness and a demonic urge to dump the contents of his plate in his lap.

Keeping a wary eye on the weather, Sloan was dismayed to watch the situation worsen. The Golden Gate Bridge was closed to traffic for hours at a time because high winds and torrential rains made driving across it perilous.

Sloan began to panic. The couples from Iowa fulfilled their stay, but the elderly couple was due to leave the following day. She had two rooms reserved for the weekend, but she was afraid tourists would hear the discouraging weather reports, which the news reporters seemed bent on painting as black as possible, and cancel their trips. Not only would that severely affect her budget, but it would also mean she and Carter would be alone. Unless she could convince him to leave—and she thought the possibilities of that were about as good as those of the rain stopping any time soon.

Her worst fears came to fruition. Within an hour she got cancellation calls from both her weekend reservations. Despondently she sat at her desk in the cramped office under the stairs and ran tape after tape through the adding machine, praying the earlier tabulations would prove to be in error. How was she going to pay this month's bills? At least worrying over money kept her from worrying over Carter. By tomorrow night, they would be in the house alone.

It was with certain dread that she picked up the telephone when it rang later that day. "Fairchild House," she said with the resignation of one who knows it must be a creditor calling.

"You sound as dismal as the weather there is supposed to be."

"Alicia?" Her heart flopped over in her chest, but she

swore to herself it wasn't out of guilt. She'd only kissed him, for heaven's sake. Well, and sort of touched . . .

"How are you?"

"Fine. The boys are fine. Nothing's wrong, I just wanted to call."

"I'll go get Carter. He's working as usual. I swear I rarely see him. He's locked up there in his room all the time. The typewriter is constantly clacking." *Easy, easy. Don't oversell it. She'll get suspicious.*

"Actually, Sloan, I wanted to talk to you," Alicia said quietly. "How does Carter seem to you?"

Sloan licked suddenly parched lips. "Seem?" She was twisting the telephone cord with rubbery fingers. "What do you mean?"

"Is he well? Happy?"

"Well? Happy?"

"Sloan, will you please stop repeating everything I say and tell me if he's all right?" Alicia said impatiently.

Sloan took several deep breaths. "Of course he's all right. Healthwise anyway. He packs away a good dinner every night." She hoped that shallow, affected laugh sounded sincere to Alicia. "I . . . I keep coffee on the stove for him. He . . . uh . . . he said he likes to drink it while he's working."

"At least he's eating. When he threatened to take a room at a hotel until the book was finished, I vetoed that. He'd live on potato chips and coffee out of a vending machine. I still think Fairchild House is the best thing for him right now, only . . . ."

"Only?" Sloan squeaked when Alicia paused. Her heart was thudding against the back of her throat.

"Only he sounds funny when I talk to him. Distracted. Distant. I know he's working and he's always preoccupied, in another world, you know, when he's into a book, but I can't help but feel a little hurt by his lack of attention."

"I'm sure you're justified in feeling that way, Alicia," Sloan said slowly. "Naturally you're wrapped up in wedding plans, but I think women put more stock in things like that than men do. He's terribly busy. I'm sure he's just concentrating on his book and his seeming indifference doesn't mean there's anything for you to worry about." A guilty conscience made the words taste brassy.

"I guess you're right," Alicia said on a brighter note. "I've got to get used to his 'dark periods' when he's brooding over a plot."

"Yes, you do," Sloan said seriously. "I've learned one thing about your fiancé. He takes his writing seriously."

"Well he should. He makes a bundle at it."

Sloan was unaccountably offended. She was sure Carter would write if he never made another penny from it, if he'd *never* made a penny from it.

". . . so I was thinking I might come up there tomorrow night and spend the weekend with the two of you."

Sloan was yanked back into the conversation in the middle of Alicia's speech. "What? Come up here? Tomorrow? That would be wonderful!" She meant it. Alicia's presence would set things right.

"Mother's offered to keep the boys. Do you have an extra bed?"

"Too many I'm afraid," Sloan said with a bitter laugh. "Please come."

"I've heard the weather is deplorable."

"So? We'll sit by the fire and visit while Carter's working."

"I'm hoping I can get him to take the weekend off."

"Let me go get Carter. I'm sure—"

"No. You can tell him I'm coming. If I'm going to disrupt his whole weekend, I'll leave him in peace today."

She told Sloan her tentative travel arrangements and estimated time of arrival, saying she'd get a cab from the airport and save her or Carter from getting out. "I'd rather you be there waiting for me with one of your scrumptious meals."

"You've got it. I can't wait to see you."

"Me, too. Bye."

Sloan felt like she'd been granted a reprieve. She approached the dinner hour with more enthusiasm than she'd known in days. Her spirit flagged somewhat when only the elderly couple came to the dining room.

"We met the other gentleman on the stairs and he said to tell you he was going out," the man said politely.

"Oh. Thank you."

He didn't come in until after midnight. She was sitting in the parlor waiting for him. He shrugged out of his coat and was shaking the rain off it when he looked up and saw her under the archway.

"What are you, the housemother? Didn't I make the curfew?"

Her lips compressed with anger and her back went as straight as a crowbar. "I don't care what time you come in, Mr. Madison. I waited up to give you a message from your fiancée."

The insolent slant of his lips fell and his shoulders slumped. He stared at his rain-splattered shoes. "I'm sorry, Sloan. I'm acting like a class-A bastard. I apologize."

His smug taunting was almost easier to take than this abject apology. He looked vulnerable and in need of comforting, standing there forlornly with rain dripping from his clothes. She supposed it was small compensation that he looked as miserable as she herself had been, but it only made her love him more.

His eyes were haunted and his voice empty when he asked, "Is everything all right? The boys?"

"Yes, everyone is fine. She's coming up tomorrow evening to spend the weekend with . . . you." She had started to say "us." But putting it this way made it sound more personal and solidified the relationship between him and Alicia.

"Ah," he nodded, his face expressionless. "That's good. Alone?" He forced interest into the question.

"David and Adam are staying with Alicia's parents. She'll be here in time for dinner."

For the first time in days they were alone. And while each was remembering moments of passion and anger, they wanted to squeeze as much time as possible out of this mundane conversation.

He couldn't help but notice that she wasn't wearing the ugly blue robe. This one was apricot-colored velour. The color highlighted the varying shades of gold and brown in her hair and the fabric molded over the shapely curves of her breasts and hips to fall softly between her legs. It was all he could do to keep his eyes off that delicate triangle so provocatively outlined.

There was nothing he could do about the congestion in his loins, but he cleared his throat against its own tightening constriction. "Did she say anything else?"

Her eyes honed in on the pulse beating at the base of his throat and stared at it, wishing she could feel its rhythm against her lips. "She asked how you were. If you were well and . . . and happy."

"What did you tell her?"

"I told her you were eating." Suddenly her eyes flew up to his. "Did you have dinner tonight?"

"I took a cab to Chinatown and ate at Kan's."

"Was it good?"

"Delicious, but too much for one person." His mouth quirked into a smile before it settled into lines of unbearable sadness.

She longed to touch it, to smooth away the tragedy she saw riding on it. It was a mouth designed to smile. Or to kiss. She tore her eyes away and said breathlessly, "I guess that's all. Good night." She brushed past him in the darkness.

"Sloan?"

"Yes?" She turned quickly to see him standing far too

close. His breath stirred her hair. She could smell the bouquet of the after-dinner liqueur he had drunk.

"What did you tell her about the other?"

"Other?"

"About whether I was happy or not."

She couldn't be drawn away from the magnetism of his eyes. Her vocal cords failed her, but she managed to make herself heard. "I told her that you were working hard and concentrating on your book."

"Is that what you think I'm concentrating on?"

He watched the blue-gray eyes go glossy with emotion and wide with confusion and cloudy with longing. God, when she looked up at him like that, how was he supposed to control his longing to hold her in his arms? After having spent hours, days, nights, tasting nothing but her lips and breasts on his tongue, feeling nothing but the satiny warmth of her skin on his fingertips, hearing nothing but the erotic purring sound she had made deep in her throat when he touched her intimately, how could she be forbidden to him? He wanted to taste all of her, touch what had been promised beneath her clothes, hear her cries of ecstasy when the crisis came.

He had had only a preview of what it would be like to love her, yet he knew that beneath her serenity beat the heart of a passionate, giving lover, generous with her affections. His body ached when, against his better judgment, he let his imagination run free. Blood galloped through his veins when he imagined her naked beneath him, receiving all the love he had to give.

He thought he would die if he had to go through life never having known all of her. He was obsessed with the thought of her sweet mystery enfolding him snugly and warmly. She would take this surging hunger, that often beaded his forehead with sweat, and appease it. His erratic heart would be quieted. But his soul would soar.

Until then, he was consumed with relentless passion. He couldn't write, couldn't sleep. Still, his fantasies of loving her were more satisfying than the act had been with other women. He wasn't about to give them up. He'd go mad if he did. Just as he'd go mad thinking of her with any other man. The thought of her graceful, slender limbs twined around any body other than his sent him near the brink of sanity. If she were this passionate with him, wasn't it practical to assume . . . He had to ask, had to know.

"That salesman, Jason?"

"Yes?"

"You said you lived with him."

"Yes," she answered hoarsely.

"You slept with him, of course."

"Yes."

"Was he the first?"

"The only."

"Did he . . . did he make you . . . happy?"

"No."

She mouthed the word. The sound didn't carry past her trembling lips. He uttered an anguished groan and his hand came up to cradle her cheek. She tilted her head and leaned into his palm. His touch seemed to infuse her with a debilitating drug that robbed her of the will to move. She could only stand there and absorb the heat emanating from him as one soaks up the healing rays of the sun. It was a strange drug, for conversely it awakened the erogenous parts of her body while anesthetizing the rest of her. She could feel her breasts filling with love, the tips tingling with burgeoning desire. A delicious, lethargic warmth seeped through her feminine domain with a steady pulsing that echoed that of her heart. Of his.

"The man was a fool," Carter said huskily.

He ran his thumb once along the moist fullness of her lower lip before he heaved a sigh of taxing self-discipline and turned away. Her heart returned to its plodding, dejected cadence. It beat in time to his footsteps on the stairs.

Five

"*I think that's selfish of you, Carter,*" Alicia said *with her mouth* beautifully pouting. "What difference does it make?"

"No one reads my manuscript before I'm finished. Completely finished. Not my agent, not my editor, not my . . . fiancée. No one."

They were in the dining room eating the meal Sloan had spent most of the day preparing. The food was delicious, the ambiance of the turn-of-the-century dining room warm and cozy, especially with the incessant rain that ran in silver rivulets down the paned windows. For once Sloan was eating her meal in the room. She had even dressed for the occasion in the same black skirt and georgette blouse she'd worn the first night Carter had been there. Her hair was swept up into a loose knot on top of her head. Pearl earrings adorned her ears. She looked as though she fit the room. Alicia did not.

She looked much too modern and sophisticated. Sloan had been lighting the fire in the parlor when the brass knocker had announced her friend's arrival. Alicia had thrown herself into Sloan's arms and hugged her with characteristic ebullience. Carter had been treated to the same unrestrained affection when he came down the stairs, having heard her cheerful exclamations.

He had taken the lively Alicia in his arms and embraced her warmly, kissing her on the cheek as she wrapped her arms around his neck. Sloan had turned blindly back into the parlor on the pretext of checking the fireplace.

Alicia's blond hair had come through the flight, the rain and wind, her wild embraces without being disturbed. Her eyes danced with customary merriment. Her lips smiled as she chattered about the impossibilities involved in leaving children with Grandma even for two days. When she came down to dinner after Sloan had showed her to her room—the one conveniently next to Carter's—she was wearing an electric blue silk hostess pajama set, having changed from her red wool pants and matching leather jacket.

Now her beautiful face was puckered with vexation. "Artistic temperament, I suppose. Do you understand why he won't at least let me thumb through his manuscript, Sloan?"

Sloan desperately wished Alicia wouldn't ask her opinion on anything concerning Carter. She toyed with the food remaining on her plate with an idle fork. "Yes, I think I can. He wants to make it as perfect as he knows how, and if he doesn't feel it's perfect yet, he's cheating both you and himself if he lets you read it prematurely."

Alicia looked at her as though she were speaking a foreign language. "I guess so. But for heaven's sake, I'm going to be his wife."

Carter, too, was looking at Sloan, and she hoped the light burning in his eyes was only a reflection of the candles on the table. "I'm sorry, Alicia. But I remain steadfast. No one reads the book till I'm done."

"How much do you lack? Can you finish it earlier than you originally thought?"

He shifted uneasily in his chair and took a sip of wine. "I don't think so. I'm not happy with the last chapter."

"It's probably wonderful," Alicia said admiringly and reached across the table to cover his hand.

Envy stabbed through Sloan's vital organs. Alicia had the right to touch his hand. She had the right to brush back the unruly hair that had fallen onto his forehead, the right to trace the mismatched arches of his eyebrows, and to iron out with loving fingertips the worried crease between them. Did Alicia even see that flagrant sign of anxiety?

"There are certainly no noises or distractions here," Alicia said with a laugh. "What happened to the autumn tourist trade, Sloan?" she asked, turning away from her fiancé.

"I'm afraid the weather is keeping them all at home. The television reports have scared them. I had two separate reservations cancelled yesterday. A group of four women due to arrive next week called today to reschedule."

"Are you worried? I thought you were barely making it as it was."

Alicia wasn't being malicious, but Sloan could easily have throttled her for mentioning her rocky financial status. It was like pointing up another of her shortcomings. Alicia's family had always had money, as had Jim's. She had never known a lean day in her life. Sloan had never known a solvent one. "Oh, I'll survive," she said blithely. "I may have to start serving hot dogs rather than gourmet dinners, but I'll manage."

"Of course you will," Alicia said. "I wish I had one ounce of your competence and common sense."

I wish you did, too, Sloan thought to herself. *And I wish I gave off the impression of feminine frailty.*

"Anyway," Alicia went on, "I'm glad you didn't start cutting back tonight. That ham was delicious." She folded her napkin beside her plate and stretched luxuriously. "Now I'm ready to curl up in front of the fire."

Sloan stood. "You and Carter make yourselves at home. I'll get started on the dishes."

"No, no, let me help," Alicia said.

"Go," Sloan said, pointing an imperious finger toward the parlor. "This is your mini-vacation. I'll have this done in no time and then I'll join you."

"You talked me into it," Alicia said, taking Carter's hand and leading him out of the room.

Sloan could feel his eyes on her as he went out, but she didn't look up from the tray she was piling with dirty dishes. She took a long time to clear things away, making breakfast preparations in the process. Done at last, she took off her apron and went reluctantly toward the parlor where she could hear Carter's rumbling laughter and Alicia's animated voice.

They were on the loveseat. Carter was sprawled in the corner while Alicia half-sat, half-reclined against him, her shoes off and her feet tucked under her thighs. She was fiddling with the buttons on his shirt. He'd taken his coat off.

"There you are. We'd about given up on you," Alicia said. "I was telling Carter about Adam's encounter with a mouse at his nursery school."

"Not too traumatic, I hope." Sloan took a chair across the room, trying to keep her eyes away from Carter's inscrutable face.

"More to the poor teacher than to Adam," Alicia said, laughing. She sighed and lay her cheek against Carter's chest, slipping her hand up to his throat. "Oh, this is so nice. Relaxing and peaceful. I can't tell you how those boys wear me out." She tilted her head up to look at Carter. "I needed to get away and see you so much."

He smiled down at her, kissed the end of her perfect nose, and lightly scratched the top of her head affectionately.

Sloan sprang out of her chair. "You two really must excuse me, but I'm extremely tired tonight. I think the rain is making me sleepy."

"But, Sloan—"

"We'll visit tomorrow, Alicia. I'm sure you'd rather be alone with Carter tonight. Please bank the fire and turn off the lights when you go upstairs. I'll see you both in the morning."

She fled the room, knowing it was rude, knowing she was a coward, and knowing that if she had stayed and watched them snuggle together on her loveseat, she would have died.

She hated herself for doing it. She stared at the door to Alicia's room and knew that if she opened it and found that Alicia's bed hadn't been slept in, she'd never forgive herself for being compelled to find out. But nothing on earth could keep her from seeing for herself where Alicia had spent the night. The brass knob turned under her hand and the door swung open and she saw the bed with its flung back spread and wrinkled sheets and dented pillow. One pillow.

Sloan weakly slumped against the doorjamb and immediately despised herself for this snooping. But she had *had* to know. She could excuse it as part of her job to go into a guest's bedroom to make the bed. Deep down, she knew she was spying on her best friend.

Last night she'd heard them as they went upstairs,

but she hadn't been able to tell if they'd gone into the same room or not. It had been a hellish night. She'd tossed and turned in her bed imagining Alicia's beautiful naked body being explored by Carter's hands and lips. She could see his hard passion driving into Alicia's willing flesh, could feel each thrilling thrust as though it were she taking that glorious pounding. It had been all she could do to keep from screaming out her emotional agony.

They had come down to breakfast together, Alicia happy and vivacious and gorgeous, Carter rumpled and haggard and surly, as though he hadn't slept much.

"But at least he slept in his own room," Sloan said to herself as she quickly made Alicia's bed. The rest of the room was straight. Alicia was scrupulously tidy.

After the hearty breakfast Sloan had fed them, Alicia had insisted that Carter take her shopping. Despite her pleas, Sloan had declined to go with them, saying she had bookkeeping to do. She did, but it was nothing that couldn't be postponed or done in half an hour. Still, she couldn't punish herself by tagging along with them like a maiden aunt.

Sloan now went into Carter's room, which looked like it had suffered the ravages of a tornado. Balls of paper that hadn't made it into the trashcan were lying on the floor nearby. The table she'd provided him was littered with sheets of manuscript. Slashes of red ink crisscrossed them like bloody scratches. He was taking his clothes to a laundry within walking distance, but shirts and jeans and jackets and sweaters were draped over the furniture in postures resembling wounded bodies.

She began the chore of restoring order by making up the bed. Never had she been so grateful for having to do that task. She was folding one of his sweaters over a hanger when he walked into the room. She spun around, not having heard him come in the front door or up the stairs. But then she'd been absorbed with handling his clothes that smelled wonderfully of him and the cologne he always wore.

"What are you doing here?" she asked on a gasping whisper. Mindlessly she was clutching the sweater to her chest. She felt trapped, caught redhanded performing some shameful act.

"I live here," he said, the corner of his lip tilting into an amused smile.

"I mean where's Alicia?"

He shrugged out of his jacket and for once neatly hung it on the back of a chair. "At Saks in the couture department trying on clothes. I'd had enough and told her I'd meet her back here when she was finished. God knows when that could be."

Sloan remembered shopping expeditions she and Alicia had taken and knew her friend could occupy herself that way for hours. "She's having a good time," she said, turning to hang the sweater in the closet.

"I'm sorry about this room. I don't think I'm doing any permanent damage."

She smiled as she closed the closet door. "None at all. I make the beds and straighten the rooms each morning. Since you've got the largest room and are paying the most, it doesn't hurt me to hang up a few clothes."

"Thanks just the same."

"You're welcome."

The world dropped away as they stared at each other. They had been granted this small piece of the universe, this fraction of time in which to be alone. But such indulgences were hazardous to Sloan's aching heart and she felt it might shatter if she stayed with him a moment longer.

"I think that's everything for now," she said, edging toward the door. "I'll leave you alone so you can work." She reached the door without his stopping her, but when she would have pulled it open, his hand was splayed wide over it, keeping it shut.

"You look good in jeans."

She couldn't look at him. She stared at the back of his hand plastered to the door, preventing her from opening it. His knuckles were sprinkled with brown hairs and dotted with light freckles. She wanted to kiss them. Instead, she pretended she still had dominance over her faculties and could carry on ordinary conversation. "I don't wear slacks except sometimes on Saturday mornings when I do heavy cleaning."

"You don't smell like you've been cleaning. You smell like freshly baked bread." He moved closer, pressing his middle against her bottom.

She barely had sufficient breath to say, "I've been baking bread, too."

"I want a bite." He lowered his head and nudged her hair back with his nose. Then she felt his lips on the side of her neck, nibbling softly. His teeth raked her skin lightly. The spot was soothingly laved with his tongue as his mouth opened over it.

"Carter . . ." she breathed, ashamed and thrilled by the molten lava of desire that spilled from the center of her femininity to flow with delicious sluggishness through her veins.

"Do you have any idea how delectable your cute little butt looks in those jeans?" he asked in her ear as his tongue outlined its translucent rim. "No you don't, or you wouldn't wear them."

"You shouldn't say—"

"To hell with what I shouldn't say or with what I shouldn't do. I'm doing what I want to do for a change. And whether you admit it or not, it's what you want me to do. Isn't it? Say it, Sloan."

"Yes," she sobbed.

"Ah, God will damn us for sinners, but kiss me."

It was far more tender a kiss than she had expected. He cupped her chin in his hand and turned her face around to his. Their mouths met over her shoulder. His lips parted and he drank of her for a moment before his tongue dipped into the silky depths of her mouth. When he withdrew it slowly, she murmured a protest. "Shhh, there's no hurry." He spoke against her lips, outlining them with the tip of his tongue.

With an indolent thumb, he stroked the underside of her chin and jaw. He used his tongue again, not urgently, but with a lazy and pumping motion that deflowered her mouth and made it entirely, exclusively his.

"Raise your arms and put them behind my neck," he instructed as his lips left a string of scorching kisses along her throat.

She did as he asked of her, lacing her fingers through the hair that brushed his collar. It was natural to angle her body along his, to stretch against him, to rest her head on his chest.

His hands began a slow, circular massage up her ribcage. Responding to a pagan rhythm that thrummed through her body, she swayed slightly, rubbing her hips against the fly of his trousers. "My God, Sloan. Yes, Love. Don't stop," he groaned.

With his head bending over her shoulder, he nuzzled his way along her shoulder, freeing the buttons of her blouse one at a time. Without haste, he peeled it away, taking the satin strap of her brassiere with it. He took love bites and sampled the texture and flavor of her skin with his tongue. He rubbed her with his chin, and the suggestion of his beard sent chills of delight racing through her body. Her fingers tightened in his hair and her back arched, lifting her breasts.

"So soft," he said, letting his hand find the top of her breast swelling over the cup of her bra. He filled his hand with her and rasped over the beguiling nipple with his fingertip. His eyes gleamed with masculine pride when it beaded beneath his coaxing. In no rush, he let his finger trace the circle of the pink areola. "This almost drove me nuts that first night. I wanted to do this." He gently rolled the bud of flesh between his fingers until its longing became more pronounced. "Then I wanted to touch it with my tongue." His voice dropped a decible, to little more than an aroused growl. "I still want to."

Sloan shivered with a seizure of uncontrollable passion when one lean, strong hand flattened over her abdomen and pressed her backward, urging her against his virility. Her muscles became gelatinous and she was plagued by a lassitude that she reveled in. She was sensuality's prisoner and Carter was the jailer. He held the key to all that made her woman. He had tapped the resource of her femininity and, like a well, it gushed forth, flooding her body, inundating her with sensations she had never experienced before.

"I want you, Sloan."

"I want you," she confessed on a ragged sigh, turning into his arms. Her arms snaked around his waist to hug him tight. She nestled her face on his chest, breathing deeply of his scent, knowing that within a few seconds she would have to let him go. But for a moment he was wanting her and she could pretend she belonged to him.

His lips moved in the mass of her hair as he held her to him, caressing through her jeans the taut, saucy derriere he'd admired. "After having made me suffer this purgatory, you'll love me now, won't you, Sloan?"

"I *do* love you," she vowed, letting her lips brush against his skin just beneath his collar.

He took her by the shoulders and pushed her away. His eyes impaled her. "You know what I mean."

"I'm not going to . . . to make love with you, no," she said quietly, but irrefutably.

He released her suddenly and slammed his fist into

the opposite palm. "Dammit," he cursed loudly. "Why?" Plowing deep furrows through his hair with angry fingers, he demanded again, "Why?"

Slowly, she readjusted her clothes and faced him with abject weariness. "You know why, Carter. Please let's not go through this again. If we ever did . . . go to bed together, it would hurt someone we both dearly love."

"Are we hurting her any less by *wanting* to?"

"No, but we won't have to feel so guilty about it afterward."

"I doubt I'd ever feel guilty about giving you my love. And I sure as hell wouldn't feel guilty about taking yours."

"You would! I know you would."

Arrogantly, he hitched his thumbs under his belt. "Don't bet on it. I don't have the same perverse penchant for self-punishment that you have, Sloan. I don't get my kicks by being a martyr."

Anger surged through her veins where passion had flowed only moments before. "It seems I gave you more credit than you deserve."

"What's that supposed to mean?"

"I didn't think you'd resort to that masculine crutch. But if it placates your male ego to verbally abuse me because I turned you down, go ahead. It won't change my mind. I still won't go to bed with you."

"Abuse?" he scoffed. "Baby, let me tell you all about abuse. Abuse is when a woman strokes a man to rigid senselessness and then tells him it's no dice."

His words struck her in the stomach like vicious fists

and made her nauseous. She swallowed scalding bile. "I don't like being called 'Baby,' " she ground through teeth clenched as tightly as her hands were. "And what you said is crude and vulgar."

His stance was one of goading belligerence. "I haven't even gotten to the crudities and vulgarities yet."

"Save them for your book." She jerked open the door before firing her last insulting shot. "I'm sure they'll fit right in."

She slammed the door before he could make a comeback.

Alicia came in a short while later, lugging an armload of packages and boxes labeled distinctively from the exclusive stores of Union Square. "Sloan, Sloan," she called, bustling in after paying her cab fare.

Sloan came out of her office where she had been poring over the discouraging tapes her adding machine spat out. "Did you leave anything in the stores?" she asked, trying not to sound like she'd been kissing this woman's fiancé less than an hour ago. Alicia's bright, childlike face did nothing to alleviate her disgust with herself. Alicia's hair was rain-dampened and windblown, and she was decked out in black patent boots and a matching vinyl raincoat.

"Wait until you see the absolutely gorgeous things I bought. Where's Carter?"

"Upstairs working," Sloan said, avoiding Alicia's eyes. "I can hear his typewriter."

"Come up. I want to try my things on for you."

"In a minute. Go on up. I'll bring some hot cider and you can give me a fashion show." She had to have more recuperative time. However, she didn't think all the time in the world would rid her of the guilt she felt.

"Okay," Alicia said as she happily tripped upstairs.

Carter's typewriter was silent when Sloan carried the tray up a few minutes later, but his door was closed. Alicia's was partially opened so Sloan pushed it with her foot as she went inside. She halted just inside the threshold, gripping the handles of the tray with knuckles gone white.

The packages and boxes were lying helter-skelter on the bed and floor. Carter and Alicia were standing in the middle of the room locked in an embrace that caused Sloan's heart to wrench painfully in her chest. Alicia's coat hung by one arm and shoulder as though she'd been arrested in the process of taking it off. Carter's hands were imbedded in her thick skein of blond hair. His mouth was working savagely over Alicia's.

Sloan felt she had been nailed to the floor. She was unable to move as her spirit deflated like a discarded balloon. Her eyes were wide and vacant with disillusionment as she stared at Carter's mouth devouring Alicia's with unleashed passion. Her own lips parted and a serrated sigh like a death rattle shuddered through them.

That's how Carter saw her when he jerked his head up from the dissatisfactory, bruising kiss. He dropped his arms from around Alicia as a spasm of self-loathing shook him. He had never felt so wretched in his life. Not only for the horrible expression he had brought to Sloan's face, but for the shabby way he had treated Alicia. She hadn't deserved that debasement. It wasn't her fault he was drowning in his own poison. The kiss had been to serve one purpose and one purpose only. And it hadn't stemmed from desire.

Alicia pressed shaky fingers to her mouth and turned, flustered, to see Sloan. "Oh, Sloan. We . . . Carter . . . he wants to see the things I bought, too. And . . . here, set that heavy tray down. You didn't have to serve refreshments, but then you're such a dear."

She chatted on, while Carter and Sloan moved mechanically and answered responsively as though the whole scene had been rehearsed and they all knew what roles they were supposed to play and what lines of dialogue to recite.

Sloan was never so relieved as when they said they wanted to go out for dinner. Of course they expected her to go with them, but she refused. Alicia pleaded. Carter was stonily silent after politely seconding Alicia's invitation. Sloan remained resolute, and finally Alicia gave up.

Alicia wore one of her new dresses and Carter looked handsome and successful in his sport coat and tie. The perfect couple. The embodiment of the American dream.

Sloan, smiling and commissioning them to have a good time, watched as they climbed into the cab. She closed the door to Fairchild House and pressed her head into the hard coldness of the door, wishing she had no more feeling than it.

Everything Carter had said had been a lie. He'd wanted a convenient bed partner, one last fling before he got married. That she was his fiancée's best friend, that the fiancée was underfoot, only made for intrigue. It was something fresh out of the pages of one of his novels. When Sloan had spurned his base advances, he'd run straight and sure back to Alicia's loving arms.

God, what a fool she'd made of herself. Twice. First she'd believed Jason could love her. Then she'd believed Carter did. If it weren't so tragic, her culpability would be laughable. Jason's rejection she'd taken with a stiff upper lip and a grim resignation that things were running true to form.

"Why does it hurt so much more this time?" she asked the walls of her room.

It wasn't easy to fall asleep, but she was almost afraid to anyway. She was afraid that if she closed her eyes, she might die of despair in the empty house.

"I think I'll go back to Los Angeles with you," Carter said quietly.

Sloan hadn't heard them last night when they had come in. She was glad. She didn't want to know if they'd shared the same room during the night. Most probably they had. Carter's lust had been thwarted once by her untimely appearance. She doubted he'd have been deterred again.

Alicia had insisted on helping with the brunch dishes, and now they were lazing away the hours of early afternoon with cups of coffee in front of the fire in the parlor.

Swearing all the while that she despised the real man Carter camouflaged behind his charm, his announcement nonetheless rattled Sloan's composure.

"Do you mean it, Carter?" Alicia asked excitedly. Sloan saw her hand grip his thigh with familiarity. "Oh, that's wonderful! David and Adam will—"

She broke off abruptly and collapsed against the back of the loveseat. "No," she grumbled. "You can't come back. Not now."

Sloan glanced at Carter but when she saw that his own surprise mirrored hers, she quickly averted her eyes back to Alicia's sullen face.

"Why shouldn't I go back home? I thought you'd want me to."

"I do, Carter," Alicia said earnestly. "But you haven't finished your book and you couldn't get it done before the wedding even if you locked yourself in your house. We'd all start hounding you just as we did before."

He shrugged. "I just won't finish it until after the wedding. It's not crucial that I meet my deadline. I can get an extension."

"Oh no," Alicia said, sitting up straighter and shaking her blond mane emphatically. "I'm not starting off a marriage with something as important as a literary masterpiece between us. You'd never forgive me for that."

"It's hardly a literary masterpiece. There would be nothing to forgive."

She looked at him with open skepticism. "I know you, Carter Madison. If your book isn't going well, you're miserable and I don't want a sad sack for a groom. You tell him, Sloan. He should stay here in Fairchild House until he's finished. Right?"

Sloan's eyes bounced from Alicia to Carter. He was carefully listening for her answer. It was much safer to look at Alicia. "I'm sure Carter will do what he feels he should without any advice from me."

"You like it here, don't you, Carter? Sloan's not mistreating you, is she?" Alicia asked teasingly.

Sloan's face paled, but Carter answered swiftly. "No, no, it's nothing like that. It's just that no book is as important as you and the boys."

"You really should go ahead and finish it, darling. You won't be happy until you do, will you?"

His eyes made a swift trip in Sloan's direction and back. "No," he admitted at last.

"And this is the best place for you to work right now. So you'll stay, though I truly appreciate your making the unselfish gesture." Alicia leaned over and planted a soft kiss on his mouth. He touched her shoulder briefly. "Now I've got to get my things together. The cab will be here in less than an hour."

Sloan watched the cab pull away, Alicia waving enthusiastically from the back seat. The car was soon swallowed by the gloom and the rain. Carter preceded Sloan into the house and went into the parlor. He was standing in front of the fireplace gazing into the flames when he said, "I tried."

She had been making a hasty retreat toward her own quarters when his words stopped her. The tension between them was palpable. How they were going to survive until the next guests arrived at Fairchild House, she didn't know.

"What did you say?"

He turned around, a dark, slender silhouette against the firelight. He hadn't turned on any lamps. The room and hall were dark save for the reddish glow. "I said I tried. To gracefully leave," he added when she still seemed not to comprehend.

"Yes, well . . . . It would have been best. I think this is the first time in her life Alicia made a decision with her head instead of her heart." She said it with derisive affection and he caught the humor. It served to lessen the tension somewhat.

He chuckled softly. "Her timing is off." He studied the carpet beneath his feet. "She's a trusting soul. She doesn't suspect a thing. She didn't even mention that we'd be here alone without any customers for chaperones."

Sloan looked away and crossed her arms in front of her. She was suddenly very cold. "She has no reason to mistrust either of us."

He sighed heavily. "No. I guess not." She grew warm again when he stopped pretending interest in the rug and raised his eyes to her. They shone on her from across the dim room. "Can you trust me, Sloan?"

"What do you mean?" The convulsive working of her throat made her voice sound unnatural.

"Yesterday. I wanted to take you to bed and you said

no and I got mean and insulting. God!" He thumped his fists against his thighs. "I don't know what made me act like that. I've never been that abusive with a woman before. If she said no, I'd tip my hat and be on my way, but with you . . ." He looked at her hopelessly and lifted his arms in appeal. "I just can't seem to take no for an answer. I was angry, physically agitated, not a little frustrated, and . . . I'm sorry. Please forgive me."

She twisted her hands at her waist. "I'm as much to blame as you, Carter. You were justified to be angry. I led you to believe that I was more than willing."

"Sloan, you know I'd never hurt you, don't you?"

Her head shot up at his agonized tone. "Of course," she pledged with soft urgency.

"You know I'd never force—"

"Yes!"

He went to a chair and dropped down, linking his hands loosely between wide-spread knees. "You saw me kissing Alicia." It wasn't a question, but a simply stated fact.

Again she felt that pain, like a spear piercing her heart. "That's what men are supposed to do with their fiancées. Kiss them."

"But they're not supposed to be in the hope of banishing another woman from their mind." He looked up at her from where he sat, his hair falling with disregard over his creased forehead. "They don't kiss them wishing they could forget how delicious another woman tastes."

"Oh, Carter, please stop." Sloan covered her face with both hands.

"That's the only reason I was kissing poor, startled Alicia. I promise you she's never known such unbridled lust. At least not from me. I had to see if I could find a trace, only a trace, of the pleasure kissing you gives me. It was a stupid thing to do. Naturally there was none. Because she isn't you."

"Don't tell me this," she cried.

"I don't know how I'll ever make love to her after we're married." He came out of the chair, across the room to her, and pulled her hands free from her tear-bathed face. "Maybe I'll pretend she is you."

"No!" She whirled around, giving him her back. The tears that had longed to be released for days ran down her cheeks. He turned her to face him again, but not as a lover, as a friend.

"Weep for both of us, Sloan," he whispered. He pressed her wet face into his shirt front and comforted her as he would a child while she continued to cry. He stroked her hair and rubbed her neck and smoothed his hands down her back.

She let him. Because she never remembered a time when someone had comforted her. She'd always been there for other people to pour out their sorrow to, but had never been allowed the luxury of revealing her disappointments. Under Carter's loving hands and melodic reassurances, she gave vent to all her brokenheartedness.

"We won't speak of it anymore, Sloan. You've been

right all along. I know my obligation, what I have to do, and it's unfair of me to hurt you like this. So we won't ever be lovers, but I'd like very much to be your friend. And as a friend, I ask you a favor."

She lifted drenched eyes to his. He swiped lingering tears from her cheeks with the caressing pads of his thumbs. "What favor?"

"Would you read my manuscript?"

Six

She knew her expression must define imbecilic. She could feel her mouth hanging slack and her eyes blinking rapidly. Carter saw the amazement on her face and seemed pleased by it because he grinned in that lopsided, endearing way of his.

"But you said no one ever reads a manuscript of yours before it's finished," she gulped out between lips that were operating like a goldfish's.

"No one does. This is an exception. I want you to read *Sleeping Mistress* and tell me what you think of it . . . honestly."

"I didn't know you were finished with it."

"I'm not. That's why I want you to read it. I'm having trouble with the last chapter. Maybe if you read the rest of the book and give me your observations, something in my head will click."

After a moment of introspection she said slowly, "Alicia will be upset."

"She'll never know. At least I don't intend to tell her you've read it."

Her eyes roamed aimlessly over his face while she pondered her decision. They lingered on the wayward hair that graced the top of his ears. That, like everything about him, made her want to touch him. "Alicia should be the one who reads the manuscript for you." Sloan never wanted to be accused of usurping Alicia's place in his life.

"She would love it, or rather she'd tell me she loved it whether she did or not. And that's not to be taken as a criticism of her. It's a truthful observation. She'd be kind at the risk of offending me."

"How do you know I wouldn't do that? Tell you what you want to hear instead of what I really think."

He laughed then, a deep, rich sound that surrounded her with warmth, that she would bask in. "You've never minced words with me before, nor shied away from saying things I didn't particularly want to hear. Even at the risk of making me furious. I don't imagine you'd start now." He saw the pros and cons parading across her face in stark disclosure of her indecision. "It won't take up too much of your time, will it? You could do it in the evenings."

She laughed then. "I don't suppose I'll be busy this week. You're my only boarder."

"Speaking of that, don't go through that servile hostess routine just for me, okay? You're lovely when you do it. I've never seen anyone handle things so competently and graciously. But let me treat you to some meals out." When he saw she was about to object he stopped her with raised palms. "I insist. It can be your payment for reading the manuscript."

"But your breakfast and dinner are included in the price of the room."

"Then we'll consider it a swap off."

"Your meals are worth more than that," she argued.

"God, you're proud and stubborn. Okay, let's say you can fix my breakfast and serve it in the *kitchen,* and we'll either go out or have sandwiches or something easily prepared for dinner. Deal?"

He stuck his hand out for her to shake. She took it and pumped it twice firmly. "Deal."

"Sealed with a handshake and"—he leaned down toward her—"a kiss."

His lips met hers softly, but firmly, in what was supposed to be a dispassionate kiss. Instead the contact of his mouth on hers sent an arrow of love shooting into her body. It imbedded itself deep in her womb and splintered through her whole being. Their lips never opened, their tongues remained dormant, the kiss never expanded into one of unleashed desire. Yet they valued it more than any other they had shared. It was a declaration not of the physical desire they had for each other, but of the spiritual need that was also having to be denied. That sacrifice was the hardest to bear.

When he pulled away, his sherry-colored eyes were misty with longing. "When do you want to start?" he asked thickly.

"Tonight."

He smiled, realizing that all her objections had been for show. His heart swelled with pride over how eager she was to read his manuscript.

Sloan's own heart was exultant. He was granting her a privilege no one else had ever had, nor ever would. It wasn't his body, or his name, or even his love. It was his life's work he was giving her. And she knew that above all else, that was most precious to him.

"Well, are you going to make me beg?" he asked from the kitchen table the next morning. She was at the range scrambling eggs.

"I'm punishing you for coming to the kitchen to eat. Breakfast is part of our deal, remember? I planned to bring it up to you on a tray."

He sipped his coffee. "I've been up for hours, pacing that room until I thought it was a decent enough hour to come downstairs. How far did you read?"

"Eat your eggs," she said, thumping the plate down in front of him and swinging away saucily.

He muttered an imaginative curse, but attacked the plate of food while she ate at a more sedate pace. Sitting across the breakfast table from him, each dressed casually, alone in the house, she indulged herself and fantasized that it wasn't temporary, that Alicia didn't exist. Fairchild House was empty save for them, yet to Sloan it had never felt cozier. It seemed to have shrunk in the rain, to have formed a chrysalis around them that sealed them off from the rest of the world.

"What did you think of the first chapter?" he asked around a mouthful. "Did you read the first chapter at least?"

"The weather man said we're in for at least three more days of rain." Being deliberately obtuse, she meticulously spread jam on her biscuit.

"All right, all right, I get the point," he grumbled. "Pass the bacon, please."

When they were done, she carried their plates to the sink, ran hot water over them, and came back to the table bringing the coffee pot with her. She refilled their cups. Carter watched each move impatiently, tapping his thumbnail against the stem of his eyeglasses.

"Your first chapter is excellent," she said after taking a contemplative sip of coffee.

His shoulders sagged in relief, but he tensed back up immediately. "You're not just saying that?" The glasses were shoved to the top of his head where they rode most of the time he wasn't actually working.

Her laugh was full throated and wholesome. "No." She shook her head. "I thought the man running down the alley in terror of the man who was chasing him was going to be the hero."

"That's what you were supposed to think."

"The way you described his ringing footsteps on the dark, wet streets, the thudding heartbeat . . . well, you know what you wrote. Anyway, I thought you set the scene perfectly. I was feeling his fear, his panic. My lungs were bursting just as his were. I was thoroughly surprised—"

"When he turned out to be the bad guy and the man chasing him was the hero."

"Yes! That was an extremely clever twist. The readers will love it. But—"

"But what?" he asked anxiously.

She shuddered. "Did you have to make his murder so brutal and bloody?"

He grinned. "It wasn't a murder, it was an execution. He was a Nazi guilty of atrocities. Besides, the hero has to be not only heroic, but dangerous. A shade beyond the pale. A large percentage of my reading audience is men. The books are a fantasy for them. And when someone's brains are blown out against a brick wall by a .357 Magnum, it's a lot more grisly than I described it. There's really no way to describe it."

She swallowed hard. "Y-you've seen . . . that?"

"Yeah. A buddy of mine is with the FBI and when I told him what I needed, he called me the next time—"

"I don't think I want to know anymore," she said quickly.

"Okay," he said smiling. "Is that as far as you got? The first chapter?"

"Through chapter four. And I like it, Carter."

"Do you? Really?"

"Really. Cross my heart." She made the childish gesture, but the gleam in his eyes as they followed the path her finger took between the lush mounds of her breasts was most adult.

As though they had adhered there, he had to peel his eyes away from her breasts to lift them back to her face. "I know it's a mess. Can you read it okay? I've been making revisions right and left since I got here. When I haven't been able to work on that last chapter, I've been attacking the rest of it with a vengeance."

"I had trouble following the editing marks in some spots, but I deciphered them well enough. The story moves so quickly and you've put the hero in an impossible situation. I can't wait to see how you're going to get him out of it." The animation that had made her face beautifully mobile, suddenly fell away as though a mask had been removed. "He's not going to die or anything, is he?"

He chuckled at her obvious distress. "No, he's not going to die."

"In that case, I can't wait to get back to it. Are you going to work today?"

"Yeah. I'm going to change a scene in chapter six before you get to it."

She had cleared the table as they talked and was now stooping to load the dishwasher. She had no idea how provocative her pose was from the back. "Why?"

"You've given me an inspiration."

She turned around, her fingers dripping water onto the spotless floor. "*I* have?"

"I told you I liked you in jeans. I want to put them in the book."

Self-consciously, she dried her hands on a dishtowel, not quite able to meet Carter's eyes. "I only wore jeans today because no one else is here and I need to do some regrouting in one of the showers."

"Don't apologize for looking sexy as hell in a pair of jeans, Sloan," he said softly.

With an attack of shyness, she tucked a strand of hair behind her ear. "I didn't . . . I mean *I* don't think I look . . . sexy as . . . as hell."

His eyes lasered into her from across the room and held her motionless. "I know. You don't work at it. That's what makes it so effective."

She might be able to stand what he was saying if he weren't saying it in that voice that reminded her of a mink glove. She'd seen it advertised in the back pages of a magazine. It was a toy, a sexual toy, designed for lovers to wear while giving each other a massage. That's what Carter's voice felt like as it stroked her ears. Mink on naked skin.

She tried not to think of it on her bare stomach and between her thighs as she stammered, "H-how can you use my . . . uh . . . jeans in your book?"

"I have Gregory getting shot in the shoulder at the end of chapter five. He wanders around in this labyrinth of a Swiss village, dazed with fever, and in pain. Lisa, who sees him in chapter four making a contact, has been following him."

"I've read that part."

He nodded. "When he finally faints from loss of blood, she has him carried up to her apartment and tends to his wound herself. He's delirious for days." He shrugged self-critically. "Trite, but effective. Anyway, when he starts to regain consciousness, I had her bending over him looking like an angel. He sat up and lay his head against her breasts like he was trying to decide if he was still alive or not. He got . . . uh . . . well, he responded to her physically, and knew he wasn't dead."

"I don't see anything wrong with that." Sloan stared at him entranced. She couldn't look away from his magnetic eyes any more than she could keep from walking toward him where he still sat in the chair at the table.

"It was okay." Carter cleared his throat of an unusual raspiness. "But instead, I think I'll have him open his eyes and the first thing he sees is this terrific feminine derriere in a pair of tight jeans. Lisa can be bending over the end of the bed, tucking in the covers around his feet or something. Yeah, that's it," he said with a spurt of inspiration, "because he's had fever and when it began to break, he kicked the covers off.

"He reaches up and touches her . . . fanny . . . like he can't really believe it's there, like it must be a part of his dream." Carter matched action to words and molded his hand to Sloan's hip. "He caresses it. It's firm and round and taut. She knows what's going on in his mind and stands perfectly still, letting him do what he will to reassure himself that he's still alive."

Carter was kneading her gently, rhythmically, and Sloan swayed unsteadily, intoxicated by his words and touch. Instinct alone brought her hands to his hair to remove the eyeglasses. Solicitously she smoothed back the mahogany strands and stroked his brow with comforting fingertips, as though he had been the one raging with fever.

"Then he brings his hand around to her front and presses it . . . here." He looked at her abdomen. The long tail of her unglamorous shirt was knotted at her waist. He lay his hand along the fly of her jeans. The tip of his middle finger was on the metal snap and the heel of his hand adjusted itself over the soft, swelling femininity.

"Eventually," he went on in that mesmerizing voice that held her spellbound in a web of sensuality, "he unsnaps her jeans and lowers the zipper."

He didn't move, but actuality couldn't have been more potent than the power of his words. Sloan closed her eyes. She could see it. Feel it happening.

"He lowers the zipper slowly until he comes to the lacy band of her bikini panties. He smiles, a half-amused, half-fearful smile, because this may still be an hallucination. Then he touches her skin with his fingertips, brushing them back and forth across her abdomen. Her skin is vibrating with life and it shimmies up through his fingers, telegraphing him that he's alive too. With a small groan he raises himself to a sitting position and lays his head against her, pressing his mouth to the woman flesh that is so soft and smooth and smells so good. He kisses her navel, probes it with his tongue."

Involuntarily Sloan whimpered and, though his hand was motionless and her skin was still covered, her flesh quivered reflexively and she could feel the damp strokings of his tongue over her navel.

"He nuzzles her, catches her panties between his teeth, and scrapes his tongue along the lacy edge. He sighs in relief. She's not an illusion. His head flops back down on the pillow and his hand falls to the bed." Carter's hand dropped from her to dangle loosely at his side. She removed her hands from his temples where her fingers had been sifting through the burnished strands of dark hair.

Carter's sigh was one of sublime peace and his whisper was a lullaby. "He closes his eyes and sleeps, knowing that because she exists, because she's real, because she's there with him, he will survive."

Ponderous seconds ticked by until he roused himself out of his fantasy and looked up at her. "How does it feel to be a Muse?"

"I'm honored," she said in a thready voice. She shook herself slightly, trying to throw off the cloak of eroticism he had blanketed her with. Her legs threatened to give way and she stumbled away from the table. It became essential that she put distance between them. "But this Muse has a shower to regrout and a contrary curtain rod to tamper with."

It was a desperate effort on Sloan's part to put things aright, to clear away the marvelous debris of an emotional storm. It was a brave, valorous gesture, but her lips were tremulous and her eyes were shimmering with tears. She would valiantly fight for the cause even if her heart wasn't in it.

He was merciful and followed her lead to let go the fantasy before it became reality. Grudgingly, but with the same spirit of bravado, he said, "And this writer has chapters to revise and one to compose."

They went to their separate jobs, but it was a long time before either of them was able to concentrate on anything but the scene they had enacted.

"This is insane, Carter."

"Come on. Just a few more yards. Where's your sense of adventure?"

"Back in my living room where it's warm and dry . . . and light. How can you see?"

"Night vision. Hey, that'd be a terrific title, wouldn't it? *Night Vision* by Carter Madison. I like that. Guess what, Granny. We're here."

She looked around her and saw only stygian darkness through a drizzling rain. "Where?"

"At the bench on the top of the hill."

Evening had already fallen when he had bounded down the stairs, telling her to grab a coat and hat and follow him. She'd obeyed and was amazed when he insisted on driving. Asking where they were going gained her nothing because he wouldn't tell her. He stopped at a convenience store and bought a loaf of sourdough bread, a bottle of red wine, a block of cheese, and a package of cold cuts. They drove across the Golden Gate Bridge. Immediately upon reaching the Sausalito side, he had taken a left turn, driven through a long, absolutely black tunnel, then up a winding road to the ridge of a hill looming over the bay.

"We walk from here," he had said as he pulled on the emergency brake of her car.

"Walk?" she had asked in a high, disbelieving voice. "To where?"

"To the top."

Now he was pulling her down beside him onto a cold, hard bench and making a broad sweep with his arm. "There, Ms. Fairchild, lies before you the finest view of San Francisco."

To their right and slightly behind them was the Pacific Ocean, dark and ominous and shrouded with fog. The mournful hoot of foghorns on the boats and tugs that had defied the dreadful weather sounded haunting in the dreary stillness. To their left and in front of them San Francisco had been set like a jewel mounted on the hilly terrain. In the immediate foreground Sloan could see the skeletal shadow of the Golden Gate bridge, its lights fuzzy and diffuse.

"There before me lies the finest view of San Francisco totally obliterated by rain and fog," she said dryly.

"You'll feel better after a cold slice of bologna," he said commiseratingly, a laugh lurking just behind his lips.

They munched on the hard bread, tearing at it with their teeth and then storing it beneath Sloan's poncho to keep it dry. The block of cheese was passed back and forth as was the bottle of wine.

"You got to read some this afternoon?" he queried with affected nonchalance.

"Yes. It felt downright sinful to be reading a book

when I'm usually cleaning or cooking, but I was so enthralled I didn't even care."

"Good. It's healthy for a body to be sinfully self-
indulgent every once in a while. Despite the less than ideal
weather conditions, you needed this outing tonight, too.
Having fun?"

She looked up at him and smiled languorously. "Yes,"
she said softly. "I'm having a wonderful time."

He looked at her mouth. It was so beautiful when she
smiled naturally and openly, not with the guarded austerity
she imposed on herself. The darkness made it impossible
for him to be sure, but he thought her lips had been
stained rosy from the wine. He couldn't think of anything
tastier, more inebriating, more sexually stimulating than
licking the taste of wine from her lips. He dragged his
mind away from that to save his sanity. "What about the
book?"

"It's pure entertainment, Carter. But it has pathos,
too."

"It didn't until I made those recent changes. Go on."

"I love it. I think it's the best you've ever done."

"Truthfully?"

"Truthfully."

"There's only one scene that bothered me." She
snuggled down deeper in her poncho. The wind off the
ocean was frigid against her back.

"Cold?"

"A little," she admitted.

"Here." He pushed her off the bench, scooted over,

and then pulled her down onto his lap. "I'll be your wind-break. Stretch out."

He sat with his long legs stretched out in front of him in a half-reclining position, bracing his shoulders on the back board of the bench. She aligned her body to his and gradually let him absorb her weight. "How's that?" he asked in her ear.

His breath was hot against her rain-damp skin. "Better." It was blissful. Despite the rain and the cold and their meager supper, she'd never felt more relaxed and fulfilled and comfortably warm in her life.

"Have another sip of wine," he urged, passing her the bottle under her arm. She took a long draught, which she didn't think she needed because her head was buzzing and her body was heavy with a deliciously sapping lethargy. His arms slipped around her beneath the poncho and pulled her close against him. The hard impression of him was firm against the cleft of her buttocks. "Now what part bothered you?"

She didn't think her floating mind could form a co-herent thought, drunk as she was by the arousing juxtapo-sition of their bodies. Carefully, her lips formed the words transmitted by her brain. "You know the scene where he comforts her after they escape from the terrorists?"

"At that old inn?"

Thoughtful fingers were strumming against her stomach. Her throat was aching from suppressing moans of animal pleasure. "Yes. Well, I think you might have short-changed it." The words tripped over each other on their breathless exit. "But who am I to tell you? I don't know anything about writing."

"I'm not offended. I asked. Go ahead."

His hand rested, palm upturned, just below her breast. "Lisa's emotions are riding right on the surface. She's been terrorized, she's experienced the exhilaration of escaping with her life, with Gregory's life."

His hands stirred and, if he had clamped them over her mouth, it couldn't have stifled her speech any more effectively.

"Go on." The murmur was actually no more than a wisp of air drifting across her ear.

"Th-that scene where he comforts her after she realizes her child was actually killed in the raid . . ."

"Uh-huh." His lips were moving against her lobe now. Not quite kisses, the meanderings were alluring enough to make her insides churn.

"You handled that beautifully. That's what she needed then. Comfort without romance. But in this other scene I don't think comfort would be enough."

"How do you mean?"

"You have him holding her. She's frantic, clinging to him almost hysterically. Then he just kisses her and she falls asleep. I'm not sure she wouldn't want something more, wouldn't want . . ."

"Intercourse?"

Her heart somersaulted and only then did she realize that her breast was gently imprisoned by his palm. Her nipple was nestled in the fleshy part of his hand while his fingers were curved around the full, soft globe with unqualified possessiveness. Even through the yarn of her sweater, she could feel his heat burning into her flesh, branding her heart with his name.

"Yes," she replied on the merest breath of sound. "I think she'd seek the ultimate outlet for the explosive emotions inside her. I think she'd want to celebrate that they were both alive in the most tumultuous way."

"You think I should have him make love to her?"

"Yes. Quickly, fiercely, almost brutally." She didn't know that her muscles were demonstratively contracting with each word, responding to the passion of the scene she envisioned, until she felt her hips squeezing against Carter's lap and heard his sharp intake of breath.

"God—" He hissed a vile curse and buried his face in the nape of her neck. "God, Sloan, you don't realize what you're doing." His breath was hot and rampant against her neck as he struggled for control. She, too, was finding it hard to regain mastery over emotions and senses plunged into chaos.

When at last the turbulence subsided, he kissed the side of her neck with utmost tenderness. "That's good advice, Sloan, very good." His fingers curled slightly and she felt her nipple hardening beneath the increased pressure. "It would work. Gregory only pulled back out of concern for her. When they first realized they'd made good their escape, I described his desire for Lisa at great length."

She hiccuped a laugh and covered her mouth, ashamed at the *double entendre* that had sprung into her mind. Hopefully Carter wouldn't catch it.

He did. Placing his mouth against her ear, he said

with a lascivious inflection, "Your mind is in the gutter,
Ms. Fairchild. Did you find a pun in my choice of words?"
She giggled again and he laughed. "You're tipsy. The prim
and proper mistress of the respectable Fairchild House is
actually drunk and not a little ribald in her private musings." He stood up, catching her under rubbery arms to
bring her to her feet. "I'd better get you home before we
catch pneumonia."

They were both relieved that the former tension had
been banished, but his arm was firm around her waist as he
led them down the steep, pebbly incline. At the car, he
gave her a loud, smacking kiss. "Thanks for the help. I'll
change the scene first thing tomorrow."

The day following their unorthodox picnic passed
much as the preceding one had. They shared breakfast in
the kitchen. Carter went back upstairs to his typewriter
and Sloan decided to polish the silver. Off and on during
the day, she read several pages of the manuscript, then a
few more. She had become totally engrossed in the story
and in the characters Carter had so admirably created.

He declared at mid-afternoon when he came down for
a cup of coffee that he was taking her out to dinner.

"Indoors?" she cooed sarcastically.

He kissed her swiftly as he passed her on his way
back upstairs. "Indoors. Someplace that has tables and
chairs and everything."

The rest of the day she worked on herself, doing her
nails, her hair, taking a long soaking bath in oil-slicked

water, pressing her best dress. It was a soft, clinging wool jersey in a subdued shade of blue that deepened the mysterious hue of her eyes.

Carter couldn't help but notice that now, as he watched her from across the candlelit table. He had selected one of the restaurants at Pier 39 that overlooked part of the marina. Sailboats and cabin cruisers rocked dejectedly in the water, looking desolate and deserted in the rain-dimmed night.

"Carter, have you ever been married?"

"No, I've never been married. I came close once."

"What happened?" A sudden rush of color painted two bright patches on her cheeks. "You don't have to tell me," she added hastily. "I can't imagine why I asked."

He took her hand and squeezed it playfully. "You wanted to know. There's no heartbreaking secret as to why I'm still single. She was a bright, beautiful young lady, a decorator with a growing list of impressive clients. She wanted me to use my architecture degree and start making tubs of money so we could play hard and live fast. I wanted to write even if it meant not making any money and not playing so hard and living quite so fast. In short, we wanted different things, had irreconcilable goals, and we parted amiably."

"Where is she now?"

"Married to a bright and beautiful surgeon and living as she wanted to."

"But I'll bet her bright and beautiful surgeon doesn't make the money you do," she said in a sing-song voice.

He assumed a disbelieving look and his eyebrow shot

up. "Why, Ms. Fairchild, I'm flabbergasted. Could it be that you have a malicious streak to your otherwise flawless nature?"

They laughed and declined the waiter's offer for more coffee. As they crossed the footbridge over Embarcadero to the parking lot, she said, "I didn't know you had an interest in architecture."

"I studied it for five long, tedious years to please a father who thought wanting to be a writer was an unambitious copout."

"What does he think now?"

"Now he displays my books on the mantel like trophies. He and Mother live in Palm Springs. He's a retired banker."

"Do you love them?"

He paused and studied her for a long time before he said quietly, "Yes. Because they gave me life and because they did the best they knew how to do at parenting an only child. I see their shortcomings and was frustrated and mad as hell when they laughed at my dreams. Now I take a little credit for myself for what I've become and try not to blame them for all that I'm not."

She cocked her head to one side. "Is there a lecture in there somewhere?"

The corner of his mouth tilted into a smile. "You're not only beautiful, you're perceptive." His expression changed as he framed her face between his hands and said seriously, "Just because your parents weren't capable of showering you with affection doesn't mean you're not worth loving, Sloan. It wasn't a failure on your part, but on theirs. They cheated themselves of your love. Don't cheat yourself."

Tears glistened on her eyelashes and there was a distinct tremor to the lips that whispered, "Thank you." Coming up on her toes, she kissed his cheek hard.

His eyes were like torches burning in the gloomy night as he said tightly, "You're welcome."

Tears blurred the last few lines of typed text, but she read each poignant word. She lowered the sheet of paper to her lap, then on impulse, flattened it against her breasts. It couldn't be wrinkled any more than it was. The corners were curled. There were markings and deletions and additions scribbled in the margins, but what was written on the page couldn't have been finer had it been engraved on silver.

They had returned home from their dinner out. Carter had bade her a regretful good night and gone upstairs. The remaining chapters of the manuscript lay so temptingly in their box that after Sloan had changed into her velour robe, she took it with her into the parlor. Stoking up the fire that had been banked before they left for dinner, and wrapping herself in a blanket for extra warmth, she got comfortable in one of the roomier chairs. Only one small lamp burned on the table at her elbow, but the whole room faded into oblivion as she stepped into the final scenes of Carter's book as though they were three dimensional.

His characters breathed. Sloan was wildly in love with

Gregory, even as much as Lisa was. Indeed, the closer to the end of the book she got, the closer Lisa resembled her in how she thought and how she reacted to life.

By the time she got to the scene they'd played out in Carter's bedroom that first morning, she felt like she'd written the story. Not that she could have told it so expertly, but Carter had captured her ambiguity, her emotions, her physical cognizance of him, as keenly as if she'd quoted it to him verbatim. How could he know her so well? Secret thoughts she'd harbored were vividly revealed in Lisa's thought processes. Yet such blatant intrusion into her innermost self didn't feel like a violation. It felt like freedom.

Carter had actually seen the person she was behind the screen of caution she used for protection. Just as Gregory had coaxed Lisa's secrets from her, so had Carter brought all that Sloan Fairchild was out into the open.

He had read her soul, touched it, expressed it with words both lancing and sweet. She couldn't feel closer to him if they shared the same heart. They were one in the spirit. They couldn't be more an integral part of each other unless . . .

Her eyes sought him as though beckoned to do so. He was standing in the shadows near the doorway, barefoot and shirtless. He was still wearing the dress slacks he'd worn to dinner. His expression was indiscernible in the darkness.

Carter knew he'd never seen a more beautiful sight. She looked like a child folded in the chair with the blanket swathing her. Her feet were tucked under her. Her posture may have been innocent, but her rapt expression was that of a woman.

His heart jumped to his throat as he noted that her hands were pressing the last page he'd written to her breasts. He'd been unable to go any farther, but he'd worked on that damn passage for one whole day, trying to get it right, trying to capture Lisa's feelings on paper. Did Sloan recognize herself?

Were those tears in her eyes? They sparkled like liquid diamonds in the firelight. Her hair was alive with light. He'd noticed that she didn't peel it back anymore, but let it flow wild and free about her shoulders. He hadn't mentioned it or complimented her on it for fear she'd revert back to that blasted bun on the back of her head. Now firelight shone through the riotous curls. He longed to warm his hands in them.

He didn't move as she carefully lowered the sheet of paper back into the manuscript box. He remained in mute and motionless enchantment as she unwound her legs from the blanket and stood up.

His pulse rate accelerated to an alarming rate and his lips parted to facilitate his rushing breath when he saw her hand go to the zipper of her robe. He watched her slim fingers close around the tassel and tracked them as she lowered it—God!—past her navel. Only a slender ribbon of skin was revealed to him, but to gaze at it was an intimate act of love. He saw the graceful length of her throat, the valley between her breasts, their plump inner curves, the haunting groove that divided her stomach, her indented navel, and . . .

Dragging his eyes up from the shadowy mystery of her body, his eyes locked with hers. She smiled beseechingly as she peeled the robe from her shoulders and let it drop to her ankles.

He heard his own rattling whisper of praise for her naked perfection. She was Venus, infused with life, injected with fire. The dancing firelight licked her body with prurient delight. Everywhere the golden flickering light touched, he wanted to know with his hands, his mouth, his tongue. He felt himself filling, swelling with a love so strong it could only be granted fulfillment inside her body.

He was moving toward her even before he heard her whispered plea.

"Carter, love me."

Seven

"*Gladly, my love, gladly,*" *he said upon reaching her and* clasping her to him. His hands sank into the mass of her hair and lifted her mouth for his fervent kiss.

His lips slanted over hers with tender possessiveness. "You can't imagine how lovely you are. I love the way you look, love your gorgeous body." His breath was warm, his words a love song against her lips. "Your mouth is so sweet. Give it to me to taste."

He nibbled at it with his own moist lips. His tongue probed at the corners, then glided without haste along her full bottom lip. When he pried her lips open, his tongue barely breached them and surveyed their slick lining with an analytical precision.

She whimpered her impatience and he raised his head slightly to tease her. "You hot little hussy."

"Yes, yes. For you I am. Kiss me." She wound her arms around his neck and curved her body up to interlock with his. Wantonly she moved against him in open invitation. His eyes went dark and a muscle in his cheek twitched.

Strong hands played wide over her hips and shoved her harder against him. The breath left her body in a long, corrugated sigh just as his lips opened over hers. His tongue pressed home, penetrating her mouth, filling it, stroking it with passion given vent.

She clawed at his hair with one greedy hand while the other examined the muscles that rippled beneath the tanned skin of his back.

Again and again his tongue assaulted her mouth, driving deeper each time. She denied him nothing. Their chests rose and fell together as they began to crave oxygen. He rested his mouth on hers as their breath was exchanged on rapid pants.

She didn't allow him to languish long, but coaxed him back, teasing his tongue with the tip of hers until his was once again inside her mouth. This time she became the aggressor. The sweet folds of her mouth tightly captured his tongue and she sucked it with a seductive rhythm.

Her breasts absorbed the vibrating growl inside his chest and she gloried in her ability to bring him such pleasure. He jerked his head back in surprise. "Good God, Sloan. I thought I was the master of symbolism."

"You're my master." Her fingertips smoothed over his damp lips, his cheekbones, his mismatched brows. The love radiating from the core of her soul made her eyes luminous. "Master me."

His eyes drilled into her the profound message of his own love. Taking up the blanket, he spread it out in front of the hearth on the carpet warmed by the fire. "Lie down on your back," he instructed softly.

She obeyed, her eyes never leaving him as he undressed. His hands went to his belt and she watched with avid interest as he undid the gold buckle. He worked the fastener next, then the zipper. With one lithe, fluid movement he divested himself of both trousers and underwear and stood over her, naked and proud and aroused.

He searched her face, looking for any sign of regret or dislike or hesitation. He hadn't felt so unsure of his own appeal since adolescence. Such modesty was unlike him. He wanted to be all she had ever desired in a man. What if she didn't like him, was repulsed by him?

But all he saw in her eyes was the shining expression of a woman waiting to be loved. He lay down and drew her under him. Their bodies adjusted to each other with the comfort of old acquaintances and the expectant excitement of a rollercoaster ride.

"I've wanted this for so long, to be lying naked with you underneath me. Tell me it feels as good to you as it does to me." Lovingly his mouth glanced over the features of her face.

Sloan's eyes closed with the pleasure of having his

weight atop her. "It feels wonderful." He buried his face in the hollow between her neck and shoulder, and she stroked through the dark shaggy strands from the top of his head to his nape.

Her hands coasted over his shoulders and down the smooth planes of his back. The muscles were firm, the skin warm. The small of his back dipped vulnerably before the tautness of his buttocks reminded her just how masculine he was. The backs of his thighs were dusted with hair.

"You're so hard," she murmured in awed appreciation.

She felt his chuckle. "Uh-huh."

"I didn't mean just *that*," she said with a shy smile. "I meant generally, all over."

"Thank you, but right now *that* is demanding most of my concentration." He lifted his head to brush soft kisses on her lips. He angled his body to one side of her and granted himself the privilege of taking stimulating liberties. "And by contrast, you're soft. Soft and sweet."

"Am I?" she sighed tremulously as he kissed her throat and the upper part of her chest. Her neck arched prettily and he dragged his tongue down its satiny length.

"Yes, yes," was his harsh whisper as his hand wrapped around her breast, gently squeezed it upward, and plucked at the rosy peak with his lips. "You taste so damn good, Sloan."

His tongue laved her nipple until it puckered with longing. She held her breath, clutching at his hair with both hands. When he enveloped her with his mouth, she exhaled on a low, satisfied moan. He flexed his fingers and his jaws simultaneously with a tugging she felt deep inside her womb. She called his name plaintively.

"Am I hurting you?"

"No, no." A curtain of hair swished around her face as she shook her head from side to side.

"Do you like this?" he asked, as his mouth moved to the other breast while his fingertips stayed to appease the one that was already shiny and wet from his loving.

"Carter, Carter." That fervent repetition of his name was the best way she knew to answer him. It was the only way she could answer him while she swirled in this maelstrom of desire. Her heart was spiraling upward out of her body and her brain had long since taken flight.

He wasn't merely doing something physically satisfying for her. And she wasn't allowing him to use her for his own pleasure. It was an exchange, and it was exhilarating. At the moment, her passion-blurred mind couldn't sort out her myriad emotions about what was happening. It defied classification. She only knew that it was the highest level of loving she'd ever experienced.

His hand drifted down her stomach, massaging the supple flesh. He levered himself up to look at her navel as his finger traced the fragile rim and tested its depth. He smiled as he played with it in studious delight, like a baby who has just discovered his toes.

But his eyes came back to hers when his hand lowered to the downy triangle that secreted her womanhood. Its perimeter was outlined by an adoring fingertip. Lightly he combed through the sweet nest and watched her eyes dilate with desire. Even as he watched that miracle of nature, his hand caressed its way down to press open her thighs. His touch was exquisitely tender, yet bold, confident yet humble, as he introduced his fingers into the moist protective petals.

"Sloan." His lips formed her name, but had she not been watching him, she wouldn't have heard it. A quiet purr in her throat was her only response. That and the gentle thrust of her hips against his hand as she arched her back. "So very woman." His exploration went beyond the bounds of timidity and inhibition.

Wave after wave of passion washed over her, leaving her a little more breathless each time. She felt herself melting against his heat, felt her nipples begging for surcease, felt herself losing her grip on reason as his fingers continued to stroke, to feather, to circle until she was gasping for breath.

"Carter," she cried as her flesh contracted around his fingers. His eyes glazed.

"You're killing me," he ground out as he withdrew his hand and poised himself between her thighs. "Sweet . . ." He gnashed his teeth in an exercise of self-control as he bathed the spearhead of his desire with her dew. He bent down and kissed her breasts, gentle, homage-paying kisses, before he slowly let himself enter the haven she promised.

"Oh, my God," he breathed into her ear as he lay his head next to hers. Full and hard, he pulsed inside her while they tried to define for their own mystified minds the wonder of it.

"You fill me completely." Her hands roved his back, trying to draw him closer, which was impossible. She turned her head and let her lips ghost over his ear and the hair that grazed the top of it. Catching his earlobe between her teeth, she beseeched softly. "Move inside me."

He growled an assent, but his motions were tentative at first. "You're so . . . small," he anguished. "Am I hurting you?"

Her fingers curled deeper into the flesh of his hips imploringly. "No."

"I can make it better for us."

"I'm disappointing you?" she asked in sudden panic.

"No, sweetheart, no. Only listen and do as I tell you and it'll be better."

His instructions were softly spoken and his praise when she complied was loving. "You're precious," he murmured as his movements became swifter to match their accelerated passion. "Precious, Sloan, do you hear me?"

She could hear him. His voice, his rushing breath, his pounding heartbeat that echoed hers. She could hear too, their harmonizing, ecstatic cries as they both lost all contact with the world.

Their descent was as sweetly loving, if not as clamorous, as the ascent had been. Her voice was drowsy, drugged with love, as she asked him, "What have you done to me, Carter Madison?"

"Loved you as you should have always been loved."

He lifted his head and rained love on her from his glowing eyes. "The real question is," he whispered, "what have you done to me?"

"Should we go upstairs?" he asked into her hair. They lay face to face, her head cradled against his chest. Lazily his fingers were twining through her hair.

"No," she said, rubbing her face back and forth over the hair-matted wall of his chest. "Not just yet. This is too . . . I don't want to move." Even after he had rolled them to their sides, he remained nestled insider her. "It feels so good."

"Does it?" With an index finger under her chin he lifted her face for a gentle kiss. She trembled. "Are you cold?" He had enfolded them both in the blanket.

"No. I'm still feeling aftershocks."

Confidentially he whispered, "So am I." He stirred inside her and she ducked her head shyly.

"That was a terribly brazen thing I did. Taking off my robe that way. Asking you to make love to me."

At the time she hadn't thought about having the courage to woo him, or the right or wrong of it. She had simply obeyed her instinct and he had heeded his own. Neither regretted it. Of that she was certain.

It was wrong. Alicia had been betrayed and everything Sloan had stood for had been compromised. But she wasn't sorry for it. Alicia would have Carter for the rest of his life. Tonight, for a few brief hours, he belonged to

Sloan. The consequences could be lamented later. The only worry that plagued her now was if she had disappointed him.

"I know I'm awkward." Her hand was self-consciously restless as it tweaked the hair on his chest.

"Sloan." He repeated her name until she met his eyes in the flickering firelight. "I am content. More content than I've ever been with a woman. You are what I need, more than I could ever hope for. Please don't insult me by belittling yourself. I love you, Sloan."

"I love you," she vowed as tears pooled in her eyes, mirroring the nearby flames. "I love you so much it hurts." She tilted her head back for his kiss. His tongue entered her mouth lovingly, with a sincerity that touched her soul.

"I think that bastard you were engaged to was an insensitive fool. Didn't he ever teach you the finer techniques of loving? Wasn't it a sharing thing?"

She shook her head. "No. At least I never felt with him what I do with you."

"You've been made to feel inferior when in fact the opposite is true. Your body is beautiful, Sloan. Except for this tragic scar."

"What scar?" she asked, pushing away from him slightly.

"Right here." He trailed his finger down between her breasts. The cleavage was more pronounced because of her position and all but swallowed his finger. "That's where your heart has been broken. The scar is invisible, but I can see it. Let me heal it now, once and for all."

He dipped his head and placed his mouth on the soft, fragrant flesh of her breasts. "Don't ever let anyone hurt you again, Sloan." He kissed her with ardent lips that indeed seemed to draw all the hurt out of her. Her heart soared with new-found freedom. "You are a beautiful woman with a tremendous capacity to love. Watch me while I take away all your pain."

Raising her head, she did watch as his nose nudged against her breasts. Their lush round shape was measured, treasured, appreciated by his hands. The shadow of his dear head spread over her breasts like healing lotion.

She saw the shadow of his tongue on her nipple before she actually felt its damp, deft touch. That gentle aggressor fanned the fires of her desire which she had erroneously thought were quenched. They burst into instant life, hotter and more intense than before. Her head dropped back onto the floor as her eyes closed. She danced again the ballet she had only recently learned, a mindless undulation that responded to the drumbeats in her head and heart and loins.

"See what a priceless woman you are." She was lifted over him, his hands covering her hips and pressing, encouraging her to feel his desire that had filled her again.

"Carter, you're—"

"Yes. Slowly dying. Now it's your turn to heal me."

She awoke languidly to lips planting tiny kisses on her neck. Even before she opened her eyes, she stretched luxuriously beneath the sheets, loving the way they slid around her nakedness. She'd never slept in any bed in the house other than the one in her room. It had been a rare privilege for many reasons for Carter to carry her upstairs during the night and establish her in the bed he'd slept in alone for weeks.

Now her breast was the object of his fondling as he trailed kisses along her shoulder. "Milady's breakfast is served."

Sloan opened her eyes and they lighted on the window. It was still raining, but the steady dripping sound was welcomed. Somehow it helped assure their privacy, set them apart, separated them from the world. It also contributed to her own sensuous birth, where all stimuli were magnified in her brain. Besides seeing and hearing the rain, she could smell it, taste it, feel it falling on her skin.

"What did you say?" she mumbled into the pillow, sighing. A silly smile curled her lips when his fingers found her nipple already distended and begging for his caress.

"I said, milady's breakfast is served." His mouth availed itself of what his fingers had tenderly prepared for it, sucking her nipple lightly. His fingertips whispered down her stomach to disturb the tawny nest at the top of her thighs with flirtatious strokings.

"Ummmm," she groaned. "What is on milady's menu?" she asked insinuatingly against that carnal mouth that had made its way up to hers.

He parted her lips with an aggressive tongue and swept it possessively as though he didn't want her to entertain any notions that his ownership had ended with the approach of morning. "An omelette, English muffins, orange marmalade, crisp bacon, and coffee."

Shoving him away, Sloan sat upright in the bed, disregarding the sheet that settled around her waist. As he enumerated the breakfast dishes, she realized that those were the tantalizing aromas she could smell. She spotted the laden silver tray at the foot of the bed and cried out in surprise.

"You really are serving me breakfast in bed!"

He wasn't looking at the tray and was paying scant attention to her surprise. Rather, he was scrutinizing her breasts, blushing with sleep and sex, and so provocatively displayed for him. He rode their sloping shape with an indolent finger. "After the way you served me last night, I thought it was the least I could do."

"Oh!" she exclaimed, grabbing his finger, bending it back to a torturous angle and saying, "Just as I thought. You don't respect me in the morning."

He pounced on her, tossing her back amidst the pillows and pinioning her naked body beneath his that was unfairly fully clothed. He ravaged her mouth with a playfully savage kiss. "It's my respect you want, huh?"

Primly she answered. "On an empty stomach, yes."

"And after breakfast?"

She lowered her lashes in a demure way that delighted him because he could see the lasciviousness of her thoughts twinkling behind the mask of false modesty. "That's for milord to wait and find out," she teased throatily.

They demolished the food on the tray. "This is delicious," she said, taking another bite of the cheesy omelette. "But I still don't think it's right that you did it. *I'm* supposed to be the hostess, remember?"

"You deserve to be indulged. And you'd better wait before you thank me too profusely."

"Why?" she asked warily, her fork poised in front of her mouth. He avoided answering by sipping his coffee. "Carter?"

"I don't clean as I go."

She set her fork down. "You're telling me that my kitchen is a disaster, right?"

"I wouldn't go so far as to say *disaster.*"

She crossed her arms under her breasts and tried to look stern, an expression that looked incongruous considering her bobbing breasts and her beguilingly disarrayed hair. Carter had a hard time keeping a straight face as she demanded. "How far would you go?"

He squinted his eyes. "Uh . . . shambles. Yeah, that's the right word. Your kitchen is a shambles."

"What's the use of having breakfast served to you in bed if you have to worry about cleaning up a shambles?"

"I guess I'll have to find a way of making it up to you," he drawled, lifting the tray from the bed.

He had a most persuasive way of taking her mind off the kitchen. It started in the shower where he soaped her body, massaging her flesh between his lathered fingers. She insisted on washing his hair and he sat on the tile bench while she worked shampoo into the thick strands. They stood together under the spray, letting the water sluice down their bodies, following the runnels with eyes and hands and lips until they fell on each other in a tempestuous kiss.

Sloan was already reclining against the pillows when he came out of the bathroom vigorously drying his hair with a towel. She watched the lithe movements of his muscles. As she had noted the first time she saw him, no motions were wasted. He was lean and sinewy, with a lethal sleekness about him that reminded her of the heroes in his books. He wasn't musclebound, yet there was about him a sense of ruthlessness lurking just below the surface. It excited her.

He dropped the towel on the floor and stepped over it negligently, looking down at her where she lay with sultry perfection on the linens. He didn't move as she reached up and took his hand.

"You're very nice to look at, Mr. Madison." Her voice held the mellow seductiveness of a silk scarf being pulled over harp strings.

"I have knobby knees."

"They are *not* knobby," she said in fierce defense of her lover. When his brow arched skeptically she assessed his knees more closely, smiled, and said more softly, "Well, not *too* knobby."

The role of aggressor became hers as she pulled him down onto the bed. Delighted with her brave interest, he submitted to her silent directives and lay down on his back. Her touch was timorous as she began to examine him curiously.

"I'm shy of you, Carter. Of your nakedness."

"I know," he said softly. "Don't be. I don't ever want you to be afraid to touch me."

He wouldn't have been surprised last night to discover she was a virgin. It had been apparent from the first that her skills were limited. But there had been no doubt as to her passion. The way she'd stood before him naked and boldly proclaiming her need had made his heart fill with pride that she'd finally recognized herself as a sexual woman.

Her fevered movements against him had been hungry and wild and he'd loved it. But he saw in her no coy demonstrations of desire, no affected sounds of mounting passion, no rehearsed caresses. She'd been totally honest, almost innocent in her passion, and God, that alone had been enough to make him love her with a ferocity that frightened him. Compared to her, all the other women he'd ever known seemed like animated mannequins who had performed for him as they thought he wanted them to.

But hadn't he, too, always performed? Hadn't his sighs and loving words been little more than scripted, often lifted out of the pages of his own books? Hadn't he recited the words he knew they would want to hear only so he could bring them to a quick lusty climax and be done with it? And hadn't the emptiness inside him afterward often been more than he could stomach? Hadn't he felt physically purged, but spiritually sullied?

Not so last night. He'd known the moment he felt her moist tightness glove him that Sloan was unique. This was what it was to love, not *make* something, but to let it happen. Sex had ceased to be a bodily function and had become an exercise of the spirit, a blending of two whole personalities and not just a meaningless, temporary fusion of the flesh.

He had loved teaching her the subtleties of it, the rapture in detention, the pleasure in finesse. And he'd wanted to kill that bastard who had cheated her out of it before. Yet that wasn't quite the truth. If Jason had loved her the way she should have been loved, she wouldn't belong to him now. He wouldn't have had the privilege of leading her into a realm of ecstasy she'd never known existed.

Now she was kneeling over him, bashfully learning his body. And he wondered how in God's name he was ever going to give her up.

She looked at him and smiled when her finger circled a prominent patella. "Not so knobby," she whispered. His thigh muscles flexed spasmodically as her hands crept up them. He held his breath when they reached the juncture where his arousal was already becoming apparent. He didn't breathe again until her attention wandered to his navel.

Before he could quite prepare himself for it, she leaned down and kissed the hair-whorled dimple fleetingly. His clenching fingers tangled in her hair, still damp from their romp in the shower. "Ahhhh, Sloan."

Praise made her courageous. Her tongue raked his navel roughly, then dipped into it in shallow forays that robbed him of breath.

She pressed her breasts against the rigid column of his thigh as she bent over him. Her hand meandered with seeming aimlessness down his torso until it encountered the thick bush of dark hair. She tested its texture against her lips as she whispered, "I love you," and unselfishly she showed him her love until he could stand no more.

He lifted her, pressed her into the pillows, and buried himself in the feminine arbor made wet with love for him. "You are mine, Sloan. No matter what happens, I want you to know that I've never loved like I do at this moment. Feel my love, take it. Please. God, please. Take it, Sloan."

"Yes, yes," she sobbed, wrapping herself around him.

Her name became a reverent chant in her ear as he patiently contained himself until she, too, had reached the summit. When he showered her womb with life, it was a rebirth for them both.

Over her strenuous objections, he helped her restore the kitchen. They were ostensibly washing dishes, though their hands were mating in the sudsy water and their lips were sealed over the steamy sink when the telephone rang.

"Don't answer," he grumbled.

"I have to. It may be someone wanting to book all six rooms for next week."

"You'll only have five available. Unless you share yours with me," he called as she raced for the extension in her room.

"Hi. Is Mr. Madison there?" an immature voice piped.

"Yes. Who's calling please?" She clutched the receiver because she knew who the caller was and felt guilt and depression as heavy as iron chains winding around her.

"David Russell."

She squeezed her eyes shut and stifled a sob. "H-hello, David. This is Sloan. You remember me, don't you?"

"Sure. My mom talks about you all the time. Do you have blond hair?"

"Yes. Sort of blond."

"Yeah, I remember. Can I talk to Carter now? It's important."

"There's nothing wrong, is there? With your mom or Adam?"

"No. My mom's not here. I'm at Grandma's house. But she gave me permission to call."

"Just a minute." She held the receiver to her chest, taking great breaths and trying to fend off the waves of despair that threatened to drown her. When at last she turned around to call Carter, he was standing in the doorway, a dishtowel thrown over one shoulder, watching her. A severe grimness had thinned his lips and she remembered thinking of that latent strain of violence in him.

Silently he reached for the phone, and listlessly, she handed it to him. When she tried to move past him, he manacled her wrist and sat down on the bed, pulling her onto his lap. She struggled, but to no avail. He held her there, his eyes boring into her chalky face as he brought the receiver to his ear.

"Hello," he said emotionlessly. He showed a bit more

animation when he said, "Hi, buddy. How's your brother?
. . . Well I miss you, too, but you knew I had to come
here to work. . . . What is it that Adam's doing? . . .
Well you're the oldest and you need to set a good example.
. . . No, it's not fair, but few things are."

Sloan hazarded a glance at him and saw that the last
had been addressed to her, not the telephone. His eyes
begged for her tolerance, not understanding, not forgiveness, only tolerance of an intolerable situation.

"Tell you what, you ask Adam not to pull hair and
you don't worry your grandmother with tattling on him. I'll
have a talk with Adam when I get back. Okay? . . . Yeah,
I can't wait either. . . . You bet. *Two* ice cream cones.
Good-bye."

Without releasing her, he replaced the telephone. For
long, silent moments she sat stonily on his lap. Finally she
said, "Please let me go."

"I can't," he said through gritted teeth. He wasn't
talking about physically releasing her right then, he was
referring to the time when they'd have to part permanently.

She didn't pretend to misunderstand. "You'll have
to," she sobbed, trying futilely to tear herself from his grip
on her upper arms.

"But not today. Not now." He burrowed his face between her breasts that were full and unfettered beneath
her blouse. His head rutted against her like a child seeking
solace, peace, sustenance. "Please don't deny me you,
Sloan. I *need* you. Please."

Mindless of anything save his heartfelt plea, she flung

her arms around his head and clutched it to her bosom. Covering the top of his head with frantic, random kisses, she echoed his words. "I need you. I was dying until you."

They were hampered but slightly by their clothing. They tore at it, groped and grappled until they were free enough to unite in a scalding, swift possession. All their frustration, anguish, fear went into each fierce thrust. They were on a timetable and the clock was running out. They raced against it. Wanting to banish the world, to rid themselves of conscience, to hold onto their shrinking piece of heaven, they ground together. The ablution came from Carter, a warm, sweet bath that cleansed them of their torment.

Afterwards, his hair clinging damply to her skin as he rested his head heavily on her breasts, he said, "Sloan, now I can write the final love scene."

Eight

For the rest of the afternoon and into the evening he worked with total absorption. Sloan checked on him periodically, sometimes taking him a fresh cup of coffee or a cold drink, sometimes just standing at the door of his room and silently watching as he deliberated over the words he was immortalizing on paper.

Since their breakfast had been so plentiful and eaten late, she fixed him "finger food" for a light supper. She cut two sandwiches in quarters and surrounded them on the platter with sliced fruit and raw vegetables. When she carried the tray into the room, he was staring at the sheet of paper rolled into his typewriter, his elbows spread wide on either side of the keyboard, his chin propped on his clasped hands. His glasses, for once, were in their proper place.

She sat the tray on the table as unobtrusively as she could and turned to tiptoe out. He caught her wrist as she went by and brought her hand to his mouth, planting a quick kiss in its palm. "Thanks, love," he said absently. His eyes never left the page. Somehow that distracted, automatic show of affection meant more to her then than a long, lingering embrace would have. He had taken it for granted that she would feel his love even if he was concentrating on his work.

She busied herself with unnecessary tasks downstairs, baked a few dozen cookies, and then undressed and got herself ready for bed. She made one last trip up the stairs to take him a plate of cookies and a thermal carafe of coffee. He was still at it, bent over a sheet of manuscript, mercilessly slashing it with his red ink pen. All the food on the other tray had been eaten. She moved it aside and put the plate of cookies in its place.

His head came up and he focused on her. "What is that heavenly smell?"

"Chocolate chip cookies."

"I'm not talking about the cookies," he said, bringing her around to the side of his chair. "I'm talking about you." Drawing her close, he parted her robe and lay his head against her stomach. "You always smell so good," he mumbled contentedly, yawning broadly.

She ruffled through his hair that she guessed had been abused by aggravated fingers. "Are you tired?"

"Getting that way. But I need to work a while longer."

"Eat some cookies. The coffee in the thermos is fresh and hot." Her words came out on short gusts of air. He was sliding his face over her silky nightgown, nuzzling her stomach and abdomen with his nose and chin. Occasionally his lips would open, and she would feel the warm vapor of his breath filtering through the sheer garment to tantalize her skin.

"So am I. Fresh and hot, that is," he snarled against the indentation of her navel.

Taking handfuls of hair in her fists, she forced his head up and said scoldingly. "But you have to work."

"Slavedriver," he grumbled.

Leaning down, she kissed him chastely on the mouth. "Good night." She turned to leave, but he caught the hem of her robe and jerked her to a halt.

"Just where do you think you're going?"

"Downstairs to bed."

"Wrong. To bed. Over there." He nodded toward the bed they had shared the night before.

"But you have to work, Carter."

"I'll work. You'll sleep. If I won't disturb you."

"That's not the point. *I'll* disturb you."

He shook his head. "No you won't. Please stay in the room with me."

She looked at him out of the corner of her eye. "Are you sure?"

"Positive. I want you with me."

"Okay, I'll take this tray downstairs and bring a book up with me. But if I see that I'm distracting you, I'll leave."

"Deal."

He was true to his word. When she came back, he was struggling with another phrase, muttering it repetitiously under his breath. She switched on the bedside table lamp and slid between the sheets. Picking up her Carter Madison novel, she adjusted it on her lap, propped herself on the pillows, and began to read. Two hours later, engrossing as the story was, she couldn't suppress her yawns and finally surrendered to sleepiness. Carter was still poring over the pages he'd typed. She fell asleep listening to the tapping keys of the typewriter and marveling over his self-discipline.

The sinking of the mattress awakened her a moment before she was cradled against his lean, naked body. "Carter?"

"It had better be," he chuckled.

"Are you finished?"

"You're so warm." He snuggled against her, finding the soft warmth of her neck with searching lips. His hands closed around her waist.

"Aren't you tired?" she asked on a yawn.

"Exhausted. What does this do?" One hand was blindly struggling with the neckline of her nightgown.

"It unties."

"Ah, there," he said, gratified when the cord loosened and fell away. He moved down her body, kissing the upper curves of her breasts. Suddenly he raised his head. "I'm sorry, Sloan. I'm a selfish beast to wake you up in the middle of the night like this."

"Yes, you're beastly," she sighed. After lowering the nightgown herself, she found his hand in the darkness and lay it on her breast. With slow circular motions she moved his hand until her nipple grew ripe in his palm. "Look what you've done to me, you beast."

His whispered words were somewhere between blasphemy and prayer. While his hand continued to fondle her breast and its responsive crown, his lips melded into hers. His tongue delved deeply, then withdrew to match hers in a darting, thrusting, rubbing skirmish. He sampled the skin of her throat and chest and shoulders with lovebites. His kisses were hot, damp, increasing the fever that suffused her flesh with a rosy glow.

Cherishing her, he peeled the nightgown away from her other breast and feasted his eyes on the erogenous display. The nipples were taut and dark from his caressing fingers. The mounds rose gently from her chest like offerings on an altar of love. And he was the high priest.

His mouth covered her with a sweet suction and drew on her nipple with tender hunger. He loved her thoroughly, his tongue honoring her with delicate strokes, his mouth closing around her as though to take all of her sweetness into himself.

Not only her consciousness was awake now, but every

cell in her body was clamoring for his. She writhed against him, twisting the nightgown and trying to kick it free with thrashing legs. He helped, shoving the garment down as his hand smoothed along the top of her thighs, in between, possessing her womanhood with a cupping, loving hand. Gently she was explored, tantalized, coaxed to a raging passion that threatened to ignite her.

Inch by alluring inch he eased down her body, at last totally freeing her of the nightgown. Letting her legs drape the sides of his body, he kissed her navel with the same talent as he kissed her mouth. His lips sipped at it, his tongue flicking into the small crevice as though it were a precious receptacle containing rare nectar.

His breath disturbed the golden tangle of curls on the slight mound and she cried out his name in astonishment and not a little fear. "No, Carter."

"I love you, Sloan. I want to experience all of you."

His adoration was bold and gentle, carnal and holy. She felt not the least bit violated, but a great deal embellished by the sweep of his lips and the thrust of his tongue. His loving was so exquisite that she was cocooned by bliss. When the crisis came, she called his name. He was there, crushing her to him, involving himself in the magic of her, and enriching it with his essence.

Thoroughly spent, he rolled them to their sides. She lay like a doll against his chest, her arms and legs sprawled limply over his. His hands smoothed her back, the swell of her hips, the length of her thighs.

"I can't believe I've lived this long without having your love," she whispered weakly.

"You have had it. I've always loved you," he said quietly, threading his fingers through her hair to press her head against his heart. "I just never knew your name."

He was sitting on the edge of the bed watching her when she opened her eyes the next morning. He was wearing only his underwear, which did more to detail his sex than to cover it. Without speaking he handed her the crumpled, ink-scarred pages of his manuscript.

She looked at him inquiringly, then at the pages offered her. Taking them, she sat up in bed, discreetly pulling the sheet over her chest. He smiled before he stood and went to the window where a watery sun was peeking through the clouds.

Line after line of the manuscript was gobbled up by her avaricious eyes. With each one, she felt another door of her soul opening up. It wasn't Gregory and Lisa living on the pages. It was she and Carter, loving without restraint, expressing their love not only with their bodies, but with their sensitivity for the other's needs. When she had read the last line, she lowered the page and with tear-filled eyes met his across the room.

"It's us, isn't it?"

He left the window and came to sit down beside her. His shaking fingers brushed back tousled strands of hair from her cheek. "Yes."

"When did you finish it?"

"Just now. I worked on it after you had gone to sleep . . . the second time. I couldn't get the love sequence right until . . . until you." His smile was half-hearted. She could see tears glossing his own eyes.

"This isn't the ending." It wasn't a question.

"I can't write the ending, Sloan."

"But you know what it will be."

"We both know what it will be."

"Yes," she said, laying her cheek in his palm and shutting her eyes. "We've always known he'll have to leave her."

"But in the meantime, they'll love each other without any regrets, as though there were no future, as though each day were an eternity unto itself."

She smiled at him tremulously. "Yes," she said softly, then repeated it with more emphasis. "Yes, yes." Clasping his face between her hands she kissed him, telling him of her love with softly parted lips and a prowling tongue. "Why don't you sleep for a while and I'll bring you your breakfast later."

"On one condition. You stay with me until I'm asleep."

For an answer, she raised the covers and let him slide in beside her. Fitting her body into the curve of his, he fell asleep in a matter of minutes. He didn't awaken when she got up, but there was a peaceful smile on his rugged face.

The days passed far too quickly and they tried not to mark the limited hours allowed them. They lived vagariously according to their appetites, their moods, their libidos. Carter had the lecherous idea of enshrining every bedroom in the house in a most appropriate way. Sloan refused, reminding him of all the linens she would have to wash and iron. His creative mind came into play and she relented to his wishes, amazed by how inventive he could be.

As she sat facing him, her legs straddling his, on the rug on one of the bedroom floors, she watched the effect of her loveplay on his nipples. "If I read this in one of your books, I'm going to know I inspired the scene."

He tilted her head up to meet his heated gaze. "Didn't you know that from now on, you *are* my inspiration." He moved deeper into her in a way that left his meaning crystal clear.

The rain, which had been everyone else's nemesis and their blessing, abated. The sun, after a few days of maidenly coyness, bared herself to the pale San Franciscans.

Sloan rebooked three rooms that had been previously cancelled. The guests were due to arrive the following week. She made more reservations for coming months and thought that with just a little luck, she might recoup the losses the unnaturally disagreeable weather had cost her.

"Hey, hey, what do you know? A bookstore!" Carter chortled. They had gone out to replenish her pantry and to soak up some sunshine. After storing her packages in the car, they had decided to walk and window shop for the sake of needed exercise. Carter now caught her arm and dragged her toward the door of the old house near Washington Square that had been quaintly converted into a two-level bookstore.

The bell over the door tinkled pleasantly as they went in. The musty proprietor peered at them over the top of his half-glasses and nodded a greeting with his bald head, then went back to his book.

"He didn't recognize you," Sloan whispered as Carter led her toward the racks of fiction.

"They usually don't. I don't mind as long as they sell my books."

"It's that dreadful picture on the dust jacket."

"How would you have me photographed?"

She hauled his head down and whispered her lewd suggestion in his ear. The whimsical eyebrow scowled in feigned disbelief. "You're a wanton broad. Did you know that?"

"Only recently."

"Well, you're in luck." He grabbed an appreciable handful of jean-covered fanny and squeezed it. "I have a lech for wanton broads."

She squirmed away and glanced nervously over her shoulder at the bookseller, who thankfully was still immersed in the pages of his book. "Yes, I know, Mr. Madison. I've read your books," she hissed.

"Wait until you read the next one. It's going to have a bathtub scene you won't believe."

"Carter!" she exclaimed, putting her hands on her hips and drawing her sweater tight across braless breasts. He had selected her wardrobe that morning. "You promised not to write about that!" Her cheeks blushed most becomingly.

"I did?"

"Yes!"

"I only promised that to get you to participate," he said with an unrepentant shrug. "You're great at orgies. And don't get all huffy because you know you loved it just as much as I did. Let's see now," he said, ignoring her indignant look and perusing the shelves. "J, K, L, L-a, L-o, L-u, Ludlum. God, I wish he'd change his name. His books are always shelved just above mine. Ah, here we are, Carter Madison."

"How many Carter Madison novels are there?" she asked, already having forgiven him.

"Twelve. And this marvelous bookstore with excellent taste has all of them in stock. *Sleeping Mistress* will be thirteen. I hope that's not unlucky."

"All twelve are best-sellers?"

"Not the first two. The others, yes."

"How many movies?"

"Two. And one television series. The credit reads, 'Based on a novel by Carter Madison.'"

She pondered his wrinkled forehead. "The fame and fortune make you uneasy, don't they?" Her intuition was founded on love.

His sherry-colored eyes sought hers and held them. "A bit, yes."

"Why, Carter?"

He sighed and leaned against the shelf, taking her hand and studying it as he answered slowly. "I don't know. Sometimes I feel like a well-paid whore."

"That's ridiculous!"

"Is it? My writing is technically correct, my style is

my own, not a bastardization of someone else's, I do what I do well, I bring pleasure. But sometimes I feel like what I've done is meaningless. A parody of the real thing. I had such aspirations and goals when I began and none of them related to money."

"Money's the barometer by which the world measures success. Just because you're paid a lot of it, doesn't conversely reduce the value of your writing."

"I suppose so," he said with a rueful smile. "Still I'd like to do a truly meaningful novel whether it was a commercial success or not."

"Why don't you then?"

His eyes whipped up from her hand to her face. It was as though no one had ever challenged him to it before. "Do you think I could?"

"I know you could. You've got the talent. Your writing is superb. Just direct it in the channel you want it to go. Please yourself with the book you want to write. I assume you already have a plot in mind?"

"Yes." He nodded excitedly.

"Okay. Write the book you want to do and then go back to writing what the public wants. At least you'll have satisfied yourself. And I can't really imagine the public scorning *any* Carter Madison book, especially one as marvelous as that one is bound to be."

He studied her quietly for a long moment, his finger stroking her cheek. She could feel the love emanating from him and seeping into her. "You're something," he mouthed.

"*You're* something," she responded in kind.

"I love you so much."

"I love you."

He scooted closer. "I can see you, imagine you rather, under your sweater. Do you think our studious proprietor would notice if we slipped into his storeroom and I—"

"Well, well, well, there's a celebrity in our midst."

The voice was snide and deprecating, having been filtered through a pinched, sanctimonious nose.

The man who had intruded on their privacy was slight, several inches shorter than Sloan. His hair was clipped close to his scalp and only brought attention to the narrowness of his head. A sharply pointed goatee gave him a sinister aspect. His eyes were as shifty and busy as a ferret's. His clothes were natty. A turtleneck sweater was anchored to his chest by ropes of gold chains.

"You're far too humble, Sydney," Carter drawled, edging closer to Sloan in what she sensed was a protective gesture. "You're as much a celebrity as I."

"A celebrity perhaps. Humble? Not at all, Mr Madison. I consider my opinions to be sterling, as do my readers."

Sloan could feel Carter's muscles bunching with angry tension. "Ms. Sloan Fairchild, Mr. Sydney Gladstone." He made the introduction out of necessity and with as little flair as possible.

"Hello, Mr. Gladstone," she murmured, not daring to offer her hand, afraid Carter would snatch it back like a mother keeping her child away from a snake.

"Ms. Fairchild," Gladstone oozed, executing a jerky little bow.

She knew who the man was. His column was run twice a week in the book section of the *Chronicle* and she knew it was syndicated to other major newspapers. She didn't read him. She found his columns to be petty and vindictive, almost always taking pot shots at the writers rather than addressing what they'd written. It was all she could do to keep from shivering as his cunning eyes toured her with lurid interest.

"We didn't hear you come in," Carter said.

He laughed, and it was a nasty, decayed sound. "Implying that you would have taken your leave sooner if you had. Really, Mr. Madison, are you still piqued by my critique in *Publisher's Weekly* of your last book?"

"I wasn't piqued. Nor am I now. It, like all your articles, was tripe."

The skinny nostrils almost closed in vexation. "Nevertheless I see you took my advice." He eyed Sloan again in a way that made her feel like she needed a bath.

"What advice was that, Sydney?" Carter crossed his arms over his chest and put all his weight on one foot in an attitude of extreme boredom. Sloan wasn't fooled. If Gladstone weren't a complete fool, he wouldn't be either.

"If you'll recall I said that the love sequences in your novels were predictable and lackluster."

"If that means my characters aren't into group sex, bedroom gymnastics, perversions, whips and chains, etc., etc., you're right and I'm flattered."

The critic sniffed fastidiously. "That's not entirely

what I meant. I think your sexual passages lack a certain excitement, depth. What I said in the critique was that your fictional love affairs had become staid, emotionless, and trite. I suggested that your readers might benefit from your getting a new love interest of your own." He slanted a crude glance at Sloan. "I see by the way you could barely keep your hands from under Ms. Fairchild's sweater that you've taken my advice."

Carter's arms dropped to his sides as he balled his hands into fists. "You son of a bitch."

"Save your gutter language for your heroes, Mr. Madison. It suits them perfectly. And I despise violence when it doesn't reside on the pages of a book so spare me your growls and feral looks. I personally am delighted that you've found a new source of inspiration. I was rather dreading *Sleeping Mistress*." His eyes cemented on Sloan's breasts. "Now I'm rather looking forward to each page," he said with a noticeable slur. "Though I doubt you let a mistress like Ms. Fairchild sleep very often."

Carter was at his throat in one lunge. The man was slammed into the bookshelf with his Adam's apple the victim of Carter's steely fingers. "You listen and you listen good, Sydney. I'd dearly love to strangle you with one of your pretty necklaces, but you're not worth the effort. Your columns are crocks of crap and anyone who reads them knows that. How the hell you think you know anything about loving a woman, I don't know. The only lust you've ever felt is when you're raking some undeserving author over the coals. And if that's the only way you can get your jollies, I pity you.

"But for what you said about Ms. Fairchild, I could easily kill you. And if you print one word about her, even insinuate anything about her, I'll come after you. I'll make it my business to see if there's anything to you to castrate. And if there is—"

"What's the trouble back there?"

The proprietor had finally been roused from his book.

"No trouble," Carter called back. Only then did he release the sagging, choking critic from his deathgrip. He wasn't done yet. His eyes and his voice slashed across Gladstone's face. "You remember what I said," was his deadly warning before he gently took Sloan's arm and led her from the store.

How her knees supported her until they reached the car, she never knew. Carter ushered her into the passenger side with tender courtesy. "God I'm sorry, Sloan," he said when he got in.

"It wasn't your fault."

"No, but it was my grudge match. I called him a pompous, no-talent ass on the *Tonight Show* once and he can't quite find it in himself to forgive me."

His attempt at humor failed miserably. She continued to stare out the windshield in a daze. The white stillness of her face caused alarm to worm through his entrails, but there was nothing he could do about it parked in a car on a public street. He crammed the car into first gear, lurched into traffic and made record time getting them to Fairchild House. Wordlessly he helped her carry in her packages and deposited them on the kitchen table.

He reached for her. "Sloan—"

"No!"

He was stunned as she dodged his embrace. He could feel his temperature dropping, his body turning cold, the fire in his soul being extinguished even as he tried desperately to keep one life-giving flame flickering.

"You can't let some bitchy, small-minded jerk like that bother you, Sloan. You're more intelligent than that. I know you are. Dammit, tell me you are!" By the time he finished, he was shouting at her in frustrated anger.

"No, no," she yelled back. "It wasn't him, it's . . ."

"What?" he demanded.

"It's *me*. What he said woke me up to the fact that I'll never be anything to you but a mistress. Oh, God. I hate that word."

"So do I. Don't ever say it again in relation to yourself."

"Why not?" she flared. "That's what I've been to you, isn't it? Not your wife. Certainly more than a friend. What would you call me?"

"Beloved," he said in a voice striving for calmness. "The woman I love."

"But not the woman you'll marry. Not the woman you'll give your name to. Not the woman who'll share your life, have your children."

"You knew that, Sloan. We both did. And we both know that there wasn't one damn thing we could do about it. You said you'd love me while you could."

"I know," she sobbed, wringing her hands. "I

thought it would be enough. It's not. I've betrayed my best friend with you. Betrayed myself. I couldn't abide having that hideous man looking at me that way, saying those things. He and everyone else will see our love as something sleazy. What's between us may be pure, but the rest of the world won't see it that way."

"Screw the rest of the world!" he shouted. "Who the hell is going to know? To care? I assure you Gladstone hasn't got the balls to print a word about you, not after what I said to him. He's all hot air and basically a coward. And even if the rest of the world did know, what would you care if what we feel for each other is honest?"

"It's *not* honest, Carter. Our love is based on deceit." She paused to draw in several deep breaths, garnering her strength and courage to do what she had to do. "You've got to leave, Carter. You can't stay here any longer."

"I can't leave you, Sloan. Not ever."

She looked at him with mingled incredulity and fury. "Surely, *surely*, you didn't intend to continue seeing me after you married Alicia," she said on a dwindling gust of air.

His failure to meet her eyes and the defensive way he shoved his hands in his pockets was as good as a confession. "No. I don't know. I can't give you up, Sloan."

"Why?" she sneered. "Because I provide you with such a great time?"

He spun around and nailed her to the floor with outraged eyes. "That's a helluva thing to say."

"Oh, I don't know," she said loftily. "Mr. Gladstone

might not have been far off the mark. I'm certainly convenient. No attachments. Now that you're going to be a married family man, you can't live the flamboyant life of a wealthy bachelor. Your romantic escapades will have to be on the hush-hush. Secretive, furtive, clandestine.

"And you know, because I've ill-advisedly poured out my soul to you on more than one occasion, that I've been a doormat for everyone all my life. My parents could look right through me. Jason used me for as long as it pleased him. Now you want to run up here, no doubt with the full, understanding endorsement of your loving wife, and use me whenever you need inspiration." The last word was spat at him.

His eyes dropped to the middle of her body with a crude implication. "Let you sharpen my quill, so to speak."

The moment he raised his eyes to her shattered features, he was steeped in self-hate. His expletive echoed off the ceiling as he tossed his head upward and then dropped his chin to his chest, trying to find some manner in which to eradicate the harmful words they'd flung at each other.

"I'm sorry, Sloan," he said at long last. Even to his own ears the words sounded hollow and dead.

"No, don't be," she said, laughing bitterly. "You are most succinct. It took you only a few words to express exactly what I had been trying to say. We have, however, come to a perfect understanding. All that could be said has been. I think you should leave. Now."

"Dammit, Sloan, you can't mean that."

"Oh, but I do,"she said with indisputable resolution.

His eyes beamed into hers incisively. "You're actually going to crawl behind that goddamn shell again, aren't you? Put yourself behind that protective shield of yours that's as tough as armor and just as impenetrable."

"Analysis isn't your forte, Mr. Madison. Stick to nouns and verbs and crude language and vulgar innuendos. You're very good at them."

"Begging isn't my forte either." He went to the kitchen door and pushed it open. "All right, Sloan, go back to your safe, lonely world and wallow in your selflessness. And when you try to sleep alone at night, count up all the rewards you have from it."

She watched him almost tear the door off its hinges as he pushed through it. She watched, too, as it swung back and forth until it came to a standstill, just as surely as her heart had stopped.

Nine

He was gone.

She didn't know how long she sat at the kitchen table staring vacantly into space. Twilight crept around the window sills and faded into darkness and still she sat unmoving. At one precise moment, she knew with stark clarity that he had left, that she was alone in the house. He had made no sound as he left. He had exited her life with no more fanfare than he had entered it.

Sloan forced herself to her feet and drifted through the dark hallways and up the stairs as one following a hypnotic command. The door to his room was ajar.

The emptiness was ominous. The table in the middle of the room looked like a carcass picked clean. Gone were the papers and the typewriter, his dictionary and thesaurus, his red ink pens. The floor was mournfully free of balled pieces of manuscript that had known his wrath and impatience with himself. The bathroom was clear of his personal effects; the closet stood empty beyond its gaping door. The bed was unmade. Its covers were clinging to it like the petals of a flower that had known full bloom and were now wilting and dying.

Sloan toured the room like a flagellant at a shrine, her eyes filling and flooding. Spying the sheets of unused manuscript in the wastepaper basket, she knelt, picked up each one, smoothed it out and made of them a neat stack. Pressing it to her breasts, she went to the door. She couldn't bring herself to clean the room just yet. Later, when she was stronger, she would prepare it for another's use. But not now. Not while her heart was bleeding.

Taking only the pages of words he had so carefully composed and then so easily discarded, she left the room, closing the door quietly behind her.

"Fairchild House," she said into the telephone two days later.

"Sloan."

The voice was so familiar yet so unlike itself. "Alicia?" *My God, no!* was Sloan's first thought. Something had happened to Carter. Why else would Alicia sound so forlorn? "Alicia," she repeated, gripping the receiver with a suddenly slippery hand, "what's wrong?"

"Nothing," she said dully. "At least not an emergency. I didn't mean to frighten you."

Sloan's heart returned to her chest, but the foreboding stayed like a bad taste in her mouth. "Y-you don't sound like yourself."

"For a very good reason."

Sloan mashed her fingers to colorless lips. She couldn't know! She couldn't have found out! Carter? No, he'd never . . . Sydney Gladstone! Had he written? . . . No, she'd been reading his columns. How could Alicia have found out?

"Can we talk about it?" Sloan said tearfully.

"Oh, Sloan, please, yes. I've got to talk to somebody." Alicia collapsed into tears.

Sloan was dismayed by this turn of events. Alicia wasn't referring to her affair with Carter, but to something else entirely. She was relieved, yet instantly concerned. "What is it?" she asked anxiously. "Alicia, please don't cry like that. Tell me."

"I can't. I want to, but . . . I've got to talk to somebody," she repeated.

Sloan bit her lower lip before saying. "Carter. Why don't you talk to him?"

"Carter's not here."

"Not *there*?"

"Didn't he tell you where he was going when he left Fairchild House? He didn't come to Los Angeles. He telephoned me from the airport saying he was going to New York to deliver his manuscript in person. He said he couldn't wait to unload it and that he wanted to get all the business taken care of before the wedding. It's next week, you know."

Sloan's heart felt like a lead weight in her chest, dragging her down into an abyss from which there was no escape. No doubt he hated his book now because it was a reminder of her. He couldn't wait to get rid of it, wanted to be free of it like a scab to a sore that had been a long time in crusting over. "N-no," she croaked. Clearing her throat, she said more crisply, "No, he just left one evening. He didn't say where he was going and I assumed he was going home."

"I assumed he would too, the minute he finished his book, but it's just as well under the circumstances that he didn't."

"What circumstances?" Sloan asked, getting back to the original reason for Alicia's call.

"Sloan, can you come to Los Angeles?"

Sloan coughed a short laugh. "Of course not. What are you talking about?"

"Please, Sloan. If you've ever loved me as a friend, come down here. Just for a day. I desperately need to talk to you."

"I can't, Alicia. You can talk to me over the telephone." Sloan wished Alicia hadn't brought up that about loving her as a friend. Judas had been an exemplary friend compared to her.

"You've got to." Sloan heard the telltale huskiness in Alicia's voice again. She was crying. "I'd come up there, only I've left the boys too much recently. I'll pay for your ticket. I'll do anything, only please come, Sloan. You don't have anyone at Fairchild House now, do you? Please."

Sloan studied the brass paperweight on her desk. The desperation in Alicia's voice was genuine. Something was terribly wrong and she was reaching out to her best friend for help. If only she knew how wretched her best friend was, she would reconsider, but as it was, she thought that she needed Sloan. Sloan had already let her down once in a way that, hopefully, she'd never know. Could she refuse to help her now? Didn't she owe Alicia more than she'd ever be able to repay?

"I have guests coming next Wednesday. I'll have to come before then."

"Tomorrow," Alicia said rapidly. "Tomorrow, please."

Sloan rubbed her aching forehead with agitated fingers. Could she *ever* face Alicia? "I suppose I could. I'll catch an early plane and take a cab to your house."

"I'll be at Carter's beach house. He asked me to go over and check on things and the kids want to play on the beach."

God, would this torment, this nightmare ever end? Carter's house! "What's the address?" she asked glumly. Refusing Alicia's offer to purchase her ticket, she promised to see her the following day.

Like a sleepwalker, she lived through the rest of the day. That's how she'd moved since Carter's departure. She had lived out of habit; sleeping, waking, eating, working in the house like a programmed robot. What joy Fairchild

House had previously brought her had now been altered by Carter's brief residence. Forever that large room in the corner of the second floor would be Carter's room. No amount of cleansers or vacuuming or air fresheners would rid it of him. Just as her heart would never be exorcised of his spirit.

At least she wasn't having to fret over lost revenue. Each day she was booking room reservations. If they kept coming in at the rate they had been, she'd have enough money to tide her over, and enough left to place ads in travel magazines. The future of Fairchild House depended on publicizing it. She was confident of the product she had to offer once people heard about it.

Things would work out. She'd live through this crisis just as she had survived other disappointments. Eventually it wouldn't hurt so much. His image would fade from her mind. Maybe a few successive nights would go by when she wouldn't read those pages locked away in a japanned box on her dresser. There would eventually come a time when she'd no longer remember how it felt to be held in his strong arms, the splendor of his loving.

The recovery would be slow, but she'd live.

She suffered a major setback when she stepped out of the airport taxi and saw his house outlined against a backdrop of sea and sky. It so reflected the nature of the man that her eyes blurred with tears as she paid her fare to the driver.

Hearing the squeals and laughter of children, she walked around the redwood deck that surrounded the

house. Alicia was leaning over the back rail calling down to
the two boys running along the beach. "Adam, stop throwing sand or I'll make you come in."

"You wouldn't be that cruel, would you?"

"Sloan!" Alicia cried and rushed to embrace her
friend. She clung to her, hugging her tight, making Sloan
choke on her guilt. "God, it's good to see you. I'm so glad
you came. Thank you."

"Don't thank me. I haven't done anything."

"You're here. That's a lot. Let's go inside."

"The boys—"

"They're forbidden to go near the water. It's too cold.
I'll keep an eye on them."

"They're growing so fast," Sloan observed wistfully
as she watched the two little bodies running gleefully in
the sand.

"Yes, they are."

Alicia slid open a floor-to-ceiling glass door and led
Sloan from the deck into Carter's house. The living room
was tall and two storied. Suede sofas and chairs in beiges
and browns were agreeably arranged around a brass fireplace. A fur rug of unrecognizable origin lay on the parquet
floor in front of the hearth. Bright prints and colorful post-
ers telling of Carter's travels around the world were hanging in brass frames on the white stucco walls. A spiral
staircase led to a loft containing only a desk and chair. Its
walls were lined with bookcases. The whole room was
washed with sunlight. Sloan loved it. She was certain
Carter had designed it.

"Lemonade?"

Alicia didn't wait for Sloan's answer as she went into the kitchen, separated from the living room only by an open bar. As she mixed pink frozen concentrate with club soda in a tall glass pitcher, Sloan let herself soak up the ambiance of the room. Carter's taste was impeccable. The reading matter in the cluttered bookshelves varied from philosophy and religion to erotica. His record collection was enviable. Seeing the things he surrounded himself with, Sloan felt as if she were touching his soul. She wanted to explore the rest of the house, but unless Alicia suggested it, she couldn't bring herself to ask.

"How was the flight?" Alicia asked as she handed Sloan a tall, iced glass.

"Noisy. There were two babies on board and neither was enjoying the trip."

Alicia made a valiant attempt to laugh. "Would you be too cold on the deck?"

"No. I'd like an unrestricted view of the ocean."

"You should have dressed more casually, but then you rarely do."

Sloan could have told her that last week she'd been tearing around San Francisco in jeans and sweaters under which she'd worn no underwear. But she doubted Alicia would ever believe it of her. Carter barely had, though that had been part of his prescribed therapy to "bring her out." "No pun intended," he'd said with a sly wink.

Today she was wearing a perfectly, if unexcitingly, tailored suit with a navy skirt and matching herringbone jacket. Her blouse was prim. Next to Alicia, in jeans and a turtleneck sweater, Sloan felt stodgy. She wondered again how Carter could prefer her to her friend. Or had he only pretended to so she'd go to bed with him?

The thought almost gagged her. No. No. No. He might have left furious, proud, and insulting, but she couldn't—wouldn't—believe that his professions of love had been lies. She *wouldn't*.

Alicia stretched her shapely body onto a chaise. Sloan took a chair facing the ocean. The boys' laughter reached them. "I want you to see the boys later, but I want to talk first. Do you mind?" Alicia asked.

"Of course not. What's the matter?"

"God, you don't know how good it is to hear your sound, practical, steadfast voice." Alicia sighed and her full breasts quivered beneath her sweater. Sloan tried not to imagine Carter touching, kissing . . . "I'm so ashamed."

Alicia's wail brought Sloan out of her disturbing musings. "Alicia, please don't," she urged as wracking sobs shook Alicia's shoulders. "What's upset you? And what do you mean you're ashamed? I can't imagine you doing anything that shameful."

"Neither could I," she said, sniffing back her tears. "But I did. And it's that I don't regret doing it that's so shameful."

Sloan sat patiently, giving Alicia time to sort her thoughts. "I went to Tahoe that weekend after I came to San Francisco. I have a friend who has been divorced for several months and she's been after me to go out of town with her for a weekend. I swear to God, Sloan, I don't know why I went in the first place, except . . . Let's skip the reason for now. I went and I—I met someone. He was a good-looking man, nice, amusing, and we had a great time skiing together all day. And that night I—I stayed in his room and he made love to me all night and it was absolutely terrific."

She seemed vastly relieved that it was out. She shuddered on a long expulsion of breath. They remained silent for a long time. At last Alicia whipped her head around and faced Sloan with a degree of defiance. "Did I shock you speechless?"

Sloan shook her head before she could find enough voice to say, "No, no."

Alicia lay her head against the cushion of the chaise. "Of course I did. I shocked myself. I know you must think I'm a tramp, sleeping with a man I barely knew and liking it so much. How could you begin to understand, Sloan? A level-headed woman like you would never let herself go like that, throw caution to the wind, let the devil take tomorrow, do something she knew wasn't right."

Sloan's heart was thudding painfully and she felt like she might pass out if the thunder in her head grew any louder. She knew exactly what it was to sacrifice everything for passion's sake!

"I don't know what happened to me. Mountain air? The only excuse I have is that I met Jim Russell when we were still so young. We married right out of college and had the boys within a few years. Then Jim was gone and I've felt so . . . old. Old and used up. Like life had passed me by before I'd even had time to enjoy it. Not that I regret my early marriage to Jim. I don't. But there's never been a time in my life when I didn't belong to someone else, when I was living solely for me." She looked down at the two children scuffling in the sand. "There will never be a time, will there?"

"Not if you marry Carter next week, no."

Alicia's bright eyes clouded with tears again. "That's why I feel so damn guilty about that weekend, Sloan. I love Carter, but . . ." Her voice trailed off and she plucked at a loose thread on her sweater. "Maybe I shouldn't confide this to you, but I've got to get it all off my chest. Carter and I have never, you know, been together. We've never gone beyond mild affection. Well, there was that one time at your house, remember when you came in my room and caught us kissing?" Mutely Sloan nodded. "You could have knocked me over with a feather! He's never been that way with me. And I . . . well, as passionate as it was, it did nothing for me. It's ridiculous, I know, but I felt like I was being unfaithful to Jim! Every time I look at Carter, I see Jim, and it's like we're cheating on him. I didn't feel that way with the man in Tahoe."

"Carter was Jim's best friend. It's natural that you'd feel that way," Sloan said for lack of anything better. A tiny beam of light was shining in the stygian darkness that had engulfed her since Carter left. She dared not hope that it could become a full-fledged ray of hope, still . . .

"In all truthfulness Carter's never . . . turned me on. He's just too good a friend. I guess after we're married I'll do what brides are expected to do. Even though he does nothing for me sexually, I have no doubt about Carter's virility. I doubt he'd tolerate a celibate marriage. We both want another child." Her voice trailed off into nothingness, its faint whisper carried by an uncaring ocean breeze.

Despite her inner turmoil, Alicia looked beautifully shy when she said, "Sloan, every time Mac—that was his name—touched me, I tingled all over. Do you know what I mean? Do you think I'm a terrible person?"

Sloan's soft smile was a trifle sad. "Yes, I know what you mean and no, I don't think you're at all terrible." With an affected nonchalance she asked, "This Mac, where does he live? Would you ever want to see him again?"

"He lives in Portland and he *said* he wanted to come see me. Of course I refused. I told him everything." She sighed deeply. "He's not really the point. The point is, I've limited my options." She sat up suddenly. "It's not that I want to be a bed-hopper. You know that, don't you?"

"Yes," Sloan said earnestly.

"I disdain that kind of life. I don't like my friend for living that way. She's probably had a score of men since the weekend in Tahoe and felt not one twinge of guilt. That's not me, Sloan. I could never cheapen myself that way, nor do that to the boys. It's just that I suddenly woke up to the fact that Jim might not be the only man I could love wholeheartedly and passionately.

"I thought that part of me was dead. It isn't. It's just been lying dormant and when Mac touched me, I was reminded that I am a woman, not just a widow and a mother and a close friend. I knew after my trip to San Francisco, after Carter kissed me that way, that he wasn't ever going to make me go weak-kneed. That's why I went to Tahoe in the first place."

"What will you do?" Sloan asked slowly. The light had become brighter and it was all she could do to sit calmly in her chair. She felt like shouting, like joining the children cavorting on the beach. Like an animal shedding its winter skin, she felt new and alive.

"I don't know," Alicia anguished. "Tell me what to do, Sloan." Pleading was in Alicia's crystal eyes and in her voice. "Tell me what a wonderful man Carter is. Tell me that with him there would be no risks. My sons and I will have security, safety. Tell me that their well-being has to come before my own selfish desires. Remind me how much Carter loves them and how disappointed and disillusioned he'd be if he found out that Jim's widow had slept with a stranger and loved every minute of it. Convince me that after we're married, when we're sharing a bed, that passion will bloom. Tell me all that, Sloan. Remind me what the decent, responsible thing to do is.

"Or," Alicia continued after a deep breath, "tell me to say to hell with what's right and to do what I want to do. If the truth were known, Carter might be relieved. He might only be marrying me because he feels an obligation to Jim to take care of us. Tell me to go to Carter and lay my cards on the table, to tell him I love him, but not in the way I should." Reaching across the space that separated them, she clutched Sloan's hands. "Sloan, for God's sake advise me."

"I can't," Sloan cried on a sudden burst of emotion. "Don't ask that of me, Alicia. I can't tell you what to do." If only she could. If only she could tell Alicia that it would be best for all concerned if she broke her engagement to Carter. One part of her was screaming, "Tell her, tell her. Make her decision easy for her. She'll be glad that you and Carter have fallen in love. Tell her."

It would take only one sentence. "I love Carter and I believe he loves me." She could tell Alicia honestly that they hadn't intended for it to happen, but it had. Now they could all have what they wanted. Sloan would have Carter. He'd have her. Alicia would be free to pursue her own happiness.

Another part of her was closing its ears to her heart's arguments. She couldn't interfere with Alicia's decision. Maybe Alicia loved Carter more than she realized. That weekend in Tahoe was the first time she'd been on a fling and she was still basking in the novelty of it. Her mind was remembering it more romantically than it had been. Later, she would realize that it was the steady, reliable kind of love that she and Carter shared that she needed.

No. Sloan could say nothing. If Alicia ever suffered any regrets because of this life-affecting decision, Sloan could never live with herself. She could never be happy with Carter if she had influenced Alicia to give him up. It had to be Alicia's decision, hers alone.

But please, God, let it be the one I pray for.

"Sloan, what am I going to do?" Lost in their thoughts, they stared at the two young boys playing on the beach. "They need a father," Alicia said quietly. "A father like Carter, but . . ." Again they fell silent, each running their separate gauntlet, fighting their way through their own hell.

Then David stopped his play and jerked his brother around, pointing toward the house. David yelled something and with the shorter, slower Adam in tow, began running toward the house, screaming at the top of his lungs.

Sloan and Alicia looked at each other in puzzlement. Then they heard David's lilting voice carrying across the wind. "Carter, Carter. Carter's back."

Turning simultaneously, they saw Carter just as he rounded the corner of the deck. When he saw Alicia's companion, he stopped with an abruptness as sure as if he'd walked into an invisible wall. The three were momentarily frozen in suspension while four sneakered feet tramped up the steps from the beach to the deck. Carter barely recovered from his shock at seeing Sloan in time to brace for the two small bodies launching themselves into his legs.

"You're back, you're back," David shouted, dancing a jig and clutching at Carter's trouser leg.

"Carter, will you buy us an ice cream cone? Mom said you could if we were good," Adam chimed in. "We've been good."

"Guess what. Our fish died. He's in Heaven with Daddy. But Mom said we could have another one."

"His stomach pooched out and he was floating on the top of the water. I saw him first and David didn't think he was dead, but I said he was."

Soulfully, Alicia looked into Sloan's eyes. Had she not been so wrapped up in her own misery, she would have seen her desolation mirrored in their smoky depths. A resigned smile tried to get a foothold on her lips, but didn't quite make it. "I really have no choice, do I?" she whispered for Sloan's ears alone.

Sloan shook her head, knowing that she had no choice but to remain forever silent, even if it killed her. "No."

"I knew that when it came right down to it, I wouldn't do anything else. I'll do what you would do. You'd do the right thing, Sloan. I know you would."

The *right* thing? Was damning three people to unhappiness the right thing to do? Yes. In this circumstance it was. Carter and Alicia would grow to love each other through the children who loved them both. Familiarity would fragment Jim's memory. They were both physically beautiful. Passions would flare when they realized that.

Yes. It wasn't ideal, but it was right.

Alicia gripped Sloan's hand one last time. Standing, she quickly turned and went into Carter's embrace. "Welcome home, stranger," she said cheerfully.

He enfolded her in an embrace made haphazard by the two boys who still clung to his pants legs. Over Alicia's shoulder he looked at Sloan.

His eyes flashed a thousand messages and she received each one. He was sorry for the things he'd said. He had missed her. He was miserable. He was tired, weary of the world, of life without her. He was also asking what she was doing here at his house. He looked reproachfully at her clothes and the tight restrictions of her hairdo.

"I was lonesome for you, so I called Sloan to come down and spend the day with me," Alicia said, pulling him toward the group of patio chairs. Sloan's shoes could have been riveted to the spot, for she hadn't been able to move since seeing Carter. In spite of the fatigue pinching the corners of his eyes and mouth and the haggard blankness in his russet eyes, he looked marvelous. He had on a casual pair of slacks and a sport shirt with the sleeves of a sweater knotted around his neck.

"Hello, Sloan."

"Hello, Carter. How was New York?"

"Cold and rainy."

"You don't seem to be able to escape the rain," Alicia said, demonstrating amazing recuperative powers. "It rained almost the whole time you were in San Francisco, didn't it?"

"Yes," he said, his eyes melting into Sloan's.

"Boys, please stop pushing and come say hello to Sloan," Alicia instructed. Obediently they each mumbled a hello to Sloan.

She responded to their greeting with a smile that she hoped didn't look as brittle as it felt. "You've become fine young gentlemen since I saw you last."

"Did you know my daddy?" Adam asked. "He died."

Sloan's eyes swept past Alicia and Carter who were standing arm in arm. "Y-yes I knew him. You're as handsome as he was."

"That's what Mom says. Carter's going to be my daddy now."

"That'll be wonderful, won't it?" Sloan didn't know how the words were surviving the crushing vise in her throat.

"Yeah, it'll be super," David contributed.

"Super, super, super," Adam sang.

"Go play now," Alicia said. "What about your book?" she asked of Carter when the boys had scampered to the edge of the deck. "Did you finish it?"

"Yes. It's already on the editor's desk. He said from what he could tell, it will be my best one."

"That's such good news, darling." Alicia squeezed his arm against her chest as she looked up at him eagerly. "You worked so hard on it."

"A lot of me went into this one." He tried not to look at Sloan, said to hell with it, and let his eyes gorge on the sight of her face.

"Does it have a happy ending?" Alicia asked.

Carter dragged his eyes from Sloan and looked down at his fiancée. At the moment her face was as innocent and guileless as her sons', and he felt like a bastard for the resentment he'd been harboring toward her. It wasn't her fault he'd fallen in love with the wrong woman. Raising bleak eyes back to Sloan, he answered solemnly, "It ended the only way it could."

As though his words had cut off her air supply, Sloan spun around frantically and rushed toward the door of the house. "I need to call a cab."

"No, Sloan, you must stay until after dinner," Alicia wailed.

"I can't. I have to get back."

"Stand right there," she said. "Don't do anything until I chase down David and Adam."

Alicia had been diverted by her sons' uncannily rapid disappearance, but not Carter. He followed Sloan into the house. With an iron will, he had to lasso every muscle in his body to keep from going to her and taking her in his arms.

He cursed the dowdiness of her clothes, the return of the bun on the back of her neck, the guarded expression that masked the animation he knew her features capable of. That thin, tight-lipped mouth didn't even resemble the smiling, tempting one that had destroyed his senses with its loving generosity.

He longed to see again the passionate woman who he knew lurked behind a wall of defeatism. Unimprisoned once, she could be freed again by his touch. But they were forbidden to each other by the dictates of their consciences.

Still, he couldn't let her go without her knowing how much he wanted her, how much he needed her, how much he loved her. He had to speak it aloud one last time or forever regret it. "Sloan, I—"

"Don't," she said through grinding teeth. Her back was to him as she braced rigid arms on the back of a chair. "Don't say anything."

"I've got to, goddammit."

"No. Please. If you do, I won't be able to stand it."

"Sloan, don't call a cab," Alicia said, stepping into the room, oblivious of the drama taking place. "The boys want to drive you to the airport so they can see the planes."

"No," Sloan objected quickly. "Carter just came from the airport."

"I don't mind."

"You stay, Carter," Alicia said. "I'll take Sloan now and you can pick her up next week when she comes for the wedding."

Sloan felt like Alicia had kicked her swiftly and firmly in the stomach. "I won't be at the wedding."

Now it was Alicia's turn to look dumbfounded. "But, Sloan, you have to be!"

Nothing on earth could compel her to sit and listen to Carter pledging his love and life to another woman. Any woman. Even a woman Sloan loved, too. "I'm sorry, but I can't. I'll have guests at Fairchild House by then. I can't leave it. You'll have to consider the trip today my wedding congratulations."

Alicia looked upset and disconsolate. "But you missed my first wedding," she said petulantly. "I can't believe you'll miss this one, too."

"I hate to disappoint you, Alicia, but I can't . . . I can't be at your wedding."

Her tone brooked no arguments, though Alicia offered a few. Carter didn't say anything.

They left a few minutes later. Alicia was explaining to

the boys how airplanes fly as she backed the car out the shell driveway.

Sloan risked one last look at the house. Carter was standing on the deck, staring directly at her. The wind was tearing through his hair. His hands were shoved into his pants pockets and his shoulders were hunched defensively, against the wind or against some internal enemy, she couldn't decide. His face, cast as it was in deep shadow, was inscrutable.

Which was just as well. Had Sloan seen the emotion shimmering in his eyes, she might not have been able to leave him no matter what the consequences.

Ten

At least I still have this, Sloan thought as she served the custard
with caramel sauce to the guests surrounding the dining
room table. Fairchild House was filled to capacity. All the
bedrooms upstairs were occupied. Save one. But that one
didn't count.

She would survive. She had before. She would again.

Fairchild House would require all her energy, physical and mental. This is what she was committed to. This
was her life. Everything she had she'd pour into making
the bed and breakfast a success.

Friday evening. At two o'clock today Carter and Alicia had been married. He was permanently out of her life.
From now on, her heart would belong to her business.

"It must have been dreadful. Wasn't it, Ms. Fairchild?"

She almost sloshed coffee onto her treasured Irish linen tablecloth. The conversation had flowed around her, but she hadn't been listening. She was startled to have a question directed to her.

"I'm sorry. What were you asking?"

"All the rain you had out here. It must have been dreadful." The woman was from the East Coast and spoke with a nasal twang. She bullied her obsequious husband without letup.

Whenever the unseasonable weather that had made willing prisoners of her and Carter was mentioned, a misty look came into her eyes. "It was dreadful if one was required to go out of doors. More coffee, Mrs. Williams?"

Her voice was cordial and soft, unobtrusive, trained to give away none of her sadness. Only if one looked closely could he note the wistfulness in her eyes.

The guests filed into the parlor, four of them deciding on a game of cards. Sloan kept the coffee, liqueurs, and herbal tea flowing for as long as anyone wanted them. It was close to midnight before the last of the guests retired upstairs. Wearily Sloan went around checking locked doors and turning off lights.

She went into her room and crossed it in darkness, switching on a lamp on her bureau. Automatically she touched the lid of the locked lacquered box where it sat in a prominent place. A poignant smile played about the corners of her mouth and her eyes filled with eloquent tears.

It never occurred to her she wasn't alone.

Absently she reached up and drew the pins from her hair, one by one, slowly, until her hair fell in heavy waves onto her shoulders. She combed both hands through it, revolving her head on her neck to ease the tension of pretending happiness when actually grief as wide and deep as a chasm had severed her heart in two.

She unzipped her skirt and stepped out of it gracefully, folding it carefully over the back of a chair. The slip she was wearing clung to her hips, dipped and curved over the feminine delta, and detailed the shape of her thighs. Her hair fell forward and caressed wan, slightly sunken cheeks as she bent her head to better see the buttons on the deep cuffs of her blouse. Then the buttons tracking its pleated front were languidly released as she stared at some inspecific point in near space, lost in her thoughts. She was peeling the blouse off her shoulders when she happened to glance in the mirror and see him sitting in the easy chair across the room.

Her heart rocketed to her throat and stoppered a scream just before she could utter it. She spun around. The sudden action and the river of blood rushing to her head made her dizzy and blurred her vision. She grasped the edge of her bureau to keep from falling.

It *was* him, acting as though he sat in that chair every night and watched her perform this ritual. One ankle was propped on the opposite knee. He was holding a hardback book on his lap. His eyeglasses were perched precariously on the tip of his nose.

"Don't stop on my account," he said in a voice as seductive as his eyes, which were touring her body with slow deliberation.

"What are you doing here?"

"Watching a most entertaining and stimulating strip-tease."

"Damn you, Carter, answer me."

All her frustration, heartache, despair roiled to the surface and she lashed out at him angrily. The torment wasn't over yet. Just when she'd become resigned to it, some malicious god had inflicted this dream on her. Or was this real? Was he really here, wearing that horrible fatigue jacket and looking much as he had the first night he'd arrived on her doorstep. "How did you get in? The doors were locked."

"Chapter five of *The Bishop's Kiss*." He held up the book on his lap. "I was just rereading it now to see that I'd done it right. The point is moot, of course. I managed to break in the back door and relock it without anyone discovering me." His grin was boyishly proud. "I think I did it as well as Slater. He's the hero of this—"

"What are you doing here?" she fairly screamed, knotting her hands into fists at her sides.

Dropping the book and his eyeglasses on the floor, he lunged out of the chair and bounded toward her, plastering her against him with one arm and clamping the other hand over her mouth.

"You don't want to disturb your guests, do you, Ms. Fairchild?" he asked silkily, trailing his tongue down the side of her neck. "I didn't want to get rough, but this is what Slater did when he broke into the heroine's apartment. Not to mention our friend Gregory. We know to what ends he'll go to accomplish his goal."

She squirmed against him, trying to speak against his hand. "I can't understand you, Sloan. And you'd just as well save your breath and energy because you're going to need them." His mouth was at her ear now, moving in her hair, touching her lobe with the wet tip of his tongue. "You see I plan to make love to you all night or until we're both senseless, whichever comes first."

He captured her scream with the palm of his hand. "Did you say get out? Why? Oh, I know. You think I'm committing adultery. Wrong. I'm not married and I won't be until you can take a few hours off and we can run down to City Hall."

She sagged in surrender and became pliant against the rock hardness of his body. Over the heel of his hand, she blinked away furious tears and stared at him in wide-eyed incomprehension. "That's better. I hate to use force. But I wasn't sure I could stop you from screaming with this much more pleasant and much more subtle method."

Gradually he lowered his hand from her mouth and replaced it with his lips. He sealed them together with a sweet adhesion. She complied, at first because she was too bewildered to resist. Then the tongue that arrogantly caroused inside her mouth extinguished all thought except that she was once again in Carter's arms and he was loving her.

Her weak arms garnered enough strength to lift themselves to his shoulders. With greedy fingers, she plundered the hair that seemed perpetually too long on his collar. Her lips parted beneath his, flowering open for his tender violation. The magic lassitude that flowed through her veins like honey every time he touched her, afflicted her again. All her strength came from him, and suppliantly her body arched against the source of his energy in silent appeal.

"God, that feels good," he murmured as his lips ravished her throat. His hands cupped her bottom through the satin slip, lifted and pressed until he was snugly tucked into the shallow valley between her thighs.

"What happened?" she asked on a moan. "Why aren't you married? Don't hurt me again, Carter. Kill me if you must after you love me, but don't leave me again."

"Never. Never. I swear it. Can this go?" he asked of her blouse. She shrugged out of it as he pushed the sleeves down her arms. "I can see your nipples," he rasped in soft pleasure. "Don't you have on a bra?"

"I don't wear one anymore unless I have to."

"I love it, I love it." He fondled her through the cups of the slip. "But what made you decide that?"

"Because going without one reminded me of you. Kiss me there," she urged on a spiraling sigh as his fingertips found her nipple peaking with arousal.

He ducked his head and closed his mouth around her, fabric and all. He wet the cloth thoroughly until it molded to and outlined her shape. "Look at you," he whispered reverently, his finger tracing the pouting point of her nipple. "I couldn't marry Alicia. I can't marry anyone but you, Sloan."

Her hands were busy divesting him of his jacket and shirt. When they were gone, her hands coasted over the fevered flesh and its crinkly blanket of dark hair. Sensuously her palms raked over his chest, back and forth until she was delirious with the variety of sensations. Her fingertips fanned across his nipples and they reacted suddenly and firmly. "Tell me what happened." Her tongue flirtatiously played with what her fingers had brought to distention.

"Sweet . . . make them wet . . . oh, God, yes, Sloan. I can't . . . can't talk when . . ." He fumbled with the fastener of his trousers. "Later . . . I'll tell you later. . . . Just know that I belong solely to you and that no one is going to be hurt by our being together."

"Carter," she breathed, repeating his name and loving the sound of it.

He hooked his thumbs under the straps of her slip and pulled it down over her love-swollen breasts. Her stomach rose and fell with agitated breath as he took the slip past it, then farther, taking her pantyhose as he went. When she was naked, his fingers sifted through the soft triangle of hair and caressed the slender thighs. His eyes swept over her like a prairie fire that crawls burningly over the plains. Taking her hand, he drew it to his pulsing desire. "Forgive me. I can't wait."

Sloan guided him to her own yielding moistness. "Nor can I." She trembled when he lifted her against him and carried her to the bed. He followed her down, shedding the rest of his clothes and kicking them free.

In one swift, sure thrust, he grafted her body to his. Exercising a tremendous amount of control, he framed her face with his palms and kissed her mouth with the same breathtaking intimacy of the other fusion. He delved deeply into its sweet wet warmth with his tongue.

"Feel how much I love you, Sloan Fairchild. From the first moment I saw you, I knew I had been incomplete until then. Know my love. Accept it. You are most worthy of it. It is I who humbly offer it. Sloan, make me whole."

Her body lay curled between his thighs, her legs and feet entwined with his. Her cheek was pressed into the hollow of his abdomen beneath his ribcage. Her hair draped him like a cloak woven of various shades of brown and gold. He threaded his fingers through it idly. Her fingers lazily circled the thick nest that housed his navel.

They lay replete after a crisis of volcanic proportions. Not once, but twice, exultantly free and guiltless passion had hurled them into another sphere. Now they were luxuriating in the sweetest exhaustion they'd ever known.

"Are you positive you're not just telling me that to make me feel better, Carter?"

"I promise. It was Alicia who asked to see me before the ceremony. We were at her parents' house. The wedding guests were already arriving. David and Adam had been spit-and-polished and were being guarded by the maid so they wouldn't get dirty. Alicia knocked on the bedroom door where I was getting dressed."

"You weren't dressed when you talked to her?"

He gathered a fistful of her hair and lifted her head. "Yes, I was dressed when I talked to her."

"Just checking," she said lightly, kissing the hair-dusted flesh with loving lips. "I'll have to keep close tabs on a husband who has a knack for breaking and entering."

"Yeah, I especially like the—"

"Entering," she finished for him. "You're shameless," she chided, twirling her finger in the well of his navel. "Proceed with the story."

"Alicia sat down on the bed and immediately burst into tears. She confessed what she saw as a dire transgression, making me feel like the biggest hypocrite in the world."

"You can imagine what I felt like when she confessed to me, saying that a woman like me would never do anything like that. And here I'd been sleeping with her fiancé. How did things ever become so complex?"

"We fell in love. No one, not even us, counted on that." He slipped his hand under her hair to massage her nape. "Then she started telling me what a wonderful father I'd make to her sons and how much Jim thought of me and how her parents thought I would be a marvelous provider. Your earlobes feel like the petals of a velvet flower."

The simple statement was so out of context that Sloan laughed. Carter drew in a sharp breath. "We're going to have another postponement of this story if you laugh again."

"Why?"

"Because I can feel the vibration of your breasts on a place that doesn't need any further encouragement to make me blissfully aroused . . . again."

"I'm sorry," she said without the least bit of contrition. Indeed, she let her hand drift farther down his torso. "I'm listening."

His breathing was jagged, but he continued doggedly. "I took both her hands and looked her straight in the eye and asked her if she loved me."

"To which she said?"

"To which she said yes."

Sloan levered herself up so she could look at him. The eyes which had been gleaming with devilish delight clouded over with turbulence. Carter ran his index finger along her lower lip consolingly. "She said yes she loved me, but not in 'that way.' And when I asked her what way she meant, she said, 'Not in the way a wife is supposed to love her husband. Not enough to share your bed. Not enough to keep from wanting to return Mac's calls which I've been refusing.' Then to her great surprise, I hugged her and kissed her with more enthusiasm than I ever have, except for one time in this house that doesn't need to be recounted, and told her that I thought she was a perfectly wonderful woman for Jim and for some other fortunate man, but that I felt she might not be the woman for me."

Sloan had propped her chin on his sternum and was looking up into his face. "What did you tell the boys? Were they terribly disappointed?"

"Oh, yes, they wept bitterly."

"Oh, Carter no!" Sloan said, ignoring his previous warning and jarring him with her shifting body.

"Oh, yes. They couldn't stand the thought of not getting to live at the beach."

Sloan's head dropped again to his chest as she slumped with relief. He chuckled and trailed a finger down the groove of her spine. "When they were assured that they could use the beach house whenever I wasn't there working, and when they were assured that I was still going to take them skating and to ball games and to get ice cream, and when they'd been served a piece of wedding cake, they were mollified."

"They do need a father."

He tensed as though to get up. "Well, if that's the way you feel, I can always go back to Alicia on my hands and knees—"

She spread her arms wide, closing her fingers around his biceps and holding him down on the bed. "They need a father, but not you."

"You're gonna keep me?"

She assessed him through narrowed eyes. "I'm giving it careful consideration," she said after a long, indecisive pause.

He closed his arms around her back and flipped her over, making their positions reversed. "Carefully consider this," he growled before he clamped his mouth over hers, his tongue plunging and dipping, circling and sampling, probing and persuading.

She panted beneath him when at last he scooted down her body and lay his head on the pillow of her breasts. "I'll certainly take that into consideration, she said breathlessly. For long moments they were still. She reveled in the feel of his hair clinging to her fingers, he to the steady drumming of her heart in his ear.

"Carter, did . . ." She wet her lips. "Did you tell Alicia about me?"

"Uh-huh," he said with casual disinterest as he blew softly on a temptingly pink nipple.

Sloan knew a spasm of guilt and shame. "What did you tell her?"

"The truth," he said solemnly, raising himself up to peer steadily into her remorseful eyes. "That you were the hottest broad I'd ever laid."

"*What!?*" she cried, pushing him off her and sitting up. He collapsed onto his back, holding his stomach as he shook with laughter.

"You should have seen your face," he said, when his laughter finally subsided.

"Of all the horrible things to say," she huffed.

"Don't give me that, Ms. Fairchild." He yanked her down on top of him again. "Sell that prim and proper act to your customers, but not to me. I saw the real woman who was hiding behind that god-awful robe you were wearing the night I got here. Tomorrow morning I'm going to personally see to it that that thing is burned." He hauled her up to his mouth and kissed her soundly while his hands smoothed over her bottom.

"In answer to your question," he said, when she was once again lying along him in docile contentment, "I admitted to Alicia that you and I had become very close friends and that I was returning to Fairchild House to see if my being engaged to her had been the only deterrent to our becoming more involved."

"And was it?"

"Absolutely. I intend to become *very* involved."

She smiled against his chest. "And Alicia didn't seem to care?"

He chuckled. "She may be more intuitive than either of us give her credit for. She cocked her head to one side and studied me shrewdly. Then she said, 'There are a lot of bedrooms in that old house and personally I think they could be put to better use.' I took that as an endorsement. In any event, she was laughing when I stripped off my necktie and asked who was available to drive me to the airport."

Sloan snuggled closer. "I'm glad," she said in a whisper. "I couldn't have ever been completely happy if *she* hadn't been the one to free *you*."

"Nor could I."

"What are we going to do?"

"Are you referring to the immediate future? If so, that's a stupid question." His hand found her breast and circled the dusky areola with a bewitching finger.

"Um, yes," she sighed. "But I mean about your house and your work and Fairchild House. I don't want to give it up, Carter."

"You won't. I'd never ask you to, and I love this old house. But, and I underline the but, there are going to be some changes made. I'm bringing a few bucks into this marriage and some of them are going to be used to hire you some help. A cook, someone to clean, someone to help you serve—"

"But I love the cooking."

"And you can still do it. Just not all the time. Some afternoons I may want you to be making wild love to me, not preparing bouillabaisse." He kissed her on the tip of her nose. "I could work here, even in this room. We can make this our base of operation, but I want you to take some time off periodically. I want to travel with you, take you places, show you things, show you off."

"Are you that proud of me?"

He could feel the tension, could sense the courage it took for her to ask that, and knew that ony a few weeks before she wouldn't have had that kind of courage. She'd have reflected that defeatist attitude that she wasn't worthy of anyone's notice, that her existence was insignificant. His eyes lovingly touched each feature of her face, and in those amber eyes she found the self-confidence no one else had ever made her feel. "I'm that proud of you. You're the most lovable woman I've ever met. You always have been, Sloan. You just picked sorry candidates to show you how lovable you are."

"I believe that," she said, lightly touching his lips. "Because of you, I believe that. I am loved."

He pressed her palm to his mouth. "You are loved."

The emotion of the moment rendered them momentarily speechless. Finally he asked, "What did you think of my house on the beach?"

"I loved it," she said, her eyes sparkling. "It's beautiful."

"So it would be amenable to you if we lived there when we felt like it and lived here when we felt like it and maybe hired a couple to run Fairchild House during our occasional absences?"

She pursed her lips in thought. "I'd be very particular about whom I left in charge, but I think I could live with that arrangement. It means a lot to me, Carter, to make a success of Fairchild House."

"You have," he whispered urgently. "And it certainly can't hurt its reputation to have a famous author in residence."

"A *humble* famous author."

"That goes without saying," he said seriously. Then his face broke into a broad grin as he settled her beside him once again. "Will you have a baby for me?"

"I'll have a baby for us," she said with quiet determination.

He murmured love words in her hair before asking, "What is in the box?"

"Box?"

"The one on your dresser. The one you came in and touched so reverently."

Slowly she disengaged herself from his embrace and walked naked across the room. Taking up the japanned box, she carried it back to the bed and silently extended it to him. He swung his legs to the floor and sat up, looking directly into her eyes as he took it from her.

He turned the tiny key with the black silk tassel dangling from it and lifted the lid. He knew at once what he was looking at without even reading the edited lines. He thumbed through the pages, before raising bewildered eyes.

"Why? You could have bought all my books if you didn't have them already."

The lock of dark hair that grazed his eyebrow was brushed back with an affectionate hand. "Anyone could buy your books. These discards were all I had left of you. No one else had ever read them nor ever would. They were exclusively mine."

"But, Sloan, they're the dregs, the trash. They're rotten."

She shook her head, fanning him with her hair. "How they read doesn't matter. To me they represent the most beautiful love story ever written. They are poetry."

In that way of his that she'd once found objectionable but now found endearing, he muttered what could have been a vile curse or a fervent prayer, depending on who heard it. She knew it to be the latter. He set her treasured collection of marred papers aside and wrapped his arms around her waist, laying his head on her chest.

"*You* are the poet. And the poetry," he whispered.

His hands skimmed her body, marveling over each texture, each swell, and each hollow, the seeming frailty of her bones and the resilience of her skin.

His mouth rubbed against her breasts. "I need you,

Sloan. I need your quiet encouragement, your intelligent insight on what I write. I need your understanding when it's not going well and your praise when it all falls together. I need the nurture of your sweet body."

A gentle push of his palm brought her nipple to his mouth and he kissed it with light fluttering kisses until she was aching with the love blossoming inside her. He took the delicate bud in his mouth and tugged on it with so sweet a yearning that her hands clenched in his hair and held his head fast.

"God, I love the way you feel inside my mouth, love to taste this." He lubricated her nipple with his tongue so it slid easily along his closed lips when he dragged his mouth across it with an erotic rhythm.

He loved her other breast just as ardently while his hands climbed the backs of her thighs from knee to hip. His fingers curled inward and upward when his mouth lowered to claim her navel. Hot kisses were rained on her and she was nuzzled by faintly whiskered cheeks. Her heart was frantic, her senses explosive.

Then his mouth grazed the golden down that veiled her femininity, and her spirit leaped to yet another level of splendor. Heeding the sweet request of his hands on the backs of her thighs, she tilted forward to receive his loving tribute.

Her fingers dug into the muscles of his back as she felt herself molding to the heat of his mouth, obeying the whims of his nimble tongue. Her body liquified in an attempt to quench his thirst.

But it could never be quenched. It was a raging thirst and one that compelled him to urge her down onto the bed and to sheathe himself in her love.

"Sloan, Sloan," he groaned in her ear as their bodies arched together. Calling her name, he experienced that small death that comes just before rebirth, and looking into her face he saw her own renaissance.

Later, when their hearts were pulsing together more sedately, he gathered her to him. "You'll coach me through writing the great American novel, won't you?"

"I'd be honored."

"You'll put up with my black moods?"

"I'll love you out of them." His hand cherished her breast without passion, but with a great deal of loving gratitude. "Will you begin right away?"

"I have two things to do first."

"What?"

"Have a honeymoon at Fairchild House."

She covered his hand and pressed it tighter against the globe of her breast. "What's the other?"

"To change the last few pages of *Sleeping Mistress*. It's going to have a happy ending."

SEND NO FLOWERS

CHAPTER ONE

It was probably the cutest tush he had ever seen.

Through the screen door he had an unrestricted view of it, a derrière roundly feminine, but trim. The cutoff jeans were tight. Denim fringe, bleached and curled from years of laundering, clung damply to taut, slender thighs.

She was on hands and knees, peering into and hesitantly poking at the fuse box near the baseboard. As she leaned down farther to investigate the intricacies of the switches, the man smiled a slow, cat-with-mouse-trapped smile of masculine pleasure. It was the smile of a gratified voyeur. He was a little ashamed of himself. But not ashamed enough to stop looking.

The cabin was dark. Her flashlight gave off a meager glow. The only real illumination came from fierce flashes of blue-white lightning.

The two young boys watching her efforts were growing increasingly restless.

"I'm hungry. You said we'd eat as soon as we got here."

"Do you know how to turn the lights on, Mom? I bet you don't."

The man at the door saw her head fall forward between her shoulders in an attitude of defeat. It lasted for only a moment. She raised her head determinedly as she drew in a deep breath. "It's just a fuse box, David. When I find the breaker switch, the electricity will come back on. It must have been tripped by the storm. And, Adam, we'll eat as soon as I can get the lights on and unload the car."

"You said the cabin was gonna be great. I think it stinks," David complained. "We should've used tents."

"Yeah, tents," the younger brother seconded.

"If you don't think I can turn on the breaker switch, what makes you think I could put up a tent?"

The rising impatience in the young woman's voice was unmistakable and the man at the door didn't blame her for it. But the two little boys looked so bedraggled that he couldn't blame them for their complaining either. They were only kids and had apparently spent hours traveling. Their arrival at the lake cabin had been inauspicious, to say the least.

He had seen the headlights of their car when they arrived. A few minutes later, he decided to brave one of the most tumultuous thunderstorms he remembered in recent history and walk to the cabin only a hundred yards from his. That hundred yards was through dense woods, which guaranteed the owners of the cabins privacy. Walking through it in a thunderstorm had been foolhardy, but he had become concerned for his neighbors. His electricity had gone out about ten minutes before their arrival and God knew when it would come back on.

Now as he listened to the whining of the boys and the near desperation in the young woman's voice he was glad he had chanced the woods. She needed help and she was alone. At least there was no husband and father in evidence.

"We should've stopped at Burger Town. David and I wanted to eat there, didn't we, David?"

"I knew this was gonna be a jerky camping trip. I wanted to use a tent and camp for real, not stay in a dumb cabin."

The young woman rose up to sit on her heels, hands on hips. "Well, if you're such a pioneer, you can go out in the rain and start hunting or fishing for our supper." The boys fell silent. "I've had it with you two. Do you hear me? This cabin was graciously loaned to us. Since we don't have a tent and know nothing about them, I thought it was best we take up the offer to use it. I can't do anything about the storm. But I'm trying my best to get the electricity back on. Now stop the complaining!" She matched her stern tone with an intimidating glare and returned to her fanny-in-the-air position to futilely inspect the fuse box.

Glumly the brothers looked at each other and shook

their heads. They were convinced their trip was doomed to disaster. "Do you think she can fix the 'lectricity?" the younger asked the older in a loud whisper.

"No, do you?"

"No."

Now was the time to make his presence known. He had never been a window peeper and was ashamed for having stood outside this long without letting them know he was there. But he was enjoying them. They were in no immediate danger. Their tribulation somehow endeared them to him. He found himself smiling at the comments of the two boys and the parental frustration of the woman. Maybe watching their dilemma was acting as a panacea for his own. Observing them had certainly taken his mind off his problem. Albeit unfair, that was human nature.

It was also human nature for him to feel a shaft of desire spear through him each time he gazed at the display of long bare thighs and that incredibly delectable tush. That wasn't fair either. It was downright lechery to lust after a wife as well as the mother of two young boys. But could a man be held responsible for his thoughts?

"Mom, I have to go to the bathroom." It was Adam who spoke.

"Number one or number two?"

"Number one. Bad."

"Well, since we haven't located the bathroom yet, go outside."

"It's raining."

"I know that, Adam," she said with diminishing patience. "Stand on the porch under the roof and aim out."

"Okay," he mumbled and turned toward the door. "Hey, Mom."

"Hmm?" She was dickering with one of the switches.

"There's a man out there."

The young woman spun around, toppled backward, and gasped in alarm. "A *man?*"

Quickly, hoping not to frighten her, he switched on his high-beam flashlight and caught in its paralyzing spotlight an impressive chest straining against a chambray workshirt tied in a knot at her waist, a tumble of blond hair that had escaped a haphazard ponytail, and wide blue eyes.

Alicia Russell gulped in air and held it, her heart pounding. A brilliant flash of lightning silhouetted him where he stood just outside the screen door. Had she locked it behind them? Would it matter? He looked huge and fearsome against the stormy sky. And he was coming in!

He pulled the screen door open. It was ripped from his hand by the force of the wind and crashed against the outside wall. She and the boys cowered. He rushed across the room and dropped to his knees in front of where she lay sprawled. Her eyes were blinded by his flashlight. She could no longer see him except as a looming hulk bending over her. She opened her mouth to scream for her boys to run.

"Are you all right?" He switched off the light and for a moment everything was black. "I didn't mean to scare you. Here, let me help you up."

Alicia recoiled and the hand extended to her was withdrawn.

"I'm f-fine," she stuttered. "Startled, that's all." She pulled herself to her feet without his assistance. Her first concern was for her sons, who were eyeing the stranger curiously. "David, go help Adam . . . uh . . . do what he has to do on the porch." If she was going to be raped and murdered, she didn't want her sons to witness it. God, where was the telephone? Why didn't the lights come back on? Who was this man and where had he come from? Her heart was banging against her ribs and pounding on the inside of her eardrums.

"Hi," David chirped. Alicia cursed herself for teaching her children to be courteous and friendly. "I'm David. This is Adam. I'm the oldest."

"Hello," the man said. Alicia thought he smiled, but it was so dark, she couldn't tell. Her flashlight had flickered out and he had kept his turned off. "My name is Pierce."

"David—" Alicia began, only to be interrupted by her eldest.

"We're gonna camp here for a week, but Mom can't turn the lights on. She's not too good at things like that."

The stranger looked in her direction, then back down at the boys. "Few moms are. But she couldn't have turned the lights on anyway. The power's off because of the storm."

"Da-vid," Alicia ground out through gritted teeth.

"Why don't you take your brother outside," the stranger suggested, "while I see if I can help your mom."

"Okay. Come on, Adam."

The screen door slammed behind them and the man turned to Alicia. "You're off to a bad beginning. The campers aren't too happy."

If he were a rapist and a murderer, he was a polite one. But then it was said the Boston Strangler had been too. And Jack the Ripper. "I'm sure once the electricity comes back on and they get something to eat, they'll be in a better frame of mind." There, that sounded good. Unafraid, in control, cool, calm, capable.

"Where are your lanterns? I'll light them for you."

So much for cool, calm, and capable. "Lanterns?" Employing that gesture that is universally used by women to give them an air of indifference and make them appear less stupid than they feel at the given moment, she reached up and made patting, straightening motions on her hair. She also gave the frayed hem of her cutoffs a swift, hard tug. "I don't know. The cabin is borrowed and I didn't have a chance to look around."

"Candles?"

She shook her head.

"You didn't bring any emergency equipment with you?"

"No, I didn't," she snapped testily, hating the

incredulity in his voice. It made her feel imbecilic. This was the first camping attempt she had braved with her sons. How good was she supposed to be the first time out? "We'll be fine when the power comes back on."

"Why don't you wait out the storm in my cabin? We'll have to walk through the woods, but it's not far."

"No," she rushed to say. He had made her feel even more incompetent than she already did. That irritation had taken her mind off the possible danger he posed. But her panic quickly resurfaced when he mentioned their going to his cabin.

"That only makes sense. I can cook something for the boys on a butane stove."

"No, really, Mr. . . . uh . . ."

"Pierce."

"Thank you, Mr. Pierce, but—"

"No, Pierce is my first name. Pierce Reynolds."

"Mr. Reynolds, we'll manage. I don't want to leave the cabin."

"Why?"

She could hear the boys playing on the front porch, letting the rainwater splash on the palms they extended past the overhang. "My . . . my husband plans to join us later tonight. We should be here when he arrives or he'll be worried."

"Oh." He rubbed the back of his neck in indecision. "I hate to leave you alone under the circumstances. Why don't we leave him a note and tell him where you are?"

"Hey, Mom, we're starving," David said. He and Adam had tired of the game and trooped back inside. "When can we eat?"

"We're starving," Adam echoed.

"I really think it would be best if you came to my cabin."

"I—"

Before Alicia had a chance to object, the man turned to the two boys. "How does chili sound? If you come back to my cabin with me, I can have it heated up in no time."

"Gee, neat. That'd be great," David said enthusiastically.

"Neat," Adam said.

"But you'll have to walk through the woods to get there," the man warned. "There's no road to drive your car through."

"We don't mind, do we, Adam?" They were already racing toward the screen door.

"Boys!" Alicia called after them frantically, but they heedlessly dashed outside.

"Come on, Mrs.—?"

"Russell."

"Mrs. Russell. I can't leave you and the boys here alone. I promise I'm not someone you need to be afraid of."

Just then another flash of lightning rent the sky in two. Alicia thought the prospect of the power being restored was nil. She had been an idiot not to have come prepared for something like this, but it was too late to do anything about it now. At least the boys could be fed. When the rain abated, they could come back and wait for morning.

With a resigned sigh and a prayer that she could trust this man with her virtue and their lives, she said, "All right." The only thing she took with her was her purse. It would be insane to unload their bags from the car in the downpour.

On the front porch, Pierce Reynolds lifted Adam into his arms and directed David to take his mother's hand. "Okay, everybody, hold on tight. Mrs. Russell." For a long moment, Alicia stared down at the strong, lean hand extended to her. Then she placed her hand against it and he clasped it tightly.

The rain drove against them like stinging needles. Wind tore at their hair and clothes and buffeted them about. Each time lightning flashed, Adam buried his face deeper into Mr. Reynolds's neck. David tried his best to be valiant, but he was fearfully clinging to Alicia by the time they saw the other cabin through the trees.

"Almost there, troops," Mr. Reynolds called over the roar of the storm.

They reached the security of the covered porch just as a clap of thunder rattled the windowpanes. "Let's leave our shoes out here," Pierce said, setting Adam down. When they were all barefoot, he led them through the front door of the cabin, which was softly lit by two kerosene lanterns and smoldering coals in the fireplace.

"I'm cold. How about everyone else?" Pierce crossed

the room and knelt in front of the fireplace to stir the logs with a poker. Glancing over his shoulder, he saw his three guests huddling uncertainly just inside the threshold. They were shivering. "David, bring me one of those logs, please." The boy picked a log from the box near the door and rushed it to the man who was definitely hero-material. "Thanks." Pierce ruffled the boy's wet hair. "You'll find towels for you and Adam and your mother in the bathroom."

"Yes, sir," David said and ran toward the door that could only lead to the bathroom. The cabin was one large room serving as living room, bedroom, dining room, and kitchen. Comfortable chairs and a sofa were arranged in front of the fireplace. A double bed was tucked under a drastically sloping ceiling, which was actually the bottom of a narrow staircase that led up to a sleeping loft. It was too homey to be rustic and was spotlessly clean.

David emerged from the bathroom carrying a stack of folded towels. After first handing one to Pierce, he took them to his mother and brother. Alicia felt a sense of unreality. What was she doing here in this stranger's mountain retreat, alone with him in a veritable wilderness? It would have been bad enough if he were old and feeble, or kindly but pitifully ugly and ignorant. But their rescuer was handsome and suave and virile, something she hadn't known until they'd entered the cabin and she had seen him in the light.

His hair was ash brown and threaded with silver. It

was carefully cut to look carelessly styled and was worn a trifle longer than fashion currently dictated. When he turned his head Alicia had seen green eyes as brilliant as emeralds beneath a shelf of masculine brows. As he added the log to the coals and fanned it to life, well-developed muscles rippled beneath his wet cotton shirt, though his physique wasn't brawny.

He made her inordinately nervous. Not because she thought he would harm them. No man who would carry a little boy through a thunderstorm, murmuring reassurances that there was nothing to be afraid of, could be a murderer. As for being a rapist . . . Well, it was clear he would never have to *force* any woman.

"I'm glad I decided to build a fire earlier tonight. It was barely cool enough then, but now—"

Pierce stopped mid-sentence. Because if Alicia was surprised to find him so appealingly attractive, her reaction to him couldn't compare to the explosion in his chest and loins when he stood and turned to face her. Her hair was wet and silkily draping her cheeks, neck, and shoulders. The chambray was soaked and plastered against full breasts and nipples peaked hard from the cold. He had a helluva time keeping his eyes off them. Her bare feet only made her legs look longer and shapelier. They were covered with goose flesh he craved to warm with caressing hands.

He dragged his eyes away from her, cursing himself and this sudden attack of rampant desire. He hadn't felt so compulsively desirous of a woman since . . . He had *never* felt so compulsively desirous of a woman. It baffled him. She was a wife and mother and doing absolutely nothing to entice him. In fact, she looked jittery and nervous, and if his expression revealed anything of what was going on between his thighs, he didn't blame her.

"I think we ought to get you out of those wet clothes. Why don't you take the boys into the bathroom and I'll see if I can find them something to wear."

"All right." Alicia herded her sons toward the sanctity of the bathroom, where she hoped she could will her breasts back into a state of repose. He had noticed her distended nipples. She knew he had.

Several minutes later he knocked on the door, though it stood open to give them light. Adam and David had been stripped down to their underpants and Alicia was rubbing them with towels. "Chili is on the stove and I found these in a drawer." He held up two UCLA T-shirts.

"Super," David said, grabbing one and pulling it on over his head. It hung to his knees.

"Say thank you, David, to Mr. Reynolds for loaning you his shirt." She stood slowly, still painfully aware of her wet shirt and short cutoffs. When she had left Los Angeles that afternoon they were enjoying an unseasonable warm spell. For an automobile trip to the woods with David and Adam, the old cutoffs and shirt had seemed like the perfect outfit.

"Thanks, Mr. Reynolds," David said as he helped Adam with his shirt. The hem came to Adam's ankles.

"You're welcome, but the shirts aren't mine. This cabin belongs to my company. Everyone uses it and leaves things behind. I'm sure they'd never be missed if you want to keep them."

"Gee, can we?" The boys raced out looking like two friends of Casper the Ghost. They were happy now that they were warm and dry and dinnertime was imminent.

"I'll have to look a bit further to find something for you." Somehow Pierce kept his eyes on her face, which wasn't hard to do at all. Her hair was beginning to dry around the edges and it coiled beguilingly along her cheek. And, God, did she have a kissable mouth. His insides were groaning.

Alicia shifted from one bare foot to the other. "I'll dry out in a minute. Don't bother." Despite his resolution, his eyes drifted downward. "Maybe we'd better get them fed," she said hurriedly, and pushed past him. The boys were already sitting at the table where four places had been set. There was a basket of saltines and a tray of sliced cheese and apples in its center. A pan of chili was steaming on the portable butane stove.

She carried the bowls to the table as Pierce ladled them up. Then he held her chair for her before she sat down. Her stomach rumbled rebelliously and he laughed. "I guess the boys aren't the only ones who are hungry."

Good-naturedly she smiled. "I didn't have a chance to eat today."

"She always says that," David piped up. "She doesn't eat breakfast or lunch because she's afraid she'll get fat."

"Yeah," Adam said after cramming his mouth full of crackers, "she exercises every morning with the girl on the television. She gets on the floor and stretches and grunts and her face looks like this." He made a grimace that made Pierce laugh and made Alicia want to kill her second-born.

"Eat your supper so we can get back to our own cabin," she said in typical motherly fashion.

"Can't we stay here?" David whined.

She looked at him with the unmistakable, but silent, parental threat of annihilation. "No, David. We can't intrude on Mr. Reynolds."

"You don't mind, do you?" Adam asked him candidly.

Pierce looked at Alicia across the table. "No, I don't mind. As a matter of fact, I was thinking that I could run back down there and leave a note for your husband. He could join you here when he arrives."

"Husband?" David's young face screwed up in puzzlement.

Alicia's heart stopped and she momentarily closed her eyes. When she had told the lie, it was in the hope of protecting herself and her sons. The boys hadn't heard her. She had never thought the fib would come back to haunt her.

"Your mom told me that your dad is going to meet you at your cabin tonight."

"We don't have a dad," David informed him. "He died."

Adam swallowed his food. "Just like our goldfish.

Except Daddy's grave is in the c'metery instead of the backyard."

Alicia felt the green eyes slicing toward her before she even looked up to meet their inquiring gaze. With what defiance she could muster, she met their stare levelly.

"He died a long time ago," David said conversationally. "I remember him but Adam doesn't."

"I do too!" Adam protested. "He had black hair and brown eyes like us."

"You've just seen pictures of him so you think you remember."

"I remember. Mommy, make David stop saying I don't remember."

While this argument was carried out, the green eyes hadn't released their captive. "I'm sure you remember your daddy, Adam," Pierce said quietly.

"He was big like you, except maybe you're bigger," David continued. "We thought Carter was going to be our new dad, but then he married Sloan instead of Mom."

Alicia's warning glances did nothing to stop the flow of words from the mouths of her babes. "David, I'm sure Mr. Reynolds—"

"I cried when Carter told us he wasn't going to be our dad," Adam expounded. "But Mom said it was okay because Sloan was our friend and we'd get to see Carter a lot and just because he didn't marry her that didn't mean he didn't still love us. Can I have some more chili, please?"

"We can still go to Carter's beach house to play. It's neat. Adam's a pig. He always wants seconds."

"Am not."

"Are too."

Alicia was able to avoid Pierce's questioning eyes as he got up to refill Adam's bowl. He would think she was a complete idiot for fabricating a husband.

"Do you have a dad?" David asked of Pierce as he sat back down.

"No. He died a long time ago. But my mother is still alive."

"You're just like us."

Pierce smiled. "I guess I am."

"Do you have a wife?"

"Adam!" Alicia admonished, ready to throttle both her talkative offspring in one fell swoop. "That's enough. Both of you stop talking and eat your supper."

"No, I don't have a wife." Pierce's eyes were laughing as he blotted his mouth with a napkin.

They finished the meal in what was to Alicia blissful silence. Finally Pierce spoke. "If you're finished, I think it's time to get you two boys to bed." He stood and began to clear the table.

Alicia panicked. "David, Adam, go in the bathroom and wash your hands."

"Do you want us to wash our hands or are you just sending us in there because you want to talk about something you don't want us to hear?"

"Go!" she said, pointing a commanding finger toward the door.

"All right," her precocious son mumbled, taking his younger brother by the hand.

When they had the water running in the bathroom, Alicia whirled on the man. She had to tilt her head back at a drastic angle to look up into his face. Until then she hadn't noticed how tall he was. Or was he just standing closer? "I'm taking my boys back to our cabin. We will not spend the night here and I would appreciate it if you'd stop trying to lure them into staying, thereby making me the villain."

"That's lunacy, Mrs.— Oh, hell. What's your name?"

"Mrs. Russell," she said peevishly. He glared and she relented. "Alicia."

His lips drew up in a quick smile, then thinned to a resolute line. "The rain hasn't slacked off. What possible advantage could it be to drag those two little boys back through the woods to that damp, dark cabin when they could sleep here?"

"Because I'd be sleeping here too."

He shrugged. "So?"

"*So?* So my mother taught me to have better sense than to spend the night with strange men."

"I'm not strange." Again that quick smile, then tight-lipped sternness. "Why did you make up that lie about a husband? To protect yourself from me?"

She tossed back her hair and raised her chin. "Yes. I

was hoping you wouldn't bother us if you thought I had a man joining us soon."

Was it only her imagination or did he lean forward slightly and did his voice lower in volume and pitch? "Am I bothering you?"

Damn right. That's what she would have had to say if placed under oath. Thankfully she wasn't. "I just think that for all concerned, it would be best if we returned to our cabin."

"I disagree. You'd be alone without power. It's cold out now and the boys aren't dressed properly, to say nothing of you."

To make his point, his eyes scaled down her bare legs. But something happened on their return trip up to her face. They softened. Dangerously so. So that when they collided with Alicia's, he and she were both rendered speechless by that nonphysical collision. Seconds ticked by, moments stretched out, and still they stared, powerless either to move or look away.

What is wrong with me? Alicia asked herself. She had taken this week off to weigh an important decision, a decision she was being pressed for. Her time was running out; they wanted an answer. She didn't need this kind of romantic distraction in her life. Not ever, but particularly not now, when she had just found her footing in the scheme of things.

Similar thoughts were parading through Pierce's mind. A week ago, he would have been highly amused by this situation. He would have given his arousal free rein and not battled to suppress it. Wryly he admitted that he would have used any tactic necessary to get this woman into bed with him. But the day before yesterday, his world had been turned upside down and he didn't know how he was going to cope. His problem was solely his. He certainly couldn't invite anyone to share it. And what he had in mind every time he looked at this woman was sharing of the most intimate kind.

"Where's my bed?" Adam's question was rolled out around a broad yawn.

Alicia and Pierce both jumped reflexively and moved apart.

She floundered helplessly. If she refused to stay now, that would be tantamount to an admission that Pierce Reynolds *did* bother her. Purely from a logical standpoint, staying in his cabin was the safest, most reasonable thing to do. She would look like a sap traipsing back through the woods during this thunderstorm with her two weary, cranky children in tow.

This would be a temporary relapse, she assured herself. It had taken her thirty-one years to learn to take care of herself. She never wanted to depend on anyone else ever again. But this was only for one night.

Pierce Reynolds's gray-flecked eyebrow arched in query and she answered with a silent lowering of her eyes. He accepted her decision graciously and without a trace of smugness. "I thought one of you boys could sleep down here with me and the other upstairs with your mom. There is a double bed up there."

"They can both sleep upstairs. I wouldn't want you to be crowded." *He would crowd any bed.*

"No problem." *I'd love to be crowded in a bed with you.*

"Then Adam can sleep with you since he's the smaller."

David's brow wrinkled as he eyed his brother jealously. Then he bounded up the stairs. "Goody, I get to sleep upstairs."

They were soon bedded down and the cabin became awkwardly quiet save for the steady cadence of rainfall and the distant rumble of thunder. The worst of the storm had been spent. Alicia began clearing the table, washing the dishes in the sink. Pierce dried and replaced them in the limited cabinet space. They worked in silence until the job was done.

"Thank you," he said.

"It's the least I could do."

"I guess I'd better find you something else to put on. Whether you want to admit it or not, I know those damp clothes are uncomfortable. Mine are."

She wished he hadn't mentioned that. His damp shirt was molded over the muscles of his arms and chest. Tight denim jeans hugged his hips and thighs like a second skin. His bare feet hinted at an intimacy she would rather not think about.

She was thinking about it just the same.

He knelt in front of a cedar bureau and began rifling

through the drawers. He had searched two, found them lacking, and closed them before he pulled open the third. His hands plowed through the garments left behind and long forgotten. The drawer produced a stocking cap, one glove, a pair of plaid bermuda shorts about a size forty-two, and three socks all of different colors.

"Ah, here's something." He pulled the garment out of the drawer, eyeing it knowingly. "Someone had a good time while he was here."

Alicia's breath stopped in her throat when he held up a slinky nightgown. Firelight shone through its black transparency. Filaments of fabric formed the shoulder straps. The lace bodice was as fine and fragile as a spider's web. On a human body, it would be no more substantial than smoke, a shadow worn for clothing.

Coming slowly to his feet, he advanced toward her, his eyes immobilizing. He laid the straps of the night-gown against her shoulders, pulled the scanty bodice into place over her breasts, and let the length of it float down over her bare legs to her feet.

He peered at her through the shimmering folds. "Perfect fit," he said in a rough, unnatural voice.

Alicia stood stock-still, not daring to move. Feeling vulnerable and much like a succulent dessert about to be devoured, she quavered, "I can't wear this."

To her relief, he stepped back quickly. He looked as though he had suddenly remembered something and whatever it was had yanked him out of a golden fantasy and plunged him into cold reality. His face went blank.

His mood changed abruptly. It was so extreme a mood shift that even Alicia, a stranger to him, saw it, felt it. It was tangible.

Maybe he *was* married.

He turned his back, angrily shoved the nightgown out of sight into the drawer, and began to pillage it again. He seemed unaccountably aggravated as he stood up and thrust a man's shirt at her. "You can wear this," he said brusquely. "Good night, Alicia."

CHAPTER TWO

She awoke stretching contentedly. Staring up at the unfamiliar ceiling, it took her a few moments to determine where she was. Then she remembered.

Sitting bolt upright, she tossed the covers back. The other bed was empty. When she had climbed the narrow stairs the night before, she hadn't thought she would sleep so deeply or so long. One glance out the small window in the atticlike loft told her that the sun was well up on a gorgeous fall day. The woods seemed to have been washed clean by the storm.

A high-pitched giggle followed by a chorus of "Shhhh" came from downstairs. Alicia tiptoed to the top of the stairs and listened. She heard the clatter of silverware against dishes and smelled the wonderful aromas of bacon and maple syrup and coffee.

"Keep your voices down and let your mother sleep. She was very tired last night."

"Can I have some more pancakes?"

"Sure, Adam. How many does that make?" There was laughter in the deep, husky voice.

"Don't know."

"About sixty," David said, and Alicia could tell that despite her lectures he was talking with his mouth full. "I told you he's a pig."

"So are you!"

"Hey, cool it, both of you. Here, David, here's two more for you too."

"You make good pancakes."

"Thanks, Adam."

"Not quite as good as Mom's, though," he said loyally.

From her hidden perch Alicia smiled. She heard Pierce's laugh and it caused a fluttering in the pit of her stomach. Her clothes had been carefully draped over the end rail of the iron bed, but they were still damp. The thought of pulling them on was repugnant. Tugging self-consciously on the hem of the man's shirt, she took the first few stairs down.

"Good morning," she said tentatively.

Three heads turned in her direction. Two spoke, one remained silent. "Hi, Mom." "Pierce fixed us pancakes and bacon." "Watch it, Pierce, you're dripping the batter on the floor."

Pierce looked properly abashed and dropped the spoon back into the large mixing bowl. He had been so taken by the sight of Alicia's legs, the soft way the shirt clung to her breasts before falling mid-thigh, the tousled blond hair wreathing her head, and the sleepy-warm flush of her complexion that he had been momentarily dumbfounded.

Alicia knew she must look like the very devil. Her makeup was now almost twenty-four hours old. Every time she moved her face it seemed to crack and she could feel loose flakes of mascara precariously clinging to her lashes. Her hair had been rained on and she didn't even have a brush with her. Knowing that a wrong move could reveal more of her thighs than needed to be revealed, she descended the staircase with stiff carefulness.

She patted each son on the head. "How early did you get Mr. Reynolds up?"

"He was already up. He jogs every morning," David provided.

"Would you like a cup of coffee?"

Having run out of things to do to avoid it, she glanced up at her host. His cheeks were ruddy, as though he'd been outdoors and kissed by an early morning mountain chill. The silver-brown hair was agreeably mussed, falling softly on the tops of his ears and shirt collar. The green eyes were as startling now as they had been the night before. He smelled of clean air, a recent shower, and a woodsy fragrance.

"Yes, please," Alicia said. Her voice had very little power behind it and came out a breathy gust that she hoped he wouldn't take the wrong way.

He poured her a cup of coffee, pointing out the cream

and sugar on the table. "Have a seat and I'll grill you a stack of pancakes."

"No, thank you."

"See, I told you. All she thinks about is getting fat."

"David Russell . . ." Alicia shook a warning finger at him and both boys collapsed into a fit of giggles.

Pierce was laughing too. "Everybody has to eat breakfast in the mountains. Besides, I haven't eaten yet. I was waiting for you. It would be unfair to make me eat alone."

Alicia sighed her consent and Pierce poured disks of batter onto the hot grill. "Since you boys are finished, why don't you go make the beds while your mom and I are eating? I don't want to see one wrinkle in the covers when you're done."

"Yes, sir," they said in unison and nearly ran over each other scrambling up the stairs. Alicia watched their enthusiastic retreat in wonder.

"How did you do that?"

"What?"

"Get them to make the beds without a fuss."

He grinned as he flipped three perfect golden circular pancakes onto her plate. "It's different when someone besides Mom asks you to do something."

"I guess you're right," she said, liberally and sinfully buttering the pancakes. Her mouth was watering. She was just as generous with the syrup.

"Bacon?"

"Two, please."

"More coffee?"

"Yes."

By the time he swung a long jean-clad leg over the back of his chair and joined her, she was well into the stack of pancakes. "These are delicious."

"Thanks." He smiled his pleasure as he watched her eat. "The power came back on sometime during the night, so I was able to use the grill. Otherwise the menu might have been boiled eggs."

She laid her fork down, realizing for the first time that the electricity had indeed been restored. Why hadn't she noticed something that important before? Was it because this cabin was so comfortable that she subconsciously dreaded returning to her own and leaving the company of this man?

"Good," she said, taking a sip of coffee with an assumed air of nonchalance. Something in the way he looked at her across the breakfast table made her uncomfortably aware of her bare thighs on the seat of the chair and that only a pair of panties kept her from being naked beneath the shirt.

She felt very naked.

"We'll have to get to our cabin and out of your way as soon as I help with the dishes."

"How did your husband die?"

The question was so out of context that Alicia felt it like a well-placed sock to her jaw. Slightly stunned, she looked at Pierce. He had finished eating and was holding his coffee cup high, just under his chin, with both hands. He stared at her through the steam that rose from it.

She saw no reason not to answer him, even though it was an impertinent question for one stranger to ask another. "He was a businessman, but his avocation was racing sports cars. One Sunday afternoon, he was racing and . . ." She lowered her eyes to her ravaged plate. "He had an accident. He died instantly."

Pierce set his cup down and folded his arms on the tabletop, leaning forward slightly. She got the distinct impression that he wanted to touch her, to offer condolence. "You couldn't have been married long."

Alicia's smile was wistful. "Long enough to have David and Adam barely two years apart. We married while still in college. I fell in love with Jim Russell the first time I saw him."

Pierce was alarmed by the jealousy that took a stranglehold on him. He was also swamped by a feeling of supreme frustration. *Why now?* Why now was he meeting a lovely woman who exuded a latent sexuality longing to be released? A woman who happened to be an unfairly young widow.

When that internal anger seized him again, Alicia was aware of it. His face changed, becoming hard and closed. Anxiety pinched the corners of his eyes and mouth. Pierce Reynolds was a man with an ax to grind. The sooner she was away from him, the better.

"We should get started," she said uneasily. She didn't

need a man in her life. Not now. Not anymore. And she especially didn't need one with problems.

Briskly she set about cleaning the kitchen. Once upstairs, she pulled on her sour-smelling clothes and hustled the boys out of their UCLA T-shirts and back into their own shirts and shorts. She disregarded their litany of protests and querulous questions.

"I can't tell you how much I appreciate your kindness and hospitality, Mr. Reynolds." God, she sounded like a paragraph out of an etiquette handbook and felt just a little ridiculous standing in the cutoffs when it was too cold for them. Her tennis shoes were like clammy weights tied onto her feet. The small group was gathered on the porch of the cabin.

"I'm glad I was here to help." Pierce's tone was just as detached and formal. "You're sure you'll be all right?"

"Yes. Thank you again."

The two boys looked about as jolly as pallbearers. Pierce knelt down in front of them. He gave each of them a quarter. "Play a video game for me the next chance you get."

When they continued to hang their heads in glum silence, Alicia prodded. "What do you say?"

"Thank you," they mumbled. David lifted his head. "Did you ever play soccer, Pierce?"

"Football."

"No kidding? Which position?"

"Halfback."

"Gee. A running back. I'm too young to play football, but I'm a forward on my soccer team. We're the Hurricanes."

"I'll bet you're a good forward."

The dark eyes lit up. "Maybe you could come see me play sometime."

Alicia's heart wrenched at the pitiful plea in the young voice. David desperately needed a masculine role model. But she had learned long ago that she couldn't simply provide her children with a father. She would be taking on a husband too. Since she and Carter had broken their engagement, there had been no serious candidates for that.

"Maybe sometime." But he knew he wouldn't. He couldn't.

"Where is your house?" Adam asked.

"In Los Angeles."

"That's where our house is too."

"Come on, boys. Say good-bye and thank Mr. Reynolds again," Alicia intervened before their departure stretched out any longer.

"Thanks," they muttered sadly as Alicia all but dragged them across the clearing, past the parked Jeep that she hadn't seen the night before, and into the woods that separated the cabins.

"Oh, we're going to have such fun," she said, warding off her own sense of loss and depression. "Just wait and see. Maybe after we get settled, we'll go fishing."

"You won't want to bait the hooks," David grumbled.

He was right. The whole idea made her queasy. But she had had to do worse. "Wanna bet? You can show me how."

Her forced enthusiasm lasted as long as their walk through the woods and past the front door of the cabin. Then the three of them came to an abrupt standstill and gazed about them in mute disbelief. The cabin was a wreck.

A tree limb, driven by the wind, had torn through a screen and crashed through a window, leaving the floor and one bed showered with glass. Heavy rain had blown in. The floor was puddled in several places. The beds and even the one sofa were saturated. The curtains hung on the window in soggy tatters. Alicia reached for the light switch. Nothing happened. The electricity may have been restored in Pierce's cabin, but not here.

She shivered to think what would have happened had they not joined Pierce last night. What if one of them had been lying on that bed when the limb crashed through the window? They had escaped possible injury and for that she would be eternally grateful. But what was she going to do now? Were it not for her boys, she would have sat down and cried.

To her dismay, her sons were jubilant. "Can we go back to Pierce's cabin?"

"Can we, Mom? We liked it there."

"We'll be good. We promise. Won't we, Adam?"

"We'll be good."

"No," she cried, facing them and immediately dousing their expectations. At their collapsing expressions, she ventured a wide false smile. "Don't be silly. We can't force ourselves on Mr. Reynolds."

"Then what are we gonna do?" David demanded.

"I don't know." If she had let her dejection show, she would have sunk to the floor and curled into a tight ball. She hated being solely responsible all the time, having to provide all the answers, make all the decisions. But wasn't that what she had set out to prove after Carter had married Sloan, that she *could* and *would* be responsible for her own life and that of her sons?

She had survived the sudden death of her husband and a broken engagement; she had landed herself a peach of a job that she loved and was good at. By God, she wasn't going to let these setbacks ruin their vacation!

She clapped her hands together. "The first thing we're going to do is change clothes. It's much cooler here than it was in the valley, so David, Adam, help me carry in our luggage."

Despondently they obeyed, but they seemed to revive when they were dressed in jeans and long-sleeved T-shirts. After a cold hasty shower and shampoo in the small bathroom, Alicia pulled on an old pair of jeans and a sweatshirt left over from college days. It was still splattered with the paint she and Sloan had used to redecorate their room in the sorority house.

"Well, it's for certain we can't stay here," Alicia said,

assessing the damage in the main room of the cabin. "We'll drive down to the lodge. They have cabins that they rent out by the week. We'll see if one is available."

"What if there isn't?"

What if there isn't? "Then we'll go somewhere else," she said with more bright cheerfulness than she felt. "Let's get the bags back in the car." She checked the ice chest she had brought along. Most of the ice had melted. If she didn't refrigerate the groceries soon, she'd have to throw them away. But that was the least of her problems.

First priority was to find them lodging, someplace where the boys could fish and hike and generally soak up Mother Nature, which she had been promising to let them do for months. Not too isolated, not too crowded, not too far from home. Woods, mountain air. This place had been perfect. Now she might have to take what she could find. Rescheduling the trip would cause innumerable problems. She had arranged with the boys' teachers to excuse them this week. Undoing all that would be a pain.

The clerk at the main desk of the lodge listened sympathetically when she told him about the storm damage the cabin had sustained.

He scratched behind his ear. " 'Course, those places up there on that ridge are privately owned."

"I know that, but I've already called my friend who owns it. She gave me permission to see that things are cleaned up and the window repaired. She'll pay the bill. Could you find someone to take care of that for me?"

"Sure, sure. See no problem with that. I can have someone out this afternoon to get started."

"Thank you. Now we need a place to stay. We'd like to rent one of your cabins for the week."

"This week?"

Alicia mentally counted to ten. "Yes, this week. Right now."

He must have had a terrible itch behind his ear, for he was scratching it again. "Don't have any available, little lady."

Alicia clenched her teeth against the chauvinistic slur and instructed Adam to keep his fingers out of the ears of the buffalo head mounted over the mantel of the lodge's fireplace. She tried cajoling. "Surely you have something. I don't care how large or how small—"

"Nothing," he said emphatically, and flipped open a reservation book. "Let's see here. . . . We'll have a cabin that sleeps six on December fifteenth. Not many folks come up here around Christmastime, you see."

When he said nothing, he meant nothing. She spent a half hour plugging the pay telephone with quarters trying to find them an alternate recreation spot within driving distance. She wasted her quarters and her time.

"I'm sorry, but there's nothing I can do." She placed a consoling hand on each boy's shoulder. "We'll have to go home and plan another trip."

"That's not fair. You promised!"

"David, I know it doesn't seem fair. I was looking forward to this week off too."

"No, you weren't. You don't care if we have to go home. You didn't want to camp. You're a silly girl. You're *glad* everything's been ruined!"

"Now listen to me, young man—"

The Jeep braked just a few feet beyond the porch of the lodge and Pierce stepped out of it. He looked breathtakingly handsome in a plaid flannel shirt with a down vest over it. "What's going on?"

Before Alicia could open her mouth, Adam and David ran toward him spouting a barrage of broken sentences that more or less told him what had happened. Over their heads, he looked at Alicia.

"David," Pierce said, fishing in the tight pocket of his jeans for a dollar bill, "will you and Adam go into the lodge and buy me a newspaper, please?"

"Come on, Adam," David said wearily. "They're gonna talk grown-up again and don't want us to hear."

As Adam followed his brother through the door, he was heard to say, "Remember when Carter had to talk grown-up to Mom? They made us go away all the time."

Embarrassed, Alicia looked up at Pierce, but he was smiling. "I think they're making kids smarter these days."

She didn't feel much like smiling, but she managed a wobbly one. "I think so too."

"Now, what happened?"

Slowly, and in more coherent detail, she explained what had happened. "They're not reconciled to the fact that this outing wasn't meant to be."

"Wasn't it?"

The soft urgency in his voice brought her head up and she met his eyes. They were hot, burning into hers. She couldn't look at them long and averted her head. "No, I don't think it was. Everything's gone wrong. I'm not the outdoorsy type and they know it. Of course they blame me for this fiasco."

He propped his shoulder against a redwood post that supported the porch's overhang and gazed out over the gravel road and into the dense woods on the other side. He was weighing a decision. She somehow knew this and stood by silently, unable to move away, compelled by some unknown force to wait him out.

He spoke with methodic precision. "Why don't you and the boys stay with me?" He turned to look at her. "In my cabin."

Unconsciously, she twisted her hands together. "We can't."

"Why? Because you know I want to make love to you?"

Four things happened at once. Her eyes rounded. Her face paled considerably. She gasped sharply. Her tongue darted out to wet her lips.

"I'm not a man to mince words, Alicia. Let's be frank. From the first time I saw you in the light, standing dripping wet by the front door, I've wanted you in bed with me. Before that actually, when you were bending over the fuse box. Even when I thought you were another man's wife, I desired you. And you knew it."

"Don't—"

"But I would never do anything about it." Her protests died in her throat from surprise. When he was certain she would hear him out, he continued. "First, you would probably be insulted if I even tried to coax you into my bed. I'd never want to risk offending you." He drew a deep breath and turned away from her again to stare vacantly into the distance. "Secondly, I have reasons not to get involved with anyone right now. Viable, prohibitive reasons. Especially since . . ."

She swallowed. "Since?"

He swiveled around to face her. "Never mind." He smiled. "Knowing that I would never take advantage of you or compromise you in any way, will you consent to sharing the cabin?"

She rubbed her forehead with her thumb and middle finger while she groped for a sound reason not to accept. His invitation was seeming less and less absurd. "I'm not afraid of you. I don't think you're a man of uncontrollable impulses."

He laughed then. "Don't press your luck. I still find you damnably attractive. If you were to come out in that black nightgown I found last night, all these vows of celibacy would be shot to hell."

She blushed and hurriedly changed the subject. "I can't let us interrupt your vacation. Do you have any idea what the boys can be like when they get wound up?"

"No," he replied solemnly. "I missed parenting altogether. But I'd love to know what it's like. Your boys are a delight and I'm already looking forward to having them underfoot."

She shook her head in bewilderment, unaware that the gesture made the sunlight shimmer in her hair. It was all Pierce could do to keep his hands out of it. "I don't think you know what you're letting yourself in for."

"Let me worry about that." He took a step forward, not too close, but close enough to smell her morning cologne, close enough to feel her body heat. "Please say you'll stay. I want you to."

Throat arched, head thrown back, she peered up into his face, trying to decide if she had heard a trace of quiet desperation in his entreaty or if she were imagining it. How old was he? Early forties? His face had the firm stamp of mature masculinity on it, but wasn't coarse. His brows were thick and often spoke eloquently for themselves. A finely sculpted nose, long and narrow and slightly flared at the nostrils, went well with a full and sensuous lower lip. Looking at his mouth made her think shamefully erotic thoughts.

For that reason alone she should refuse his invitation. There were many reasons not to accept. Capsulizing them, it was just plain stupid and highly irresponsible to spend a week with a total stranger. Despite his manners and cultured voice and obvious intelligence, she knew nothing about him beyond his name and that he had a living mother and no wife. But instinctively she trusted him. She chose to trust her instincts. "Are you sure?"

His answer was a broad grin. Just then the boys came bounding out the door of the lodge with Pierce's newspaper. He scooped Adam up in his arms, straining biceps Alicia couldn't help but be impressed by. "Guess what, fellows? You're going to stay with me this week. So the only place you're going now is to help me unload your car at my cabin."

They whooped with noisy glee. "Can we ride in the Jeep? We've never ridden in a Jeep before."

Pierce laid a hand on David's shoulder. "Yes, you may ride in the jeep, but first you have an apology to make to your mother, don't you?"

Both Alicia and David looked up at him in bewilderment. "What for?" David asked.

"I heard your tone of voice and what you said to her when I drove up. You were blaming her for something that was beyond her control. Do you think that's fair?"

David's chin fell almost to his knees. "No, sir," he mumbled into his chest.

"You're the man of the family. As such, you should know to accept things graciously when there's nothing you can do to change them. Don't you think so?"

"Yes, sir." The boy turned to his mother. "I'm sorry."

Alicia knelt down and hugged him hard. "Apology accepted. Now let's concentrate on having a good time, all right?"

David smiled tremulously. Pierce curved his hand around the back of the boy's neck and steered him toward the Jeep. "Why don't you sit in the front seat this time and help me navigate?"

"Can I too, Pierce?" Adam wanted to know as he trotted after them on his chubby legs.

"Next time." He glanced over his shoulder to see Alicia standing where they had left her. "Coming?" he asked softly.

She nodded. "I need to make arrangements with the clerk for the repairs on the cabin. I'll follow in our car." As she watched them go, she wondered why there were tears in her eyes.

The day didn't lack for activity. It was a chore to unload her car and find a place for everything in the cabin. Then Pierce took the boys on a wood-gathering mission while Alicia prepared a lunch of soup and sandwiches. In the afternoon they hiked around the lake, and returned to cook steaks on the outdoor barbecue someone had had the foresight to build when the cabin was constructed. The dinner was sumptuous, but the boys yawned through theirs. Immediately afterward they were bathed and put to bed.

Alicia went to sit on the front steps of the cabin, to soak up the silence, the crisp night air, the star-studded sky undimmed by city lights. Pierce joined her, carrying two mugs of coffee, one of which she accepted with a soft thank you. Rather than being an intrusion, she found that his presence enhanced her sense of peacefulness.

"They're already asleep."

"I hope Adam's snoring doesn't keep you awake."

"I've been told I snore too."

Alicia wondered how many women had told him that. To keep her mind from wandering in that direction, she guided it to neutral territory. "You said your company owns the cabin. What company?"

"Ecto Engineers."

"What kind of engineering?"

"Aeronautical."

"You design airplanes? Military planes? What?"

He settled and she liked the sound and feel of his male body shifting comfortably. "We do some military contracts. Mostly we work with private aircraft firms, design corporate jets, that kind of thing."

"Are your designs brilliant and innovative?" She was teasing.

"Yes," he answered honestly and smiled a dashing smile. They both laughed softly.

She glanced over her shoulder toward the dark cabin. "What would the owners of your company say if they knew you had invited a widow and her brood to share their cabin with you?"

"Well, since I'm a full partner in the company, I'm entitled to invite whomever I want." She might have guessed that he wasn't a wage earner. He reeked of success. Even his casual clothes bespoke good taste that one paid a high price for.

"What about you?" he asked. "What work do you do?"

"I'm an assistant fashion coordinator for three boutiques. Glad Rags we're called." His eyes took in her ponytail, paint-smeared sweatshirt, jeans, and sneakers. She laughed. "You're too polite to make a sarcastic comment." Her elbow found his ribs and because he was as warm as a stove, she didn't move away as quickly as she should have.

"I'm the epitome of diplomacy," he said, wishing she hadn't moved away after touching him, even if it was with her elbow. She was so damned soft, so indubitably feminine. "What does an assistant fashion coordinator do?"

"Helps plan the overall fashion statement the stores are going to project for a particular season."

"In plain English, what the hell does that mean?"

She laughed and marveled at how relaxed she was. "For instance, are we going to be trendy or understated? Do we push ensembles or coordinates? Are we going to be avant-garde or classical? Does that make sense?"

"More or less. Do you like it?"

"I love it. I've been preparing for it all my life and didn't know it. Despite what you see here"—she bowed her head mockingly—"I love clothes, have a knack for putting things together, and shopping has always been one of my favorite pastimes. Now I can do it with someone else's money." Her face clouded as she remembered her dilemma.

"What is it?"

"I don't want to burden you with my problems."

"I asked."

Setting her coffee mug aside, she studied him for a moment before she began. It felt good to talk to an adult, someone objective, uninvolved. She had eliminated her parents and good friends, even Sloan and Carter, as able to give her an unbiased opinion.

"My supervisor is expecting a baby next month and has decided to leave for good. It's her cabin I was borrowing," she said as an aside. "Anyway, the owners of the stores have offered me her job. They know a lot about merchandising and money management and absolutely nothing about taste and fashion. I have until the end of the month to give them my answer before they start looking for someone else."

"What will you decide?"

She leaned back, propping herself up with straight arms. If she had realized how that pose emphasized the shape and size of her breasts and the effect it had on Pierce, she wouldn't have sat that way. "I don't know, Pierce." It was the first time she had said his name, and she swung her head around to see if he had noticed.

"I like that much better than Mr. Reynolds," he said softly. He tugged on a wayward curl before tucking it behind her ear and lamented the multitude of reasons why he couldn't smooth his palm over her breast and seek the nipple with his thumb. "Do you want the job?"

"Yes. It's challenging and exciting. I'd make much more money."

"Well then?"

"It's a demanding job that requires long hours and some travel. I worry about short-changing the boys as it is. They have only one parent. Don't I owe them my undivided attention? I feel guilty if I'm five minutes late getting home."

"You owe something to yourself too. Adam and David will be on their own one day. If you've devoted your life exclusively to them, where will that leave you?"

"I've thought of all that," she said slowly. She had argued with herself until she was blue in the face and the solution to her dilemma still eluded her. Her time was running out. She must make a decision.

But not tonight.

"Thanks for being a sounding board."

"My pleasure." He took her hand. "You'll make the right choice, Alicia."

It was a long time before she could find the will to

pull her hand from the warm strength of his. She knew being held in his arms would feel even better. They would be even warmer, stronger. "I think I'd better go upstairs now."

"Who is Carter?"

CHAPTER THREE

His question caught her hunched and ready to stand up, but brought her bottom back down onto the wooden porch with a jolt. "Why do you ask?"

"Because the boys refer to him constantly. Carter said, Carter did. Just about everything in their world is measured by how Carter would respond to it. I'm curious."

"Carter Madison." She knew full well it wasn't strictly curiosity that had caused him to ask. His face was too tense for mild curiosity. "He's an old friend."

"Carter Madison, Carter Madison." Pierce repeated the name like rapidly snapping fingers. He was trying to place it and when he did, he turned to her. "Carter Madison the writer?"

"You've heard of him. He'd like that."

"I've read most of his novels."

"He'd like that even better."

"I've seen him interviewed on television talk shows. Charming, glib, good-looking guy. What happened? Why didn't you marry him?"

So, he remembered the tale the boys had told him the night before. No wonder he was inquisitive. "He married my best friend, Sloan, instead." Pierce's face went blank, as though he thought he had committed an unpardonable blunder. Alicia relieved his mind by explaining. "Carter was my husband Jim's best friend. After Jim was killed, Carter was marvelous. He felt responsible for me and sheltered me from some of the most unpleasant aspects of recent widowhood. He helped me with the boys. Eventually he became an essential factor in our lives. I hated to admit it, but we took him for granted. He asked me to marry him and I accepted. I felt lost, lonely. Carter was a familiar, safe bulwark to lean against for protection."

She smiled with fond memories. Husbands and wives should be good friends, but good friends should never become husband and wife. "I sent Carter to Sloan's bed-and-breakfast house in San Francisco so he could finish a book before the wedding. They were instantly attracted to one another. It didn't take him long to realize that he was marrying me for the wrong reasons. Almost simultaneously I realized the same thing. We broke off the engagement the day of the wedding and he married Sloan a few weeks later. They're very happy. She's expecting their first child."

Pierce sipped his coffee, which had to be cold by now. Alicia thought he did it more for something to do to cover his unwarranted interest than because he wanted the coffee. "No regrets?"

"Absolutely none. I love Carter. I always did, as Jim's and my friend. I love Sloan, who remains my best friend. I'm very glad to have been instrumental in bringing them together. They needed each other."

"There's been no one else in your life since Jim's death?"

"No."

She had tried the singles scene for a while, but found that kind of life wasn't for her. Before she and Carter had acknowledged what a mistake they were making, there had been a skiing weekend in Tahoe. A friend, who was much more accustomed to the singles life than Alicia, had enticed her to go. She had had a good time, met a very nice man named Mac, and ended up staying the night in his room. It had felt good to be held, to be loved. Her relationship with Carter had never gone far beyond the platonic. Mac's affection had been just what she needed at the time.

But later, when he had come down from his home in Oregon to see her, he was still nice, he was still attentive and affectionate, but the magic of having a weekend fling in Tahoe was missing. They had endured a strained dinner together and he had said good night at her door, both of them chagrined and a little sad that it hadn't been the same. He hadn't pressed the issue or tried to force anything. She had appreciated that and was glad he didn't call again.

Well-meaning friends, erroneously under the impression that she was grieving over her loss of Carter, paired her with any number of eligible men. Most of those evenings had been disasters and it was a relief to both her and her escort when they were over.

She had frequented the singles bars and discos with girlfriends who were currently unattached. They hovered like circling vultures waiting for an available man to drop before swooping down on him. The whole scene seemed tawdry and sleazy and Alicia felt cheapened by it. She started making excuses not to go, until they stopped calling to invite her. The well of her social life dried up about the time she found her job and after that she didn't miss it.

Only now, in retrospect, did she realize how she had missed talking to an adult. A man. *That's a euphemism, Alicia. What you've missed is the scent and strength of masculinity. And admit it, it feels good having this man near you.*

She missed something else too. But she couldn't allow herself to think about that. The love she and Jim had shared in their marriage bed had been so special, she never wanted to settle for anything less. Still, Pierce was extremely attractive and she felt that just beneath his veneer of polished manners, sexuality seethed like a cauldron ready to boil over. What kind of lover would he be? Tender and relaxed or fierce and intense? Or an exciting combination?

She yanked herself out of her musings and stood up quickly. "Well, good night."

"Good night. Don't forget the fishing trip first thing in the morning."

She groaned. "David and Adam were ecstatic about the fishing boat, but I'm concerned. They've never been on a lake in such a small boat. Do you think it's safe?"

"We'll lay down the maritime rules and regulations before we even embark." He saluted and she laughed.

"I know I sound like a mother."

"You sound like a sensible, caring, loving woman."

The way he said it made her throat go dry. There was no moisture with which to wet her lower lip when she dragged her tongue along it.

"Alicia, are you glad you stayed?" Shadows kept her from seeing his face, which was just as well. Longing and desire were nakedly apparent.

"Yes." She tried to sound cheerful and bright and peppy. She sounded breathless and aroused and languorous.

"Good," he said, nodding slowly. "Good."

In vain, she tried to wet her lips again. "Are you coming in? Shall I turn off the lights?"

He shook his head. "No. I'll be in shortly."

The screen door closed behind her and he heard her soft tread on the stairs to the sleeping loft. He could still smell her hair, still see her eyes reflecting the moonlight, creating twin clusters of sapphires and diamonds beneath perfectly arched brows, still detail the shapely swell of her breasts.

He didn't follow her in because he knew if he did, he couldn't have stopped himself from taking her in his arms, pressing her softness against him, kissing her deeply and without restraint, touching her, tasting her, and making her his.

Alicia awoke from her second night under Pierce's roof the same way she had the previous morning, well rested and with a feeling of contentment. Stretching luxuriously, she glanced at the other twin bed, and, as on the first morning, David had already left it. Lazily, she indulged herself and lay still for a moment, enjoying the concert of the birds in the trees outside.

It came to her suddenly that that was the only sound she heard. This morning there was no commotion in the kitchen. The boys were being awfully quiet in light of the fact that they were going fishing.

Alicia threw back the covers and padded to the stairs on bare feet. She had slept in her own nightgown last night, but it covered little more than the borrowed shirt had, despite the fact that it came to her ankles. Its scooped neckline showed an expanse of creamy California-tanned décolletage. The sleeveless bodice left her arms bare.

She tripped down the stairs, becoming more panicked with each step. There was no movement in the house. It was sleepy and quiet. Maybe they had gotten up and gone without her, but she doubted Pierce would leave her to worry like this. She ran toward the front door, which was standing slightly ajar, pulled it open, and scanned the grounds surrounding the cabin. Nothing. Yes, they had probably gone without her.

Just then she heard rustling movements behind her and whirled around. My God! Pierce was sound asleep, alone in the double bed. Alicia's heart began to pound out danger signals. She gave the forebodingly empty cabin one more hasty inspection before she crammed her fingers against her mouth to stifle a whimper of panic, at the same time bolting for the bed.

"Pierce!" The heel of her hand landed hard on his shoulder with the impetus of her lunge behind it.

"What?" His eyes popped open wildly as he struggled to sit up. He shook his head to clear it. "What?"

"The boys are gone." The words were clipped, emphatic, rapid, like bullets being fired from the barrel of a gun.

He stared at her blankly for a moment. Didn't he remember her, recognize her? "The boys are gone?" he repeated.

Her head bobbed in frantic confirmation. "I don't see them anywhere outside. They're gone." Her voice cracked on the last word, and that seemed to finally alert Pierce to her distress. The covers were flung back and he sprang off the bed.

His hands closed around her shoulders. "They're

okay. I'm sure of it. They probably just wandered off."
His palms were moving up and down her arms, warming
her, the way a paramedic would try to revive a victim of
shock. "Maybe they're on their way down to the boat."

"At the lake? Oh God. They won't know the danger.
What if they try to get in the boat?"

He pulled her to him quickly, hard, crushing her against
his body and pressing her face into his chest. "It's all right.
I promise it is." He whispered urgently into her hair,
willing her to believe him. "Hurry now. Let's dress and go
look." He pushed her away and peered into her eyes.

She nodded mechanically and turned to run up the
stairs, catching her nightgown in a damp fist and hiking
it high. In minutes they met at the front door. "They
were so excited about the fishing, I think the pier is our
best bet to start," Pierce told her as they scrambled
down the steps of the porch.

"So do I." Even the pinkish golden rays of the new
morning sun didn't relieve the pallor of her face.

Pierce took her hand and they ran down the over-
grown path that led from the cabin toward the lake. He
did his best to push aside tree limbs and warn her of
roots that snaked across the trail, but she stumbled along
behind him, fear and dread making her blind to the haz-
ards. By the time the lake came into sight like a silver
platter lying amidst the woods, she had been scratched
and bruised.

"Do you see them?" Anxiously she stepped around
Pierce where he had halted on the edge of the clearing.

"Yes," he said, letting out the word on a long exhalation. Alicia knew then that he had been just as concerned as she, but had remained calm for her benefit. He pointed in the direction of the pier. Both boys were sitting on it, legs dangling over the water. They were happily chatting, blissfully unaware of the chaos they had caused in their mother's heart.

Pierce took her hand and they jogged down the gradual slope to the pier. The boys heard them coming and ran to meet them. "We're gonna catch millions of fish. We've been watching them, haven't we, Adam?"

"They swim right up to the pier."

The two young faces turned up to the adults were flushed with excitement and high color. "Are you ready? The poles are in the boat. Adam and me checked."

Alicia paled again to think of them climbing in and out of the boat that was moored at the water's edge. They had taken swimming lessons for the last three summers and both could swim fairly well. But a neighborhood pool where the depth of the water was clearly demarcated and the cold, murky waters of a lake were two different things entirely. "David, Adam, I was scared out of my wits!"

For the first time the boys realized that their mother and Pierce weren't smiling and their exuberance was immediately snuffed out. Their smiles deflated and they took steps backward, away from the wrath they felt coming.

"It was extremely dangerous for the two of you to

come down here alone." Pierce's brows were as scolding as his tone of voice.

"We didn't do anything wrong, honest, Pierce," David said in a small voice.

"You left the cabin without permission. That was very wrong. Your mother woke up and you weren't there. She was worried half to death and so was I."

David and Adam looked mournfully at each other. Adam's lip began to quiver. "David wanted to get to the lake early."

"So did you!" David said, wheeling on his brother. "He came upstairs and woke me up. He——"

"It doesn't matter whose idea it was," Alicia said with forced calm. Now that she knew they were all right, she was trembling on the inside from the aftershocks that still assailed her. "Don't ever, *ever* wander off like that without letting me know where you are."

"Are we in trouble?"

"Can we still go fishing?"

"Did you understand what your mother said?" Pierce's voice was so intimidating that even Alicia flinched. "You are never to disappear like that again." Both boys hung their heads in contrition and answered with meek "Yes, sirs." They were miserable, but Pierce didn't relent. "Let's go back to the cabin. We want a cup of coffee and I think you should eat some breakfast before we get started."

"Then we still get to go?" David asked, bravely, hopefully.

Now that they seemed to have learned their lesson, it was all Pierce could do to keep from smiling. "Alicia and I will talk about it on the way back. It might make a difference if, when we get back, we find the beds being made and the cabin straightened."

David streaked off toward the trail, Adam doing his best to keep up with him.

Alicia slumped as the tension ebbed out of her. She gazed at her sons, realizing, as parents are wont to do after a crisis, just how tenuous their lives were and how important they were to her. "Thank you." Her voice was husky with emotion. "I was ready to light into them out of fear and anger. You handled it perfectly by properly chastising them but also making sure they understood their mistake."

He laughed shortly. "They're not my kids. That makes it a helluva lot simpler."

"But you were worried too."

"I was worried too," he admitted ruefully. He touched her arm. "You okay?"

She shuddered briefly to shake off the last traces of trauma and looked up at him. "Yes, I'm fine now."

Their eyes melted together. Realization of what had happened only minutes ago dawned on them at the same time. It had had a stunning impact on them, but they hadn't been able to pause and dwell on it then. The indulgence had been postponed until now, now when they could afford the time, could devote to it the concentration such an occurrence deserved.

Her mind tracked backward and Alicia could see him coming off the bed, a study of virile grace and power, naked save for a pair of briefs that hid nothing and emphasized much. There was much to emphasize.

Her palms began to perspire.

The chest hair that matted the hard curves had tickled her nose as he held her tightly against him. He was an even toasty tan color all over. She had longed to explore him slowly, to drink in with the sensors on her palms the varied textures. He had offered her comfort when she needed it, but at the same time he had acquainted her with his rawly masculine body.

Pierce was remembering too. But his recollections were of softness, the kind a man is compelled to cover, to protect, to mate with, the kind of softness hard virility yearns to be nestled in. Blond hair was riotous around her head, much as it was now. It fell on skin the color of ripe peaches and he had longed to taste it. He had wanted to taste her mouth, too, a mouth that seemed in perpetual need of kissing.

Her breasts had swayed lush and heavy and heavenly beneath her nightgown. When she was bending over him, shaking him awake, he had seen their full glory displayed under the gaping neckline of the gown. Almost as enticing were the dusky shadows of her nipples that shyly pushed against the cloudlike cotton when she was standing straight. He remembered what it felt like to hold her against him, to feel the blatant femininity that roused every sleeping cell in his body.

And now it had become just too much to resist. He simply had to kiss her.

One hand cupped her jaw and tilted her face up. The other went inside her jacket. His arm curved dictatorially around her back and hauled her close.

"Pierce—"

His mouth came down on hers, slanting over surprised, slightly parted lips that didn't stand a chance against the onslaught. It was a potent kiss and had an immediacy about it that coerced her lips to relax against the thrusts of his tongue. It was buried in the soft, sweet recess of her mouth, where it refused to be stilled and continued its stroking.

Later, Alicia assured herself that she had struggled and that his greater strength had overpowered her. She lied to herself. For actually her body inclined toward his and her feet followed with tiny baby steps that brought them between his hard straddling legs. There was no denying that he wanted her in the most primeval way. He was a steely hard pressure against the fly of her jeans.

But his mouth was softly persuasive. Against such gentle persuasion, she had no argument. His kiss made her feel as if she were the most desirable woman in the world, the only woman in the world, and that if he didn't have her, he might perish.

When at last he lifted his head, he seemed impatient with himself. The hand securing her jaw dropped to his side and the other was withdrawn from her jacket.

"We'd better get back and see to the boys," he said gruffly before turning in the direction of the cabin.

Left with a sense of loss, Alicia forlornly followed him. She hadn't invited his kiss. It shouldn't have happened. But since it had, she wished he had cuddled her for a while afterward.

Such romantic sentiments were utter foolishness. She didn't want this man. Did she?

Fishing in the boat turned out to be a complete success. Pierce instructed the boys on what they could and could not do in a boat that small and they returned to the pier with a creel of fish and four slightly sunburned noses.

In the afternoon, Alicia opted for a nap while the "men" went into town for groceries. She handed Pierce a shopping list and a twenty-dollar bill.

He frowned at the money. "I insist," she said firmly, forcibly curving his fingers around the bill.

"Let it be noted that I concede under protest."

"Fine. Just so long as you concede."

She was glad that the kiss that morning hadn't put a wedge of tension between them. By the time they reached the cabin to find the downstairs bed already made and the ones upstairs being worked on, he was conversing as though nothing had happened. She tried to ignore that he went out of his way not to touch her or be alone with her. His avoidance both relieved and piqued her, so it was wiser not to think about it at all.

"Which bed are you going to sleep in, Mommy?" Adam asked, feeling important since it hadn't even been suggested that he stay behind to take a nap rather than accompany David and Pierce. "You can sleep in mine and Pierce's. We wouldn't mind, would we, Pierce?"

The corners of Pierce's lips were twitching with suppressed laughter as he cocked a rakish eyebrow at a blushing Alicia. "No. While we're gone she can sleep in any bed she chooses. She has the run of the place."

"In that case," she said, buttoning up David's jacket and futilely finger-combing his dark hair, "I may make a pallet under the trees."

"You won't either. You'd be afraid of snakes and bugs and stuff."

She tweaked her eldest son on the nose. "You're right."

The boys raced for the Jeep, fighting over who would get to sit in the front seat first. "You're sure you don't mind staying alone?"

Her laugh was spontaneous and genuine. "Are you kidding? Do you know how rare these precious occasions are?"

"Okay," Pierce said. "Just don't open the door to strangers," he warned with a mocking grin.

Alicia waved them off with a glowing feeling warming her from the inside out. But on the fringes of that energy source, away from that tingling heat, there lurked an indefinable sadness.

When she woke from her nap—she had slept in the upstairs twin bed—Pierce and the boys were building a fire in a ring of stones well away from the cabin but not too close to the trees.

"Hey, Mom," David called out when he saw her looking at them from the upstairs window, "we're gonna cook the fish in the coals of the fire. Pierce knows how. Are you coming down now?"

"Have the fish been scaled and gutted?"

"Yes."

"Then I'm coming down."

While they tended the fire and wrapped potatoes, ears of corn, and seasoned fillets of fish in foil, Alicia baked a double batch of Toll-House cookies. "Those smell scrumptious," Pierce said from over her shoulder as she dropped the balls of dough onto the cookie sheet.

"Better than raw fish," she said, wrinkling her nose and sniffing the air.

He laughed. "Just wait till you taste it." Reaching around her, he scooped up a fingerful of the dough from the mixing bowl and plopped it into his mouth. She spun around to confront him.

"Pierce! You're worse than the boys."

"Am I?" His eyes were dancing emeralds of mischief as he laughed down at her. He bent forward quickly and Alicia thought he was going to kiss her, possibly on her nose. But just as suddenly as it had sparked, the light in his eyes went out and he pulled back. Turning away, he went through the screen door and she was left staring after him as she had been that morning, wondering what she had done to turn him off so abruptly.

The boys enjoyed that meal more than any other they had ever eaten. They all ate outside, sitting around the fire. The boys hung on to Pierce's every word as he told them how he had learned to cook over a campfire on a hunting trip with his father. Once again Alicia was grateful to him. She could never have made the week such fun. He was just what her boys needed, a masculine presence, a role model. It was plain to see that they had awarded him a place next to their other heroes, their late father and Carter Madison.

For a man who had never had children, who wasn't even married, Pierce showed infinite patience with them. Unless he was a very good actor, he was enjoying the boys' company as much as they were his. When they talked to him, they held his attention. He gave everything they said importance and credence, when she often tuned out their chatter, listening with half an ear and recording only what she deemed important.

"Off to bed, you two," he said after they had carried the dishes into the cabin.

"Oh, please, can we stay up longer?"

"Nope," Pierce said, shaking his head. "If you go to bed without an argument I may have a surprise for you tomorrow."

"What?"

"Can't tell."

"He can't tell, David, or it wouldn't be a surprise."

Pierce laughed. "That's right, Adam. Good night or no surprise."

After hasty kisses aimed in the general direction of Alicia's mouth, the boys went into the cabin. "More wine?" Pierce asked Alicia once they were alone. Only the occasional stirring of autumn leaves and the crackling friendliness of the fire broke the pervading quiet.

An aluminum bucket had served as their wine cooler. He had surprised her with it after dishing up their campfire supper. "White, of course, madam, to go with your fish," he had said in a sonorous tone and executed a stiff formal butler's bow. Alicia's dumbfoundedness had given way to delight as he poured her a liberal portion into a tin cup.

"No, thank you," she said now. "It was delicious, but no more for me."

"Half a glass? It's good for the soul."

"If my soul gets to feeling any better, I'm going to fall over in a stupor."

He laughed. "A woman who can't hold her liquor, huh? That could prove dangerous."

They lapsed into silence, smiling, looking at each other. Then, because looking at each other proved to be unsettling, they stopped looking at each other. Then stopped smiling. The longer the silence stretched out, the more awkward it became. Finally Alicia got up, dusted off the seat of her pants, and said, "In spite of my nap, I'm sleepy. Thank you for a wonderful dinner, Pierce. I'll do the dishes before I go upstairs."

How he moved that quickly, she never knew. By the

time she leaned down to pick up her cup of wine and turned toward the cabin, he was standing inches away blocking her path.

"I shouldn't have kissed you this morning." His body was rigid with self-enforced control.

"No," she said, her head down, eyes staring at his boots, "you shouldn't have."

"I shouldn't kiss you now either."

"No."

"But I'm going to anyway."

Before her reflexes, dulled by the wine, could respond, she was being folded into his arms and molded against his hard frame. His lips plundered again, but more sweetly this time. They savored her as they whisked back and forth over her mouth before they settled and pressed. His tongue parted her obliging lips to tease the sensitive inner lining. When he heard her murmur of arousal, it plunged deeply and with authority to investigate her mouth at will.

What little resistance she had initially fell away like melting wax. She craved the tutelage of his mouth, for surely she had never been kissed with such expertise. His passion frightened and thrilled her. It reminded her body of its long abstinence from all things sexual. Her sense of shame was diminished by the sweet flow of wine through her veins. She arched against him invitingly.

The sounds he made in his throat were wonderful to her ears. They were guttural, animal, the sounds of a

male mating—or desperately wanting to. It was grati-
fying to her ego that she, a mother, a widow, could
excite an exciting man like Pierce.

He left her mouth and swept hot airy kisses on her
cheeks and nose, her jaw and earlobes, on her temples
and in her hair. One hand slipped past her waist and
secured her hips hard against his. The other pushed
aside the collar of her shirt. He planted his mouth at
the base of her throat. When his lips parted, she felt
the scalding caress of his tongue, rasping and velvety
at once.

"I swear to you, this is not why I encouraged you to
stay," he said thickly. His lips sipped at her neck.

"I know." She didn't remember when she had set
down her cup and raised her arms, but now her fingers were tangled in his hair and she was holding his
head fast.

"I tried to keep my hands off you. I swear I did. I
couldn't any longer."

His mouth met hers in another fiery kiss. An erotically
gifted instrument, his tongue made love to her mouth.
With rhythmic, wild, savage thrusts he deflowered it and
left no question as to his claim of absolute possession.
His hand was once more inside her jacket, bolder now
than it had been that morning. It tensed around the slim-
ness of her waist and slid up her ribs to mold to the
undercurve of her breast. She held her breath.

A long sustained sigh soughed through her lips when

his hand covered her with strong warmth. He massaged her through her sweater, rubbing the soft angora wool back and forth over her fevered skin until he felt her nipple bud in his palm. He pressed it with his thumb, circled it, stroked.

"Oh, God." He strained the curse through clenched teeth and Alicia bit back a protest of outrage and frustration when he released her and stepped away. He turned his back. She ran for the cabin and let the door slam behind her. Fury and humiliation battled within her. Never in her life had she felt both emotions so keenly.

It took long minutes before she was restored. She forced herself across the room to the kitchen area, where she methodically began to wash dishes. She wasn't about to run upstairs and hide her shame like a thwarted teenager. Rejection tasted brassy and bitter in her mouth, but she'd be damned before she'd let him know it.

He stepped through the door. "Are you all right?"

Her whole body was flashing hotly and freezing cold, her nerves were in pandemonium, she was quaking with unrequited desire, all five senses were shooting off like skyrockets and he wanted to know if she was all right. At that moment she hated him and could barely garner enough civility to gnash out, "Of course. As you said, you shouldn't have kissed me. It was better to end it there. No hard feelings."

Frustrated in his own right, his arm shot out and he wound a handful of her hair around his fist and pulled her around to face him. Amazingly it was almost a caress of tenderness, for he didn't hurt her.

He didn't speak until she raised hostile eyes to meet his. "I wanted to kiss you, Alicia, and to go on kissing you." He pulled her closer, still not making his hold painful. "And I didn't want it to end there. I didn't want it to end until we had made love so many times we were exhausted. Can't you tell how much I want you?"

She could now, now that he had moved closer still and the lower part of his body was stamped against her thigh. He laid his hard cheek along hers; his lips moved against her temple. Every pore of his body secreted anguish, a pain she couldn't identify. "It's important to me that you know how much I want you and that my reasons for not making love to you are insurmountable. Otherwise . . ." He heaved a regretful sigh and stepped back. Gradually he let go of her hair. He studied her face, all but flaying off the skin and reading her every thought with those piercing green eyes. Then he said abjectly, "Go upstairs. I'll finish up here."

She didn't dare argue. If she stayed with him for as long as another heartbeat, she might very well make a fool of herself and beg him to take her despite whatever problems prevented it.

What could it be?

Alicia studied Pierce from the upstairs window. It was early. Miraculously she had awakened before the boys and hadn't been able to go back to sleep as she reviewed the disturbing events of the night before.

Pierce had been jogging this morning. His warm-up suit was drenched with sweat. Obviously he had driven himself to the limit of his endurance. He was propped against a tree, staring up through its branches. His face was twisted with his private turmoil. He wiped perspiration out of his eyes and Alicia heard him curse.

Whatever it was that tormented him, whatever that insurmountable obstacle was, it was terrible and something he couldn't eliminate with his own resources.

Alicia couldn't let it worry her. At the end of the week they would go their separate ways. In the meantime, she had her own problem to grapple with and solve. Her mind must remain occupied solely with that.

Yet, looking down at Pierce's bowed head, she confessed that objectivity where he was concerned had vanished the moment he had kissed her. Whether or not he had invited her to be, whether or not he wanted her to be, she was already involved.

The surprise he had promised the boys turned out to be mopeds, which Alicia was coerced into riding. They rode doubles, David behind Pierce and Adam clinging to her waist and demanding that she go faster.

The next day it rained in the morning and Pierce entertained the boys with games of checkers and lessons on whittling until the sun came out. Alicia baked brownies and made a savory stew for their supper. They checked on the other cabin and saw that the repairs had been done satisfactorily. No one suggested that Alicia and the boys should move to it, but during those two days Pierce didn't make a romantic overture. Their relationship returned to that of friendly companionship. What had taken place after their cookout might well never have happened.

"I'd like to stay close to the cabin today, if you think we can keep the boys busy." They were having a last cup of morning coffee. David and Adam had finished the chores Pierce had assigned them and were playing with a soccer ball in front of the cabin.

"Sure. Whatever. Please don't feel you have to entertain us every minute. If there's something you want to do by yourself—"

"It's not that." He set his cup aside and she could tell he was uneasy. "I'm expecting a guest tonight for dinner."

"Oh, Pierce, you should have said something sooner!" She leaped out of her chair like a wound-up spring let loose. "We'll leave immediately and make the cabin available—"

"Sit down," he said, laughing and grabbing her wrist and forcing her back into the chair she had vacated. "I want you to stay and be here for dinner."

She looked at him dubiously. "When you have company coming?"

His eyes locked into hers. "It's not actually company. It's my daughter."

CHAPTER FOUR

Chrissy Reynolds arrived as the sun was sinking behind the woods. Braking a red Porsche to a stop in front of the cabin, the tall, attractive, slender young woman alighted. She was welcomed by David and Adam who, disregarding Alicia's instructions that they not race out the door, bounded through it and down the steps to admire the car that was to them the ultimate status symbol.

"Well, hello." Chrissy laughed as she was flanked by the boys, both of whom were staring up at her curiously. "Do I have the right cabin?"

"Yes, you do." Pierce took the front steps down to greet his daughter. Though he walked with a somewhat calmer stride, he was just as anxious to see her as the boys had been. "Hello, Chrissy."

Watching from behind the security of the screen, Alicia saw Chrissy's smile brighten bashfully. "Hello, Daddy," Alicia heard her say hesitantly. His daughter was actually shy of him. Alicia didn't wonder at this after what Pierce had told her that morning.

"Your daughter!" she had exclaimed almost soundlessly. "Your *daughter?*" She had sprung out of the chair again and for the second time he pulled her back down. She yanked her hand away but remained seated. "You told me you didn't have any children."

The first thing she suspected was that he had a wife and God knew how many children waiting for him at home. She might have had one fling in Tahoe since her husband's death, but that was the extent of her romantic adventures. Being kissed and kissing back a married man was something else again.

She was hurt beyond reason and out of proportion to the extent that she was involved with Pierce. He hadn't seemed the type to lie so deviously.

"Alicia, don't jump to conclusions before you hear me out. I told you I'd had no part of parenting. I never said I didn't have a child. My wife and I divorced soon after Chrissy's birth. I abdicated my responsibility for rearing her to her mother, something that I bitterly regret. I wanted to see my daughter this week. It's become very important that I spend time with her. That's why I invited her to come up here one evening and have dinner with me."

She had been mollified, but still felt that he had misled her. "We'll leave before she arrives. I'm sure she won't expect you to have other guests when you made a special point of inviting her to join you."

"She doesn't expect anything one way or another. I wasn't exaggerating how I neglected her while she was growing up. The occasions she's visited me are embarrassingly few in number. Her mother and I can barely tolerate the sight of each other, so at the time the custody papers were being drawn up, it seemed best for all concerned if I stayed out of their lives."

Instinctive female curiosity began to crawl over Alicia like an annoying tiny insect that one can't see but can feel. She tried to brush it away. But she'd been bit. She was dying to know the details of his marriage and its breakup. However, if a man didn't even call his ex-wife by her first name, he wasn't going to talk about her. Alicia had remained silent.

"I thought I'd cook beef stroganoff for dinner," he said. "Do you think that will be okay?"

He was nervous! She could tell by the anxiety lacing that otherwise innocuous question that Pierce had misgivings about this reunion with his daughter. That vulnerability, so unusual in a man with Pierce's confidence, touched a chord deep inside her.

"Beef stroganoff sounds delicious," she assured him softly. "Pierce, are you sure you want us around tonight?"

"Yes," he answered swiftly. Too swiftly.

"To act as buffers? Are you expecting a fight? A scene?"

His grin was lopsided and self-deprecating. "No. Nothing like that. I just want it to be a pleasant evening for her, that's all."

"I'll fix something special for dessert."

"No, no. Don't feel that you have to do that."

"I don't. I've got a sweet tooth."

He knew better, but he accepted her generous offer with appreciation.

Now as Alicia watched father and daughter embrace, she could tell such displays of affection were infrequent and awkward for them both. Pierce hugged Chrissy to him, but briefly. He pushed her away to look at her. "You look terrific as always. Did you get your hair cut? I like it."

"Do you? Thanks. Mother had a fit. She didn't want it cut before the wedding."

Wedding? Whose wedding? Hers or her mother's?

"The big day is fast approaching. Any premarital jitters?"

Ah-h, Chrissy was the bride-to-be.

"A few," she admitted with a soft laugh. "But that's natural, I guess."

Pierce's brows knitted as he studied his daughter. He sensed that she could elaborate but had chosen to be reticent. He swung an arm around her shoulders. "I don't know if I'm willing to give you away yet or not."

The girl's face glowed with happy surprise, and Alicia saw tears standing in her eyes—eyes like her father's. "Thank you for inviting me up here this week, Daddy. I needed an evening away from . . . everything."

He squeezed her shoulder. "We should have done more of this long ago. I'm just now realizing how much of you I've missed. Old age has the advantage of wisdom, I guess."

She poked him in the ribs. "You're hardly sliding over the far side of the hill." She glanced down at David and Adam. "And you've sure got young friends."

"Pardon my rudeness," Pierce said, laughing. "Chrissy, my friends David and Adam Russell. Boys, my daughter."

"She sure is old," Adam said. They were disappointed. When they had been told Pierce's daughter was coming for dinner, they had obviously conjured up an image of someone closer to their age, not an ancient twenty-one-year-old.

Chrissy put her hands on her hips. "She's not too old to play soccer. Whose ball is that?" She pointed to the ball that had rolled beneath an evergreen bush.

"Mine," David said, his frown lifting slightly. "I'll let you play with it if you'll let me ride in your Porsche. It's super. I have a poster of one in my room. I wanted Mom to buy one but she said it wasn't prac... part... pract—"

"Practical," Pierce supplied, and Chrissy laughed.

"Well, she's smarter than Daddy then. He gave it to me last Christmas. You've got a deal about the soccer ball and the car." Chrissy turned to her father and gave him an arch look. "Have you known David and Adam long?"

"Since Sunday night. I rescued them during a thunderstorm."

"You're kidding!"

"No, he's not. He did!" David said.

"Yeah, he carried us and Mom back to his house and it was raining real hard and lightning, but I wasn't scared," Adam added.

Chrissy had also inherited her father's expressive eyebrows. One curved high as she eyed him shrewdly. "Well, the boys are certainly cute. How about Mom?"

Alicia blushed to the roots of her hair and tried to duck into the shadows of the cabin before she could be caught eavesdropping. But Pierce turned around and called out to her. She had no choice but to push through the screen door and take the steps down to be formally introduced.

"Alicia Russell, my daughter Chrissy."

"Hello, Chrissy," Alicia said, suddenly feeling like a scarlet woman. And why? She, better than anyone, knew that nothing had happened between her and this girl's father. But how would Chrissy react to her and the boys sharing Pierce's cabin?

"Hi. It's nice to meet you." Her smile was wide, pleasant, friendly, and guileless. "Did he really rescue you during a thunderstorm?"

"I hate to admit it, but yes. And when we couldn't find other lodging after our borrowed cabin was damaged by the storm, he insisted we share his." Alicia felt compelled to explain quickly, lest Chrissy draw the wrong conclusion.

Mischievously Chrissy slid her eyes in her father's direction. "He's a regular knight in shining armor," she commented dryly, but without rancor.

No matter about Alicia's rapid explanation, Chrissy had summed up the situation in her own mind the moment she saw Alicia. She might not know much about her father, but she knew that he was a connoisseur of women. Alicia Russell's wholesomeness was a departure from the kind of woman he usually squired around. Nonetheless the sexual currents radiating between them were real and alive and popping. Stand too close when they looked at each other, and you could get singed.

"What's a night in shiny armor?" Adam asked.

"Why don't we discuss that over a cold drink?" Pierce suggested, and began shepherding everyone inside.

Alicia liked Chrissy immediately. She was chatty and animated, shy only when she looked directly at her father. It was as though she wanted to fling her arms around him and hold him tight but was afraid to. It was apparent every time she looked at him that she admired him and loved him, but that she didn't feel completely comfortable around him yet. Alicia got the impression that the young woman desperately wanted his approval and affection.

Chrissy enlightened them on her progress in art school, and because she aspired to design women's clothing, she and Alicia launched into a long discussion on fashion.

Bored, David whined, "Can we play soccer now?"

Pierce stood. "You ladies excuse us. I'll take them out and run off some of their energy."

"No," Chrissy said, rising. "I promised. Come on, boys." They raced out ahead of her.

"Your daughter is lovely, Pierce. A vibrant, intelligent young woman."

"Isn't she?" he said proudly as he watched her through the screen door. "I only wish I could claim some credit for the way she's turned out."

"You can."

He shook his head. "I was never around. She deserved a father, a good one, one she knew cared about her. What happened between her mother and me wasn't her fault, but she's the one who paid for it."

"I think she knew you were there if she needed you," Alicia said quietly.

He turned to her and his green eyes speared straight through her. "I'd like to believe that, Alicia. I need to believe that."

"She doesn't seem to be holding a grudge. She looks at you with love, not resentment. Maybe she needs to hear how you feel about her. Have you ever told her you love her?" He pondered that for a moment, his brows drawn together. "Go on out with them and I'll set the table for dinner."

"I can't leave you to do all the work."

She pointed toward the door. "Go." She used the same no-nonsense and no-backtalk voice she used on her boys.

"Yes, ma'am." Before she could react he smacked a sound kiss on her mouth and went out the screen door.

Twenty minutes later Alicia called the boys inside for a bath before dinner. They complained and grumbled, but she finally got them indoors and into the bathroom. She carried a tray with two glasses and a bottle of chilled white wine out to Pierce and Chrissy, who had collapsed in fatigue on the front steps.

"I'm sorry this is all we have in the way of a predinner drink," Alicia said, setting the tray down.

"Where's your glass?" Pierce asked, patting the spot beside him on the porch to indicate that she should sit down.

"I'm supervising the bathing or they might flood the bathroom. Take your time. The rolls still have to bake. I'll call you when dinner is ready."

Pierce reached up and touched her hand. "Thank you." His look carried with it gratitude and something else. He was grateful to her for providing him and his daughter this moment alone. And the something else? Alicia couldn't quite define it, but it made her insides seem anchorless.

As she was putting the food on the table, they came in hand in hand. Chrissy was saying, "That was the

Christmas you sent me the pony, remember? I've never seen Mother so furious. I only got to keep it for one day before she sent it back to the stables."

"She's always been a b-i-t-c-h."

"I know what that spells," David piped. "Bitch."

"David Russell!" Alicia was horrified.

Pierce looked embarrassed and Chrissy said, "See what calling Mother bad names can get you?"

"It wasn't a bad name. It was a factual name. And I'm not sorry I said it, only sorry that David heard it. It's an impolite word, David, so don't let me hear you using it."

"Yes, sir."

Dinner was a happy time. The group lacked for nothing to talk about. Pierce had done an excellent job on the stroganoff, though he complimented Alicia on boiling the noodles to just the right tenderness. She missed the frequent entertaining she and Jim had done and had put all her culinary talents into a lemon meringue pie that won everyone's approval.

The boys hadn't forgotten the promised ride in the Porsche. Chrissy handed Pierce the keys. "Will you do the honors while I help Alicia with the dishes?"

"That isn't necessary," Alicia said quickly.

"I want to. We didn't get to finish our debate about next year's hem lengths."

"Then I'm all too glad to take the boys out." Pierce hooked a young Russell under each arm and carried them screeching gleefully out the front door.

Chrissy caught Alicia fondly and wistfully smiling

after them. Embarrassed, Alicia began clearing the table. "I understand you're getting married soon. What kind of gown have you picked out?"

Chrissy described her gown and the color scheme she had chosen for the wedding. Conversation was no effort between them. Alicia found herself telling the younger woman about Jim and his death. Her life as a widow, her job, even about Sloan and Carter.

"Have you slept with Daddy?"

That was something else Chrissy had inherited from her father, the ability to shock one speechless with an incisive, out-of-context question.

Alicia's hands were submerged in the soapy water. At the audacious, presumptuous question, they balled into fists. "No," she said softly. Lifting her eyes to Chrissy's, she repeated slowly, "No, I haven't."

"I think you should," Chrissy remarked. She wasn't looking at Alicia, but was concentrating on lining up the glassware in the cabinet.

Alicia couldn't believe the girl's candor. "Why?"

Chrissy looked at her, smiled, and shrugged. "Why not? You obviously find each other attractive. Don't get me wrong. I don't believe in sleeping around. I just think . . ." She paused to stare into space for a moment. Then she turned to Alicia again. And just as Alicia quelled under Pierce's steady stare, so did she under Chrissy's, for they were identical. One couldn't hide one's thoughts from those eyes. "There's something wrong with Daddy."

"Wrong? What do you mean?"

"I don't know. He's different. Even his inviting me up here is uncharacteristic. Always before on my visits, he's been in a hurry. I got tired just trying to keep up with him. He was always moving. Now he's meditative, sentimental. He's doing things that aren't like him at all."

"Like inviting a poor widow and her sons to stay the week with him?"

Chrissy laughed and boldly assessed Alicia's shape. "Surely you've figured out why he did that. If you had looked like a troll, I'm sure he would have been polite and seen that you were safe, but I doubt if he would have been quite so hospitable." Discomfited, Alicia looked away. Chrissy took her hand and forced Alicia's eyes back to hers. "If he asks you, will you sleep with him?"

Alicia swallowed, too overcome by surprise to be offended. "I don't know."

"I hope you will. I think he needs you."

"I'm sure a man like your father doesn't lack for female company."

"I'm sure he doesn't either. I'm not talking about sex. Not exclusively anyway. I think he needs all that you are, your warmth, compassion. And I think being with him would do you a world of good too."

Alicia thankfully heard the return of the Porsche and was glad the conversation couldn't go any further. The boys were put to bed upstairs so the adults could continue their visit. They bid a solemn farewell to Chrissy, and Alicia knew they hoped to see her again. Chrissy knelt down and kissed their cheeks and neither moved away from the caress they usually avoided whenever possible. It was late when Chrissy said she had to start back.

"Do you have to?" Pierce questioned. "We could make room for you."

"I have a class in the morning and a wedding gown fitting at noon. Mother would freak if I didn't show up for that." She took both Alicia's hands. "It was so nice to meet you. I'm officially inviting you and the boys to the wedding."

"Thank you. We'll see."

Chrissy shocked Alicia then by pulling her into a swift hug. "Remember what I said. I give you my permission." Chrissy winked before she turned away and Alicia avoided Pierce's inquiring eyes.

"I'll walk her to her car," he said.

For half an hour, Alicia sat in front of the fireplace, flipping through a magazine. Their voices occasionally drifted in to her. Once she thought she heard Chrissy crying, but couldn't be sure. At last she heard the growl of the Porsche's engine and the crunch of tires as it rolled onto the narrow gravel road.

Pierce was a long time coming in and, sensing that he might wish to be alone, Alicia headed for the stairs. She certainly didn't want him to think she had waited up for him. Her foot had just touched the bottom step when he came in.

"Are you going to bed?"

"Yes, I thought—"

He stretched out his hand. "Will you sit with me for a while, Alicia?"

Her heart began to beat heavily and she couldn't say exactly why. Perhaps because it was quiet and they were alone. Perhaps it was because she had turned out all the lights save one soft lamp and the cabin was dim and whispered intimacy from every corner. Perhaps it was because of his slightly raspy, highly emotional voice and the way he had spoken her name. For whatever reason, she was trembling with feeling as she retraced her steps to the sofa and took the hand held out for her. He pulled her down beside him on the deep, age-softened cushions.

"Thank you for taking over the dinner."

"It was nothing. No, really," she said when she noted his skeptical look. "I enjoyed playing hostess."

"Well, anyway, I appreciate it. I think Chrissy had a good time. It temporarily took her mind off the circus her mother is making out of her wedding."

Alicia squelched common sense and ventured onto ground she knew was as potentially explosive as a mine-field. She trod softly. "Chrissy doesn't seem very excited about her wedding. Does she love her fiancé?"

"I think she must feel some affection for him. He's

not a disagreeable young man. But I don't think she loves him."

"Then why—"

"She's being pushed into a 'good marriage.' Good by her mother's standards, that is."

"I see."

"No, you don't, but I'd like to explain. It's a long, boring story."

"I'm not doing anything else," she said, smiling, sensing his need to talk.

"You could be sleeping."

"I'd rather listen."

"I can't unload on you."

"I talked out my problem with you the other night. Sometimes strangers are the best listeners."

"Are we still strangers?" She was the first to look away from a long, puissant stare. He sighed heavily. "Okay, here goes. I married young and foolishly. Dottie considered me a good catch, a promising engineer. She had a pretty face, a terrific body, and an obliging attitude toward sex. I walked into a velvet trap and she sank her claws into me before I knew I'd been had. We were mismatched. We had different goals, different priorities. It was doomed to failure."

He went on to explain that his wife, who had come from an affluent family, got extremely upset when he put most of his savings and a small legacy into a new, struggling engineering firm rather than going with an already established one. Money was tight and they could no longer be members of the country club and move with that set. Then she had gotten pregnant.

"I was made to feel like a sexual deviate whose lust wouldn't let him take time for contraceptives, when in fact our bed was the only place we were the least bit compatible." Alicia swallowed a knot and was alarmed to discover that it was cold, rank jealousy. "I threatened to kill her if she even thought about an abortion. By today's standards I'm sure my attitude would seem intolerant and incredibly puritanical. Nonetheless, that's how I felt. How I still feel.

"Soon after Chrissy was born, we agreed that our lives would be much happier if we never saw each other again. Dottie hates me for causing the one failure in her life. I'm the only thing she ever wanted, went after, but couldn't have."

He ran his hands through his hair. "But I blame myself for the failed marriage because I never should have married her in the first place. And as a parent, well, that speaks for itself. I don't even know my daughter. I missed her childhood, her youth, her adolescence. Now she's gotten herself committed to a marriage that is going to make her miserably unhappy and I can't do a damned thing to stop it. Any interference on my part would be like declaring World War III with Dottie. Yet I feel that I have to do this one important thing for my daughter before—" He broke off suddenly.

"Before what?"

"Never mind. It's just that I think she wants help in getting out of this mess and doesn't know how to ask for it. I told her to stand up to her mother. I know she won't."

"Chrissy's an intelligent woman. She won't be forced into a marriage she doesn't want."

"You don't know Dottie. She's as shrewd a strategist as George Patton. And about as humanitarian as Nero. When she sets her mind to something, people have a way of cowering and going along to prevent a fight."

"You didn't."

His head swiveled around and his eyes held her motionless. "No, thank God, I didn't. I only hope Chrissy will see her mistake in time. Hell, her mother wants that young man for a son-in-law because of his last name. She probably harbors a terrible dislike for him and can't wait to rearrange his life too. Everyone but Dottie will be unhappy."

"When the time comes, Chrissy will know what to do."

"Will she? She won't have me to thank if she does. I've salved my conscience for being a lousy parent by giving her presents—ponies and Porsches. I've never given her guidance, a sense of values, anything that's really important. God, it's a wonder she doesn't despise me."

Of its own volition, Alicia's hand stroked back

strands of disheveled hair that lay silvery-brown on his forehead. They slid through her fingers in a silky caress. "You're not the reprobate you paint yourself to be, Pierce. And ·don't worry about Chrissy. She's got a good head on her shoulders."

"I told her tonight that I loved her," he said in a low voice.

So, her subtly given advice had been taken. "What did she do?"

He smiled. "She cried and hugged me and told me that she loved me too."

"I'm glad, Pierce. Very glad for both of you."

He raised one knee so he could face her. Leaning forward, he searched her eyes. "I have you to thank for tonight's success. I can't tell you how important it was to me."

"It would have happened sooner or later. You wanted it to. So did Chrissy. I only gave you a nudge to do something you already planned to do."

He touched her cheek with his fingertips. "What makes you so easy to talk to? So understanding? So tuned in to other people and what makes them tick?"

"I'm not. I've never been anything but purely selfish."

"I find that hard to believe." His voice was deep and soft and low. It touched her in places that shouldn't be touched, like her breasts, her stomach, and between her thighs. She felt his voice in each erogenous spot like a kittenish, lapping caress.

"Believe it. I've been known to think only of myself,

otherwise I wouldn't have always turned my life over to other people to take care of. First my parents, then Jim. I didn't worry about anything but my own happiness and what they would do to bring it about. When I lost Jim I transferred the responsibility for my life to Carter. It's safer to do that, you see. Then you can't be blamed when things go wrong."

She shook her head sadly and for emphasis she covered his hand with her own. "Pierce, deep inside I knew Carter didn't love me, even before he met Sloan. I almost let him ruin his life, destroy his chance at happiness, in order to secure my own future."

"Don't be so hard on yourself. You had your boys to think of."

"I used them as my excuse." Lost in her own thoughts, she fiddled with the buttons on his shirt. The familiarity didn't seem at all unnatural. "I finally woke up to the fact that I was an adult, that I had to take full responsibility for my life and that of my sons. For the first time in my life I'm standing on my own two feet. I like myself better for it, but it's a shaky perch at times."

"I don't know anyone who doesn't feel afraid at one time or another." His eyes turned introspective, and for a moment she thought that he might draw away again. Instead he raised her hand to his mouth and pressed his lips against her palm. "What did you and Chrissy talk about?"

He must have felt her pulse leap beneath his stroking thumb on her wrist because his eyes lifted to hers.

His lashes were dark and long and ridiculously lavish. She wanted to run her finger over them. "Girl talk. Nothing much."

"Did she ask about us?"

"Yes."

"What did she want to know?"

She knew where the truthful answer might lead. In this instance, it would be best to avoid the truth. But she didn't want to. She wanted to be led straight into the jaws of temptation. Damn the consequences. "Chrissy asked me if we were sleeping together."

"What did you tell her?"

"I told her no."

"What did she say to that?"

Alicia wet her lips with the tip of her tongue. Jealously he watched it disappear back between her lips. "She said she thought we should, that it would be good for both of us."

"I'm inclined to agree. I know it would be damned good for me." He cupped her face between his hands and drilled into her eyes with the hot, emerald brilliance of his. He saw in her eyes a need, a longing, a desire as clamorous as his own. "What about you?"

"I think it would be mutually satisfying." The die was cast.

"I can't get involved. It would be bed, that's all. I don't want you to be hurt later."

"I understand."

"Do you? Do you, Alicia? Because I have to know now."

"I can't get involved with anyone either."

"We're two people who know what we're doing, right? Consenting adults."

"Yes."

"No regrets later."

"No regrets."

"It's only for tonight. Nothing binding. We attach no special significance to it, just take it for what it is, a physical release, a pleasurable exchange of flesh. Right?"

"Yes." The last word came out a plea as passionate as the way her body curved longingly against his.

His thumbs outlined her lips, detailed their shape before his mouth took them under his kiss. Without preamble or apology, his tongue pressed into her mouth and moved freely, rampantly, stroking, delving, tasting all of her.

Wrapping his arms around her, he stood and brought her to her feet. Never letting his mouth leave hers, he held her full length against him and carried her to the bed. He let her slide to her feet and the dragging motion of her body along his brought moans of desire from their throats. Deftly he tugged her shirttail free of her waistband.

He ducked his head and kissed her breasts through the cloth even as he unbuttoned her blouse. When he parted the garment and peeled it down her shoulders her breasts were damp from his mouth and their crests were rosy and taut beneath her sheer brassiere.

Forcibly he calmed himself, commanded himself to slow down, not to ravage but to savor. His hands closed with tender possessiveness around her breasts and he fondled her with gently squeezing motions.

"You are wonderful to touch," he whispered along her neck.

Her hands folded around his neck and she laid her cheek against his thudding heart. He smelled of that elusive, expensive, woodsy cologne and she breathed it in greedily.

Nimbly his hands went around her back and unfastened her brassiere. When he pulled it away from her and dropped it to the floor, she faced him demurely. But his eyes showered praise on her. "Your breasts are beautiful, Alicia. Beautiful."

His eyes, his words, then his hands and lips testified to that. He brushed light kisses on the soft flesh, lifting her breasts to his mouth with his palms. Her nipples beaded beneath the sweet coaxing of his fingertips and his tongue circled them in lazy contrast to the fury building inside them both.

"Do you want to undress yourself?" he asked, his throat throbbing with self-imposed restraint.

"Do you want to undress me?"

"Very much."

She stepped out of her shoes and stood before him,

compliant. His eyes rained liquid heat on her as they slid over her tremulous breasts, down her stomach to her waist. He released the slender belt and slowly unbuttoned and unzipped the flannel slacks she had worn for Chrissy's visit. Putting his hands inside them on either side of her hips, he lowered them down her legs until she could step out of them.

"I already knew your legs were beautiful," he whispered playfully as he straightened. Hooking his thumbs in the elastic of her panties, he started to pull them down. He felt her tense suddenly and immediately withdrew his hands. "Did I do something wrong?"

"No, it's just . . ." Embarrassed by her sudden attack of virginal modesty, she sought to make amends by laying her hands on his chest and unbuttoning his shirt. His chest hair looked fuzzy in the soft light and she longed to rub her face in it but didn't quite have the courage. He stood still and let her examine him. His nipples were dark and flat. Inquisitively she touched one with the tip of her finger and it distended. His breath hissed through his teeth. Was that good or bad? She never remembered touching Jim there.

I'm no good at this, she thought dismally. *He won't like me. I don't know the right things to do.* She and Jim had been married so long ago. Now she felt ignorant and callow and distressed.

Sensing it, Pierce lay comforting hands on her shoulders. "Why don't you lie down."

She turned toward the bed and folded back the covers while he took off the rest of his clothes. She lay down, refusing to look at him, though she could see from the corner of her eye that he was naked. He approached the bed and knelt on it with one knee.

"Alicia?" he asked softly. He bent down and took one of her hands and laid it high on his thigh. She squeezed her eyes shut and her chest heaved with fear. He rubbed the back of her hand with his palm. "Do you want to stop? Tell me."

The concern in his tone compelled her to look at him. She saw his sleek nakedness, the intriguing dusting of body hair, the corded muscles, the toasty skin, the masculine strength.

But stronger than his desire, than his body, was his character. Even now, he was willing to let her call it off. An emotion feeling very much like love welled in her throat. She remembered his talking with her boys, making them sit still with rapt attention, making them squeal with laughter. She remembered the times she had caught him looking at her with tenderness, a yearning that surpassed sexual desire. Despite what he had said about himself, he was kind and caring and she wanted to experience this man.

Slowly her fingers curved around the outside of his thigh and she moved her hand in a light caress. "No, I don't want to stop."

Without haste, he lay down beside her and gathered

her beneath him. He held her for a long time before he kissed her. When he did, his lips honored hers softly and she relaxed against him. Sliding his hands down her torso, he removed her panties, taking care to go slow, not to frighten her.

His eyes took in her nakedness and she lay submissive beneath them. When he looked again into her eyes, his were shining with pleasure and his smile was a silent endearment. He caressed her earnestly, unhurriedly, delaying the supreme gratification by heightening the anticipation. Her body hummed and purred beneath his hands and lips.

He watched his hands as they smoothed over her skin, visually enhancing his pleasure in her. Alicia marveled that she wasn't burning with embarrassment. Rather, her own arousal was embellished by watching his every move, meeting his eyes with a lover's gaze.

With a soft touch he parted her thighs and acquainted himself with her mystery. Alicia felt like a rare treasure being discovered by someone who could appreciate her rarity. She was malleable and moist to his seeking fingertips and he murmured his approval as he moved above her. Alicia felt his passion, hard, so hard. It rubbed against the nest of tawny hair between her thighs. His lips were softly urgent against her breasts, on her nipples.

He made no lunging, thrusting motions, but suddenly she felt his intrusion and arched against that sublime, invading pressure. He filled her competently, completely, and the pleasure of his possession went on and on, rippling over her like trickles of sensation from a magic waterfall.

"Oh God, it's good," he whispered in her ear. "So good, Alicia."

"Pierce." Softly she cried his name as he began to stroke her with shallow thrusts that gradually deepened. Frantically, her hands groped along his shoulders. Her body bowed and bucked. Had she just forgotten or had it ever felt like this before?

"Shhh," he said quietly without breaking that tantalizing rhythm. "We're in no hurry. This isn't a contest. Relax. Just let it happen, darling. Feel me love you. Just feel."

That's all she could do. Her insides coiled tighter and tighter as he reached higher and higher inside her to touch the very gate of her womanhood. She didn't want to make a fool of herself or do anything she'd be ashamed of later, but when she felt herself quicken and knew that she was about to be swept away on a tidal wave of emotion, her limbs curled around him and she burrowed her face in his chest. "Pierce!" she called as her world exploded into dazzling fragments.

From far away she heard his own soft cries and they were all her name. And they were exultant and . . . sad.

Chapter Five

He twined golden strands of hair around his fingers and tried to count the jeweled facets in her eyes. He kissed the plump curve of her breast, nuzzled it. "You're so sweet." The words vaporized damply on her skin.

"Am I?"

"Very, very, very." He punctuated the confirmation with tiny kisses on her throat. Shifting his weight, he resettled them against the pillows. "How long since Jim died?"

"Three years."

"You've been three years without a lover?"

"What makes you say that?" Had she been that unpracticed and awkward? Her body strained away from his.

He smiled affectionately and drew her back close beside him. "I could tell, but it's certainly nothing to be defensive about." His lips wandered along her hairline and his hand seesawed in the deep valley of her waist between ribs and hip. "It's a nice thing to know."

His saying that pleased her and she snuggled closer. "There was one," she confessed quietly.

"Carter."

She laid her hand on his chest and let her fingers idly strum through the crinkly forest of hair. Smiling privately, she hoped that the trace of jealousy in his voice wasn't a product of her imagination. "No, not Carter."

"Not Carter?"

She shook her head. "I told you my relationship with Carter wasn't like that. If we had ever made love, even if we had been married, I think we would have felt like we were betraying Jim. Carter and I were too good friends to be lovers."

"Then there was someone else?"

"He wasn't a 'someone.' He was one night, that's all. He was very nice, but it meant nothing beyond waking me up to the fact that I wasn't dead even though Jim was. And that I was being unfair to myself by taking the first man available to me. Not to mention how unfair it was to Carter."

For long moments Pierce lay quietly. His hands were no longer adoringly caressing her. He barely breathed. Had she been wrong to tell him about that night in Tahoe?

"You lied to me, Alicia."

Startled, she propped herself up and peered down into his shadowed face. "Lied?"

He wrapped his hand around the back of her neck and massaged it lovingly. Her hair was a magnet that attracted every ray of light as it tumbled around his hand and arm, down onto his chest. "You lied when you said tonight wouldn't have any special significance." Knotting handfuls of hair in his fingers, he pulled her face down for his kiss. It was an infinitely tender one. "For you this is more than just sex, isn't it? It means something?"

He watched her eyelids lower, watched the diamond-like tears form on the thick row of lashes, watched as she once again lifted those swimming eyes to his. "Yes. It does," she said hoarsely. "It would have to or I wouldn't be here."

"Alicia." He encircled her waist with his arm and pulled her atop him. The soft weight of her breasts was cushioned against his chest. The slender columns of her thighs aligned to his. This time the kiss wasn't so tender. Every measure of passion he gave, she returned.

Her lips were throbbing and moist when at last they were released. Pierce's, too, were damp. She ran her finger along his lower lip, taking up the moisture, loving the feel of his mouth, loving the taste of herself that lingered on it. "Were you lying, too, Pierce?"

He pressed her head into the hollow of his shoulder. His eyes closed against the exquisite pleasure of holding her nakedness against his. His hands smoothed down the satiny length of her back and over the firm roundness of her derrière. He stroked the backs of her thighs and when he heard that rattling sigh in her throat, he knew that he would make love to her again. Again. And again.

"Yes. To you and to myself, I was lying."

Just before dawn Alicia left Pierce sleeping, gathered her scattered clothes, made a brief stop in the bathroom, and crept upstairs. She slipped on her nightgown and managed to get into bed with Adam without waking him. She felt ridiculous, sneaking into bed like a teenager who had come home too late, but morality was hard enough to teach children these days. If she were ambiguous about last night, how would her boys have taken her sleeping with Pierce?

It seemed that she had only just fallen asleep when she heard them begin to stir. Whispering, they went downstairs. Moments later she heard the commode flush. Then she heard Pierce's low, "Hey, are you two already up? Is your mother still sleeping?"

She would have to get up and face them all sooner or later, but she stayed beneath the light covers dreading that time. What was Pierce thinking of her now? What did she think of herself? Why one minute was she breathless and giddy over what had happened between them last night, and the next minute scaldingly ashamed of it?

Nothing in her adult life had prepared her for sharing a bed with Pierce. There wasn't an inch of her body that he hadn't explored thoroughly and didn't now know intimately. Jim had been a sweet, earnest lover, but their bed had been modest and immature compared to the sheer ecstasy of Pierce's.

His lovemaking utilized his whole body, not just his hands and lips and sex, but his skin and hair and all five senses, his heart, and his mind. Perhaps it had been his total concentration on her that made her feel that no woman in history had ever been so loved.

Recollections of all that she'd done, all that had been done to her, made her blush like a maiden aunt. People who knew her well would be shocked by her wanton behavior and boundless responses. Her parents, her friends, Sloan and Carter. Well, maybe not Sloan and Carter, she thought with a smile, remembering the sexual passages in Carter's recent books.

But that was them and this was her. A new her. One she had only met. The old Alicia Russell was delighted, and horrified, and intrigued by the woman in her who had emerged last night.

She had put it off long enough. Breakfast was already in full swing downstairs. It was time she joined them. She pulled on a velour sweat suit, ran a brush through her hair, and timorously approached the steep stairwell.

Adam spotted her first. "Hi, Mom. Did I kick you last night?" He turned to Pierce. "Every time I sleep with her she says I kick."

"I didn't notice it last night." She didn't quite look at Pierce, who was leaning against the drainboard sipping coffee. Her nervous eyes merely glanced over him. He had pulled on a pair of jeans, but his chest and feet were bare. Her heart picked up its tempo and her stomach did a cartwheel. She knew the texture of his skin, knew how his body hair felt against her palms and cheeks and lips.

"Good morning, David."

"Hi. Your face is red."

"It is?" Alicia clapped her hands up to her burning cheeks. Her hands were icy.

"Why is your face red, Mom?" Adam asked around a slurpy spoonful of cereal.

"I—I don't know."

"You're sure acting funny," David commented. "Pass the jam, please."

Alicia lunged for the jar of grape jam, wishing she could clout her son on the head with it. It took a long, awkward moment before she had enough gumption to look at Pierce.

"Coffee?" he said softly.

And that was enough. His eyes, his mellow expression, the confidential inflection, let her know that everything was all right. Tension ebbed out of her like the remnants of a wave receding from shore. "Please."

He poured coffee for her and she took a seat at the table before her jellied knees gave way. The snap of his jeans rode an inch below his navel. The spot mesmerized her. Had her tongue actually been there, investigating in the dark? She ached with the need to touch him, to give him a good morning kiss that said thank you for a wonderful night—it was thrilling; I've never felt so feminine and desired.

"Would you like some breakfast?"

"Maybe just toast. I'm not very hungry."

"Neither am I."

For a moment that stretched out noticeably long, they stared at each other, transmitting a thousand and one silent, private messages. Eventually David asked Alicia a question and she roused herself enough to answer him. Pierce brought a plate of toast to the table and sat down across from her.

"You look pretty in that color of lavender."

The sweat suit was too nice to actually sweat in. "Thank you."

"Sleep well?"

His mouth was so beautiful. "Yes. You?"

"Dreams kept me from sleeping too soundly."

And that mouth had made her feel very beautiful. "I'm sorry."

He remembered all the times and all the places he had kissed her and his eyes dilated. "I didn't mind. They were good dreams."

"We're just like the people on the box, Mom."

Alicia dragged her eyes away from Pierce's and looked down at Adam. "I beg your pardon," she said vaguely.

"See." He pointed to the bright picture on the cereal box. "They're all sitting around the table eating breakfast. The two boys, that's me and David, and the mom and dad."

"That's not like us, stupid," David said. "Pierce can't be our dad. He would have to marry Mom first."

Adam's bottom lip stuck out belligerently. "Yeah, but then it'd be the same, wouldn't it, Mom?"

She didn't answer. She was too alarmed by the sudden paling of Pierce's face and the sexy cloudiness in his eyes being frozen out by hard, cold, brittle light. "Sort of the same. And, David, please don't call your brother stupid," she said distractedly. Her heart, which had been dancing joyously, now felt heavy. It was trying to sink into a vat of despair and she was holding on to it for dear life. "Why don't you two go outside and play if you're done?"

They were glad to be excused and headed for the door. "It'd be neat if Pierce was our dad, wouldn't it, David?"

"Yeah, we'd be just like the other kids and Chrissy could come see us and we could ride in the Porsche again."

"Gee. Would she be our sister or our aunt?"

"Our sister. Don't you know *anything*?"

"She sure is old to be a sister."

The screen door slammed behind them. Its loud banging only emphasized the ominous silence in the cabin.

Pierce set down his coffee mug. He did so with great care as though if he didn't, he would likely hurl it and its contents against the nearest wall. Sightlessly he stared into the cup. His jaw was as rigid as iron. In his temple, a vein ticked with pulsing blood. He swept his hair back with a raking gesture of tense fingers and then clenched them into a tight fist.

The transformation terrified Alicia. Not because she was afraid of him, but because she suspected what such a metamorphosis meant. "They're just little boys, Pierce." She couldn't help the pleading sound in her voice. "They don't realize the implications of what they said. They just know that our family isn't complete and the fact that they don't have a father bothers them. Please don't attach any special significance to what they said."

His smile was mirthless, frosty. "That sounds vaguely reminiscent of what we said to each other last night. But it *did* have 'special significance,' didn't it, Alicia?"

"I thought we'd already established that it did." She plucked at a loose thread. "Is that any reason to get angry?"

"Dammit, yes!" he shouted, vaulting out of the chair. Luckily the boys were yelling loudly at a squirrel and didn't hear him. Alicia did, however, and winced at his level of rage. "Yes, I'm angry."

"Why?" She recovered quickly. After last night, wasn't she entitled to know what his hang-ups were? "How can you get angry over a five-year-old boy mentioning marriage?"

"I'm not angry at Adam. My God, Alicia, give me some credit," he snapped. "I'm angry because last night was so damn good, because you are a woman I could fall very deeply in love with, because I want to be a father to your boys and make up for the mess I made of it the first time."

She gazed around her, waving her hands helplessly. "I don't understand you. Why is any of that bad?"

He grabbed her shoulders and shook her slightly. "Because none of it can happen." Each word was driven out of his mouth, holding on tenaciously, reluctant to be uttered.

He released her suddenly and she reeled. He turned his back and went to stare out the window, watching Adam and David as they picked up kindling wood and stacked it on top of the logs he had piled against the cabin the day before. He closed his eyes to the poignant sight and only wished he could close his ears to their conversation.

"This is the way Pierce taught us to do it."

"How come he knows so much stuff, David?"

"Because he's old, like a dad. Dads know lots of stuff."

"Do you think he'll be proud if we stack all this up?"

"Sure. He's always proud of us. Remember? He said so."

Alicia willed him to turn around and explain himself. When he didn't, she took the initiative. She was pushing and she knew it, but she wasn't about to leave him never knowing or understanding. "Why can't it happen?"

"Believe me, it can't."

"Why?"

"Drop it, please."

"Is there another woman?"

He turned toward her. His eyes swept her body and there was no disguising the desire that was still smoldering in them. "I wish it were that simple. To live with you, sleep with you every night, I'd give up any other woman I've ever met."

A small moan escaped her. "Then what is it, Pierce? Tell me."

"No."

"Why?"

"Because you're better off not knowing."

"Who made you the judge of that? After the intimacy we shared last night, can't we talk to each other openly and freely about anything?"

"Not about this."

"How could we possibly harbor secrets from each other after the way we've loved?"

"I didn't let myself think about it last night. This morning I *have* to think about it."

She laid her hands on her stomach, splayed wide. "I'm still carrying a living part of you inside me. But you can't confide in me? There's no logic in that."

The character lines were ironed out of his face as the skin stretched tightly across it. He stared at her hands where they pressed against her lower body. "My God," he strangled out. "You're on the pill, aren't you?"

"No."

His expletive was vicious and to the point. "Why didn't you tell me?"

"I don't recall your asking," she shot back. Her whole body was bristling with anger now. He had staggered away from her, but she reached for his arm and spun him around. "Don't worry, Mr. Reynolds. I'd never come begging after you with a baby on my arm."

"It's not that," he snarled. "I don't want to leave you pregnant, that's all."

"Leave me? This is it, then?"

He drew in a deep sigh and his eyes softened considerably. "Yes. You knew that before you ever consented to stay the week here."

Yes. He had been honest about that. "I can't get involved," he had said. He had repeated it last night. She knew it, but she had ignored it. Their loving had been special, not just an exchange of flesh, but apparently Pierce Reynolds was stubbornly clinging to his reasons for not getting involved.

All right. To hell with him.

To save what scraps of pride she had left, she turned away from him and began to clear the table. Pierce went into the living room and finished dressing. When the dishes had been washed and neatly stacked—never let it be said that she and the boys had taken advantage of his hospitality—she went to him.

"I'm going back to L.A. this afternoon. It's a day earlier than I'd planned, but under the circumstances I think that's best." He was sitting on the couch, his hands folded between his widespread knees, staring at the floor. "Pierce?" she said impatiently when he didn't respond. His head came up. He looked at her and nodded tersely.

On the verge of tears, she fled upstairs and began throwing things into their suitcases.

Pierce stared after the car until it disappeared into the trees. The engulfing silence was cacophonous and hurt his ears.

Go after them, you idiot. You damned fool. How could he let them leave? He wanted the woman. He wanted the boys.

He didn't move because he knew he couldn't. In the long run it wouldn't be fair to any of them. He'd lived in a vacuum for almost a week. He'd remain there until he knew the answer one way or another. And either way it came out, he couldn't chance involving them.

He cursed his luck, cursed his life, and slammed the cabin door behind him as he entered its gloomy interior. He couldn't abide its shrouding depression. Shadows and sounds stalked him as he ranted through the small house. It would drive him mad to stay. He'd return to Los Angeles, too, just as soon as he could pack.

"It's your fault," David accused from the back seat. "He liked Adam and me but you made him mad. That's why we had to leave."

"We were going to leave tomorrow anyway." David and Adam were acting as though the Wicked Witch of the West was an angel compared to their mother. They had cried and whined and argued ever since she had virtually shoved them into the car and headed for home.

"Yeah, but tomorrow, not today."

"I didn't want to leave today either, David."

"Then why did we?"

Oh God, she was tired of his harping on her. She craved peace, silence, solitude. She didn't want to make explanations because she had no explanations herself. Why couldn't she just go away someplace to lick her wounds, remember, savor, analyze, agonize? "Pierce wanted us to leave."

"Maybe he wanted you to, but he didn't want us to. He liked us."

"All right! That does it!" She drove the car off the highway and braked it to a teeth-jarring stop on the shoulder. Her face fierce with anger, she whirled around to face the boys. "I'm the bad guy. Okay, I've admitted it. Now shut up about Pierce and the cabin and the whole week. Got it? I don't want to hear any more about it."

Four eyes had gone wide and round with apprehension. Rarely did she lose her temper with them to that extent. "Say, 'Yes, ma'am,' " she instructed.

They responded tearfully, fearfully, their eyes watery and their lips wobbly. Her shoulders sagged. Everything inside her sagged. "Thank you."

She pulled back onto the highway and when she looked around several minutes later, both boys were asleep. David had a protective and comforting arm around Adam. Adam's thumb was in his mouth, something he hadn't done in a long time.

Alicia felt wretched for yelling at them, but her nerves were shot, her heart was broken, and she, more than anyone, felt like crying. Hours of hard sobbing sounded like a supreme luxury. She wanted to wallow in self-pity.

Why was she so unlucky in love? When would she learn to use some common sense, to practice caution, to beware? When would she grow up and stop being so gullible? Would she ever look beyond the surface of things? Why did she waltz blindly and foolishly into hopeless situations? Why had she had to fall in love with a man who wanted to race sports cars and get himself killed? Why had she thought herself in love with a man who liked, but obviously didn't love, her? Why now had she fallen in love—

The car nearly swerved off the road.

Had she fallen in love with Pierce?

Tears trekked from the corners of her eyes and rolled down her cheeks. Her bottom lip was pinched by bruising teeth. Her breasts heaved painfully.

Yes, she had. She was in love with Pierce. And a helluva lot of good it was going to do her.

• • •

"Good morning," Alicia greeted the saleswoman the following Monday morning as she pushed open the glass door and entered Glad Rags.

"Alicia! Hi. Have you heard the news since you got back?"

"I guess not. What news?"

"Gwen had her baby last Thursday night."

"Oh?" Alicia walked to the back of the shop, her footsteps soundless on the lush baby blue carpet. She hung her purse and jacket in the crowded employees' closet. The saleswoman followed her.

"It was almost a month early, but weighed over six pounds. A little girl."

"How wonderful. How's Gwen?"

"Fine. Came through it like a charm."

"Good. I need to call her about the work that was done on her cabin."

"Can I get you some coffee?"

Alicia looked at her quizzically. "Awfully solicitous, aren't you? Is there something you're not telling me? Have I been fired in my absence?"

"Hardly." The woman lowered her voice. "The powers-that-be are in a meeting and asked me to send you in when you arrived. I think they want your decision today, Alicia."

"Hmm." Alicia accepted the coffee and took a sip. She hadn't expected it to come so soon, but she knew now what her answer would be. "Well, to the trenches."

She winked at her cohort, checked out her appearance in the hall mirror, and took the stairs to the chain's executive offices on the second floor.

"Hello, Alicia, they're expecting you. Go right in," the owners' secretary said with all the cordiality of an undertaker.

"Thank you."

Summoning all her poise, Alicia opened the heavy oak door and entered the inner sanctum. She was greeted by a cloud of cigar smoke and hearty hellos.

After being politely seated, offered coffee, and queried about her week of vacation, they put the important question to her.

She had almost blown it again. She had almost let herself slip into that old habit of dependency on someone else for her happiness. She had two wonderful sons, two healthy legs to stand on, a keen mind, and creative ideas. After several hours of hard weeping, more hours of cursing and stomping, and two days of soul-searching, she had decided she didn't need Pierce Reynolds. She didn't need anything except her own ingenuity.

"My time and talents are expensive," she told them bluntly. "I want five hundred dollars a month more than you offered."

They conferred and met her terms.

"Well, sirs, you have yourself a new Fashion Coordinator. Shall I outline some of my ideas?"

Her smiling enthusiasm captivated them.

• • •

"I love it," she said, knocking on the plate glass window. The window dresser turned around and gave her the thumbs-up sign. She pushed through the door.

"Thanks for the idea. I think it looks terrific."

"It does," she said, glad that her idea of featuring belts in the window had sparked such a creative response in him.

"You look terrific too."

Because of her promotion and the hefty increase in salary she had splurged on the outfit. The skirt was a long swirl of lightweight ivory wool. The blouse she wore with it was teal silk. She had slung a fringed paisley print shawl over one shoulder and belted it at her waist with one of the designer belts she was featuring in the window. Pale stockings and bone pumps completed the businesslike, but softly feminine, ensemble.

She curtsied. "From our Beverly Hills store."

He whistled long and low. "Wrap them up. I'll take a dozen. If the girl comes with them, that is."

She tilted her head to one side and put her hands on her hips. "What would your boyfriend say?"

He grinned at her. "We're open-minded. He'd be delighted to have a lady like you join us one night."

She laughed and shook her head. "I'm afraid I'm not quite that open-minded."

"I was afraid this was going to happen." He sighed

theatrically. "One week with a new title and she's too prickly to have a good time with us commoners."

Alicia swatted a hand at him and went to answer the ringing telephone. She could see that the two saleswomen were with customers.

"Glad Rags."

"Is Mrs. Alicia Russell there, please?"

"This is Alicia Russell."

"Mrs. Russell, this is Westbrook Clinic calling. We have your son here."

All the air rushed out of her body at once and she slumped against the counter. "My son? At the hospital?"

"David. He had an accident at school. The principal brought him in."

"Is he—"

"He's fine, but he's crying for you. Can you come right away? I'm afraid we need you to sign—"

"Oh God, yes. I'm on my way."

She slammed the phone down and, picking up her purse again, raced for the door. "David's been taken to the hospital," she called over her shoulder to the saleswoman who had noticed the nature of the call and was standing nearby. "I'll probably be gone the rest of the day."

"Is it serious? Do you want someone with you?"

"I don't think so. I don't know. No. I don't want anybody with me."

The California sunshine struck her eyes like a laser,

but she didn't take time to put on her sunglasses. Her hands were shaking uncontrollably as she tried to unlock the door of her car. Traffic was snarled on the avenues and sluggish on the freeways. Her eyes were tearless, but her throat was clogged with the need to cry.

Was it a broken bone? A scratch? What? Why hadn't she asked? Was he bleeding? And where the hell was Westbrook Clinic? Oh, yes, on Montgomery Street near the boys' school. Thirty minutes from here.

When at last the clinic came into sight, she screeched the car to a stop and dashed for the entrance. Automatic doors slid open and she ran through them. "David Russell," she said breathlessly to the nurse behind the reception desk.

"Are you Mrs. Russell?"

"Yes, how is he? I got here as quickly as I could." She could easily have slapped the nurse for her cool, calm efficiency and the slightly reproachful curl of her thin lips.

"He's in treatment room five down this corridor. I'll bring the papers in for you to sign before we can treat him."

She wanted to ask if they'd let a child die because some damned form hadn't been signed, but she didn't want to waste her breath or her time. She ran down the corridor, her heels striking hollow thuds that matched her heartbeats.

She heard his whimpers of pain even before she

reached the door and pushed it open. The first sight that greeted her was a blood-saturated towel lying on the floor. Nausea gushed to her throat. "David?" A man was bending over him. He straightened and turned around. It was Pierce.

CHAPTER SIX

What are you doing here?"

"David had them call me."

"Mommy?"

The pitiful, frightened cry superseded her shock over seeing Pierce. Rushing to the side of the examination table, she looked down at her son and barely stifled a gasp. His right eye was almost swollen shut. An inch-long gash had been cut from the middle of his eyebrow to well past the outer corner. It had stopped bleeding, but the raw flesh lay open . . . obscenely open.

"David, baby, what happened? Oh, Lord! Are you in pain?"

"It hurts, Mommy." Blindly he groped for her, catching a fistful of her shawl.

"I know, I know it hurts, sweetheart." Frantically she looked up at Pierce. "Have they done anything for him? What about his eye?"

He shook his head. "They wouldn't let me sign the

permission for treatment. He can see out of his eye. I already tested him on it."

"Thank God," she breathed as she gripped David's hand. "We're going to get you fixed up. I promise."

"Don't leave me, Mommy," he cried when she began to draw her hand from his.

"I'm not going to leave you. I'm only going to get the doctor."

Just then the nurse swished in crisply. "Mrs. Russell, if you'll please sign this form and give me the name of your insurance company and your policy number, I can give David a shot to relieve his pain."

"I don't want a shot," David screamed and began to cry.

"Hey, hey, what was that promise we made each other about being brave? Hmm?" Pierce lay a consoling hand on the boy's shoulder and bent over him.

Alicia fumbled in her handbag for her wallet, where she kept her insurance cards. When the forms had been properly filled out, the nurse prepared a syringe with a mild sedative. "It won't hurt so bad in his hip."

Alicia and Pierce, working together, got David's belt unbuckled, turned him over, and lowered his jeans. He was crying copiously. Alicia's heart was wrenching.

"Now we'll let that take effect while we wait for Dr. Benedict," the nurse said.

"What do you mean wait?" Alicia demanded heatedly. "I want my son seen to immediately. What's wrong with you people?"

"Alicia, I took the liberty of calling Frank Benedict," Pierce said calmly. "He's a plastic surgeon, a friend of mine. I thought you might want a plastic surgeon to suture David since the cut is in such a visible place on his face."

"Oh," she said in a small voice. "Of course. I probably would have done that myself. Thank you, Pierce."

The nurse looked at her smugly as she went out the door. No doubt she had assessed Alicia as an unfit mother who couldn't be found when her son was injured. She had assumed Pierce was her lover.

Wasn't he?

The staff doctor, looking alarmingly young and breezy, bustled through the door. He was wearing jeans and jogging shoes with his laboratory coat. "Hi. Which one of you is David? No, let me guess. You," he said, pointing to the boy, "the one with the busted eye. What did you run into, buddy?" He coaxed a shaky smile from the patient.

In a nonchalant and what seemed to Alicia unsympathetic-to-pain manner, he swabbed the cut with antiseptic. When his fingers separated the lips of the wound and she saw the depth of it, nausea surged burningly into her throat again and she slumped against the wall. Strobe lights went off behind her eyelids. Had it not been for a pair of strong arms suddenly supporting her, she would have collapsed to the floor when her knees gave way to rubbery weakness.

"Hang in there. David's going to be all right."

God, his voice sounded wonderful. How had she lived for a whole week without hearing it? His hands felt good, strong, sure, safe. She leaned against him. His body was warm, tough, and solid, able to ward off the worst of nightmares. She allowed herself only a precious moment of actually touching him, then she straightened.

"David had you notified?" she asked, tilting her head up to look at him.

He nodded. "When you couldn't be located, he gave them my name and the name of the company."

"I must have been in transit between stores."

"Don't blame yourself. You can't be expected to sit by a telephone all day long. As soon as I spoke with the principal of the school and he told me what had happened, I rushed right over."

"Thank you. I'm sorry."

"Sorry?" He frowned. "For what?"

"For your being . . . called, involved in this."

He scowled and looked away from her for a moment. She could almost hear him mentally swearing. When his eyes came back to her they were seething with anger.

Taking the coward's way out, she avoided the issue. "I—I still don't know what happened."

"It was just after recess. The kids were being rowdy. Someone slung open the classroom door and David caught it with his eye."

She covered her mouth with her hand. Her fingers were cold, unworkable, stiff. They were clasped and warmly chafed. Pierce rubbed heat and life back into them. "He'll be fine. I know it," he whispered. His flare of temper had disappeared as quickly as it had come.

"Naw, the Cowboys don't stand a chance against the Rams' defensive line," the doctor was saying to David.

"They're pretty good."

The doctor snorted derisively. "Not a chance. I'd lay money on it. There, all done. Clean as a whistle. That fancy stitchin' doc will have you lookin' good in no time."

He sailed out and they were left alone.

Alicia leaned over David and brushed back strands of his hair from the pale, clammy forehead. How vulnerable he looked lying on that sterile table. She hated it.

The shot was taking effect and he was drowsy. "Mommy, I got blood on Miss Thompkins's blouse. Do you think she's gonna be mad at me?"

Tears trickled down Alicia's cheeks, but she smiled. "I don't think so. If she is, I'll buy her a new one."

"I'm sorry you had to leave work."

"No job is as important to me as you are."

"Is this the first time I've been in the hospital?"

"Except for when you were born."

"Daddy was there then."

"Yes, he was."

"I'm glad Pierce is here this time. Aren't you, Mommy?"

Alicia's eyes sought out his. He was holding David's hand and rubbing the knuckles with his thumb. He lifted his head and looked at her across the table and she knew how much she had been missed. His eyes told her so.

"Yes, I'm very glad Pierce is here."

The door was pushed open. "Pierce?"

"Hi, Frank." The two men shook hands. "This is Alicia Russell and her son David, friends of mine."

"Hello," the doctor said cordially. He was a man about Pierce's age, shorter, balding, and paunchy.

"David had an altercation with a door and the door won."

Dr. Benedict peered down at David's eye. Now that the banalities were out of the way, he was all business. "I'll say it did." He patted the boy on the knee. "I'm going to give that cut some medicine to put it to sleep."

"Shots?" David asked tremulously.

"Little tiny ones that you won't even feel. Then I'm going to sew you up with a needle and thread. Do you know what silk is?"

"Like Mommy's blouses?"

"Yeah. Only the thread I'll use is even softer than her blouses."

"Gee."

The doctor began rolling up his shirtsleeves to wash his hands. He turned to Alicia and Pierce, who had moved aside while he was examining David. "Why don't you wait outside?"

"But—" Alicia began to protest.

"It'll be easier, Mrs. Russell, I assure you. Wait outside."

She looked imploringly at Pierce, but he nodded agreement with the doctor. She took David's hand and squeezed it. "When I see you again, it'll all be over." She kissed his forehead and let herself be led out the door as the nurse came through carrying a tray of medical implements.

"Will he be okay?" Her question was as anxious as the hand clutching his sleeve.

"Frank's great with kids. He has four of his own."

"David looked so little, so helpless, lying there."

"I know. It scared the hell out of me too when I first saw him."

They heard David cry out sharply and then sob painfully.

Alicia rushed toward the door, but Pierce detained her with a steady arm across her shoulder. "It's all right. He's okay. You know that." He leaned back against the wall and pulled her into his arms, pressing her head down onto his chest. "Shhh, it's okay," he repeated in comforting whispers. His body absorbed her trembling as she wept.

David wasn't crying any longer. They could hear the doctor talking to him in muted tones. The words were indistinct, but the inflection was lulling.

Alicia's own distress subsided beneath the healing power of Pierce's touch. His fingers sifted through her hair, massaging her scalp. His other hand soothingly rubbed her back. "You look beautiful today. I've never seen you dressed up."

She laughed against his starched shirt front. "I was hardly haute couture at the cabin, was I?"

"I like you both ways."

"Do you?" Her words were barely audible.

"Yes."

"I've never seen you in a jacket and tie either."

"And?"

She raised her head. His was the most perfectly masculine face she had ever seen. Not as handsome as some, not even as classically handsome as her dark and dashing Jim had been, but the features were so arrestingly arranged; the man was so sensuously appealing. Even dressed for business as he was, his hair was still styled casually. His face bore the marks of the wind and rain and sun from his week in the woods. His cologne was painfully familiar and stabbed her lungs with memories each time she inhaled.

She wanted to tell him that she didn't care how he was dressed, he always looked good to her. She wanted to say that she was so glad to see *him*, she had barely noticed what he was wearing.

But she didn't say anything because she didn't know what his being here might mean and because she was worried about her son. So rather than having to think up something appropriate to say, she simply settled against him again and basked in the feel of his arms around her.

For right now, she needed him and he was here. It might turn out to be a foolish indulgence, but she wasn't going to deny herself his comforting.

Twenty minutes later, the nurse summoned them at Dr. Benedict's request. "His eye is fine," he said to Alicia immediately as she entered the treatment room. She flew to David's side and took his hand. His right eye was covered by a white gauze bandage. "If he complains of blurred vision or anything out of the ordinary, you should have an ophthalmologist check it, but I don't anticipate any trouble. I don't think he'll have much of a scar, but we'll monitor the healing process closely."

"Hi, Mom. Can I wear the bandage to school tomorrow?"

Dr. Benedict laughed. "Let's give it a few days, David, until the swelling goes down."

"How many stitches did you say I got?"

"Only seven on the outside, but a whole lot more underneath. You be sure and tell the other kids that."

"Okay!" David beamed.

The doctor went over treatment of the incision with Alicia and gave her a prescription for an antibiotic. "Thanks, Frank, for coming so soon," Pierce said.

"No problem. You'll get my bill," he said jovially.

"No. Send the bill to me," Alicia said. Both men looked at her, stunned. She hadn't intended her words to sound so emphatic and waspish, but that's the way they had come out.

"Yes, well, of course," the doctor blustered. "Good-bye, David. I'll see you in a week to take out the stitches. Call the office for an appointment," he said to Alicia.

"I will. Thank you." She was embarrassed and wondered what the doctor thought her relationship with Pierce was. What *was* her relationship with Pierce?

David insisted on walking, though Pierce offered to carry him to the car. He was woozier than he thought and they supported him between them until they reached the parking lot.

"Pierce, thank you so much for coming—"

"I'm driving you home."

"That isn't necessary."

He gnawed on his bottom lip in vexation. "Here, David, get in and lie down." He opened the back door of her car and helped the boy in. Then he shut the door and, turning, stormed toward Alicia, grabbed her arm, and dragged her out of hearing distance.

"Will you stop being so damned defensive? Frank was making a joke about his bill."

"I know that," she said, freeing her arm with a vicious tug. "I spouted off before I realized it. I'm sorry if I embarrassed you in front of your friend. But I didn't want him to think that I was . . . was . . ."

"Well?" he demanded impatiently. "What didn't you want him to think?"

"That I was a kept woman who depended on you to pay my bills. A mistress."

"Oh, come on," he cried. "What history book did you dredge up that word from?"

"You know what I mean."

"Yes, I know what you mean." He ran his hand through his hair. "You can't stop people from jumping to conclusions, so don't worry about what they think. We know we're not involved that way."

"That's right. We do," she said furiously. "God knows I've heard it often enough from you. So what are you doing here? Do you blame me for being defensive? You with your sexy bedroom eyes across the breakfast table one minute and your accusations that I might trap you by getting pregnant the next."

"I never made any such accusation," he growled.

"Didn't you?"

"I was concerned for you, not for me."

"I think I heard that line on a soap opera once."

"It's the truth."

"So that's what this is about? *Concern* for the little widow and her two children?"

"Yes. Partially."

"You rushed over here today, disrupted my life again out of human compassion, benevolence, Christian charity?"

"Whatever you want to call it."

She wanted to call it love, but didn't have the nerve. She wanted to fling the word in his face just to see how he would react. Instead they stared at each other across the space that separated them, breathing heavily, each feeling a little ridiculous about this argument taking place in a public parking lot.

Finally Pierce stepped forward and curled his fingers around her upper arm. She knew it would be useless to try to free herself this time. "You're in no condition to drive. I'm taking you and David home and you can read whatever you like into it."

She surrendered because she didn't feel like fighting with him anymore. But mostly because, for whatever his reasons, she wanted him to come home with her.

Spineless, stupid female, she silently berated herself. But she meekly followed him. He seated her in the passenger side of her car. "What about your car?"

"I'll pick it up later. Let me lock it up."

It was low, foreign, lean, and mean. It was like the cars the long, leggy girls climb out of in pantyhose and perfume commercials, trailing skeins of hair and yards of mink behind them. And it perfectly suited the man. Alicia wondered how many leggy women had climbed out of that car under Pierce's escort. Frank Benedict hadn't seemed surprised to find his friend taking care of a woman. Probably he had seen Pierce in that role many times before.

He slid beneath the steering wheel. "How's the patient?"

"He's fallen asleep."

"Still dopey, I guess. What about Adam?"

Alicia consulted her watch and was dismayed to see how late in the afternoon it was. "He'll already be home with the after-school sitter. I hope David's car pool driver heard what happened to him."

"The principal said he'd take care of it."

That was a worry that hadn't even occurred to Alicia. What had the boys' elementary school principal thought of Pierce when he showed up at the clinic? What had David told him about Pierce? "D-did you meet Mr. Jenkins?"

"Yes." He could read her like a book, or so his wry grin told her. "I told him I was an old friend of the family's."

"Oh."

Adam was suitably and jealously impressed with David's bandage, the plastic hospital wristband with his name written on it, and all the attention his older brother was getting. Once David was changed into pajamas and in bed, Pierce invited Adam to drive with him to the drugstore to pick up David's prescription. That appeased his sense of fair play. When they came back, his arms were full of comic books and small board games.

"Me and Pierce bought them for you," Adam said, dumping the prizes onto the bed.

"And a new video game," Pierce added.

"It's busted," David said dismally.

"Oh?" Pierce squatted down in front of the video unit. "Maybe I can fix it."

Alicia groaned. While he was on the errand, she had telephoned her parents about David's accident and they were on their way over. She had hoped Pierce would be gone by the time they arrived. No such luck. They came to the door with Jim's parents in tow and both sets of grandparents swarmed into the sickroom in time to see Pierce sitting with Adam in the middle of the floor, the entrails of the video equipment strewn around them, and a seemingly recovered David peering over his shoulder and offering advice.

"Such a nice man," Alicia's mother commented with studied indifference. Someone had gone out for fried chicken. After the indoor picnic, Alicia's mother had insisted that she help clean up. Alicia just wanted everybody to go home. Her head was pounding and she imagined her nerves to look like the frazzled ends of overpermed hair.

"Who?"

"Alicia, how many men do you have repairing your television sets and replacing unreachable light bulbs?"

"Oh, Pierce. Yes, he is nice."

"Have you known him long? I'm surprised that David would call him before he'd call us."

She hadn't told her parents about their week in Pierce's cabin. When they had asked about the vacation, she had simply told them that she and the boys had enjoyed a very good time and thanked her lucky stars that David and Adam hadn't been around to fill in the details. Some things a girl, no matter how old, never told her mother. "I haven't known him too long," she replied evasively, "but the boys like him."

"He's older than most of the men you've dated."

"We're not dating. Exactly."

Exactly what were they doing? She couldn't be accused of sleeping with him on their first date. They hadn't had a first date.

By the time the grandparents left and David and Adam were settled for the night, Alicia felt like collapsing in a heap and never getting up. "Here, drink this," Pierce said, handing her a glass.

"What is it?"

"I'm not sure," he said with a twisted smile. "Your supply of spirits is limited, to say the least. I had to search until I found this labelless bottle on the top shelf of the kitchen pantry."

"I think it's the brandy I used to pour over a Christmas fruit cake."

"Drink up." He tilted the glass toward her lips. She sipped and sputtered on the fiery liquor. Pierce set the glass on the coffee table. Laughing softly, he lifted amber droplets from her lips with the tip of his finger. Their eyes locked, his laughter subsided, and they became very still.

He painted her lips with the brandy on the tip of his finger. His eyes dropped to her mouth that waited soft and moist and fragrant with the bouquet of liquor. His tongue tasted it first as it flicked lightly over her lips. "Whatever it is, it's delicious," he whispered.

"Is it?"

"This way it is." His arms closed around her. Her lips needed no persuasion to open beneath his. They did so willingly, sacrificially, and took his tongue deep inside. The kiss was long and thorough, heady with emotion, intoxicating. When they at last surfaced for air, they were both dizzy and clung to each other.

Pierce lay his lips against her ear. "Your bath water is getting cold."

"My what?" Her voice sounded like a cello string that had been plucked and didn't know whether to vibrate or not. She didn't want to move. She wanted to stay molded against him for the rest of her life. "My bath?"

He disengaged them. "While you were saying good-bye to your folks I drew you a hot bath. Come on."

Taking her hand, he led her into her bedroom. She looked around it as though expecting it to have undergone a change since he'd been in it. It was remarkably the same. Her bathroom was steamy from a scented bubble bath in the deep tub.

"That looks heavenly." She sighed.

"Take your time. I'll run interference, answer the phone, that kind of thing. And," he said, laying his finger across lips that had started to speak, "if anyone should call, I'll identify myself as a cousin or brother or something."

"I don't have a brother."

He kissed the tip of her nose. "Take your bath." The door closed behind him.

When she emerged from her bedroom she was wrapped in a blue silk kimono and a haze of sexual excitement. "Any word out of the boys?" she asked softly.

Pierce was sitting on the living room sofa watching television. At the sound of her voice he switched off the set and stood to face her. His eyes went wide with appreciation, then narrow with hunger. "No. I just checked on them. They're both sleeping."

She rustled into the room, trying to act normal, trying to pretend that her thighs weren't melting and her insides weren't churning. With feigned negligence, she pinched a dead leaf off one of her plants. "I like your house," Pierce said, his voice rough.

"Thank you." Stucco walls, Italian tile floors, shutters on the windows. Her house was as it had been since she bought it soon after Jim's death. But suddenly everything around her seemed alien. She felt that the only place she would ever feel at home was in Pierce's arms. The notion was absurd—but stimulating. "I want to do some redecorating, buy new furniture, but I'm going to wait until the boys are older."

"That's probably smart."

They were talking about nothing, playing at conversation, pretending this was a casual encounter between old friends and not an electrically charged rendezvous between lovers.

Pierce was cursing himself. Why was he standing here talking like an idiot when what he wanted to be doing was holding her, caressing her, kissing her? Was she really naked beneath her robe or was that just a depraved hope of his warped mind?

"What about work?" he asked. She was naked. Faintly visible through the soft fabric were the dusky areolas and the sweet impudence of her nipples.

"I called them and said I wouldn't be in tomorrow." He looked rakishly attractive with his shirtsleeves rolled up. His jacket and tie were draped over the back of a chair. Three buttons on his shirt were undone. She wanted to rip the rest open, to see all of his chest and not just that inviting wedge with its forest of soft, crinkly hair.

"I mean about your decision."

"I accepted the job." Her smile was confident, proud, and he smiled with her.

"That's great. Do you like it?"

She tossed back her hair and said a trifle breathlessly, "It's a challenge." His eyes were burning the kimono off her body. She could feel their heat as they toured her. Why didn't he come to her and embrace her? "I've never been so busy. I'm going to New York next spring to buy the fall lines."

"You'll do a good job." God, he wanted her. He needed her.

"I hope so."

"I'm sure of it."

"Thank you for the vote of confidence."

She felt anything but confident. It had been so long since she had entertained a man. How did one go about it? Was he waiting for her to make the first move? Did he think that after their argument of this afternoon she didn't want him? Couldn't he tell that she was dying to be loved? She took a step toward him.

"Would you like some— What's that?" An automobile horn was honking outside.

He took a long time answering. "A cab," he finally stated in a flat, dead tone. "I called for one while you were in the bathroom. I can't stay. I have to go, Alicia."

She glanced at the door, then back at him, disbelief replacing her expectant expression of a moment ago. His eyes pleaded for understanding, but as he watched, her face stiffened into an expressionless mask. "Of course," she said tightly. "Thank you for everything."

"Don't, please."

"Don't what?"

"Don't get angry and make it harder for me to leave than it already is."

She laughed harshly. "I don't know why you find it hard. You've had so much practice at it."

The horn honked imperiously. Pierce jerked open the front door and shouted, "I'll be right there."

"I ain't waitin' for free, mister."

"So start your meter."

He slammed the door closed and advanced into the room. "I must go. If I stay—"

"So go!" she shouted.

"If I stay, I'll make love to you."

"God forbid."

"And I'll spend the night, making love to you all night."

"And you don't want to get involved," she mocked.

"It's impossible."

"I understand."

"You don't."

"Explain it to me then."

"I can't."

"Oh, damn you!" she cried and turned her back on him. Immediately she spun around again, her eyes afire with anger. "Why did you even bother, Pierce? Why didn't you just act like you'd never heard of David Russell when they called from the school? Why did you come home with us? Why any of it, Pierce? *Why?*"

Three long strides brought him to her and he closed hard fingers around her upper arms and pulled her to him. "Because I care. Because I adore your sons and wish like hell they were mine. And because I want you so bad I can't do anything without seeing you, feeling you, tasting—"

An anguished sound was torn from his throat just a heartbeat before his mouth fused with hers. He kissed her fiercely, his tongue plowing deep with undisciplined passion. Her head fell back over the arm supporting her shoulders. His lips only followed to plunder her neck and throat before taking her mouth again.

His hand pushed aside the robe and found her breast.

He kneaded it possessively. Her nipple pearled beneath the finessing of his thumb and they both shuddered under the impact of inundating desire.

His mouth tempered its lust slightly as it continued to ravage her mouth, but sweetly, so sweetly. Her fingers tunneled through his hair. Anger had only given her passion impetus. She was wild with her need for him. All the trauma of the day reared up to become unbridled desire. Her body arched against his, straining for fulfillment. She reached for him. Touched him.

He swore savagely. He prayed. He rubbed himself against her hand. "I want you," he whispered raggedly. "I want you, your mouth, your breasts." The words tripped fervently from his busy lips. He clasped her to him as though he would never let her go and planted his mouth in the hollow of her neck. "Can't you feel how much I want you? Do you think I've forgotten how it feels to be inside you? Do you know what it's doing to me to leave you now?" He cupped his hands around her face and dragged his thumbs over her kiss-swollen lips. "I want you, my darling, but I can't have you."

And with that, he was gone and she was alone.

The days passed in a grueling, hectic routine that should have exhausted her enough to sleep every night through without waking. But Alicia was plagued by insomnia. She was prone to weep every night at bedtime, hugging her pillow to her and wishing for Pierce's strong warmth, his ardent kisses, his erotic caresses.

In the daytime, two emotions warred within her. She was furious with him. She hated him. How dare he do this to her again? It was cruel beyond measure to torment her this way. But he wasn't a cruel man. So what game was he playing? Or was it a game? Would she ever see him again? And that's when the second emotion would set in. That's when a black, fathomless loneliness would enclose her and she was powerless to fight her way out of it.

She could easily murder him for what he had done to her—twice. But on the other hand she was constantly looking over her shoulder in the hope of seeing him.

That's why, when the doorbell rang on the evening of the day David had his stitches taken out, she jumped reflexively and her breath and pulse rate accelerated madly. Was it he? Was he coming by to check on David? Was he coming to beg her forgiveness?

Wetting her lips and combing trembling hands through her hair, she went to the door. She took a deep breath and pulled it open.

"Oh my God, what's happened?" was her startled cry.

CHAPTER SEVEN

Is Daddy here?"

Chrissy Reynolds's eye makeup had bled down her cheeks on what must have been a torrent of tears that wasn't yet checked. Her expensive dinner dress was wilted and wrinkled, her stockings had a run. A well-maintained short hairdo had gone haywire.

"Chrissy, what in the world?" Alicia exclaimed, pulling the girl through the door. Thank heaven the boys were already asleep. They would have been frightened to see Pierce's daughter in such a state. "What's happened to you?" Had she been attacked?

"Daddy's not here?" she wailed.

"No." Alicia led her to the sofa and she sank down on the cushions, burying her face in her hands.

"I thought he might be here. I've been calling his house, but there was no answer. I looked up your number in the phone book at a telephone booth and realized I was so close that I came by rather than calling. I have to see Daddy. Do you know where he is?"

"No, I haven't heard from him in a week. David hurt his eye and—"

"Oh, I'm sorry, Alicia. Daddy told me about that. How is David?"

Pierce had told her? He hadn't called, though he had sent David a different card every day. "He's fine, but what's happened to you?"

Chrissy's snorting laugh lacked humor. She sniffed back tears. "I created a scene at the party tonight. It was held in honor of my fiancé and me. Only he's not my fiancé anymore."

Alicia took Chrissy's hand and said calmly, "Tell me."

The distraught young woman seemed only too glad to have a sympathetic ear. "Oh Alicia, I don't know what happened to me. Just suddenly there were too many false people, wearing too many false smiles, offering us empty wishes with trite phrases. I looked at my fiancé, and wondered what in the hell I was doing there with him then and what I was going to do with him the rest of our lives." She laughed again. "I said, 'Do you love me?' And he stared at me as though I'd lost my mind. I took off my engagement ring, handed it back to him, and made the announcement over the bandleader's microphone that the wedding was off."

Alicia covered her laugh with her hand. "You didn't."

"I did."

"I'm sorry, I don't mean to laugh, but I can just visualize the stir that must have caused."

"I thought Mother was going to have a stroke."

"Wasn't your father there?"

"Earlier, but he had left. That's why I thought he might be here. He didn't have a date tonight and seemed in a hurry to get away. Mother, of course, was furious with him for leaving right after dinner."

Alicia wanted to pursue the reason Pierce didn't have a date. The way Chrissy had said it led her to believe that his behavior tonight was quite a departure from the norm. She, too, wondered where he was at this hour. Maybe he had a late date with a woman unsuitable to attend his daughter's engagement party. The thought gave her such pain that she thrust it aside.

"What are you going to do?" she asked Chrissy.

Heaving a sigh, Chrissy reclined against the cushions of the sofa and let her head drop. "Beyond the moment, I don't know."

"Well then, let's concentrate on the moment," Alicia said cheerfully. "I don't think you need to be driving around the streets of Los Angeles this late at night as upset as you are. Why don't you take a hot bath and spend the night here?"

"I couldn't impose on you that way."

Alicia could tell that, despite her protest, the idea appealed to Chrissy. She looked emotionally and physically exhausted. "It's not an imposition. The boys will be thrilled to find you here in the morning."

Chrissy smiled, but then she groaned. "I can't stay, Alicia. Mother will have the FBI out looking for me.

She'll call Daddy and get him upset. And I really want to talk to him."

"I'll keep trying to reach him." The girl would never know how much it cost Alicia to offer that service. "Let's get you out of that dress," she said, standing. "I'll find something for you to sleep in." Pierce had offered to do that for her at the cabin. A vision of the black nightgown he had found came to her mind. He had held it up to her, his eyes had . . .

Chrissy was ensconced in the guest room and Alicia checked to see that it was stocked with everything she would need. She tapped on the bathroom door. "Everything all right? Feeling better?"

"This is just what I needed. Thanks so much, Alicia."

"I'm glad to have you." She paused. "Uh, Chrissy, what is your father's telephone number? I'll try to call him for you."

Chrissy told her and during the next several minutes she dialed it twice. There was no answer. Chrissy joined her in the kitchen, where she was sipping a cup of herbal tea. She had put on her nightclothes. Chrissy was wrapped in a borrowed robe.

Chrissy stirred honey into her tea after Alicia set it in front of her. She took a tentative sip. The contents of the cup seemed to intrigue her. She stared into it for several long moments. "Alicia," she said hesitantly, "it's none of my business, I know, but how is it that you didn't even know Daddy's home telephone number?"

Idly Alicia stirred her own tea. "I've never had occasion to call him."

"Then I was wrong? There was nothing going on between the two of you that week at the cabin?"

"Your father is a very attractive man," Alicia said, squirming uneasily in her chair.

"But not your type?"

Exactly her type. If one was a woman, Pierce was her type. "He's probably not accustomed to romancing a woman with two active little boys tagging along."

"He's crazy about your kids. He told me so." She sipped her tea and watched Alicia over the cup. "He's crazy about you too."

"H-how do you know?" She tried to act disinterested. She failed. Chrissy's eyes were pure mischief.

"I asked him if he got lucky and scored with you." Alicia's shocked face made her laugh. "No, I didn't. At least not in those words."

"What did he say?"

"Oh, he carried on for a full five minutes about how you were intelligent and fun and charming and beautiful and a good mother and a good listener and lovely and soft and feminine. So I said, 'Well?' and he said, 'There are problems.'"

"Oh."

"What problems? Are you still hung up on your husband or something?"

"No."

"Then I don't get it. Daddy's always been a ladies' man. I hope you don't mind my saying that."

"That would be obvious to anyone."

"So, what problems? Any woman he's ever been attracted to, he went after and usually got. If she wasn't so inclined, his attitude was to hell with it."

Alicia was shaking her head. "I don't see your point."

Chrissy laid her hands flat on the table and leaned over to stress her meaning. "Look, I'm not blind. You two couldn't wait to jump on each other's bones. Now whether you did or not, I don't know. But whatever's happened, you're both walking wrecks now. Daddy looked like pure hell tonight, and when I asked him why, he said he wasn't sleeping well. And frankly, you don't look so great either. So what's with you two? If you're that hot for each other, what have you got to lose?"

Alicia could have asked that of Pierce herself. "There are problems," she repeated softly, sadly.

"Well," Chrissy sighed and stood up, "who am I to give advice to the lovelorn? I have just jilted one of the most sought-after bachelors in southern California." They laughed, but each was lost in her own thoughts. "I'm off to bed, if you don't mind."

"Of course not."

"If you're going to be up for a while, will you keep trying Daddy? I could call Mother and tell her where I am, but I don't want to cope with one of her tirades right now. Do you understand?"

"I understand." Alicia smiled kindly. "Good night."

Chrissy leaned down and kissed her cheek. " 'Night. Thanks, Alicia, for everything."

It was only an hour before dawn when he answered the telephone. Alicia had called every half hour. She told herself that her diligence was for Chrissy's sake and that she wasn't able to sleep anyway. The real reason was that she was worried about Pierce herself. Or was that, too, a rationalization? Was she driven by jealousy to know where he could be at that time of night and with whom? Anyway she kept dialing until he answered with a brusque, "Yes?"

"Pierce?" His abrupt, anxious tone had caught her off guard.

"Yes, this is Pierce Reynolds. Who is this?"

"Alicia."

"Alicia!" he exclaimed. She could almost visualize him checking his watch for the time. "Is something wrong?"

"No, I—"

"Then can I call you back? I'm trying to keep the line clear. Something's happened to Chrissy."

"She's here."

"Where?"

"Here. At my house."

Pierce sank onto his bed and let his head drop forward as his shoulders slumped in relief. "Is she all right?"

"She's fine, though she was terribly upset when she arrived."

"When was that?"

"About midnight. I've been trying to reach you since then."

He heard the question in her voice. Did she think he'd been out with another woman? If only he could tell her he'd been trying very hard to get very drunk. It hadn't worked. Even alcohol couldn't dull his memories of her nor dilute the ghost of her that danced in front of his eyes just out of reach.

Finally, he'd gone to an all-night coffee shop and eaten breakfast. He hadn't been able to push a bite past his throat at the fancy dinner Dottie had thrown in honor of Chrissy and her young man. It had been more to honor Dottie for making a good match. The whole thing had sickened him.

"I've been out."

"Oh."

God, he wished he could tell her how much he missed her. "I guess Chrissy told you what she did at the party. Her mother called here just as I was coming in about fifteen minutes ago. She was hysterical, but that's not unusual for Dottie."

"Chrissy wanted desperately to talk to you, but otherwise she was okay." She paused, knowing it wasn't her place to ask. "Pierce, you're not angry with her, are you?"

"Hell, no. I'm glad she's out of it."

Alicia was relieved. She knew Chrissy would be

devastated if her father censured the daring action she'd taken. "Good. She's so anxious to talk to you. She needs to know you'll stand behind her decision."

"She's got my endorsement. Should I come over?"

"She's sleeping now."

But you're not, Pierce was thinking. *And I'm not. And I'd love to be holding you. Lying in bed, holding each other close until the sun came up.* "Then I'll wait till morning."

"It is morning."

Was there reproach in her voice? "Later in the morning."

"All right. I'll tell her you'll be over about nine, say?"

"Fine. Good night."

"Good night."

Not good night, my love. Not good night, darling. Not even good night, Pierce. Just good night. She was put out with him. And he didn't blame her one bit. He had been a bastard. If only she knew he had had to be one for her own good.

He got there at eight-thirty. He hadn't been able to sleep so he had showered, shaved, dressed, and killed time until he thought he could arrive and still not appear too anxious to see her.

Alicia saw him coming up the sidewalk when she opened the front door to get the morning paper. She had to agree with Chrissy's opinion that he looked like hell. But to her he was beautiful, and she wanted to wrap her arms around him. Instead she said a cool, "Hello, Pierce. Thank you for sending David the cards."

"How is his eye?"

"The stitches came out yesterday. It's amazing what a week can do. The scar's just a faint pink line. I told him that, in a year or two, that scar will drive the girls crazy."

He grinned. "What did David have to say about that?"

"Yuck. And that's a quote." He laughed and she shushed him. "They're still asleep."

"Our offspring seem intent on bringing us together," he remarked softly. "First David's accident, now this incident with Chrissy."

"Yes, it seems that way."

Then one of those silences descended and their eyes latched and held. Gluttonously they feasted on the sight of each other. He took in her wan complexion and she noted the dark bruises of fatigue ringing his eyes. He watched her breath shudder up through her chest, making her breasts tremble. He wanted to touch them, feel their lushness against his fingertips. She watched his pulse tick in the triangle at the base of his throat. She wanted to press her lips there, feel his heartbeats against her lips.

Her eyelashes fluttered down to screen desire-clouded eyes. "Why don't you go in and talk to Chrissy while it's still peaceful? She's waiting for you. I'll bring in some coffee."

He reached for her hand and slowly drew her close to him. "Thanks for being her friend last night." He cupped her head, tilted it back, and kissed her softly on the mouth. Their eyes drifted open when they reluctantly backed apart. "Is she in the guest room?"

Alicia nodded dumbly and he went down the hall. Her heart was racing and her blood had heated with the merest touch of his lips. Damn! she cursed silently as she prepared a tray of coffee and cups. She had sworn to play it so aloof and here she was, quaking and quivering in front of him like a virgin before a god of fertility. One look from those green eyes, from beneath those sexy eyebrows, and her breasts had filled, the nipples swelling and tingling. Between her thighs . . . oh Lord.

So, he cared about the health of her son. So, he was a father, worried and vulnerable where his daughter was concerned. So, he was the best damn kisser in the whole damn universe. Was that any reason to come all undone? *Show some spunk, for heaven's sake. Some backbone. Don't let him get to you.*

Resolved not to be made a fool of again, she tapped on the door and Chrissy called for her to come in. They were sitting on the bed, which Chrissy had already made up. They were holding hands and Pierce was smiling. "Coffee?" Alicia asked and they both smiled a yes. She poured them each a cup, then made to leave.

"No, stay," Chrissy said, stretching out a hand and

pulling Alicia down on the bed with them. "I'm just getting to the good part," she said with an impish grin. "When my future mother-in-law realized that I was serious, she said, 'Wherever will I wear that gown I bought for the wedding? It's quite unsuited to any other occasion.' "

They all three laughed, but Pierce heard Chrissy's sigh and touched her cheek. "No regrets, I hope."

Her matching eyes met his. "Only that I didn't see what I was letting myself in for sooner. How could I have been so stupid?"

"But you realized your mistake and did something about it. I'm very proud of the courage it took to do what you did."

"Daddy." Chrissy leaned forward and hugged him tight. They embraced warmly, unselfconsciously. Gone was the awkwardness between them. Alicia's throat knotted with emotion.

Before the scene became too maudlin, the door burst open and David and Adam came piling through it.

"Pierce, Chrissy!" they yelled in unison and hurled themselves onto the bed.

"Is this the day we're going to Disneyland?" David shrieked.

"Careful of the eye," Alicia called out warningly.

What ensued was an exchange of greetings and news that rivaled the noisy exchanges in the lobby of the United Nations. Everyone talked at once. Finally Adam shouted, "I want my breakfast."

• • •

"So what will you do now?" Pierce asked his daughter after the pancakes had been served. They were crowded around the table, but no one seemed to mind the bumping elbows.

"Today? Start looking for an apartment."

"You have an apartment," Pierce said, puzzled.

Chrissy was shaking her head. "That's Mother's apartment. She found it, furnished it, she pays the bills."

"*I* pay the bills," Pierce said.

"Oops, sorry," she said. "Anyway I want a place of my own choosing. I want to start supporting myself. It'll be tough with classes and all, but I really want to do it, Daddy."

He winked his approval. Alicia was thinking. "Chrissy, could you do some sketches? Large, splashy, high-fashion ones?"

Chrissy laid her fork aside. "What did you have in mind?"

"To frame some sketches for the walls of the shops."

Chrissy's eyes widened. "You mean it, Alicia?"

"Yes. I've been thinking that the stores needed a face-lift. I can see bright prints in brass frames. Very dramatic, very stylized, like the old covers of *Vogue*. They might just as well be your drawings."

"You wouldn't buy them simply because they were mine. I mean, if they weren't any good—"

"Make them good," Alicia challenged with a sly smile.

"Deal." Chrissy thrust her hand across the table and they shook hands hard.

She left a while later, wearing a pair of jeans and a sweater borrowed from Alicia. "I'll stay in touch."

"Do that," Alicia and Pierce called out at the same time as they waved to her from the front door. Her tread was jaunty and confident as she stepped into the Porsche.

"Can we go, Pierce? Can we?"

Alicia turned around to see David and Adam fairly dancing with excitement. "What is this about Disneyland?"

Abashedly, Pierce scratched his temple. "I promised David a trip to Disneyland if he was brave while Dr. Benedict sewed up his eye."

"I was brave."

"He was brave," Adam, who hadn't even been there, testified.

"Your mother and I will talk about it while we clean up the kitchen. Straighten your rooms, get dressed, brush your teeth, then we'll see."

"Yea! 'We'll see' usually means yes, Adam."

"Yea!"

Off they ran. Pierce took Alicia's hand and dragged her toward the kitchen. As soon as the door closed behind them, he pulled her against him and sought her lips with his.

She angled her head away. "I thought we were supposed to be doing the dishes."

"To hell with the dishes. I can't wait another minute to get my hands on you." He fastened his mouth to hers.

She was still angry with him. Why was she letting him do this? Why was she standing here like warm putty waiting to be molded by his caresses? Beneath the mastery of his mouth, all her resolutions and hostility and avowals of avoidance vanished. She couldn't resist.

Not when his tongue was working its magic inside her mouth, pumping erotically, swirling lazily, igniting sparks of desire in every forbidden place of her body. Not when his hand was sliding beneath her top and covering her bare breast with a warm massaging palm. Not when his fingers were lightly plucking her nipple into a bead of passion.

The rational Alicia argued with the emotional one. She was doing it again, blindly plunging headlong toward more heartache. Masochistically, she was asking for rejection again. But at the moment she didn't care. How could she say no to him when everything inside her was crying out yes, yes, yes?

Pierce's brain was screaming admonitions to him, too, but his body had long since stopped listening to his brain. He had denied himself for as long as he could. Damn the future and the risks. He'd take them. He wanted to give her the love that had filled his heart to bursting. Somehow he must convey to her that he knew now that his spirit was incomplete without her. Surely she knew how much his body required hers. The evidence pressed hard and throbbing between them.

"Don't do this to me again," she moaned into his mouth. Even as she spoke the denial, her hands locked around his neck and her tongue darted friskily past his lips.

"I'm sorry for every time I've hurt you." The heels of his hands coasted down the sides of her breasts. "I never wanted to hurt or disappoint you, Alicia. I swear that." His lips were ardent on her neck and the words he whispered across her flesh were erotic and scandalous and she loved every one of them.

He raised her top and dipped his knees to bring his head even with her breast. It filled his hand. The crest was flushed and tight with need. He rolled his tongue over it again and again until she was delirious. "Pierce, Pierce." His name slid through her lips sibilantly. He closed his mouth around her nipple and tugged with a sweet, rhythmic heat.

"God, this is insane." He came back to her mouth and regretfully lowered her top over a breast wet and shiny from his kiss. "Come here," he said roughly and hauled her down onto his lap as he sat in a chair. He burrowed his head between her breasts and nuzzled them. "If we don't stop I'm going to take you on top of the breakfast table."

She bent her head over his, holding him tight to her, draping him with her hair. "I might not object to that."

"Ah, God, please, Alicia, don't move your bottom. You're killing me." But his hands went to her hips and held her securely over his lap. "How can anything that feels so damn good be such torture?"

Her lips found his ear and nibbled. "I sat on your lap that night at the cabin. You didn't seem to mind then." Her voice was a seductive drawl that emphasized the playfulness of her tongue.

"Then I wasn't zipped into a pair of jeans." He groaned as she lightly ground herself against him. "All right," he growled threateningly and her pulse nearly leaped out of her veins. "Two can play this game." Once again his hand slipped under her top. "I was kissing your breasts then, remember?"

"Uh-huh." Her eyes closed and her breath started coming fast and uneven.

"I was touching you with my tongue here." His fingertip slid down the outer curve of her breast. "Here." He outlined the deep bottom curve. "Here." He touched her nipple and she jumped in violent reaction. "Like this." He fanned her nipple with his fingertip and she cried out with remembrance and renewed longing. She collapsed against his chest.

He brought his hands from beneath her top and sank all ten fingers into the wealth of her hair. He pressed his forehead against hers. "Now is not the time nor the place, my love, or believe me, I'd already be deep inside you."

"Pierce!" She sighed, lifting her mouth from his kiss. "Will there ever be a time and place?"

He enfolded her in the tightest embrace. "God, I hope so. I hope so."

His lips opened over hers. He sealed their mouths

solidly in a loving covenant. Her arms linked behind his head and she responded to the fervency of his kiss.

David and Adam bolted through the door. They all but skidded to a stop. Alicia and Pierce sprang apart.

"Mom and Pierce are having sex," David sang out to a tune of his own making. "Mom and Pierce are having sex."

Shocked by their sudden appearance and what her elder son was singsonging, Alicia sat motionless on Pierce's lap, her arms still looped around his neck.

"David Russell, where did you hear that?"

"I made it up."

"Well, stop saying it. You don't even know what it means."

"I do so."

"What then?" she asked daringly, confident that he was boasting.

"It means hugging and kissing and lying down in bed together."

Her mouth fell open and she stared at him with rapidly blinking eyes. She turned toward Pierce in mute disbelief. He was grinning, one eyebrow cocked humorously. He shrugged. "You asked."

"See, I told you I know what sex means," David said, grinning proudly.

"I know too," Adam claimed.

Alicia stared at her children as though she'd never seen them before. Pierce was trying his best to suppress laughter but his shoulders were shaking. As solemnly as he could, he addressed David. "You may know all about it, but it's not something gentlemen discuss while ladies are around." Pierce nudged her and asked out of the side of his mouth, "Did that sound too prudish?"

"Don't ask for my opinion. I didn't even know he knew the word."

"Why haven't you had a man-to-man talk with your sons before now?"

"I'm not a man."

His eyes slid down her front. "I noticed that," he said and the words slurred.

"Well, can we go? Why aren't the dishes done? We're ready."

"The dishes aren't done because Pierce and I were . . . talking about Disneyland," Alicia said primly. She hopped off his lap and straightened her top and ran her fingers through her hair.

"You were not talking, you were kissing," Adam stated flatly.

"Well, yes, we were . . . a little," she admitted red-faced.

"Can we go?" David had a one-track mind.

Alicia glanced inquiringly at Pierce. "Yes, we can go!" he said. Over their squeals he shouted, "Go get jackets and caps, whatever you want to bring, while we do the dishes."

David dashed out, but collided with Adam as he ran back in. "Are you going to do the dishes this time or are you going to start kissing again?"

"We're going to do the dishes," Pierce said, drawing an imaginary X across his heart. "I promise."

"Okay. Come on, Adam. Gee, can you believe it?"

Alicia and Pierce watched them go. They looked at each other and began to laugh. For long, wholesome, healthy minutes they laughed. "Do you really want to spend your Saturday off at Disneyland?" he asked, pulling her into his arms.

"Is that where you're going to be?" She laid her hands just inside his shirt collar and sifted her fingers through his chest hair.

"It looks like it."

"Then that's where I want to spend the day too." He ducked his head and kissed her. "You promised David you wouldn't start kissing me again," she murmured around his lips.

"I'm breaking my promise."

CHAPTER EIGHT

The boys had the time of their lives. Pierce and Alicia were rarely without smiles. They strolled the Disney compound arm in arm or hand in hand, but somehow always touching. When they had to separate, their eyes remained in close contact. To anyone observing them, they were a couple in love.

Today belonged to them. Their conflict—to Alicia still a mystery—was shelved. They indulged their mutual fantasy. They pretended they were a family.

They ate and drank and laughed and clowned and finally coaxed a reluctant Adam to ride The Matterhorn.

"Don't be a baby," David scoffed. "It'll be great. Honest."

"Adam and I can sit this one out," Alicia offered.

"No!" Adam said, not wanting to lose face. "I want to ride it, only . . . can I sit by Pierce?"

Pierce ruffled the boy's hair. "Sure thing. Who do you think I was counting on to hold my hand?"

Adam sat sandwiched between Pierce and Alicia. Eyes shut and body tensed, he hunkered down between them. But he loved the ride and begged to ride it again. This time he rode in the front of the car, David behind him, then Alicia and Pierce. They straddled a padded seat.

"Pierce!" she said in a shocked whisper the moment their car entered the dark cavern. His hands went around her and wandered at will.

"Hmm?"

"I don't think that's allowed at Disneyland." No longer aware of the jerking, rocketing speed of the roller coaster, her head dropped back onto his chest. The boys were screaming in delight, playing spaceship, oblivious to the adults behind them.

Pierce's searching lips found her ear. "It's allowed if they don't catch you." His tongue feathered her earlobe. "Besides you've got no room to talk. Do you realize what you're doing to me?" He spread his hand wide over her stomach and drew her back even closer against him. She gasped when her bottom made contact with his crotch. He chuckled and kissed her neck and continued the heavy petting until the ride was over.

When they stepped back into the sunshine, Pierce's grin was that of the proverbial cat who got the cream. "As far as I'm concerned, we can't ride The Matterhorn often enough." Rosy color stained Alicia's cheeks and she quickly slipped her sunglasses on in hopes of hiding her blush.

"Come here, woman," Pierce growled caveman style and pulled her into his arms.

"Uh-oh," Adam said to his brother. "I think they're gonna start kissing again."

"No, we're not," Pierce said, laughing. "I'm just going to tell her a secret." Lifting her hair, he whispered something in her ear. Alicia pulled back and looked up at him in surprise. "How does that sound?" he asked.

"W-wonderful," she stammered. "But are you sure? Will you be too tired?"

"Will you?" She shook her head, smiling broadly. "Then go make your phone call. We'll be waiting in line at Dumbo."

When she joined them five minutes later she told Pierce, "All set."

"Terrific." He hugged her.

"What's all set?" David asked.

"Would you like to spend the night with Nana and Grandpa?"

"Do I look all right?" Alicia asked nervously as she gazed at herself in the mirror.

"Sure, you look fine," David said, not even lifting his head from the book he was flipping through. Adam yawned. His Mickey Mouse ears were sitting catty-cornered. He was so tired he didn't notice.

"Thanks a bunch," Alicia muttered. What had she expected? To them, she looked only like Mom. She wanted them to tell her she looked beautiful, ravishing, stunning. That's how she wanted Pierce to see her on this, their first actual date. She couldn't believe it when he had whispered the invitation in her ear while they were surrounded by the racket of Disneyland.

"Would your parents mind having the boys pawned off on them for one night? I'd like to take you to dinner, dancing, anything you want. Then I'd like to show you my house." That she was invited to spend the night had been implied. It had been hours ago, but her heart hadn't calmed down yet. She shouldn't go. *You can be hurt, Alicia,* she warned herself. But she wanted this night alone with him. What about tomorrow night? And the one after that?

"Why are you dressing up so much?" David interrupted her thoughts.

"I want to look nice for Pierce. He's taking me to dinner."

"Why can't we go?"

"It's a grown-up restaurant."

The doorbell rang. "I'll get it," the boys shouted in unison and raced from her bedroom. Adam was suddenly wide awake again.

Alicia was grateful for the few moments alone. She needed them to collect her wits. Did she look sophisticated, as if she went out with an attractive, successful man every weekend, as if it were nothing unusual?

No. She looked flustered. She *was* flustered. Her hands were shaking as she misted herself with her most precious perfume.

What had happened to the campus beauty queen who had had young men vying for dates? She had fallen in love, married, borne two children, lost her love. Firsthand knowledge of life's risks left one feeling less self-confident.

Somehow she had managed to bathe, shampoo and style her hair, and do her nails in a miraculously short time. She had chosen to wear a slinky black dress that clung to the curves of her body. The neckline draped and dipped low over her breasts, the hem swirled softly around her knees. She had on a smoky shade of stockings and high-heeled black shoes with rhinestone clips on the toes. Her hair was swept up into a loose knot and she'd purposefully disregarded the wispy tendrils that escaped it. Diamond studs adorned her ears and served as her only jewelry.

Assessing herself in the mirror, the verdict was that the lady-of-the-world image belied the trembling woman on the inside.

Taking up her purse and the overnight bag she had discreetly packed for herself, she switched out the light and left the safety of her bedroom. For a moment she stood in the living room door watching as Pierce read to the boys from the Peter Pan picture book, David's souvenir from Disneyland. He had a boy under each arm snuggled close to him.

When he glanced up and saw her, he did a double take. Captain Hook could remain forever imperiled by the crocodile for all Pierce cared. The words of the story froze in his throat. The boys lifted their heads and, somehow sensing the intense emotion of the moment, remained blessedly quiet. Slowly Pierce disengaged himself and stood up. He came to her like someone induced by a hypnotist to walk. Indeed he was entranced.

"You look fabulous." He took her hands in his and dropped a reverent kiss on her cheek.

"Thank you." Her voice was silky, tremulous, infinitely but accidentally sexy.

"Ready?"

She nodded. They gathered up everything the boys were taking for their overnight stay at their grandparents' house. It wasn't easy, but they all managed to squeeze into Pierce's car. Her sons' enthusiasm over the car and their accumulated hyperactivity after a day at Disneyland combined to make Alicia tremendously glad to see her parents' house come into view.

Once the boys were handed over, good-byes were said, and Pierce and Alicia were alone in his car, he asked, "What did you tell your mother?"

"About what?"

"About why you wanted the boys to spend the night."

She twisted the small gold chain on her beaded handbag. "I said it would be simpler than getting them up in

the middle of the night to take them home. I told her we
planned to be out late."

"Do we?"

"Don't we?" Had she read him wrong? Was it only
wishful thinking on her part that they would spend the
night together? God! Did she look like an overanxious
widow trying to trap a husband?

He reached across the console and took her hand,
bringing it to his mouth. He raked his lips across her
knuckles. "This isn't an audition, Alicia. We're playing
it by ear. Why are you nervous?"

She laughed with shallow breathlessness. "I know
it's ridiculous."

"Not ridiculous. Endearing," he said roughly.

"I just don't want you to think that I assumed—"

"I don't think anything except that you're the most
desirable woman I've ever known. And I'm not only
speaking in terms of sexuality. In every way, I find you
fascinating. I need you in every way a man can need a
woman. Your sweetness, your laughter, your caring."
He turned her hand over and tickled her palm with his
tongue. Sensations fluttered up from her thighs, through
her womanhood, through every vital organ, to her
breasts. "I'd love to share my bed with you tonight. But
if not, it won't alter how I feel about you. I love you."

He braked the car in the driveway of the restaurant
and, propping his arm on the back of the seat, turned to
her. She stared at him speechlessly. He stroked the back

of her hand with his thumb while his eyes ravished her face. "Alicia, no matter what happens, no matter . . ."

He stopped, looked down at their clasped hands, then began again. "I want you to know that today was one of the finest, most productive days of my life. I love your boys. I love you. With all my heart. Nothing, *nothing* can or will ever change that."

Leaning across the console, he laid his lips on hers and kissed her. With only their hands and lips touching, he drew her to him as inexorably as if he had wound velvet cords around her and reeled her in. She laid her free hand on his lapel and tilted her head for a more cohesive contact with his mouth. She felt that all she was was flowing into him, melding with him. Her lips parted as his tongue slid sinuously between them to touch the tip of hers.

The door on the driver's side was suddenly opened. "Ooops, sorry, Mr. Reynolds."

"It's okay," Pierce said to the valet. He withdrew from her but kept his eyes on her face. "We're ready to go in now."

Alicia wasn't sure she was. At that moment she didn't know if she could walk, stand, breathe. Her reflexes were chasing recklessly through her body, her mind was spinning, her soul was soaring. She had been completely disoriented by Pierce's spellbinding embrace and had willingly given herself over to its obsessive power. She had wanted to be held its bewitched victim forever.

His kiss, like a magic vapor, had wafted through her body, stroking the back of her throat, her breasts, her stomach, the cleft between her thighs, the backs of her knees, the soles of her feet.

Still dazed, she was handed out of the car. Adroitly, Pierce ushered her through the glass doors of the restaurant, outrageously tipping the valet who had disturbed their kiss.

The restaurant wasn't one of the glitzy places where celebrities and would-be celebrities came to flash newly installed Hollywood caps, try out new face lifts, and spot Rodeo Drive chic. It was refined, understated, elegant. The decor was as subdued as the music being played by the violin and piano duo. The army of waiters was deferential and all but invisible and silent.

"Your table is ready, Mr. Reynolds," the maître d' murmured as he greeted them. "This way."

As they followed him, heads turned in their direction. Without conceit Alicia had to admit they made a striking couple. Pierce's suit was dark charcoal, almost black. His shirt was ivory and the silk tie and the handkerchief he had arranged in his breast pocket were the color of vintage burgundy wine. His hair gleamed and looked well-groomed, but still retained that roguish dishevelment, as though a whimsical breeze, or a woman's fingers, had lightly tossed through it.

When they were seated and Pierce was looking over the wine list, Alicia remarked coolly, "Everyone seems to know you. Do you come here often?"

He grinned at her less-than-subtle display of jealousy. "I entertain potential clients here frequently."

"They should be impressed."

"They are. After a dinner meeting here, we're usually guaranteed the job." He mischievously didn't satisfy her female curiosity about any woman companions he might have brought to the restaurant. They were irrelevant anyway. "What are we going to eat? Do we want red or white wine?"

She couldn't have said later what she ate. All she knew was that it was delicious. Her taste buds were awakened to delightful textures and varied flavors. But all her senses were heightened. She was high and it had nothing to do with the wine.

"My stomach won't know what to think." The waiter was taking away her entree plate. "It's used to hamburger and fast foods."

"I'm glad you enjoyed it. I recommend the strawberries Romanoff for dessert."

"I couldn't, really."

She could, she did, she loved every sinful morsel.

"Pierce?"

"Hmm?" He took her hand across the candlelit table and their waiter, knowing they wouldn't need him anymore, intuitively glided away.

"Forgive me if I'm prying," she began. "You often put down your professional success, make light of it. Why? Most men would flaunt it."

He turned her hand palm up and tracked the faint

lines with his fingertip. "I don't feel successful, Alicia. Recently I woke up to the fact that everything in my life could be measured by a financial chart. Is that success? Once I thought so. Not anymore."

"You seem to have your priorities straight. However, financial and professional success aren't anything to be ashamed of."

"When they're all your life truly counts for, maybe they are."

"I don't understand you," she said, shaking her head. "Why are you so self-critical?"

"Where are the wife, the children, the home a man my age should have? After my failed first marriage, I never saw fit to commit myself to another, mostly because of indifference and downright laziness. Only in the last couple of weeks have I been any kind of parent to my daughter. God, I regret all those years Chrissy and I could have meant something to each other and didn't. And it sure as hell wasn't her fault. In the areas of life that really should count for something, I feel like a bum. I have nothing to be proud of." He cradled her cheek in his palm and she leaned her face into it. "That's why I wish . . ."

"Wish what?"

His eyes fell away and the seconds ponderously ticked by. At last he looked at her again, and his introspective expression had changed. She knew he had closed the subject. "I wish you'd go dancing with me tonight. Do you like to dance?"

They went to one of the posh new clubs where virtually any shape, form, and age of human being could be spotted. From punks with pink and blue hair to ladies swathed in chinchilla, all types were represented. The mirrored floor reflected the madly gyrating bodies. Motion pictures, everything from Charlie Chaplin to erotica, flickered on the walls. The music blared, an insult to any discerning eardrum.

"Are you the same man who bought a Donald Duck T-shirt this afternoon?" Alicia had to scream to her partner over the pounding bass and shrill treble.

"The same. And are you the lady who likes ice cream cones and merry-go-rounds?"

"I confess." She twirled, showing a good portion of thigh. "But this is fun too."

"The only problem is—"

"What?" she shouted, holding a hand to her ear.

He came closer and put his hands on her waist. "I said the only problem is that they never play any slow dances. The guys never get to hold the girls."

"That's because too often they can't tell one from the other."

"That's true," he said, laughing. "But I sure can tell you're a girl." His hands slid up her sides, the heels of them brushing her breasts and applying a slight, but unmistakable, pressure. There was also no mistaking the gleaming heat in his eyes. "I know a place where we can slow dance."

Alicia didn't protest when he took her hand and

guided her through the raucous crowd. He drove with his right hand on her knee when it wasn't shifting the gears of the sports car. His house was in the hills overlooking the city and Alicia, whose family had always been affluent, was awed when he drew up to iron gates and opened them with a transmitter. The lawn was landscaped and immaculate, the driveway wide. He pulled the car to a stop in front of a sprawling ranch-style house.

"Don't be too impressed," he said derisively. "It's only a big, empty house."

"A beautiful house."

"That's why it's such a pity that it's empty. Someone should be enjoying it. No one ever has."

The interior of the house was everything the exterior promised. The rooms were spacious and well laid out, tastefully and expensively decorated in California casual. Area rugs dotted shining hardwood floors. The ceilings were high and beamed. Immodestly undraped windows offered breathtaking vistas of the city lights spread out in a twinkling blanket below.

"It's beautiful, Pierce."

"It is now." He pulled her close and hugged her hard, slowly swaying back and forth. "You do wonders for this house and it feels so right having you here."

His lips were warm as they moved over hers. Lightly, briefly, tantalizingly. They slid to her neck, across her jaw, behind her ear, down her throat. "Would you like something to drink?"

"Would you have to stop doing this to fix it?"

"Yes."

"No, thank you."

His smile melted against hers and his tongue imbedded itself in the warm, wet silkiness of her mouth. His hands massaged their way down her back, past her waist. He cupped her derrière and boldly urged her against his hard heat. She adjusted herself to it and felt the rumble of approval and arousal in his chest. Her arms, feeling weighted down with a delicious lassitude, but oddly defying gravity, lifted languorously around his neck. Her fingernails teased the lobes of his ears.

"I thought we came here to slow dance." His expression was teasing as he raised his head. His nose batted playfully against hers.

"By all means. I was only biding my time until you asked me. Where's the music?"

He coiled an arm around her waist and guided her to a wall of bookshelves where the components of a stereo system were arranged. The control panel looked more intricate than that of an airplane, but with a flip of several switches, soft music began to emanate from strategically placed speakers.

Alicia floated into his embrace once again. His arms folded behind her back at her waist. She crossed hers behind his neck and laid her head on his chest.

His lips moved in her hair. "Do you know what I first noticed about you?"

"My stupidity. You couldn't believe anybody would go to the woods for a week without a lantern."

He laughed. "Before that."

"So you *did* think I was stupid."

"Maybe just a little scatterbrained."

"Well it couldn't have been my looks that captured your attention because as I recall I looked like a drowned rat. It must have been my sparkling conversation."

"You were stuttering."

"How chivalrous of you to remind me."

"Give up? It was this." He caressed her fanny, sliding his hands over the gentle swelling.

She pushed away from him, feigning indignation. "Of all the base, rude, prurient, chauvinistic, sexist—"

"It was all I could see," he claimed self-defensively, and brought her back to him swiftly with a soft thud of her breasts against his chest. "It's about the cutest fanny I've ever seen."

"And you've evaluated many, I suppose?"

"Jealous?"

"Pea green with it."

"Good."

She was rank with jealousy, jealous of every woman who had ever been held in his arms, caressed by his hands, kissed by his mouth. How many had he brought to this house on the pretext of a slow dance? How many had been moved through the rooms in what, not by any stretch of the imagination, could be called a waltz?

"You've got no reason to be jealous of anyone." His whispering lips found hers again. It was a kiss that drew all the life out of her, drained her, yet made her feel more alive than she ever had.

When at last he freed her mouth from the sweet suction of his, her eyes opened reluctantly. She hadn't noticed when they'd left one room and entered another. It had all been one sensuous journey through time, through space. Now she noted that they were in a game room and her bottom was being pressed against a billiard table. "Do you, uh, play?" Her voice was mere puffs of air that somehow fashioned themselves into words.

"Uh-huh." Delightfully imprisoning her against the table by pressing his middle into hers, he began to remove the pins from her hair. Each one was sought after by nimble fingers, pinched between them, and extracted with utmost care, slowly, as though he were peeling away a garment. Her hair cascaded over his hands like spilled molten gold. He nestled his face in it.

"Is it hard to do?"

"Uh-huh."

"Are you very good?"

"Expert."

His hands were on her breasts now, rubbing softly, and she moaned. "You must have developed a winning technique."

"It's all in the way you line up your balls and aim your cue."

She dragged her mouth from beneath the drugging power of his and looked at him through eyes narrowed with suspicion. "Are we still talking about pool?"

His eyebrows jumped mischievously. "Of course. What did you think?" His hands spanned her waist and easily lifted her onto the table. It took no more than a gentle pressure of his hands on her shoulders for her to lie back. He followed her down onto the green felt, covering her body with his. Insistent lips claimed hers. His tongue swept her mouth like a torch and set off a wildfire that uncontrollably spread through her body.

With his fingers buried in her hair, he rolled them over until she was on top. She kissed back fiercely, seduced by the hedonistic promise of his mouth. Making increasingly urgent sounds in his throat, he lowered the zipper of her dress with measured care and then brought his hand around to her front. Hooking his index finger in the cloth, he lowered the loosened bodice. The tops of her breasts swelled over the lacy border of her brassiere. He caressed her with his eyes, then with his fingertips, then with his mouth. He raised his head off the table, his passion mounting with each kiss.

"Pierce," she sighed. She moved against him sinuously, like a cosseted pet against its owner. "This is decadent."

"Purely decadent." His chin scoured her gently. He nipped her lightly with his teeth. "You're delicious."

"I'm the mother of two children," she groaned softly. His tongue was lashing her thrillingly.

"And you have the sumptuous breasts to prove it. Oh God, Alicia, I need you."

He turned them again and stared down at her with the question burning in his eyes. Her hair was fanned out behind her head on the green felt, lending her an air of defenselessness. Her eyes were limpid with desire and her lips were soft and moist and inviting. She lay with her arms flung to her sides, vulnerable and wanton. She looked both an innocent and a temptress. Pierce wanted them both.

Without a word he helped her off the table and led her down the hall into the bedroom he had showed her earlier. He offered no apology for the romantic ambiance he had purposefully created. The lights were dimmed. Music was piped in from some unknown source. In a silver wine bucket, a bottle of champagne was chilling.

On their way through the living room, he had picked up the overnight bag she had left there earlier. He handed it to her now and smiled tenderly. "Don't feel like you owe me anything. I'll take you home now if you want."

She had never loved him more than she did at that moment. He was thinking of her, not of himself. She touched his mouth with her fingertip. "I'm staying. And, Pierce," she said, lowering her voice and looking away timidly, "I saw my gynecologist and took care of . . . you know." She didn't meet his eyes before she moved away.

In his opulent bathroom she found something that surprised and touched her with its blatant sentimentality. It bespoke a request that Pierce would never verbalize. She smiled tenderly as she began to undress.

Before she opened the door she switched off the light, so she stepped into shadows. He was sitting on the side of the bed opening the champagne. He lifted his eyes to her and they gleamed hot and green from across the room. "Let me see you."

As she moved, the black negligee floated around her as sheer and soft and alluring as a fallen angel's wings. "When did you get this?"

He stood up. He was wearing a short wrapper like a karate pajama. It came to mid-thigh. It was grey and piped in green. He looked wonderful in it, his chest wide and hair-dusted in the deep V opening that came to a point at his waist. His legs were lean and well formed, muscled from his jogging regimen.

"I stole it from the cabin when I left." His shy confession made her heart ache with love. "I didn't plan ever to see you in it. I just wanted to keep it." When he came to her, he encircled her neck with his fingers. "I've imagined you wearing it a thousand times, but you far surpass any fantasy."

Her body was clearly defined beneath the transparent fabric. His eyes adored every nuance. It took unbearable discipline, but he contented himself with kissing her softly, brushing his lips over hers. In his mind, this was their wedding night. He was going to treat her like his bride, cherish her. "Drink some champagne with me."

He poured only one glass and offered it to her first. She drank. The bubbly wine was deliciously cold and biting on her tongue, but not nearly as intoxicating as Pierce. She imbibed his scent, the color of his skin and hair and eyes, the textures of his body, the planes and angles of his face.

While she still held the glass, he lifted it to his lips and drank, tasting more of her than the champagne. Then setting the glass aside, he drew her down on the bed. While she watched in avid fascination, he loosened the knot at his waist and shrugged out of the wrapper.

His virile nakedness excited her and made her insides curl warmly and gravitate toward her pulsing center. She wanted to lasciviously gobble up every inch of him with her eyes. How could she, Alicia Russell, be so brazenly lustful of the naked male body? But it wasn't just that alone. It was Pierce. And she loved him. As splendid as the body was, it was the whole man she reached out for.

He knelt beside her. Starting with her face, he surveyed her lovingly. His eyes were poetic in their appreciation. "I love your mouth." He outlined it with his finger. "The way it's shaped, the way it feels." She dared to touch his fingertip with her tongue. His gasp was quick and sharp. Emboldened, she closed her lips around him and sucked lightly. "My God, Alicia," he murmured. He lowered his head and, removing his finger from between her lips, replaced it with his tongue.

They almost got carried away. He forced himself to lift his head from her kiss. His hands combed down her chest and smoothed over her breasts. Her nipples pressed against the gossamer confines of the nightgown. Bending over her, he licked one, his tongue scratching over the lace.

"Oh, Pierce, Pierce." She tossed her head on the pillows and caught handfuls of his hair in restless fingers. His caresses were bold and proficient and soon she was writhing beneath his fervor.

Her response made him a little wild. He kissed her stomach randomly, examined her navel with an inquisitive tongue, caressed lower until she felt his touch on the mound of her femininity. Gently he nudged her thighs apart and lay between them. He raised the gown. She felt the moist caresses of his mouth on the skin of her abdomen, in the soft triangle of down, on her thighs. Between them.

Deftly he caressed with suppliant lips and agile tongue. She approached that divine death again and again, only to be brought back, detained, postponed by bliss. No longer able to breathe, she cried out for fulfillment. He obliged. He touched the source of all her desire and lifted the floodgate of her passion.

Her heart exploded in a blinding light. Her body quickened and surged against him. She knew the most intense rush of pleasure she'd ever known and sobbed when the ecstasy of it tore through her chest and belly. When she finally coasted down from the pinnacle, she was appalled at herself and turned her head away when he raised himself above her. Her cheeks were stained with tears.

"You're so beautiful to me. All of you. Please don't cry." The words stirred against her mouth. With a finger under her chin, he forced her to look at him. "I would never do anything to offend you. I love you, Alicia. I only wanted to demonstrate how much."

She flung her arms around him. "Oh, my darling, it's nothing you did that's making me cry." Tears were leaking from the corners of her eyes, but they were joyous tears. "I just can't believe that anyone could love so unselfishly, could love *me* so much."

They kissed. Her hand scaled down his body in an orgy of feeling, cataloguing each discovery. His chest was wide, furred, sculpted. His stomach was flat and taut. The hair tapered down to a silky ribbon that her fingertips tracked. She ventured farther and his breathing began to rasp loudly in her ear. When her fingers closed around him, he buried his head between her breasts and moaned her name. Wanting to give back a portion of his gift to her, she caressed until he could bear no more.

They came together in one swift, plunging fusion. He held her tight, not moving, only savoring the unspeakable rapture of being gloved by her body. Then slowly he began to stroke her.

"Never forget that I love you," he whispered urgently. "I love you, Alicia. Remember that always. I love you."

"And I you." She wrapped herself around him, bringing him as deeply into her as possible. "I love you so much."

"Darling, my love." He held back until she shuddered beneath him again, her body milking his. Then he surrendered his soul and let his body bathe her with his love.

"... and Nana made pizza for our supper except it wasn't the frozen kind like you cook. She made it out of a bowl."

"Thanks, Nana," Alicia said dryly, and Pierce smiled. From the time they had picked them up, the boys had talked nonstop, reporting everything that had transpired since they had left them.

"Grandpa played checkers with us, but I think he let us win."

"We ate popcorn while we watched television. And Nana made waffles and sausage for breakfast." Adam's good times were measured by his stomach. "She gave us candy because we ate all our breakfast."

Alicia rolled her eyes heavenward. "Next week we'll be going to the dentist. A day at Disneyland and overnight with Nana is like taking an injection of sugar into every tooth."

"We had a great time," David said. "Did you have fun too?"

Pierce slid a meaningful glance in Alicia's direction and she blushed, something she thought she would never do again after the night they had shared. "Yes, we had a terrific time," he drawled.

"What did you do?"

"Oh, lots of fun things," was Pierce's blithe reply and Alicia's cheeks went a brighter pink. He laughed out loud.

At the door of the house she told the boys to take their overnight bags into their rooms and unpack them. "Put everything back where it belongs, please."

Just before entering the hall, David turned back. "I almost forgot. I wanted to ask Pierce something."

By tacit agreement, Alicia and Pierce weren't keeping their affection a secret from the boys. He had his arm around her shoulders and her arms were loosely around his waist. Her head was resting comfortably on his chest.

"What's that?" Pierce asked.

"My Cub Scout pack is going on an overnight campout. Since I don't have a dad they said I could invite somebody else. I was gonna ask Carter. But I'd rather ask you."

"Thanks for the honor," Pierce said, smiling. He fingered Alicia's hair in an absently loving manner. "When is it?"

"Next month."

Alicia felt Pierce's withdrawal immediately. He seemed

to shrink away from her, draw into himself, erect an invisible wall and close them off. His hand dropped from its caress of her hair, the arm around her shoulder tensed, then fell away to dangle lifelessly at his side. His whole body went stiff and resistant.

Her head came up; she pushed away to better see him. His face was blank, his eyes hollow. She knew he had retreated into that no man's land again. But this time rather than feeling despair, she felt anger. How dare he do this to her after yesterday, after last night, after all his avowals of love.

"Will you, Pierce?" David asked.

"We'll talk about it later, David," she said, forcing gentleness into her voice when she felt like screaming. "Go do as I asked. You and Adam rest in your rooms for a while, watch television. Pierce and I want to talk."

"Okay," he said dispiritedly and ambled off down the hall.

Pierce was staring at the floor. When David was out of earshot, he raised his head. His eyes were cold. "I won't be able to go with him. Please make my excuses."

"Like hell I will," she spat out. "Who is going to make your excuses to me? You're about to pull another disappearing act, aren't you?" She gripped him by the upper arms and shook him as hard as she could. She'd never been a fighter, a person who sought a physical outlet for her anger, but she was trembling with fury and wanted to strike him. "Well, this time I want to know why. How can you freeze up like this after last night?"

"Last night was the most beautiful night of my life. I meant it when I said I love you."

"Then why?" she shouted. "Why are you walking out again? And that's what you're about to do, isn't it?"

"Yes."

"And this time there will be no family intervention, will there? You won't be coming back, will you?"

His eyes bore into hers. His jaw was rigid. "No. I won't be coming back."

She recoiled. She hadn't thought he'd say it with such absolute conviction. He had called her bluff and now she was sorry she'd forced it. "After yesterday?" Her voice wasn't cooperating. It was breaking up with pain when she wanted it to reveal all the angry hate she felt for him at that moment. "After yesterday, you can just walk out without a backward glance?"

"I have to."

"Stop saying that. You don't!"

"I do."

"Why?"

"I can't afford to stay with you, with the boys, any longer. It will only make things harder if I do. Believe me, it's best for everyone if we break it off now."

"I don't believe that."

"Believe it."

"Last night meant nothing to you?"

He rounded on her and grasped her shoulders. He brought her against him hard. The impact took her breath. His face was fierce, the words were strained through his teeth. "Last night meant everything to me. It was my deepest wish enacted. I could pretend that we were married, that we belonged to each other, that we had a future."

"Oh God, Pierce." She wanted to tear at her hair, to claw at her skin in frustration. "How can you say all that when you plan to leave me? How?"

"Don't you know how difficult it is for me to walk away from you? Don't you know that your body, since the first time we made love in the cabin, is a part of mine? I'd as soon cut out my heart as leave you. It will be the same. You're a part of me, Alicia. Forever. The sweet personalities of your boys are a part of my soul now and always will be." He squeezed his eyes shut and enunciated each word precisely. "But I can't see you anymore."

She was crying. She damned the tears, but they collected in her eyes and rolled down her cheeks anyway. She damned herself for begging, but she had to. He couldn't leave her. She wouldn't let him. She caught handfuls of his shirt in her hands and lightly beat her fists on his chest. "Tell me why. *Why?*"

"Don't make it harder than it is."

"It couldn't be any harder."

"You don't want to know."

"I do."

"You don't."

"Tell me."

"No."

"Tell me, damn you!"

"I'm dying!"

CHAPTER NINE

No, he wasn't dying. She was.

Life leaked out of her body by slow degrees. The tears were instantly checked as though his announcement had dried up everything inside her. She stood perfectly still, not so much as an eyelash moving.

It was he who moved. He gently pried her hands off his shirt front and backed away. He felt her pain as keenly as if someone had plunged a knife into his heart. It wracked the features of his face. Distorted them. He couldn't bear her suffering and turned away from it. He went to stand at the window. It was a clear, smog-free day. It didn't deserve to be.

Alicia stood there, petrified, for an interminably long time. Neither of them was counting the minutes. At last she drew in a staggering breath that seemed to puncture her lungs as though they were virgin. The blood finally, sluggishly, began to pump through her body again. Her veins seemed unwilling to accept it, filled to capacity as they were with misery. She wiped her cheeks with the backs of her hands. Her face was stiff from the salty tears drying on it.

She looked at him and the tears started again, but she didn't let them fall. He was so hard, so solid. She searched for, but couldn't find, one trace of frailty in him. She knew, didn't she, his strength, his endurance? My God! She could still feel his power bursting inside her.

"That's impossible."

He looked at her over his shoulder. "That's what I said when they told me. It's possible. Not for certain, but very possible."

She shook her head in miscomprehension. "Don't talk to me in half-truths and riddles. Please."

"Sit down," he commanded softly. "You look about ready to drop."

She stumbled her way to the sofa and folded down onto it like a collapsible paper doll hinged at the joints. "There's nothing wrong with you," she insisted.

"I couldn't believe there was either. I went in for my regular yearly checkup. It was an inconvenience, a nuisance, something that I had to juggle my schedule around in order to do. I certainly didn't worry about the outcome." He paced as he talked. "It's something in my blood. They told me it could be a condition treatable with proper medication or—" He stopped abruptly and looked at her. "A rare disease that is degenerative and terminal."

She covered her mouth with cold fingers to keep her lips from quivering. She wanted to weep, to let go and sob hysterically, to bang her head against the wall, to scream. But she knew she couldn't. "They don't know for sure?"

He shook his head. "They told me it would take about three weeks to get a firm diagnosis. They had to send blood samples back east somewhere for extensive and sophisticated testing. The symptoms of the conditions are so similar that it takes a while to establish which it is. Some of the cultures take days." Impatiently he flung his hands wide. "I don't want to talk about that." He raked back his hair. "I found out two days before I met you. That's why I had gone to the cabin. To think. To adjust to the fact that in a few months I might be dead."

A garbled cry escaped her lips before she could clamp a hand over it. Tears spurted from her eyes. He rushed forward and knelt in front of her. "Alicia, don't. This is why I never wanted you to know. You would have been better off thinking I was a sonofabitch who took what I wanted from you and then skipped."

She touched his hair. "You're not sick. You can't be sick."

He sprang up and began his pacing again. He was angry. "I argued that point too. It's damned unfair. I jog, I take vitamins. When I noticed the first sign of a paunch, I joined a health club, lost fifteen pounds, began working out religiously three times a week. I eat right. I don't drink too much. I stopped smoking years ago when the first breath of warnings against it were sounded. I think I could accept what they told me if I felt bad, if I were in pain, if I were weak, if I couldn't make love to you all night and feel ready to do it again with the slightest stimulation."

She looked away because the reminders were too vivid, the recollections too fresh. "When will you know?"

"In a few days I suppose. The three weeks are about up."

She raised her head hopefully. "Maybe——"

He was shaking his head adamantly even as he interrupted her. "No, Alicia. I have to plan for the worst. I couldn't base anything on hope because . . . Well, I couldn't. I couldn't stand the disappointment."

Her chest caved in on itself. She could feel everything inside her sinking, shrinking, sagging. He sat down beside her and took her hand. "Do you see why I told you from the beginning that I couldn't get involved? I didn't want to hurt you. If you hadn't been you, if you'd been just another attractive woman, I'd have had you in bed that first night. I would have used you to relieve my mental anguish, I would have emptied all my despair into your body and wouldn't have cared if I never saw you again."

He released her hand and went to the window again. His voice was low, deep, rife and rusty with emotion.

"But you *were* you. And I knew that if I had you once, I wouldn't want to let you go. You were exactly what I needed. But I knew I was the last thing you needed."

He faced her. "You are a young woman who has already lost one man. You have two sons who need a father. You need a man who can make a home for you, give you years of happiness and love."

He sat on a chair opposite her and pleaded for her forgiveness with his eyes. "I knew it was wrong of me to make love to you that night Chrissy came to the cabin, but I couldn't stop myself then. And I couldn't stop myself from coming back each time I did, knowing damn well that I shouldn't ever see you again. That night after David's accident, I knew you wanted me to stay. I wanted to. You needed comfort and love and the reassurance that you weren't all alone in the world. I couldn't give you that security. Even though I knew it insulted you, hurt your pride, made you angry, I forced myself to leave. You and the boys were like a gift handed to me, but you came too late."

He stood again, thumping his fists against his thighs. He looked like a man frustrated past his limit, who at any moment might fly into a raging fit. "I've taken stock of my life. One starts doing that when he realizes his mortality. You and David and Adam were like a breath of fresh air. I wanted the chance you afforded to make something meaningful out of my life. I would have loved to be a husband to you, to make love to you every night, to share confidences and laughter and even heartaches. I would have loved for us to have a baby. I would have liked to be the father your boys need, to watch them grow up, help them when I could, encourage them from the sidelines when I couldn't. I want all that, Alicia. But it's too late. Too damn late." He returned to his position by the window.

They didn't speak for a long while. She wanted to comfort him, alleviate his suffering. But she couldn't. He wouldn't tolerate pity. And who would comfort her? Her heart had finally healed itself after Jim's death. With time it had knitted itself back together, repaired the break. Now, where her heart used to be, there was only a giant, gaping wound. This time she didn't think it would ever heal.

"What will you do?" she asked at last.

"You mean if—"

"Yes."

"Sell my part of the company to the other partners. Liquidate everything. Visit my mother. Then leave. Disappear. I couldn't bear a deathwatch."

She flinched against the word and shuddered as though the temperature in the room had dropped drastically. "Does Chrissy know?"

He shook his head. "No one. That's how I wanted it."

"That's cruel, Pierce. Your mother and Chrissy should be told. You've only just established a relationship with your daughter. She would want to know."

"Would you have wanted to know that Jim was going to die that day?"

Her mouth twisted with hurt as though he'd slapped her. Furious with himself, he cursed. "I'm sorry. I'm sorry," he repeated, shaking his head. "This isn't how I wanted it to be. I wanted it to be a clean, quick break. Leaving you angry would have been so much better than this. I can't stand myself for forcing this sorrow on you." He took a deep breath. "I'm leaving now, Alicia."

He went to the door and she vaulted off the sofa, desperate not to let him out of her sight. "I'll never see you again?" she asked frantically.

He closed his eyes briefly and shook his head. "No" was his quiet answer.

"But—" She stopped herself. How could she be so selfish? She had been on the verge of telling him to call her if the worst proved false, if the blood tests wrote a happier ending to the story. *Call me if everything is all right, but don't bother if it's not.* That was the essence of what she was about to say.

He understood. He came to her and tenderly stroked her cheek with the backs of his knuckles, a bittersweet smile on his lips. "We've said everything that needs to be said. More. I ask nothing of you, Alicia. I knew from the beginning that anything between us would be impossible, but I couldn't help involving you." His eyes rained love over her face. "Forgive me. I loved you too much."

The door closed behind him. And still she stood in the middle of the room unable to move.

• • •

"I've never done this before."

"Drunk champagne in a hot tub? It's a must for every orgy."

"What are you looking at?"

"Your breasts."

"That's what I thought."

"I love the way the water bubbles over your nipples." He took champagne in his mouth, lifted her high against him and fastened his lips around her nipple. His mouth was cold against her hot skin.

"Oh, how can anything feel that good?" Wet hands gripped his wet hair.

He lifted her out of the tub and laid her on the redwood decking. Taking up the bottle of champagne, he tilted it and dribbled the sparkling wine over her. She shivered. But not from cold. From the tongue that followed the naughty rivulets of champagne.

"The candles were a good idea. I should have thought of them."

"I love candlelight."

"I love the way it looks on your skin." She could feel his eyes traveling the naked length of her back as she lay with her chin propped on his breastbone. Her thighs lay between his. "I like the way your hair spills across my chest. It's a very erotic picture."

"The candles smell good." She breathed deeply and the scent of flowers and spices filled her head.

"You smell good." Idly his fingers feathered up and down her sides, making her shiver.

"So do you."

"What do I smell like?"

She lifted her head and stared at him dreamily. *"Like man. Like me. Like us. Together."* His fingers sifted through her hair, massaged her scalp. *"What do you taste like, Pierce?"*

His hands stilled. He held his breath as she seductively inched down his body. Her fingers touched him. He groaned. Her lips. He died. And then he was reborn.

"I can't brush my hair while you're doing that." They were dressed and almost ready to leave. Her arms were raised to her hair as she stood at the bathroom dressing table. He was behind her, reaching around her to fondle her breasts.

"Why bother? I'll probably just mess it up again. Thank you for not wearing a bra today."

His thumbs were doing provocative things to her nipples. Slowly, softly, softly. Alicia watched his hands in the mirror, watched the response of her own body, saw the smoky hues of passion rising in her eyes, in his. She lowered her arms and dropped the brush with a clatter that went unheeded. Her bottom pressed snugly against the hard ridge beneath his fly. *"We're already dressed,"* she complained breathlessly.

"Uh-huh." His grin was wicked. Clothes would be no deterrent to him at all. He turned her around, unzipped her

slacks, unzipped his. He drew her close. Close. So close. Until they were one.

Alicia sat up in bed, sweat and tears pouring down her face.

All day she had coped. She had been a good mother, meeting the physical needs of her sons. She had fed them when she didn't think she'd ever be hungry again. She had listened to their chatter when she wanted to scream at them to be quiet and leave her in peace. She went through the ordeal of preparing them for bed and getting things ready for school the next day when she didn't want to move, but only wanted to curl up in a fetal ball. The last thing she felt like doing was smiling, but she had even forced smiles onto her lips when the boys expected them.

She had done all that and managed to perform an act of believable normalcy. On a day when her limbs felt like strapped-on weights that didn't want to budge, when her body knew a lethargy, an apathy for life that was frightening, she had survived by a sheer act of will.

But now, in her own bed, she could pamper her dejection. Her memories were thieves of sleep and unconsciousness. They wouldn't let her forget or ignore. They haunted her.

Forgive me. I loved you too much.

She rolled to her side and wept, wept bitterly and wetly, until she was drained of tears, of spirit, of hope.

• • •

For the next two days she lived in a vacuum, acting out her life. At work she was devoid of ideas and quick to criticize those offered by others. Everyone noticed the change from her usual effervescence. One cohort was brave enough to ask if something were wrong. Alicia snapped back, saying that she was just tired.

She tried to keep her despair at bay around the boys. But, of course, they bore the brunt of her mood. She hated herself every time she showed them her temper when she didn't think she could stand their incessant chatter any longer. Unfortunately, like most children, they didn't take hints too well and often brought Pierce's name into the conversation.

"Is Pierce going on the campout with me?"

"I don't think so, David. You'd better ask Carter. Or maybe Grandpa. He'd like that."

"But I want Pierce."

"Well, he can't go."

"Why?"

"Eat your dinner."

"Why can't Pierce go? Why doesn't he come to see us? Did you make him mad again?"

"Eat your dinner!" She stood up, flung down her napkin, and ran from the room so they wouldn't see her tears. Later she spent a long time with them over a bedtime story, tucking them in and kissing them good night. They didn't mention Pierce again, but she could see the questions in their soulful eyes. Hopefully they would soon forget him.

Everyday activities seemed Herculean tasks. Lifting a milk carton out of the refrigerator, getting dressed for work in the morning, driving the car pool to soccer practice, all required more energy than she could garner. She felt like doing nothing but sitting motionless, talking to no one, staring into space, demanding of God what horrendous thing she had done to deserve punishment like this.

That's what she was doing on Wednesday morning when the telephone rang. The boys' ride to school had picked them up. Alicia hadn't finished dressing, but she was absently sipping a cup of coffee, dreading the rush hour traffic, the day, the rest of her life.

"Hello."

"How's my favorite girl? Ouch! Damn, Sloan, those nails are sharp. Boy, pregnant ladies can sure get mean." Kissing sounds. "Make that, how's my second favorite girl?"

In spite of her black mood, Alicia smiled into the phone. "Carter? Sloan?"

"You remember us? We were beginning to wonder. We haven't heard from you."

"I'm sorry." Listlessly she plucked at the telephone cord and watched it wobble. It was good to hear Carter's voice. A friend. Tears were blurring her eyes. "I've been busy. I took that job I told you about."

"That's terrific. She took the job." He was passing the

news on to Sloan. "Ask her what? Hey, wait a minute. I can see how this is going to go. Why don't you take this extension and I'll go to the one in the office."

"Hi, Alicia," Sloan said.

"Hello. Everything all right with you and baby?"

"He's brutal. Kicks me day and night. Carter loves it, of course."

Alicia smiled, so glad for their happiness, so envious of it.

"Okay, I'm here now," Carter said from the other phone.

"How do you like your new job so far?" Sloan asked her.

She briefly outlined her new duties and responsibilities. Even to herself she sounded as excited as someone terrified of flying about to embark on a trip across the Pacific.

"It all sounds wonderful." Alicia could hear Sloan's forced enthusiasm. "Are you sure it's what you want? I mean—"

"She means you sound like hell. What's the matter with you?" Carter had never been known to mince words. And he knew all of them. "Are the boys all right?"

"They're fine." She told them about David's eye injury, leaving out Pierce, and reassured them that beyond having a faint scar his eye was fine.

"Well it sounds as though everyone is rocking along just dandy and peachy keen." Carter could also be sarcastic.

"Yes, we're fine." Alicia lapsed into silence, but her despondency came through the line loud and clear.

"Alicia, what's wrong?" Sloan asked with the quiet sincerity of an old friend.

Alicia drew in a serrated sigh. She wanted to cry. Her throat ached from holding tears back. It would be good to share it with someone. She didn't think she could bear the heartache alone any longer. "I met a man. A wonderful man."

"That's bad?" Carter asked. "Oh, wait, I know. He's not as good-looking as me. Right? Few are, darlin', but they can't help it. Don't let that get you down."

Alicia could appreciate his attempted humor and laughed. "He's just as good-looking. But he's another type."

"Would we like him?"

"Yes." For the first time Alicia sounded animated. She described Pierce to them and had them laughing incredulously when she told them how she'd met him. "You should have seen us. We looked like three survivors of a shipwreck. David and Adam were blabbing all the family secrets to this total stranger. I was afraid for their lives and my virtue."

"But he turned out to be Prince Charming."

"Yes." Alicia blotted at the tears that were making mud of her eye makeup. "He was wonderful with the boys, so patient and entertaining. They loved him immediately. His daughter—"

"He's married?" Sloan asked.

"No, he's been divorced for years. His daughter is twenty-one. She's lovely. She came for dinner at the cabin one evening. We stayed the week with him, you see."

"So much for your virtue," Carter said, smacking his lips. "The plot thickens."

"Are you in love with him, Alicia?"

She gave up trying to hide the fact that she was crying. "Yes, yes."

"And how does he feel about you?"

"He . . . he said he loved me. I believe he did. He adored the boys."

"You're speaking in the past tense," Carter softly pointed out.

"We can't be together. We have . . . had a problem."

"What?" Sloan asked.

"He's a woman beater? An S and M freak? He moonlights as a pimp?" Carter's mind was always thinking up plot twists.

"No, nothing like that."

"Carter, please," his wife admonished gently. "Tell us, Alicia. What's keeping you and Pierce apart?"

"He's terminally ill."

Sloan murmured a soft, "Oh God, no." Carter's response was crude and considerably more explicit.

"At least there's a good possibility he is. Tests are being run now. It might turn out to be a treatable illness, but he's proceeding as though it's not. I must too."

The two calling from San Francisco were silent for a moment, then Carter asked, "Why?"

"Why what?"

"Why must you assume he's going to die and act accordingly?"

Defensively Alicia lashed back. "I've already lost one husband, Carter. If Pierce is dying—"

"We're all dying."

That took her breath. Her argument was stifled, corked in a quickly closing throat. "What? What are you saying?"

She could visualize him collecting his thoughts, Sloan sitting and listening quietly, which was her way. "Alicia, from the time we're born, we're all dying. Life doesn't carry any time-limit guarantees."

"But we don't live with the knowledge that it will happen at a given time."

"No, we don't. So why are you? You're not even sure that Pierce's condition is fatal. What if it isn't? The two of you are throwing away a damn good thing. Your reasoning is crazy."

"Carter," Sloan cautioned again. She knew that once he got wound up, once he set his mind to something, it was like trying to move a mountain to change it. "What did you say when Pierce told you?" she asked Alicia.

"Nothing, really. I was too shocked. I couldn't very well ask him to come back if he were going to live but to stay away if he were going to die." She moaned and covered her face with her free hand. "I would have begged him on bended knees to stay if it were only me. But how could I do that to my boys? They want a father so badly. How could they stand to lose Pierce like they did Jim?"

"Do you think they're better off without him at all, for any length of time?"

She thought over the last few days. They had been moving around as ghostly as she, their usual exuberance tamped out. They weren't happy. They were miserable. Their sulkiness was a silent accusation that she had driven Pierce away. "No, they miss him terribly. They love him."

"And what about you? Are you better off without him even if he is ill?"

She didn't even have to think to answer that one. "No."

"Alicia, let me ask you something," Carter said. "If you had known Jim was going to die when he did, would you still have wanted him for the time you had him? Would you have given up one single day you shared with him, one minute? Given the choice, would you have sacrificed having your sons with him, living with and loving him?"

"Oh, Carter." Crystal-clear realization of what he was asking dawned on her mind. "No, no, I wouldn't have. I would have greedily lived each day to the fullest."

"That's the way you should approach this. We only get one day at a time. Any of us. Are you living today the way you want to? Are you living it as though it were your last? What would you want to be doing if this were the last day of your life? Who would you want to be sharing it with?"

Pierce and David and Adam. She didn't even realize she had spoken the names aloud until she heard Sloan laugh softly and say, "Well then? What are you talking to us for?"

Alicia's body was surging with new life. She could hardly contain the energy suddenly gushing through it. "But he might not agree," she said nervously. "He might hold back, thinking we'd be better off in the long run."

"Convince him otherwise," Sloan said.

Alicia was laughing now. "Yes, yes, I will. I'll hang on until he gives in. Oh, I love the two of you. I love you."

"Tell that to Pierce. We already know you love us," Carter said.

"All right. Good-bye. I've got to go——"

"Call and tell us what happens," Sloan rushed to say.

"I will. Good-bye."

For a moment Alicia stood in the middle of the kitchen floor wringing her hands. There was so much to do, she didn't know what to do first. The dishes? They could wait. She had to get dressed.

She dashed toward the bedroom, repaired her makeup with fumbling fingers, threw on her clothes, and managed to pull herself into some semblance of order. Leaving a note for the sitter apologizing for the messy house, she ran for her car.

"I don't even know the address of Ecto," she said to her dashboard as she started out of her driveway. She slammed on the emergency brake, jumped out, wrestled with the key in the back door of the house, found her lost phone book, tore through its pages, ran back to the car.

Architecturally the office building looked like something out of *Star Wars*. She rushed inside, breathless, a rumpled whirlwind in the cool, dignified foyer. "Mr. Reynolds, please."

"Third floor," the receptionist said. "The elevators are behind you."

"Thank you." She paced in front of the elevator doors as she waited, rehearsing what she was going to say when she saw him. He would argue. She needed ready ammunition to shoot down every argument.

There was a secretary sitting at a desk in the outer office. Behind her was a door with Pierce's name stenciled on it in gold leaf. "Mr. Reynolds, please."

The secretary looked puzzled and glanced down at the agenda on her desk. "Did you have an appointment?"

"No, but I think he'll see me. Tell him it's Alicia Russell."

"I'm sorry, Ms. Russell, but Mr. Reynolds isn't here."

She stared stupidly. "Not here?"

"He called in this morning and said he wouldn't be in all day. If you care to make an appointment or see someone else . . ."

"No. No, thank you," Alicia said vaguely and turned away, retracing her way to the parking lot. She felt deflated. Lost. Aimless. A missile without a target.

Now what? Wait and see if he contacted her? No, no! She had to find him. Today. Now.

She got in her car and drove to the nearest public phone booth. There was no answer at his house. Chrissy was probably not home either. Didn't she have classes—

"Hello."

"Chrissy," Alicia gasped in relief. "Do you know where Pierce is? Is he by any chance with you?"

"No. He should be at his office."

"I've been there. He isn't working today."

"Is something wrong?"

"No, no." She didn't want to alarm Chrissy. "I just wanted to see him."

"Well, I'm glad to hear that. I talked to him yesterday and he sounded like a man in the depths of despair. He told me you weren't seeing each other anymore. I wish you two would get your act together and stop all this pussyfooting around."

Alicia smiled weakly. "I'm going to try. Beg if I have to."

"Good. I think he'd like to be begged a little. Something about middle-aged ego and all."

Middle-aged? "Well, sorry to have bothered you, Chrissy. I'll find him."

Alicia learned one thing from the conversation—
Pierce was holding firm on his decision not to tell his
daughter about his illness. Maybe he was right not to.
But how could he stand the loneliness, the pain of facing something like that alone? He wouldn't. Not if she
could help it. Alicia gunned the motor of her car and left
the phone booth with a squeal of tires.

She parked outside the iron gates. The Jeep he'd had
at the cabin was parked at the side of the house, but his
car wasn't in the driveway. He wasn't home. So she
would wait. She rolled down the windows of her car.

I'll wait for as long as I have to.

She waited for hours, but she didn't mind. The time
passed quickly as she closed her eyes and remembered.
Everything. From the beginning. *"Mom, there's a man
out there."*

The myriad ways she loved him were itemized and
reviewed and counted again. When she saw the sleek
foreign car prowling its way up the hilly road, she
calmly got out of her car and was standing in front of the
gate when he reached it.

His face was blank when he climbed out of the car.
She went to him purposefully and confidently, wrapping her arms around his waist and laying her head on
his chest.

"I love you, Pierce Reynolds. I need you with me for
as long as I can have you. If it's forty years or four days,
I've got to have you. Please stay with me."

His arms were like the strongest of steel bands as they

closed around her. He bent his head over hers and pressed his lips into her hair. So close was the embrace that she could feel the steady beat of his heart against hers. "My love," he whispered fiercely. "My dearest, dearest love."

CHAPTER TEN

Can we have the cake now?" Adam asked.

"*May* we have the cake now. And, yes, you may."

"Give up on correcting his grammar, Carter," Alicia said. "I've tried. It doesn't work."

"He'll catch on, won'tcha, Adam?"

"Sure," Adam mumbled, his mouth full of birthday cake.

"Sloan, cake?" Carter asked his wife.

"No!" she exclaimed, warding off the enormous slice he offered her. "I'm trying to get my figure back."

"And succeeding," he snarled lecherously. "What about Jeffrey Steinbeck Madison? Can he eat cake yet?"

"*May* he eat cake," Adam chortled, and everyone laughed.

Alicia smiled as she held her friends' baby boy on her lap. She had been introduced to him only that morning, when Carter and Sloan arrived for their visit. The patio party was in celebration of Jeff's three-month birthday. While Carter finished cutting the cake and passing slices to David, Chrissy, and a young man she had brought as her date, Alicia lovingly cooed to Jeff, who was somehow managing to sleep despite the commotion.

"I wish Pierce could have been here," Sloan said quietly as she sat down beside a subdued Alicia.

Alicia sighed deeply and scanned the faces of those she loved collected around the patio table. "So do I, Sloan. He would have loved all this, the birthday cake, the children. He wanted to see your baby so badly."

Chrissy detached herself from the others and came to join Sloan and Alicia. "Don't be sad," she said, placing an affectionate arm around Alicia's shoulders.

"I'm not," Alicia said brightly, too brightly. "Honestly, I'm not."

Chrissy's smile wilted. "Well, I am. I miss Daddy being here."

Alicia took Chrissy's hand and squeezed it tightly in unspoken understanding.

Carter came over. He balanced a plate of cake in one hand as he squatted down in front of Alicia. "Are you going to eat this, or am I going to have to feed it to Jeff?"

Alicia laughed. "I'm not hungry, thank you anyway."

"Well, Jeff my boy, eat up." He scooped a generous portion of cake icing onto his fingertip and poked it into his son's mouth. Jeff began sucking and lapping noisily.

"Carter, don't you dare give that baby any more," Sloan scolded.

"He likes it." Carter was totally enthralled with anything his son did.

"It will rot his teeth."

"He doesn't have any teeth."

"Oh. Well, when they come in they'll be rotten."

Alicia smiled at their bantering. They were so apparently happy with each other, so obviously in love. Again tears welled in her eyes.

"What's wrong, Alicia?" Sloan asked gently. Even Carter's cheerfulness faltered as he looked at Alicia's bleak expression. Chrissy's eyes, so like her father's, were clouded.

"I miss Pierce. God, I miss him so much. How can it possibly hurt this bad?"

"It will get better," Sloan said. Distressed over Alicia's sadness, she patted her back consolingly.

But there was no consoling her and they fell silent, listening as the boys grilled Chrissy's date on the Lakers' season.

"Did you save me a piece of cake?"

Alicia almost dropped Jeff as she jumped up and whirled around at the sound of his voice. He was framed in the back door, grinning broadly. "Surprise! I got away early."

"Pierce," Alicia breathed, heaving Jeff into Sloan's arms and launching herself toward her husband. "Pierce," she repeated as she crashed into him and they wrapped their arms around each other.

"Daddy! Daddy!" the boys shouted. Deserting their new friend, they clambered across the patio, hurdled outdoor furniture and Alicia's carefully cultivated begonias to throw themselves against Pierce's legs. Giving his wife an "I'll get to you later" smile, he knelt down and heartily hugged the boys. "Did you bring us something?" "We were good." "We didn't bother Mom, just like we promised we wouldn't."

"Gosh, I missed you two rascals," he said, rubbing his hands over their dark heads affectionately. "And, yes, I brought you something. But first I want to visit with our guests and see the new baby."

With much fanfare, Pierce was introduced to baby Jeff. He kissed Sloan on the cheek and congratulated her on having a beautiful baby. "He gets his looks from his mother, of course," he said with affected malice as he shook hands with Carter.

The author laughed. "Still jealous of me, I see. Hey, what are you complaining about? You won her in the long run." The two men had met at the wedding and liked each other immediately. A strong friendship was developing. "Where have you been? Did Alicia say Atlanta?"

"Yes, I personally had to deliver a jet we had redesigned for a corporation. I couldn't rearrange the schedule they had set up. I'm sorry I wasn't here to welcome you when you arrived."

"I'm glad you showed up when you did. We've been through two boxes of Kleenex as it is," Carter teased, tugging on a lock of Alicia's hair. "I'd curtail the business trips for a while if I were you, Pierce. She can't handle your being away from her."

"This was the first time since we married." He kissed Alicia lightly. "Believe me, I got back as soon as I could."

"We didn't expect you at all," Chrissy said, wedging her way up to her father and hugging him enthusiastically. The awkwardness between them was no longer there. They were demonstrative in their feelings for each other. "Daddy, I'd like you to meet a fellow artist, John. He's a commercial illustrator."

Pierce shook hands with Chrissy's date. The two men appraised each other and apparently liked what they saw, for they both smiled congenially.

"I'm glad you got back," Chrissy said. "Alicia's been a basket case for three days. Not a whole lot of fun to be with."

"Were you weepy?" he asked, lowering his head confidentially.

"Yes," she answered softly. "How was Atlanta?"

"Cold and lonely." He spoke for her ears alone and pulled her close.

"But you talked to me on the phone last night."

"Not quite the same as having you in bed with me." He lifted a curl from her cheek and fingered it lovingly.

"You gave me no hope that you'd be back until Monday."

"I told them a bodacious lie this morning about my son cutting his eye at school and that I was needed at home."

"It wasn't quite a lie," she said, snuggling against him. "Whatever, I'm glad you're here."

"So am I." He cupped her jaw in his hand and tilted her face up for his kiss. His lips barely touched hers, and it wasn't near enough. Regardless of their audience, they turned into each other and lent themselves to a hungry kiss. When his tongue pressed into her mouth, she slid her arms around his neck.

Chrissy propped both fists on her hips in pretended agitation. "For goodness sake, you two, what is my new young man going to think?"

"I think he's got the right idea," John said and, taking hold of her wrist, led her away.

"Uh-oh," Adam said dismally. "We're never gonna get our presents now."

David was shaking his head with seven-year-old wisdom. "Once they start kissing, it takes them a long time to stop," he told Carter and Sloan solemnly.

"Does it?" Carter asked, smiling at Sloan.

"I've got to feed Jeff," she whispered and let her lips flirt with his ear.

"Goody. That's my favorite thing to watch," he said, his eyes lighting up.

"You're in charge of cleaning up the patio. Recruit David and Adam to help."

His face fell. "You're no fun, Sloan, no fun," he called after her as she disappeared into the house, trailing laughter. As Carter passed Pierce and Alicia, still locked in their embrace, he muttered, "Show a little restraint, will you? You're making me horny as hell."

Gradually they pulled apart, their eyes simmering

with awakened desires. The corner of Pierce's mouth tilted into a sexy grin. "I know the feeling."

Carter and Pierce cooked steaks outside while Alicia prepared the rest of the meal in the kitchen. It was about twice the size the one in her house had been and since her marriage to Pierce she had taken a renewed interest in cooking.

They ate in the dining room that until now had been used so infrequently. It was a boisterous meal. David and Adam loudly competed for Pierce's attention. Jeff set up a fuss until Sloan was forced to leave the table to change his diaper. John was as chatty as Chrissy and seemed not to be affected by the noise and confusion. He fit right in. Pierce and Alicia exchanged approving glances.

With far more chiefs than Indians pitching in, the kitchen was finally cleaned. Chrissy and John took their departure with promises to come back soon and to buy Carter's newest book. The boys were put to bed. Jeff was tucked into his portable crib. Since Carter's beach house was being remodeled to make room for the baby, they were talked into spending the night.

"You're sure you have room for us?" Sloan asked Pierce.

"For years I rattled around in this house all by myself. I can't tell you how glad I am to fill it up with people."

"I'm sure it seems to have shrunk since David and Adam moved in," Carter said, smiling.

Pierce reached for Alicia's hand. "I like it this way."

The Madisons retired to one of the guest bedrooms after sharing a last cup of coffee with Alicia and Pierce.

"Want me to wash your back?"

Pierce, water streaming over him, turned in time to see his wife of four months stepping into the shower with him. He reached for her and pulled her against him. "You have to ask?" His lips were on her neck, nuzzling, nibbling.

"Where's the soap?" she asked huskily. His hands slipped over her wet skin, found her breasts, caressed, teased, then stepped back to visually appreciate his handiwork.

He handed her the scented bar of soap. As they kissed, their mouths rapacious, she lathered her hands with soapy foam. Reaching around him, moving slowly, sensuously, she rubbed his back. Her breasts grazed his hair-matted chest.

"Miss me?" she asked. Her capricious tongue tested the distention of his nipples.

He groaned his pleasure. "Every minute. I was miserable."

"So was I." The skin of his back was sleek and wet under her palms. His waist was nipped in neatly, his buttocks were taut and firm. "Did you look at other women?"

"What women? There were no women in Atlanta." Her laugh soon became a tremulous sigh of desire. Lightly he squeezed the peaks of her breasts between his fingertips. He ripened them further with gentle flicks of his tongue.

"I'll bet women looked at you. You've got cute buns." Her hands honored the objects of her admiration.

He shrugged. "Maybe a few hundred gave me 'come on' glances. Can I help it if my buns are cute?" He let out a yelp when Alicia smacked him with the palm of her hand.

They laughed playfully but their mouths eventually found each other beneath the steamy spray and melted together in a mind-stealing kiss. His tongue caroused rowdily. Her hands stroked down the backs of his thighs as far as they could reach, then tiptoed up the insides.

He moaned, "Alicia?"

"Hmm?" Her mouth was busily tasting his, sipping water from his lips.

"My front needs washing too."

Taking up the bar of soap again she slowly worked up another lather. She watched him through the mist swirling around them, through the shower's spray, her eyes telegraphing her body's sexual awareness of him.

She laid her hands flat on his chest and rubbed in widening circles. She drew bubbly patterns on his chest hair. The hard muscles were massaged with talented fingers newly trained in the art. They worked their way down his ribs, detailing each one. An indolent index finger traced that satiny arrow of hair down his stomach, past his navel, into the dark thatch that housed his sex. Her hands were slippery, wet, sinuous. He was hard, warm, smooth.

Bending his knees slightly, he lifted her against him, his hands supportive beneath her hips. Under the guidance of her hand, slowly, driving upward, he possessed her.

She pressed his head against her breasts, unselfishly giving of herself. He cradled her in his arms. The gentle way he held her was in contrast to the turbulence of their passion.

Long after the tumult came, they stood under the spray, trembling with the aftershocks, vibrating with love, until the water cooled their fevered bodies.

Later they lay facing each other in their bed, warm, drowsy, seemingly sated. His emerald eyes roamed her face. Lazy fingers fiddled with strands of her hair.

"I love you," he stated simply.

"I know."

"Do you know how much?"

"I'm learning every day. I hope I never know the extent of your love because then the next day wouldn't be filled with discovery."

He kissed her palm and she felt his smile against it. "You should quote that to Carter to use in one of his books. That's good."

She outlined his lips with her fingertip. "It's true. I

didn't know how much I loved you, how vital you are to me, until you went away." She combed her fingers through a clump of chest hair and kissed the contoured muscles beneath it.

"We won't ever be separated again."

She made a defeated sound and flopped over onto her back. "Oh, Pierce, I forgot. Next week I have to go to Dallas. A designer is having a trunk show there and I'm supposed to meet him and try to induce him to come to Glad Rags. And then that trip to New York is looming close."

His eyes traveled over her, feasting on her shape, the peachy texture of her skin, the delicacy of her frame, the lushness of her breasts, the allure of her femininity, which was soft and downy and shadowy in the faint lamplight. "I'll invent business trips and go with you." He touched her breast, kissed it. His hand wandered lower.

She covered his caressing hand with her own, pressed it against her. "I was hoping you'd say that. We've rarely been alone since we got married."

"That weekend in the cabin with David and Adam doesn't count as a honeymoon?" he asked teasingly.

"Well, at least we shared the double bed that time." She laughed softly and laid her hand on his silvery-brown hair. "Few men would even want to date a widow with two rambunctious sons, much less marry one and take on that responsibility."

"I would have wanted you if you'd had ten sons. As

for the boys being a responsibility, you know how I feel about that. They're a privilege, a gift I never expected to have. I love them."

"I know you do. You're a wonderful father. The best."

She allowed his hands to wander at will over her body, lying still and compliant, basking in his obvious adoration. "Do you know what I love most about you?" he whispered.

"Yes, you told me once. My tush."

He chuckled. "No, I said that's what I was attracted to first."

"Oh, I stand corrected." She smiled, but she could see that he was serious.

"I love you most because you were willing to brave anything with me, even death." He laid his hand along her cheek and his eyes were shining as they delved into hers. "You speak to me of making a sacrifice in taking on the boys. But do you realize the sacrifice you were willing to make for me?"

"I made no sacrifice by running after you, Pierce. It was a purely selfish decision. I wanted you, needed you, right then. I had to have you. Not out of necessity. I had learned to live on my own and take care of my family, but it was an empty achievement. I proved to myself that I could do it, but I didn't want to be alone. You were necessary to my spiritual self."

"It still took courage to come to me without knowing that the results of those tests were negative." Closing his eyes, he shook his head. "To think that I was at the doctor's office hearing the good news at the same time you were deciding you wanted me in any condition."

"In sickness and in health. Had the tests been positive, I still would have wanted you." She kissed him softly. "I'm just so very grateful to God that they weren't."

"So am I." He hugged her close. "From the first moment I saw you, I wanted to live to a ripe old age. I wanted to have at least fifty years to look at your face."

She murmured his name against his lips before they kissed long and deep. Her thumbs stroked his cheekbones as they parted. "You'll have at least that long. The doctor said your blood irregularity is already clearing up with that medication he gave you."

He was surveying her body with hands sensitized to the feel of her. "If I get to feeling any healthier than I do right now, I'm going to die of overexertion." He pressed her back into the pillows and followed her down with his own body.

"Pierce," she protested on a sigh when at last he released her mouth to kiss her neck. "Making love in the shower where no one can hear us is one thing, but we have guests in the house, remember?"

Tenderly but firmly, he clasped both her wrists in one fist and raised her arms above her head so that nothing restricted his view of her nakedness. He even moved aside stray tendrils of hair by blowing on them softly. His warm breath struck her skin in airy puffs that elicited goose bumps. With tantalizing leisure, he dragged his index finger down the underside of her arm to her breast. Whimpering softly, she raised her hips restlessly and shifted her legs against his. Each depraved movement belied her mild objections.

With his free hand, he cupped her breast and pushed it up slightly. A skillful thumb toyed with the nipple. "Carter and I made a pact. We're not to listen through our walls and they're not to listen through theirs."

"But Jeff is only three months old." She gasped as his tongue curled around the tip of her breast.

"You know what a creative mind Carter has." He drew her into his mouth and sucked gently. Her womb contracted with the sheer eroticism of his caressing tongue.

She had forgotten what they were talking about. His hands and mouth were tuning her to a fine pitch of desire. She knew the signals well by now, but they never failed to surprise her with their intensity. Each time they made love, it was unique and added another dimension to how much they loved each other.

"Open your thighs. Let me touch you," he murmured.

His hand glided down the smooth expanse of her stomach and abdomen. He fanned through the soft tuft of hair, then palmed the slight mound. Curving his fingers downward, he found her dewy with desire for him. "Oh, you're sweet," he breathed.

With loving, questing caresses he paid tribute to

her womanhood. He watched as her eyes grew hazy with mounting passion. Lightly he scratched his evening-stubbled chin across her breasts, her stomach. His tongue sponged her navel as his fingers treated her to ecstasy.

"Pierce, love me."

"I am, my darling."

"Inside. Please, now!"

Draping her thighs over his, he slid his hands beneath her hips and lifted her to him. The velvety tip touched her, probed, was laved with her lotion. Then his hard fullness sank into her loveliness, deeper and deeper, until he knew the sweetest entrapment.

Deftly stroking, he told her of his profound love. Whispered love words were poured in her ear, a chant that accompanied the undulating movements she arched to meet. His palms coasted down her sides, smoothed over her hips, thighs, then back up to fondle her breasts, which to him represented all that was sex, all that was woman, all that was love.

They clung to each other as the crisis thundered through them. It was riotous, but excruciatingly tender. Long after the crashing fury of it was spent, ripples of sensation shimmied through them.

He stayed, nestled deep. Raising himself, he gazed into her eyes. The depths of love beckoned him and he drowned in them willingly. She touched his cheek, his hair, his mouth. Her voice was whiskey-flavored with emotion. "I never knew what it meant to really love until I loved you."

His fingers buried themselves in her hair. He kissed her eyebrows, her nose, touched her mouth with his. "I never knew what it meant to really *live* until I loved you."

And life and love were celebrated long into the night.

TONY HAWK'S
900 revolution

VOLUME 1

Tony Hawk's 900 Revolution

is published by Stone Arch Books
a Capstone imprint, 1710 Roe Crest Drive, North Mankato,
Minnesota 56003 www.capstonepub.com Copyright ©
2012 by Stone Arch Books All rights reserved. No part of this
publication may be reproduced in whole or in part, or stored
in a retrieval system, or transmitted in any form or by any
means, electronic, mechanical, photocopying, recording, or
otherwise, without written permission of the publisher.

Cataloging-in-Publication Data is available on the Library
of Congress website.
ISBN: 978-1-4342-3214-4 (library binding)
ISBN: 978-1-4342-3451-3 (paperback)
ISBN: 978-1-4342-4006-4 (paperback)

Summary: Omar Grebes never slows down. When he's not
shredding concrete at Ocean Beach Skatepark, he's kicking
through surf or scarfing down fish tacos from the nearest
roadside shop. Soon, his live-or-die lifestyle catches the
attention of big-name sponsors. But one of them offers
Omar more than he bargained for . . . a chance to become
the first member of the mysterious 900 Revolution team
and claim his piece of history.

Photo and Vector Graphics Credits: Shutterstock.
Photo credit page 122, Bart Jones/ Tony Hawk.
Photo credit page 123, Capstone/ Karon Dubke.
Flip Animation Illustrator: Thomas Emery
Colorist: Leonardo Lto

Art Director: Heather Kindseth
Cover and Interior Graphic Designer: Kay Fraser
Comic Insert Graphic Designer: Brann Garvey
Production Specialist: Michelle Biedscheid

Printed in the United States of America in North Mankato,
Minnesota.
012012
006567R

TONY HAWK'S 900 revolution

DROP IN

BY DONNIE LEMKE // ILLUSTRATED BY CAIO MAJADO

VOLUME 1

STONE ARCH BOOKS
a capstone imprint

1

"Bleck! You call this a fish taco?!" shouted Tommy Goff, spitting out chunks of tortilla and battered sea bass onto the Imperial Beach Pier. "Where'd you fish it out of, your toilet?"

"You better watch that mouth, kid!" said the street vendor in a nearby food truck. The plump, red-faced cook leaned out of the truck's tiny window and waved his greasy tongs at the teen.

"Or what?" asked Tommy. "You going to stick me in your deep fryer? I'd probably taste better than this garbage." Tommy threw his remaining taco onto the ground and smashed it through the pier's wooden planks with his skate shoe.

"Why, you little —!" began the vendor.

Before he finished, the man squeezed back into his truck like an angry turtle into its shell.

"Ha! Thought so," said Tommy. He spun around toward his friend and continued to laugh. "Tell me you recorded that, Omar! I can see the headlines now: 'World's Biggest Chicken serves up World's Worst Fish.' Man, we'll get, like, a billion YouTube hits with that clip."

Omar Grebes looked down at the small, digital camcorder strapped to his palm. The red standby light glowed back at him. "Negative," he replied, pressing the Record button and watching the light turn green.

"Dude!" exclaimed Tommy. "This is exactly what I've been talking about. You want to find a skateboarding sponsor? Then you've got to keep your eyes open. Opportunities don't fall into your lap. They sneak up from behind and hit you like a sack of —"

SPLAT!

A large, black garbage bag struck Tommy in the back of the head, splitting open and covering him in a gooey mess.

Omar quickly raised the camcorder to his eye. Through the lens, he watched tiny bones and pinkish-red slime fall from Tommy's hair. "Fish guts?" he asked his friend, trying to hide a smile.

Tommy's upper lip started to quiver, his nostrils flared, and his eyes narrowed into thin black shadows.

Omar lowered the video recorder. "Uh, you okay, man?" he asked. Although Tommy had played some pretty cruel pranks in the past, Omar had never seen his friend this angry.

For a moment, Tommy stood silent, watching the bloody remains of the food truck's "Catch of the Day" drip off his white cotton tee and onto the skateboard at his feet. "Never better," he finally said.

"In fact," Tommy continued, grasping the bottom of his shirt with both fists and lifting it toward his mouth. "I've been jonesin' for some sushi all day!" He twisted his tee like a wet dishrag, and the thick red liquid spilled onto his smiling face.

"Dude, that's sick!" said Omar, wincing with disgust.

"You know what? You're right," Tommy replied. He spit out the fish juice and wiped his mouth with the cleanest part of his shirt. "You got to be crazy to eat sushi without wasabi!"

"Well, then I guess that nutjob would be all for it!" shouted Omar, pointing over Tommy's shoulder in surprise. The food vendor sprinted toward the boys, swinging another trash bag above his head like a lasso. "And, unless you want seconds, I suggest we *vamos!*"

"Huh?" asked Tommy, puzzled.

"Let's get out of here!" yelled Omar.

The teens hopped on their boards, pushed hard, and quickly left the rabid cook in their concrete wake. They sped down the sidewalks of Seacoast Drive, weaving in and out of palm trees and angry tourists. They ollied off curbs, carved around streetlights, and popped kickflips over waist-high bike racks.

Then, a few blocks away, Tommy skidded to a halt.

"What up?" asked Omar, stopping next to him.

Tommy wiped a sweaty clump of bleached blond hair from his forehead and held out his hand. "Give me it," he ordered.

Omar followed his friend's gaze to the recorder still clutched in his palm. "This?" asked Omar, holding up the digital camera. "Chill out, man. It was funny. You should have seen your face —"

"Funny? We're not out here making cute videos for your friends at Mar Vista High," said Tommy. He swiped the recorder from Omar's hand and punched the Rewind button. "The footy on here is almost enough to get you noticed. Almost."

"Whatever," Omar replied. "You know that tape is airtight."

"Oh, really?" said Tommy.

After a moment, he flipped the recorder's viewfinder toward Omar and pushed Play. Highlights of the day's skate session replayed on the tiny screen.

"What kind of sponsor would shell out for some no-namer poppin' nollies and heelflips down a 5-stair? You gotta go big, Omar, or you ain't going anywhere but home," said Tommy.

"Thanks for the advice, Dad," Omar shot back.

"Man, if your dad was still around," added Tommy, "he'd tell you the exact same thing."

"Yeah, and look where he ended up," said Omar. The teen stared out at the ocean and watched the sun dipping below the horizon. Several surfers had just paddled out, hoping to catch a few glassy waves before dark. Omar imagined his father's final swell. He had to imagine it because he hadn't been there.

Nobody had.

But between police reports, surf reports, and a few tall tales, Omar had pieced together enough information to know that his father's last ride at Killers was a monster. A beast. A fifty-foot behemoth that could smash you into the Baja rocks and then drag you back to the shores of Japan. Omar liked to believe that his father had ended up there — alive and well, a half-world away.

Maybe for the past two years, as Omar had once dreamed, his father had simply been sipping sake, noshing sashimi, and waiting for the perfect wave to ride back home.

But, of course, that wasn't reality. "My dad's dead," said Omar.

"Dude, Zeke is a legend," Tommy replied.

"To who? Your *brahs* at Billy's Board Shop?" asked Omar. "No one east of the I-5 ever gave two craps about him. What makes you think they'll notice me?"

Omar stepped away from his friend and squinted his eyes to get a better look at the nearby surf. He spotted a brown-haired girl wearing a black rash guard and pink bikini bottoms take off on a small roller. She carved across its glassy face in a series of long, slow, arcing turns. Before the wave closed out, she popped her hips and quickly cut back to extend the ride. When the wave finally flattened, the surfer girl dove lazily off her board into the smoldering twilight water.

Omar felt a hand on his shoulder. "Maybe they won't," Tommy whispered in his ear. "But she will."

The teens stared out at the ocean and watched the girl surface. They watched her spit a playful stream of saltwater into the air, shake out her long dreads, and pull at the rash guard that clung to her body like wax.

After a brief moment, the girl grabbed on to her surfboard and started paddling out again.

Omar turned to his friend. "Well, what are we waiting for?" he asked with a smirk.

Tommy held up the video camera and pressed the Record button. "After you," he said, returning the smile.

ELCOME

SNOW KEY TRUS

APERIAL BEAC

GREBES BROTHER

TIDAL WAVE ZEK

VISIONS SURFIN

REVOLUTION NEEL

2

Without hesitation, Omar took off on his skateboard. Tommy followed closely behind, trying hard to keep up and keep Omar in the viewfinder's frame. He wasn't worried about losing him, though. Just like Tommy knew how to change Omar's mind, he also knew exactly where his friend was headed. The two had been tight since before either of them could remember, and by now, Tommy could predict Omar's every thought.

They were practically brothers, after all. Growing up less than three blocks away from each other, the teens had always shared much more than an area code. They shared a love of skateboarding, primo fish tacos, beach bunnies, and punk rock.

In a way, they even shared a father.

When Tommy's dad had bailed on him and his mom, Zeke Grebes took in the boy like a second son. He taught him to skate, to surf, and to be his own man. In return, Tommy watched out for Omar like a big bro, even though he was less than two years older than him. And, now that Zeke was gone, Tommy continued to look after his friend. But to him that didn't mean keeping Omar safe. It meant pushing Omar to the limit. It meant, in the words of Zeke Grebes himself, "Staying radical."

A few blocks later, Omar stopped where the boys had started. At the entrance gate to the Imperial Beach Pier, the skies had darkened, but rows and rows of lights lit up the boardwalk like a runway.

"You back for some more stale fish, bro?" asked Tommy, rolling up alongside his friend and pointing to where he'd smashed his nasty fish taco onto the ground.

"Nah," replied Omar with a smile, "I thought about trying something a little fresher this time."

"What, like *ceviche*?" Tommy joked.

"Not that kind of grindage," said Omar. He snapped his board up to his hand, spun 360 degrees, and then stopped. "More like an Imperial 5-0. What do you think?"

"Ha!" Tommy laughed, but soon noticed Omar wasn't joining in. "Dude, you're not serious, are you?"

"You're the one that said 'Go big, or go home,'" answered Omar. He knew Tommy's allegiance to his own father's words, and, like all younger brothers, Omar tested this devotion whenever possible. "What, too *radical* for you, Tommy?"

"Dream on," his friend replied, scoffing at the suggestion. "I just thought you were too whacked out on energy drinks to even remember that trick."

Omar hadn't forgotten. But it had been the competition, not the caffeine, that had him amped that day three months ago. The teens had been in an all-day, all-out, trick-for-trick skateboarding battle up and down Seacoast Drive. The rules were simple: live or die. Well, at least that's how Tommy and Omar saw it. When one boy threw down a challenge, the other would take it and live on, or die of shame. Of course, like in a heated game of S-K-A-T-E, each player needed the *cojones* to back his own smack. If he couldn't, he lost.

The Imperial 5-0, as the trick had since been nicknamed by the boys, was Omar's final throwdown that day and his first chance to take out Tommy in battle. Despite being a superior skateboarder, Omar had never beaten his big bro.

Like the pros, Omar always skated freakishly clean, but Tommy skated like an adrenaline freak. He would hit any ramp, jump any gap, or grind any rail. More importantly, he knew Omar wouldn't.

To finally win a battle, Omar had decided to flip the switch and turn his greatest weakness into his greatest strength. On that day, he had challenged Tommy to skate the length of the Imperial Pier, 5-0 grind on the safety rail, and return without getting nabbed by beach patrol. Tommy refused. Of course, Tommy hadn't been afraid of the trick — any noob could perform that stunt — and the five-story fall into the churning waters of the Pacific hadn't scared him, either.

Tommy simply wanted to watch his friend punk out.

Since his father's death, Omar hadn't set foot near the ocean, a place that had once been his second home. He had stopped surfing, stopped skimboarding, and couldn't step more than twenty feet onto the pier without tweaking. It wasn't hard for Tommy to predict that Omar's epic trick was bound to be an epic failure. And he was right. On that day three months ago, Omar skated halfway down the pier, and chickened out.

However, today was different. Maybe it was the hottie surfer girl, Tommy's constant nagging, or his fifteenth birthday the next day.

Whatever the reason, Omar was finally ready to take his father's advice and slay his own fifty-foot monster.

"Just keep filming," Omar told Tommy.

"Never stopped," said his friend.

Omar stared at the video camera, and the Record button stared back at him like a stale streetlight. "Time to go," he whispered to himself. Omar sped away, and Tommy followed closely behind.

The boys shot through the entrance gate, passed by the crazed food vendor, and were halfway to the Tin Fish restaurant at the end of the pier in a matter of seconds. Their skateboards clapped loudly over each wooden planks, but Omar barely noticed. His ears tuned to the lapping waves far below. The deep, thunderous crashes echoed the beat of his racing heart.

Omar kept moving.

He pushed harder and harder, ignoring his fears, dozens of "No Skateboarding" signs, and angry strollers along the boardwalk. He didn't look back. He didn't care if Tommy had kept up with him or not. He didn't care if this trick got caught on tape or made his sponsor-me video. This grind would prove something to himself and, better yet, prove Tommy wrong.

Soon, Omar neared the end of the pier and quickly spotted a six-foot section of the wooden safety rail.

Two lamps shined down on the rail like a spotlight. The edge looked clean, slick, and level enough to grind. Omar focused. He replayed the motions in his mind, visualizing a trick he'd executed dozens of times across ramps, curbs, park benches, and handrails. He picked up speed, moved his back foot toward the tail of the board, and tucked in.

Then pop.

Omar ollied high into the air. At the peak of his jump, just as planned, he locked his back truck onto the safety rail and began a 5-0 grind across its ledge. For a moment, everything stopped. He no longer heard the crashing waves, felt the worry in his gut, or tasted the uneasy sweat on his lips. He was nine years old again, grinding the coping on a mini ramp for the very first time with his proud father looking on. Omar wished he could hold the trick forever, transform into some kind of gnarly gargoyle, and become a permanent fixture on the end of the pier. But his momentum was already slowing, and Omar prepared to land back onto the boardwalk and back into reality.

Just then, Omar heard a loud screech overhead. The sound made him glance toward the darkened sky. A large black-and-brown bird swooped past his head like a kamikaze jet, nearly clipping Omar's left ear.

The brief encounter was enough to kill Omar's concentration and knock him from his perch. Suddenly, he was falling and all his senses came flooding back. The waves thundered in his ears, stomach acid burned in his throat, and a helpless scream burst from his lips.

Like all skaters, Omar had taken a couple hits, fractured some bones, and picked up a few battle scars. Still, as the dark ocean water quickly approached, Omar realized that rising from this fall would require some kind of miracle.

Then everything went black.

3

Moments later, Omar felt himself floating again, but he was no longer in the air. When his eyes opened, he was deep beneath the sea. The saltwater didn't sting, and somehow, his bones didn't ache. Like a fetus in the womb, he felt comforted by the isolation, the warmth, and the weightlessness. He wasn't breathing anymore, but he wasn't holding his breath either. Omar scanned his surroundings. He searched for something to indicate if he was dead or alive.

Far below, on the ocean floor, Omar spotted a glowing green dot. At first, it appeared to be nothing more than speck of luminescent plankton, but as Omar swam closer and closer, the object grew larger and larger.

The glowing green light throbbed like a radioactive beacon. Omar could feel its energy pulsate into his toes and out of his skull. He thought about turning back, fearing the object was some sort of alien meteorite or hazardous nuclear waste, but the neon light lured him in like a powerful magnet.

When he was only a few feet away, Omar recognized the object in front of him. There, on the ocean floor, resting amongst sea urchins and thousand-year-old coral, sat the wheel of a skateboard. Under different circumstances, Omar might have questioned the absurdity of this find. At that moment, however, his very presence seemed like something out of a very bad dream. So instead, Omar simply reached down and attempted to grab the wheel from its resting place.

Suddenly, the bulbous head of a snake lashed out from beneath a nearby rock. It lunged at Omar's hand again and again with its long, venomous fangs.

As Omar quickly backed away, the snake slithered toward the glowing green light with hungry eyes. The deadly reptile unlocked its jaw and prepared to swallow the skateboard wheel in one massive gulp. But it never got the chance. The black-and-brown kamikaze bird that had knocked Omar from the pier streaked down through the water.

The bird snatched the wheel from the ocean floor, and darted back toward the surface.

Omar watched the bird disappear, and then stared back down at the snake in disbelief. It continued slithering toward him, hissing angrily and swinging its head from side to side. Omar tried desperately to move, but he couldn't. He felt a heavy weight pressing again and again against his chest, holding him down, not allowing him to escape. The snake slithered closer and closer. It opened its jaws wider and wider, tensed its body, and then struck at Omar's face.

"GAAAAAH!" Omar screamed, hacking up water, gasping for air, and swinging his arms like a prizefighter.

"Dude!" said a voice above him, but Omar kept swinging, screaming, and struggling for air. His body ached, his lungs burned, and his nostrils stung. "Dude, chill out!" the voice said a second time.

Finally, Omar opened his eyes, half expecting a snake to be hanging from his bottom lip. Instead, through his blurry vision, he saw a young woman hovering over him like an angel. Omar immediately recognized her long caramel dreads, black rash guard, and pink bikini bottoms.

"Surfer girl," he whispered to himself.

"Who?" the girl asked.

"Um," Omar hesitated. Tommy had been right. Well, sort of. The trick had certainly gotten the girl's attention and, even though his body was on fire, Omar tried to stay cool. "Is this h-heaven?" he mumbled.

"Very funny," replied the girl, wiping Omar's mouth-to-mouth spit from her lips. "You could have been killed, you know? What kind of stupid stunt were you trying to pull, anyway?"

"An Imperial 5-0," answered Omar.

"A what?" asked the puzzled girl.

"Never mind. My bro and I were just —" Omar stopped. He sat up and finally took a look at his surroundings. Somehow, he had managed to survive the fifty-foot fall and ended up on the beach more than a dozen blocks away. To his right, Omar could see the pier in the distance. Dozens of red and blue police car lights twirled near its entrance gate. Flashlights and spotlights scanned the dark surf below for a missing teenage body.

"Some bro," said the girl, following Omar's gaze. She stood up, grabbed her surfboard, and prepared to leave. "You know, you probably shouldn't stick around here. When they don't find anything beneath the pier, they'll start working their way down the beach."

"Of course," Omar agreed. He struggled to his feet, wiped sand from his faded T-shirt, and fished seaweed from the pockets of his cargo shorts. Then, the disheveled teen began searching the beach for his missing skate shoe. "Well, I guess I'll see you around," he added, playing it cool and not lifting his head.

"Look," said the girl after a moment. "I live a couple houses down. My dad's at work. If you want, you could come hang there for a while, and, like, dry off and stuff."

"For real?" asked Omar, looking up with surprise.

"Yeah, you know," said the surfer girl, "on account of me feeling sorry for you and all."

"So this is just a pity invite, huh?" asked Omar, hesitating slightly and then examining his shameful state. "I'm cool with that."

The surfer girl rolled her eyes, turned, and started walking up the shoreline toward Seacoast Drive. As Omar followed, he spotted a black-and-gray tattoo on the girl's leg. The strange vision he'd nearly forgotten about came rushing back to him. The wheel, the bird, and there, spiraling down the back of the girl's left thigh, was the inky image of that nasty snake. Its jaw opened at the bend in her knee, and each time the girl stepped, the serpent snapped its angry fangs open and closed, open and closed, open and closed.

"See something you like?" asked the surfer girl, catching Omar leering at her backside.

"Nah, I mean, yeah — I mean, I wasn't," Omar stammered. He wanted to ask the girl about her tattoo. He wanted to tell her about his crazy, out-of-whack, tripped-out vision and how her ink was giving him some pretty gnarly flashbacks. But he didn't. "Uh, what did you say your name was?" he said instead.

"I didn't," replied the surfer girl. She walked to the top of the beach, bent down, and pulled a vintage longboard out from behind a row of bushes. Then she looked back again. "But it's Neelu."

Omar hobbled beside her and extended his hand. "Nice," he said with a cocky smile. "I'm Omar, by the way."

Neelu placed the longboard into his open hand. "Looks like you could use this more than me," she said, pointing down at Omar's missing shoe. A limp tube sock hung from his toes like a sloppy piece of toilet paper. "Just try not to fall, okay?"

4

As the girl started north up Seacoast Drive, Omar placed the longboard on the ground and hopped on. The old deck bent slightly under his body weight, and Omar could feel the soft, natural wood beneath his one naked heel. He kicked out, and began to glide smoothly down the sidewalk like a glassy wave. It was the closest Omar had come to real surfing in a really long time.

"Say, Neelu," Omar began, rolling up next to the girl. "How come I've never seen you at Mar Vista?"

"Probably 'cause I don't go to school there," she replied bluntly.

"Oh, right. That's cool," said Omar. "I got a lot of friends who've dropped out. I thought about bailing myself one of these days."

"For what?" asked Neelu. "You planning a career at the In-N-Out Burger or something?"

"No, actually, I was hoping to become a —" Omar started to explain. Then he saw Neelu take a sudden right onto Citrus Avenue. Omar quickly bent his knees, pressed his toes into the edge of the board, and tried carving sharply around the corner after her. The longboard responded, but not as quickly as Omar had expected. He flailed his arms wildly, bounced off the curb, and nearly lost his balance.

A few feet away, Neelu had stopped in front of a small white bungalow. She had seen the entire wretched scene, and stared at Omar like some pathetic noob. "Yes?" she asked with a smirk.

"— a professional skateboarder," whispered Omar, wishing he hadn't had to finish that sentence.

"BAHAHAHA!" Neelu let out gut-busting belly-laugh, waking every dog from Tijuana to Chula Vista.

"Well, at least I'm not a dropout!" Omar shot back. "I was just trying to make you feel better, you know?"

"I didn't drop out," replied Neelu. She started up the driveway of the bungalow. "I'm homeschooled."

"Seriously?" asked Omar. He followed her onto the stoop and leaned the longboard against the side of the house. "Are your parents in a cult or something?"

"Not quite," she said.

Neelu unlocked the front door, stepped inside, and flicked on the lights. Omar walked in after her and nearly collapsed. Surfing artifacts and memorabilia covered every inch of the tiny, twelve-by-twelve foot room. A hundred years of surfboards — from Hawaiian hardwoods to three-fin thrusters — hung horizontally from the floor to the ceiling of each wall. They had been signed by some of the greatest surfers to ever rip, including Kelly Slater, Tom Curren, Larry Bertleman, and even the Duke himself.

"Awesome," whispered Omar, spinning 360s on his heels, trying to take in each and every item.

"Yeah, my dad's a bit extreme," explained Neelu, leading Omar toward the laundry room. "But I'm sure you can relate to that, huh?"

"Nah, my old man passed away," said Omar.

"Oh, right, I'm sorry —" Neelu began.

"That's cool. You didn't know," Omar assured her. "He would have freaked over all of this stuff, though."

Following Neelu through the living room and into a hallway, Omar browsed the continuing collection of mint-condition boards: a 1961 Velzy, a 1978 Mark Richards, a 1982 McCoy, and there, at the very end of the hallway, stood a 1965 Greg Noll Slot Bottom.

Towering nearly ten feet tall, the turquoise-green gun stretched from within inches of the ceiling to within inches of the floor. A massive board for monster waves. "Actually, he had a board just like this," Omar added. "His favorite."

"Only the best," said Neelu.

"He called it his killer, you know," added Omar. He reached out and ran his fingers up and down the board's familiar wood grain center stripe. The crusted salt sticking to the corners of his eyes suddenly made them start to water. "I guess he was right about something."

Omar let out a nervous laugh and then turned. Neelu stood behind him, holding a pair of oversized board shorts and a baby blue polo shirt. "Sorry," Omar said, wiping at his eyes. "I didn't mean to —"

"These should fit," interrupted Neelu, holding out the clothes and trying to avoid the subject. "You can change in the laundry room, if you want." She pointed toward a door on the other side of the hallway.

Without saying another word, Omar took the clothes, entered the laundry room, and shut the door behind him. For the first time that night, he was alone. And, like a ground swell from a distant storm, Omar could feel a wave of deep, distant emotions building inside of him. The room started spinning and shaking.

Two years of anger, sadness, and fear was about to come crashing down, and Omar was riding directly in the impact zone. He quickly stumbled to the nearby window, flung it open, and let out a violent scream.

A cool, Pacific breeze comforted Omar and dried the tears that now spilled down his cheeks. They were the first tears since his father's death. The funeral hadn't even brought them out. But for some reason — maybe the accident, the vision, or the board — Omar felt different somehow, as if his life were about to change.

"Is everything cool in there?" asked Neelu from outside the laundry room door.

For a moment, Omar had forgotten where he was and wondered if the hottie surfer girl had heard him screaming like a wuss.

"Totally," he answered as calmly as possible. Then Omar quickly pulled off his crusty T-shirt and slipped on the baby blue polo. "Just a sec." He removed his belt. He emptied the contents of his cargo pockets onto the washing machine and started taking off his shorts.

"Omar! Open up!" shouted Neelu frantically. She pounded several times on the door, and then burst into the room, slamming the door behind her.

"Whoa!" exclaimed Omar. He quickly pulled up his shorts and zipped his fly.

"I'm not that kind of guy —" he joked.

Neelu pushed her hand over Omar's mouth. He could feel her palm shaking against his lips. "Shut up," she whispered nervously. Then she leaned toward the door, stopped, and listened.

Another door slammed closed on the other side of the house. Omar heard what sounded like footsteps in the living room.

Neelu spun around, grabbed Omar by the collar of the polo shirt, and pulled him close. "You have to get out of here," she said.

"Why?" asked Omar, shocked by the sudden turn of events. "Who is that?"

"My father," Neelu replied.

"Dude, don't worry about it. I'm great with parents," said Omar. He reached toward the handle of the laundry room door.

"No!" shouted Neelu, slapping his hand away. "I mean, not yet, Omar. I shouldn't have brought you here. You have to leave."

"What? How?" he asked. "In case you haven't noticed, we're kind of stuck in this room."

Neelu released one of her hands from Omar's collar and pointed toward the open window behind him. "Take the longboard," she said.

Omar thought about arguing with the girl, but she looked like he had felt only moments before. Neelu wasn't going to budge.

Omar moved toward the window, and then looked back. "By the way, in case I don't see you again, thanks for saving my life," he said. He leaped onto the windowsill and started lowering himself into the backyard.

"Omar!" he heard the girl call after him.

Neelu came to the window, leaned out, and grabbed Omar by the collar again. "You will," she said. "And you're welcome."

Neelu pulled his face toward hers, and their lips touched for the second time that night. A half-second later, when she let go, Omar fell to the ground with a thud. He stared back up at her, dazed, hypnotized by the brown-haired bunny. If their first kiss had brought him back to life, this one had knocked him on his butt.

"Now git!" Neelu whispered down at him.

5

Without hesitating, Omar stood and hobbled around to the front of bungalow. An old-time VW van was now parked in the driveway. Vintage surfboards were strapped atop the green and white relic. Omar crept onto the stoop. He grabbed Neelu's longboard from where he'd left it, and then started back down the stairs.

Just then, through a small opening in the window blinds, Omar saw the back of a man standing in Neelu's living room. He wore a pair of oversized board shorts, like the ones Omar had nearly changed into, and had a large tattoo on his right calf. Omar crept closer to get a better look. Pressing his nose to the window and squinting his eyes, the black-and-gray ink suddenly became much clearer.

An owl? Omar thought, staring at the wide-eyed bird. The predator's wings stretched above the man's knee and its talons nearly scraped against his ankle. Within its clutches, the owl strangled a long checkered snake, which writhed and wrapped its wicked tail around the man's sandaled foot. The man turned and the bird disappeared, replaced by a pale shin moving toward the window.

"Time to ditch this *cult*-de-sac," Omar said to himself. He leaped from the stoop, threw the vintage longboard beneath his feet, and landed on the driveway in one smooth sequence. He pushed hard and didn't look back. Soon, Omar was rolling down Seacoast Drive and halfway back to the Imperial Beach Pier.

Several squad cars still surrounded its entrance gates and dozens of gawkers had stopped, hoping to catch a glimpse of a body washing ashore. Omar knew they wouldn't get that twisted luxury. He also knew he couldn't risk being recognized by witnesses.

Omar made a quick left onto Elm Avenue. Then, starting to groove with the longboard, he carved right onto Second Street and sped toward his house near Reama Park. On the way, he skated past Tommy's place, and spotted a light coming from his friend's bedroom window in the basement.

Two hours had ticked by since they'd last seen each other, and Omar figured Tommy would be worried sick. After all, he didn't even know if Omar was alive.

Omar grabbed the longboard off the ground and crept toward the open window. As usual, he planned to avoid crazy Mrs. Goff and slip into the basement unnoticed. As he approached the house, however, Omar heard his friend arguing with someone.

"Great," Omar said to himself. "Looks like Tommy and his mom are fighting again."

Omar considered turning back, but then he thought he heard Tommy say his name. Omar crept closer. He kneeled near the basement window, placed the longboard against the side of the house, and listened.

"Dude, I told you already!" he heard Tommy shout. "He's gone . . . at the bottom of the sea."

Omar peeked in the basement window. Tommy hadn't been arguing with his mother. He was talking on a cell, pacing back and forth from one end of the room to the other. "What else do you need me to do?" he continued to shout. "What else do you want from me?!"

Omar heard the longboard starting to tip, sliding and scraping against the side of the house. He reached out, trying desperately to snag it and avoid blowing his cover, but the deck fell to the ground with a loud thud.

"Who's there?!" exclaimed Tommy, moving toward the window.

Omar grabbed the board, turned, and started walking away.

"Yo, Omar?!" Tommy yelled after him. "Is that you?"

Omar stopped and glanced back over his shoulder. "Oh, hey, man!" he said, faking surprise. "I didn't know if you'd be home."

"How — I mean — what are you doing here, bro?" asked Tommy, seemingly caught off guard by his unexpected visitor.

Omar turned and started walking back toward the basement window. "Is that any way to greet a guy who's just come back from the dead?" he asked.

"Must have been yuppie hell," joked Tommy, spotting Omar carrying the vintage longboard and wearing a polo shirt for the first time. "Love the color, though. Baby blue?"

"It's a long story —" Omar began.

"What, you have somewhere you got to be? I'm not keeping you from a tennis match or anything, am I?" replied Tommy with a laugh.

"Bite me," Omar shot back, setting down the longboard again, and then slipping through the small basement window.

"Dude, I thought you were dead!" said Tommy, finally greeting his friend with a punch on the shoulder. "I mean, that was some fall."

"Yeah, tell me about it," said Omar. "Actually, I kind of thought you'd be out searching for me — or at least waiting for my body to wash up on shore like the rest of those whackos."

"Yo, didn't you see all those cops out there? You'd think they were handing out free donuts or something," replied Tommy. "You know I can't risk another run-in with the police."

Omar knew all about Tommy's troubles. His big bro had been in and out of juvie since grade school. Drugs, petty theft, assault, and even arson charges had landed him in the kiddie clink a half-dozen times or more. Luckily for Tommy, Omar's father, Zeke, had always been around to bail him out.

From the looks of the basement, however, his friend had since reverted to some of his old ways. Against the far wall, Omar spotted three touch-screen monitors, an ultrathin wireless keyboard, and a juiced-up gaming computer. In his hand, Tommy held a high-tech satellite phone, something Omar had only seen in the glass display cases at RadioShack.

"Who were you just talking to?" asked Omar.

"What? No one," he replied. "I'm the only one here."

"I heard you, Tommy," said Omar. "On the phone. I heard you talking about me. About the accident."

"No — I mean, well, yeah," Tommy explained. "I've been calling around about you, Omar. I thought maybe someone would have seen you, bro. You know, been able to tell me if you were all right."

"Like who? Brody? Rico?" asked Omar. "They the ones that lifted that sat phone for you?"

Tommy looked at the high-tech phone in his hand and then back at Omar. "What? This?" he said, flustered by the sudden accusation. "Oh, I picked this baby up in Tijuana a few weeks ago. Talked the guy down to thirty bucks. Looks real, don't it? Yeah, well, it doesn't work for crap."

Omar pointed at the 50-inch computer monitors on the far wall. "Must've been tough smuggling those across the border, though, huh?" he added.

Tommy glanced in the direction his friend was pointing. "Yeah, strapped them to the moped, right?" he said, letting out a nervous laugh and pretending to rev the accelerator on his dusty old motorbike. Then he moved toward the high-tech equipment and placed his hand on one of the displays. "Nah, man, these are the real deal — fully loaded and fully paid for."

"Where did you ever get that kind of money?" asked Omar, scoffing at his friend's explanation.

"Not me," answered Tommy. "*Us.*"

"Dude, I'm not throwing down for this junk," Omar exclaimed.

"You don't understand," said Tommy. "This stuff is ours. Free and clear. You don't have to pay a dime."

"Sure, Tommy," said Omar. "You and I both know that we ain't getting nothing in this world for free."

"Not free," Tommy replied. "Think of this stuff as an advance. People out there want a piece of you, Omar — a piece of your talent — and they'll pay for it. They gave me this equipment to cut your sponsor-me tape. You know, finally get it out there and get it noticed."

"Who's 'they'?" asked Omar, still skeptical.

"Don't worry about it, bro. Just get me some more of that gnarly footage, and everything else will fall into place. Oh, and speaking of falling," Tommy began with a laugh. He leaned down and pressed a button on the ultra thin, wireless keyboard. Suddenly, the tape of that day's skate session simultaneously appeared on the three monitors, paused to the exact moment Omar had lost his balance and began to fall from the pier. "What do you say tomorrow we give that Imperial 5-0 another shot? You know, 'go big or go home.'"

Omar turned and walked toward the basement window.

"Wait!" Tommy shouted after him. "Where are you going?"

"Home!" replied Omar. "You've got to be crazy if you think I'm trying that trick again!"

"But, dude, you were so close," said Tommy. "You can't give up now. This could be your big break. I mean, if your dad was still around, he would have told you —"

For the second time that night, a wave of emotions flooded Omar's mind. He rushed at Tommy with a clenched fist, but stopped just short of hitting him.

"Shut up, Tommy! Shut up!" Omar shouted, cocking his fist again and again. "Say one more word about my father, and I swear . . ."

"Chill," said Tommy, knowing his friend didn't have the guts to hurt him. "I just meant, not many people get a second chance to slay their own dragon."

"Yeah, and not many people survive a fifty-foot fall, either," said Omar. "If I didn't know better, I'd think you wanted me dead."

Omar lowered his fist and started back toward the window. Without saying a word, he slipped outside, grabbed the longboard from the side of the house, and made his way toward the sidewalk.

"Omar!" Tommy called after him.

Omar stopped but didn't turn.

"He was my father too," said Tommy.

Omar slapped the longboard onto the concrete and hopped aboard. After a brief moment, he turned back toward his friend, who was staring out from the basement window.

"No, he wasn't," Omar finally said. Then he pushed hard and took off down Second Street.

6

Omar rolled past the next few blocks wishing he could take back the words he'd just said. Maybe Tommy was right. Maybe he had survived the five-story fall for a reason. Maybe his father would have told him to give it another shot. After all, what other chance did he have to get noticed? How else would he get himself and his mother out of this godforsaken town?

As Omar approached his house, a pair of high beams suddenly lit up near his driveway. *Whose car could that be?* Omar wondered. He knew his mother wouldn't be getting home this late. She should already be inside, worried sick about her precious little boy.

Omar stopped and squinted, trying to get a better look.

Through the blinding light, he spotted the shadows of several objects on top of the oversized vehicle.

Surfboards, Omar thought, suddenly recognizing the vehicle from earlier that night. *Uh-oh.*

Before Omar could even react, he heard the Volkswagen's wheels start to squeal on the asphalt and saw the headlights coming toward him. Omar quickly pressed his right foot onto the back of the board and spun 180 degrees. Facing the opposite direction, he started pushing hard and fast back down Second Street, but the van wasn't stopping. The driver barked on the horn and revved the engine. Soon, the VW was nipping at his heels like an angry dog.

Omar bent low and dug his heels into the left edge of the board. The longboard turned sideways, and its wheel skidded perpendicular to the road. Omar leaned back and put his hand down for balance. His palm scraped against the pitted concrete, but he managed to stay upright and — except for a little road rash — he came out of the turn unscathed. The chase, however, was far from over. The VW screeched into the alley as well, tossing one of the surfboards as it came around the corner on two wheels.

Omar pushed through the alleyway, weaving in and out of cars, dumpsters, and potholes.

Then, on the far side of the alley, he spotted a bright yellow speed bump. He didn't hesitate. Omar rushed at the foot-high hop without fear. He pushed harder and harder and bent so low his butt scraped the board. Then pop. Like earlier that night, he launched his board into the air, and ollied the 60-inch plank over the bump with ease.

He landed on Evergreen Avenue. Cars, buses, and motorcycles whizzed past him at fifty miles per hour. Drivers honked their horns and screamed out their windows at the crazy kid. Omar didn't stop. He laid into the asphalt, pushing harder, and speeding through oncoming traffic like a slalom course. Then he carved another quick right turn and circled back toward Second Street and his house.

Even though he couldn't hear the van anymore, Omar didn't look back. He snatched the longboard off the ground, hopped his front gate, ran over the lawn, and rushed inside. Slamming and locking the door behind him, Omar fell onto the entryway floor in a sweaty heap. For now, his troubles were behind him — well, at least that's what he thought.

"And just where have you been, young man?" Omar heard his mother say before he even looked up. "Do you know what time it is?"

Omar glanced at the clock hanging in the living room. It read 12:02. Even on the weekend, that was way past his curfew. "Time for some birthday cake?" joked Omar, trying to lighten the situation.

Standing at the top of the stairs, his mom cracked a tiny smile, but then quickly straightened her face and folded her arms across her chest. "Not funny," she said sternly. "Now, get to your room! We'll talk more about this in the morning."

Omar didn't say another word. If he played it cool, his mom might let him off easy. He tucked the vintage longboard under his arm and walked slowly up the stairs.

"Where'd you get the board?" his mom asked as he passed her.

Reaching the second floor, Omar turned and looked back at his mother. "A girl — I mean, a friend," he stammered.

"A *girlfriend?*" his mother teased.

"Goodnight, Mom," said Omar, avoiding the question by heading into his bedroom and closing the door behind him.

Inside his bedroom, Omar dropped the longboard onto the floor and crashed face first onto his bed. He couldn't remember the last time he'd been so exhausted.

"If this is fifteen," Omar said to himself, "sixteen must be a nightmare."

A few breaths later, Omar drifted off to sleep and into the first of many dreams. His underwater vision played backward and forward, again and again. The diving bird, the snake, the glowing wheel, all swirled in his head like an underwater whirlpool. And then, she was there. Surfer girl. She smiled at him, flicked her caramel-brown dreads, turned away, and the tattoo on her right thigh came alive. The black-and-gray snake swirled up her leg, around her abdomen and her throat. The evil reptile struck at her again and again, eating her bit by bit, piece by piece, from her skull to her toes. And when it was done, it slithered away, leaving only a bloody stain on the sandy shore. Omar rushed to its side. He grabbed at the scarlet granules of sand, trying to kiss them as they fell through his fingers. And then, from far offshore, Omar heard someone calling his name, speaking to him in Japanese. The words sounded familiar, but he couldn't understand them. And when Omar looked up, he saw Tommy riding a monster wave atop a 1965 Greg Noll Slot Bottom. He cut back and forth, and the swell grew bigger and bigger. The beast towered above him like a midnight dragon and then, an instant later, came crashing down.

Wham!

"Ah!" cried Omar, reaching up and grabbing at a sudden pain on his forehead.

When he removed his hand, a sliver of blood trickled down his palm and through his fingers. Omar looked around. He wasn't at the beach anymore. Tommy, the snake, and the surfer girl weren't there, either. It was just him, alone on the bedroom floor, and more confused than ever.

"A dream," Omar said to himself. He spotted a small speck of blood on the corner of his nightstand, and then pressed his fingers against his aching forehead again. "It was all just a dream!"

Omar pulled himself off the floor and raced into the hallway. From the top of the stairs, he could smell bacon and eggs cooking in the kitchen. On any other day, Omar would have considered that another strange event, but today was his fifteenth birthday. His mother always made something extra special for her only son.

"Mom, you'll never believe the dream I had last night," started Omar, reaching the bottom of the stairs and walking into the kitchen.

As predicted, his mother stood in front of the stove, frying up a pan full of greasy goodness.

Sitting at the kitchen table, however, was someone he never imagined he'd see again.

Surfer Girl.

"Omar, we have a visitor," said his mother, pointing her spatula toward Neelu and smiling politely. "I assume this is the friend you were talking about last night?"

For a moment, Omar didn't say a word.

"You hurt your forehead," said Neelu.

Omar stood in the doorway, debating whether to take a seat or turn and run. "What are you doing here?" he finally asked the girl. "Are you stalking me, too?!"

"That's no way to greet a guest!" said his mother.

"It's all right, Mrs. Grebes," said Neelu, standing up from the kitchen table. "I should probably be going anyway." The girl reached into her satchel and pulled out Omar's wallet. "Just thought you might need this. Got your address off the school ID inside."

"Wasn't that thoughtful, Omar?" his mother chimed in. "I think you owe someone an apology."

As Neelu walked past him toward the front door, Omar felt somehow drawn to the girl. She had saved his life, given him his first and second kiss, and died in his dream. Still, he couldn't bring himself to ask for her forgiveness. He watched the surfer girl walk out the front door, and then close it behind her.

"What was that all about?" said his mother.

Omar took a seat at the table. "Don't ask," he replied.

His mother placed a plate in front of her son. Then she grabbed the frying pan and started dishing out scrambled eggs for him. "Omar," she said with a slight hesitation. "Maybe we should have a little talk —"

"Mom!" Omar interrupted, slamming his head onto the table with embarrassment and spilling a pile of mail onto the kitchen floor. "I'm fine, Mom! I'm not like Tommy. There's nothing to worry about." Omar lifted his head and started picking up the spilled envelopes, bills, and second notices. On top of the pile, he spotted a letter addressed to him. "What's this?" he asked.

His mother placed two strips of bacon on Omar's plate and took a quick glance at the envelope. "I thought my big boy wanted his privacy," she answered.

Omar gave her an annoyed glare.

"Must've come in the mail this morning," she continued. "Maybe it's a birthday gift from your grandma."

"Nice!" said Omar. He ripped open the end of the envelope and gave it a quick shake, half expecting a scribbly twenty-dollar check from his grandmother to spill out. Instead, a small white note card fell onto the kitchen table. On the front of the card, the words THE REVOLUTION had been typed in bold red letters.

Omar flipped the card over, and on the back he read a simple message:

"Congratulations, Mr. Grebes. You have been chosen to ride for us. Our offices are located on the corner of Evergreen and Atwood. Please stop by at your earliest convenience for more information.

— Eldrick Otus."

"Dude!" Omar exclaimed, leaping up from the kitchen table and spilling his plate of bacon and eggs onto the ground. "Do you know what this means?!"

"Yeah, now I have to clean the floor," answered his mother.

"Forget about that, Mom," said Omar, holding out the card and beaming with pride. "You may never have to clean another floor again — not here and definitely not at that crappy job of yours."

"That job puts food on this table," she replied, and then spotted Omar glancing down at the spilled breakfast. "And don't even say it, young man. I'm not in the mood for your jokes."

"I'm serious. Just look," Omar said, handing the card to his mother. "Someone wants to sponsor me, Mom. *Me*! Can you believe it? This is what I've been working for. All those bruises and broken bones. All those late-night sessions. It's finally going to pay off!"

"How?" asked his mother.

"Thanks for the vote of confidence, Mom," said Omar.

"No, I didn't mean it like that, Omar," she explained. "I just meant how did they find out about you?"

Omar snatched the card back from his mom, giving it a second look. "Not sure," he replied. "Maybe Tommy sent them my sponsor-me tape. I didn't think it was finished yet, but he probably sent copies out without telling me. Typical Tommy, you know?"

"Be careful, Omar," said his mother, still sounding skeptical. "I mean, there's a lot of scams out there."

"What? Like that slap chopper thing you bought online?" said Omar, pointing at a dusty gadget on the kitchen counter. "I'm not going to fall for some slick salesman."

"I know," his mother replied. "It's just — well, you can't trust anyone these days."

"Okay, Mom," said Omar, rolling his eyes and walking out of the kitchen. "I got to call Tommy. Maybe someone around here will be excited for me —"

"Omar!" his mother shouted after him.

The teen turned and looked back at his mom, frustrated by her lack of enthusiasm. "What?" he asked.

"Your father would have been proud," she said.

Omar watched a tear fall from the corner of each of his mother's eyes. He knew only one of those tears fell for him. The other fell for his father, who had gone missing exactly two years ago. On a morning just like this one, Zeke had slipped out early to catch a few waves before his son's thirteenth birthday breakfast. Omar and his mother sat at the kitchen table waiting for him to return. They watched his eggs get rubbery and cold, the bacon turn a fatty shade of white, and the coffee stain a ring in his mug. Eventually, Omar's mother stood, exited the kitchen without a word, and started making a few phone calls.

A week later, the food was still there, stinking up the kitchen like a bad memory. The San Diego Police Department, the bros at Billy's Board Shop, and even a private investigator couldn't give her an answer.

"Maybe he just left," some of them had suggested. "You know, got tired of the real world and bolted."

But she couldn't accept that explanation. Wouldn't accept it. Zeke was a decent man, a good husband, and a great father. And, even after the police had declared him dead and the family had spread the ashes of his belongings across the shores of Todos Santos, the uncertainty surrounding his disappearance must have been killing her.

For Omar, however, it kept him alive.

"Thanks, Mom," Omar finally replied. He knew that anything more — a hug, a kiss, or even a simple "Is-everything-all-right?" — could send her spiraling back down that whirlpool of doubt.

Instead, he ran up the stairs, grabbed his cell phone and the longboard from his bedroom, and then dashed out the front door.

"Happy Birthday!" his mother yelled after him. "And don't forget to call me!"

"Thanks, Mom," shouted Omar, starting down the sidewalk on the longboard. "I will!"

8

Riding down Second Street, Omar checked his cell. He knew Tommy would never be up at this time of the morning. Besides, after last night, he figured a warning shot before showing up at his friend's house unannounced couldn't hurt. However, a message scrolled across the phone's display screen: 1 TEXT FROM TOMMY GOFF 12:21 AM.

Omar figured his friend had beaten him to the punch and called to apologize late last night. He clicked Enter on his phone, and the message popped up on the tiny screen:

I AM SORRY OMAR. IT'S NOT ME. IT'S THEM. THEY ARE THE SNAKES OMAR! THEY ARE THE SNAKES!!!!

Omar skidded to a stop in front of Tommy's house. He recalled the vision from the previous day, the black-and-gray tattoos, and the dream. The text message appeared to be a warning, but against what? His friend couldn't have known about any of these events. Omar hadn't told Tommy about the vision, the surfer girl, or her lunatic father.

"Or did I?" he wondered aloud.

Omar sprinted across Tommy's front lawn to the basement window. He rapped on the glass and waited. After a moment, when his friend hadn't answered, Omar peeked inside. Against the far wall of the basement, the monitors, the wireless keyboard, and the high-tech computer were all gone — and so was Tommy.

For a second, Omar considered knocking on the front door and asking crazy Mrs. Goff about her son and the missing equipment. But then again, he thought, maybe this bad situation was actually a good direction. Maybe their little talk last night had finally woken Tommy up. Maybe he had decided to stop lying to himself and return the stolen equipment. Sure, Omar knew his thinking was wishful, but he wasn't about to rat out his big bro before they had a chance to talk.

Omar took off on the longboard, continuing toward the location on the note card in his back pocket.

A few beats later, he arrived at the corner
of Evergreen and Atwood. He hadn't remembered
a skate shop in the area, and he didn't see one now.
Rundown bungalows, rusted-out cars, and chain-link
fences lined the sidewalks as far as Omar could see.

Maybe Mom was right, he thought. *Maybe this was all
some sort of scam or another one of Tommy's pranks.*

Omar double-checked the directions in his pocket.
When he looked back up, he spotted a small concrete
building on the opposite side of the street. No bigger
than a school bus, the building looked like some kind
of 1950s A-bomb bunker, except each and every wall
had been tagged from top to bottom with technicolor
graffiti.

Omar skated closer. He tried to decipher the
bombs, slashes, and scribbles, but like faces in a crowd,
the identities of the words and symbols were totally
unfamiliar. Then, above the building's front doorway,
Omar recognized the bold, blocky letters of one
of these straights: T H E   R E V O L U T I O N

Omar held up the note card in his hand and quickly
compared it with the simple tag.

"This must be the place," he said, confirming the
similarities. He grabbed the rusted handle of the front
door, paused, and took a deep breath.

During the past twelve hours, Omar had felt caught in the barrel of a wave, unsure if he'd get shacked or come out of this tube ride alive. The next few minutes, however, would almost certainly determine that fate.

Omar stepped inside the bomb bunker and into a whole other world. The rough exterior of the building completely masked the sickest shop Omar had ever seen. Skate decks covered every inch of every wall like some kind of rock star sheetrock. From floor to ceiling hung some of the wickedest woods to ever ride a ramp, including Tony Alva's Dogtown deck, Aldrin Garcia's highest-ollie hardwood, a Chris Cole skateboard, and a Powell-Peralta ripper board signed by the original Bones members.

Browsing the collection, Omar could hardly believe that a hella-cool place like this could fly under his radar. Then again, some of the best skate and surf spots in SoCal were also some of the best-kept secrets. If it wasn't on the DL, any fresh hangout would soon be flooded with kooks, posers, and wannabes.

A million questions raced through Omar's mind, and he scanned the store for an employee to answer them. Instead, near the rear of the shop, Omar spotted a tall pedestal with a glass display case on top, illuminated by a single spotlight from the ceiling.

Omar moved closer and peered into the display. Inside, floating in the middle of the large glass cube, hovered what appeared to be a small shard of plywood, no bigger than a flash drive. Omar leaned even closer, trying to identify the mysterious object, and his warm breath fogged up the glass of the display.

Suddenly, the wooden shard started glowing!

A bright green light burst out of the object in every direction. Omar shielded his eyes with surprise. Then, figuring he had set off some kind of security alarm, Omar quickly grabbed the tail of his t-shirt and wiped his spitty breath off of the display. When his hand brushed against the glass, an electric bolt of energy shot through Omar's body, quivering from the nerves in his hand to the nerves in his toes. Omar couldn't move. His hand stuck to the glass like a magnet. Omar fell to his knees, his body jerking and flailing wildly in a full-on seizure. And then, the visions began again . . .

Like rapid-fire clips in a music video, hundreds of pictures flashed through Omar's mind, but this time the series of images looked somewhat familiar. High atop a half-pipe stood Tony Hawk. Sweating and exhausted and with thousands of fans cheering him on, the Birdman stared down the face of the wicked ramp with a look of pure determination.

After a brief hesitation, he dropped in. He soared from side to side, and then unleashed a vertical vortex. Two and a half rotations. Nine hundred degrees. And when the Hawk finally came back down to Earth, he hoisted his skateboard into the air like a Spartan sword and celebrated his monstrous feat.

Still hypnotized by the visions, Omar suddenly felt a sense of power, courage, and accomplishment course through his veins. Like a spectator, he watched the Hawk lift his 900 deck higher and higher into the air.

But then, a nanosecond later, everything changed.

Omar's warm, fuzzy feelings quickly turned into cold-blooded fear. Tony's skateboard started warping, twisting, and expanding like a violent balloon. Fans and onlookers scattered in all directions, running and fleeing the scene in terror.

Then, *BAM!*

The 900 board shattered into dozens of pieces, leaving only a bright white light behind — and leaving Omar unconscious on the skate shop floor.

9

Moments later, through what sounded like a concrete culvert, Omar could hear his name. "Omar? Omar?" the voice called to him again and again.

Omar slowly opened his aching eyes. He soon recognized his surroundings, but not the person standing over him. The tall, silver-haired man, wearing board shorts and a polo shirt, extended his hand toward the teen. "Welcome to the Revolution, Omar Grebes," he said, offering to help him to his feet.

"Huh?" asked Omar, still a little confused.

"I've been waiting for you," the man continued.

Omar accepted the stranger's hand and pulled himself off the floor. "How did you know my name? I mean, who are you?" he asked.

"Those are two very different questions, Omar," replied the man with a smile. Then he bent down and picked up the note card, which Omar had accidently dropped onto the floor. "Let's start with the second one. My name is Eldrick Otus —"

"Mr. Otus!" exclaimed Omar, recognizing the man's name from the invitation and suddenly feeling a little embarrassed. "I'm so sorry. It's just — I took this major spill yesterday, and I haven't been feeling myself since then, you know? I hope this doesn't ruin my chances of riding for you or anything."

"Of course not," said the man. "And call me Eldrick."

"Cool," said Omar, feeling a little more comfortable. "Then I assume you've seen the tape?"

The man nodded. "Yes, we've seen the tape, Omar," he replied.

"Great!" Omar exclaimed. "But you should probably know that the video wasn't finished. I mean, if you guys are having any doubts about sponsoring me or anything, I'd totally be down for shredding a little demo or whatever you need —"

"Perhaps, there's been a bit of a misunderstanding, Omar," interrupted Eldrick. "We're not interested in sponsoring you."

Omar felt that barrel of hope begin to close out.

"You're not?" he asked, puzzled.

"No, son," answered Eldrick. "We have other plans for you."

The strange man turned and headed toward the back room from which he'd come. And that's when Omar saw it — the tattoo of an owl stared back at him from Eldrick's calf. The image was unmistakable. The wide eyes. The razor-sharp talons. The tortured snake. He'd seen the whole thing only hours before while peering through the blinds of Neelu's living room window.

Omar needed out of the situation and fast.

As Eldrick exited the room, Omar spun around and turned to run. *WHAM!* Instead, he smashed directly into the display pedestal, which wobbled for an instant and then fell to the ground in a thunderous crash.

Eldrick rushed back into the main room. "Hey!" he shouted angrily. "Where are you going?"

Without hesitating and without thinking, Omar grabbed the small shard of wood out off the shattered display on the floor. The powerful energy returned to his body, but this time it surged through him like a rush of pure adrenaline.

Omar felt alive, unafraid, and unstoppable.

WELCOME TO THE
REVOLUTION
STALEFISH

WITH HIS NEWFOUND ENERGY, OMAR RACED DOWN ATWOOD AVENUE, CUTTING IN AND OUT OF TRAFFIC LIKE A RAZOR.

I MUST BE DREAMING.

HIS LINES HAD ALWAYS BEEN TIGHT, BUT THIS WAS INSANE.

LIKE A HIGH-TECH LASER BEAM OMAR'S EYES SCANNED THE LANDSCAPE IN FRONT OF HIM.

OMAR DIDN'T STOP TO CELEBRATE.

CLACK!

HE TUCKED IN . . .

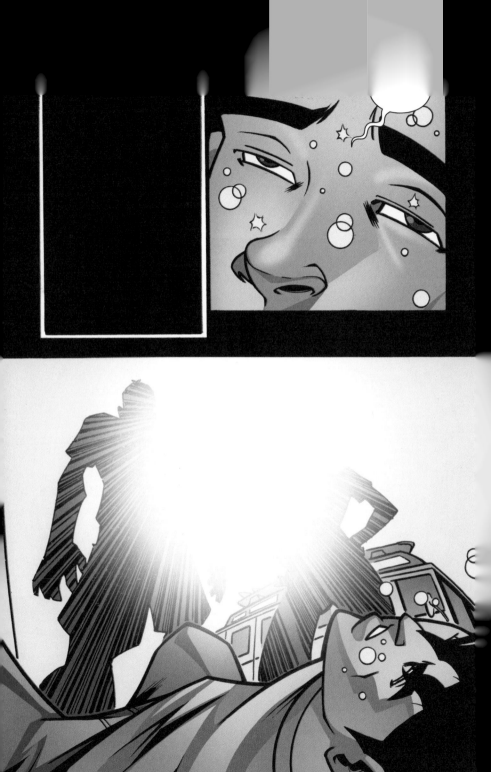

10

A few minutes later, Omar felt a large hand grasp the top of his head, and then yank off a dark hood with a few strands of his hair. Sitting cross-legged in front of him was a man who no longer needed an introduction.

"Eldrick Otus," Omar spit from his bloodied lip.

"Correct," said the man. "And you're Omar Grebes. But I believe we've already established that."

Omar glanced around the van for a way to escape, but instead of windows and doors, dozens of miniature LED monitors lined the interior walls. Videos of teens just like himself played on the display screens. Skaters, surfers, snowboarders, freestyle BMX bikers, and other athletes were all represented.

"What is this? My competition or something?" asked Omar, even more frightened and confused. "Because I can make your decision a little easier. I'm out! There's no way I'm competing for this job."

"You're not here to compete, Omar," answered Eldrick. "You've already been chosen."

"For what?!" shouted Omar.

"The Revolution," replied the man.

"Dude, I don't know what you're talking about," said Omar, "but I think I'll pass. Thanks, though."

Omar rose to his knees and motioned toward the rear double doors of the van. At the same time, he spotted Eldrick reaching into the pocket of his board shorts and half expected him to pull out a knife. Instead, the strange man unveiled the small shard of wood from the skate shop, pulsing with energy.

"Do you know what this is?" Eldrick asked, holding the piece toward the boy.

Omar sat back down, but didn't respond.

"It's called a Fragment," continued Eldrick, answering his own question. "One piece of a very important skateboard."

"Big deal," said Omar. "I've been in your shop. It's probably the sickest collection I've ever seen. You've got dozens of boards."

"None like this," said Eldrick. "Without this board, the others wouldn't even exist. Without this board . . . neither would we."

"Dude, you really are whacked!" said Omar, letting out a gut-busting laugh. "I mean, when Neelu told me she was homeschooled, I figured you must be in some kind of cult, but this is out of control!"

"When did the visions begin, Omar?" interrupted Eldrick.

Omar immediately stopped laughing. "How did you —?" he started, but a nervous bubble rising in his throat made him stop.

"The same way you pulled off that massive feeble grind out there," explained Eldrick. The wooden shard in the man's hand glowed brighter and brighter, and tentacles of electric energy slithered around his wrist and down his arm.

"That?" asked Omar, pointing toward the glowing object. "What? Does it have some kind of superpowers or something?" He let out another nervous laugh.

"We're not exactly sure," answered Eldrick with a straight face. "Only a chosen few can unlock the extraordinary powers within the Fragments."

"Fragments?" repeated Omar. "Like, more than one?"

"Many."

"And where did they come from?" asked Omar, wanting to hear the end of the man's foolish tale.

"I believe you already know," replied Eldrick. He grabbed Omar's wrist and, like a surge of electricity, the Fragment's energy flowed from his hand and into the boy's body. Suddenly, those rapid-fire images of Tony Hawk ripped through Omar's mind once again. With thousands of screaming fans cheering him on, the Birdman dropped in, executed the world's first-ever 900, raised his skateboard into the air in celebration, and then, like a megaton bomb, the deck exploded into a bright white light.

A second later, Eldrick released the boy's hand, and for a moment Omar sat in stunned silence.

"The 900?" the teen finally asked. Omar knew all about this monumental skateboarding trick. He'd been born the day it happened — July 27, 1999 — a fact his father had never let him forget. "What does Tony Hawk have to do with any of this?"

"Everything," answered Eldrick, raising the wooden shard again. "The Fragments are pieces of that board."

"Dude, I'm totally not following you," said Omar, growing frustrated by the situation. "None of this makes any sense!"

"We don't completely understand it either,"
added Eldrick. "But somehow, the 900 opened
of portal — a tunnel between two worlds. So
witnessed that explosion. Others have no recollection
of the event. But the Fragments are real, Omar. They
exist. Individually, they hold great energy and strength,
but together — well, their power is unimaginable."

"But why me?" asked Omar. "Why are you telling
me all this?"

"You are one of the chosen few," said Eldrick,
pointing at the miniature LED screens surrounding
him. "The first of the many Keys who are conduits
of this energy, and the only ones who can locate it."

"Okay, fine! Let's go find these so-called Fragments,
and get this whole thing over with," replied Omar,
hoping to satisfy the madman.

"It's not that easy, son," said Eldrick.

"Of course not," Omar scoffed.

"You see, when the 900 board shattered, the
Fragments were scattered across the globe," explained
the man. "The whereabouts of these pieces are difficult
to determine, at best."

"Yeah, yeah," Omar interrupted. "Why don't you let
the 'Chosen One' worry about that, huh?"

"There's more," said Eldrick.

"Others seek the Fragments as well," said the man. "But unlike us, they do not wish to secure and protect this extraordinary power. They plan to unleash it onto the world — and, like snakes, prey on the weakest among us."

Omar's heart started pounding in his chest, beating faster and faster in rhythm with the pulsating shard of wood. Tommy's text message from early that morning suddenly scrolled through his mind like the ticker on a sports broadcast: IT'S THEM. THEY ARE THE SNAKES OMAR! THEY ARE THE SNAKES!!!!

Omar popped to his feet. He plowed into Eldrick like a running back, pushing and shoving his way toward the van's double doors.

"What's wrong?!" Eldrick exclaimed. He grabbed the boy in both arms and tackled him to the floor of the van. "What did I say?"

"Tommy warned me about you!" cried Omar, struggling to free himself from the man's grasped. "He warned me, and I didn't listen!"

"Warned you about what?" asked Eldrick.

"YOU! THE SNAKE!" Omar screamed out. "What have you done with my friend?"

Eldrick followed Omar's gaze toward the tattoo on the back of his calf.

"I can explain, Omar, but you need to calm down," he said, pressing the boy onto the floor again and again. "You've got it all wrong, son."

"Quit calling me that, you freak! I'm not your son!" shouted Omar. "My father is dead!"

"I know all about your father," said Eldrick.

Suddenly, the wall of LED monitors went black and then, after a brief moment, they flicked back on and formed a single, vibrant blue video image. It was the ocean, recorded from high above on some sort of aerial helicopter camera. The roar of a distant wave echoed through the van. The camera pulled out further, revealing a massive swell, throbbing and rippling like the skin of a giant beast. It grew bigger and bigger.

And then, the camera zoomed out even more and, atop the monster's back, a tiny surfer cut back and forth down the face of the wave. Even from this distance, Omar recognized the turquoise gun with the wood-grain center stripe. A 1965 Greg Noll Slot Bottom.

"Where did you get this tape?" shouted Omar.

"Watch," said Eldrick, still holding down the boy.

The massive beast started curling and closing out. The surfer raced toward the bottom of the wave, trying to outrun its foamy fangs. It nicked at the board, and the rider came closer and closer to certain doom.

"Let me go!" Omar screamed, violently flailing his arms and legs. "I'm not going to watch my father die!"

"Just look," Eldrick ordered him again.

Out of the corner display, another surfer sped into the larger picture. He darted toward Omar's father like a bullet, slipped in front of him, and stole ownership of the wave. However, neither Zeke Grebes nor the snake could outrun the killer behind them. The monster wave suddenly closed out, collapsing onto itself and spraying a squall of water a hundred feet into the air.

On the floor of the van, Omar collapsed as well, and a flood of tears spilled from his eyes. Eldrick placed his hand on the boy's shoulder, trying to comfort him the best he could.

"Get off of me! Get off of me!" shouted Omar. "Why would you show me that?! Why does any of this matter?"

As the video continued rolling, Omar heard the hum of a wave runner vibrate through the van's speakers. Then, on the displays and out of the fog of water, the machine appeared, ridden by large man wearing a jet-black wetsuit and scuba tank. The man leaned to the side and extended his hand toward the surface of the ocean. From beneath the surf, another hand appeared, flailing wildly and grasping for help.

The man in black grabbed it, and pulled a teen out of the breaker and onto the waver runner. Alive.

"Tommy," whispered Omar, rubbing his watery eyes in disbelief at sight of his friend. "But I don't understand."

"We don't expect you to, Omar," said Eldrick.

"*We?*" asked the boy.

11

Omar hadn't even noticed that the van had stopped until he heard the rear double doors start to open. And there, on the other side, stood Neelu. "I'm sorry, Omar," she said. "I meant to tell you, but it wasn't the right time. That's why I left the card at your house."

"That was you?" asked Omar.

Neelu nodded.

"This is crazy!" Omar cried out. "I mean, you lure me to your shop, kidnap me, show me one stupid video, and what? You expect me to believe that I'm some kind of prophet, that these Fragments are more powerful than nukes, and that the fate of the world lies in my hands. And then, on top of all that, you tell me that my big brother killed my father. Is that about right?"

"Your brother didn't kill him, Omar," Eldrick added.

"Oh, right," Omar shot back, his hands shaking in fear. "It was an evil organization out to rule the world. I mean, how did you even get this tape? Did you piece it together on some kind of home editing software or something? Nice work, man. You're officially smarter than my grandmother, but you're not fooling me!"

Omar pushed passed Neelu, scooted out of the van, and scoped out his surroundings. He didn't recognize the area. They were parked in an abandoned lot, and a hundred feet away near a cliff overlooking the ocean stood a UH-60 Black Hawk helicopter. The blades on the high-tech aircraft spun around and around, whirling faster and faster and priming for takeoff.

Omar felt a hand on his shoulder. He looked back and saw Eldrick standing behind him with a smile on his face.

"We're the eyes in the sky," said Eldrick, pointing toward a high-definition camera mounted on the Black Hawk's landing skids.

Neelu walked to the aircraft, lifted one leg up into the side door, and looked over her shoulder. "So, are you with us?" she yelled back at her friend. Wind from the spinning rotors of the Black Hawk helicopter whipped through her hair and down the back of her rash guard.

The shirt flapped in the breeze and lifted slightly above her waist, just long enough for Omar to spot a second tattoo on the small of her naked back. A falcon. The lightning-fast predator was in a full-on dive, streaking toward that wicked snake on her left thigh.

"Birds of a feather, right, Omar?" added Eldrick, following Neelu into the aircraft and allowing the boy to make his own decision.

Omar's brain was spinning faster than the helicopter blades. Like parts of a skateboarding trick, he tried piecing together the events of the day into something solid and real. The accident. The visions. The Fragment. His father. Tommy. None of it made any sense in his head. So instead of thinking, Omar decided to follow his instincts — as he often did at the skatepark — and continue this gnarly ride.

Before he knew it, Omar was sitting inside the tricked-out heli, flying south across the Pacific Ocean. Inside the cockpit, Eldrick fed the pilot instructions. Neelu fiddled with some high-tech equipment in the rear of the aircraft like some kind of self-taught hacker.

"You were right, Neelu," said Omar, finally finding the courage to speak again. "Your dad is a bit extreme."

Neelu let out a cautious laugh. "Would I lie?" she replied, looking back at her day-old friend.

"Good question," said Omar. "Did you know about my father? Did you know about Tommy?"

"Yes," answered Neelu. "Yes, I knew."

"Then why?" asked Omar. "I've grown up with Tommy my whole life. He was — well, you know — like a brother to me."

Neelu moved toward Omar, kneeled in front of him, and held out a large GPS watch. "Tommy wasn't always one of them," she said, "but at some point they turned him."

"Did my father know?" questioned Omar.

"Have you ever heard the expression 'Keep your friends close, but your enemies closer'?" she asked.

"Of course," he replied, holding out his arm and allowing Neelu to strap the high-tech device to his wrist.

"Well," continued the surfer girl, "your father took those words to heart. He kept Tommy close to protect the Fragments, protect you, and protect all of us. And, until now, he succeeded."

"What do you mean?" questioned Omar.

Eldrick stepped out of the cockpit and into the rear of the aircraft. "She means they're close," he said.

"To what?" Omar asked, hoping he didn't already know the answer to his question.

"Another piece of the board," said Eldrick, confirming those fears.

"Yes, but now we have you, Omar," Neelu added. "You can help us find the Fragment before them and continue your father's legacy."

"But how?" asked Omar. "I don't even know where to begin."

"You will," said Eldrick. He grabbed the handle of the Black Hawk's sliding side door, pulled it open, leaned out, and let the wind rush through his silvery hair. "You will."

Neelu pressed a small red button on the GPS watch, and the gadget on Omar's wrist started beeping. "Don't worry, Omar," she said, leading her friend toward her father and the helicopter's door. "That device will track your location. No matter where the current takes you, we'll be close behind."

Omar glanced outside. On the distant horizon, he spotted the small twin islands of Todos Santos, but directly beneath them, nothing but the churning midnight waters of the Pacific Ocean could be seen.

Omar quickly stumbled away from the door, feeling his hydrophobia suddenly take hold again. "You want me to jump?!" he exclaimed.

"It's the only way," Neelu replied.

"Time is running out," added her father. "Soon, they'll have the Fragment, and we'll all be facing much deeper waters."

"How can I trust you?" asked Omar.

"You can't," stated Eldrick. "From this point forward, the only person you can trust is yourself. But if you're asking for my advice, Omar, follow your instincts . . . and drop in."

Take the challenge or die of shame, Omar thought, considering his options. Less than twenty-four hours earlier, he hadn't backed down from Tommy, and he wouldn't do it today either.

Omar rose to his feet. He glanced at Eldrick and Neelu, and then out at the horizon. "Stay radical," Omar whispered to himself, echoing his father's infamous words.

A moment later, he sprinted toward the helicopter door, and took a leap of faith.

12

Omar fell wildly through the air, uselessly flapping his arms and trying to control an out-of-control dive. Then, as Eldrick had instructed, the young man allowed his instincts to take over again. And soon, like his avian namesake, Omar dove gracefully through the sky like a black-and-brown grebe bird, speeding toward the deadly breakers below.

A split second later, Omar lifted his arms above his head and cut through the surface like a bullet. He darted deeper and deeper, and the waters grew darker and darker. Down, down, down, Omar swam into the abyss until he was skimming along the colorful, jagged coral and passing by surfperch, striped bass, and Chinese mitten crab at the bottom of the sea.

Kicking along the ocean floor, Omar experienced a tightness in his chest and a caffeinated pressure in his eyes. Unlike his underwater vision, he no longer felt like a fetus in a comforting womb; he was a newborn baby with an undeniable need to breath. Omar wanted to unlock his lips, open his throat, and let a tidal wave of saltwater fill his shriveled lungs.

But he didn't.

A far greater force kept his mouth shut, his throat closed, and the floodwaters at bay. He sensed something familiar about his surroundings. The warm waters, the thousand-year-old coral, the spiny black sea urchins, and there — resting silently on the ocean floor — sat that glowing green wheel of the skateboard.

As in his vision, the 900 Fragment throbbed like a radioactive beacon, luring Omar closer and closer like a powerful magnet. And again, when he was only a few feet away, Omar reached down and attempted to grab the wheel from its resting place.

Suddenly, something lashed out from behind a nearby rock, but instead of the black head of a snake, the black-gloved hand of a scuba diver struck at Omar again and again. The masked man wrapped his arms around the boy, squeezing him, holding him down, and waiting for him to die.

Omar bucked, wriggled, and writhed, trying desperately to escape the diver's grasp. He kicked wildly and threw his elbows from side to side.

Finally, in one last exhausted flail of his arms, Omar connected. His elbow cracked into the side of the diver's head with a powerful thud, dislodging his scuba mask and sending him floating, unconscious, toward the coral reef below.

Omar didn't hesitate. He streaked down through the water, snatched the glowing wheel from the ocean floor, and darted back toward the surface. The Fragment's incredible energy coursed through his body again. He kicked harder and faster, and soon the shallower waters grew bluer and brighter. *Just a few more feet*, Omar thought, and he would be able to breathe again and be safe inside the UH-60 Black Hawk helicopter.

But then, like a zombie pulling him back into a grave, something snagged Omar's foot from behind. When he looked down, Omar saw a face more frightening than the undead.

It was Tommy.

Omar's neighbor, his best friend, his big bro tugged violently at his foot, trying to pull him back down into the deep dark waters. Tommy had been the one in the scuba mask.

Tommy had been searching for the Fragment as well, and no amount of history, no family connections, no brotherly bonds would stop him from getting it.

With little oxygen remaining in his bloodstream and no other choice, Omar clutched the Fragment tightly in his hand and looked Tommy straight in the face. His best friend's upper lip quivered, his nostrils flared, and his eyes narrowed into thin black shadows.

For a moment, Omar wondered if he could have seen this coming. Had he mistaken the slippery schemes of a snake for brotherhood? Evil manipulations for love? Only one thing was certain: Eldrick had been right. From this point forward, Omar could trust no one but himself.

Without another thought, Omar gave his big bro a swift kick to the brow. Once again, Tommy's lifeless body drifted toward the ocean floor.

This time, however, Omar watched until nothing remained but the deep, midnight waters of the Pacific. Maybe he would see his friend again someday, or maybe the beach patrol at the Imperial Pier would finally find that missing body of a boy.

Either way, Omar knew that nothing would ever be the same.

Then, with a few more kicks, Omar surfaced.

And there, hovering nearby in the Black Hawk heli, were his new friends — his new family — Eldrick and Neelu. They quickly pulled Omar back into the aircraft and set off toward off the horizon.

"Are you okay, Omar?" asked Neelu, wrapping her arms around their hero.

Omar handed her the glowing Fragment. "What now?" he said, avoiding the question.

"Your quest continues," added Eldrick.

"You mean —?" Omar began.

"Yes," Eldrick interrupted. "This is only the beginning. We have many more pieces to find and many more members to recruit."

"But what about my mother?" asked Omar. "I can't just leave her behind."

"Don't worry, Omar," said Eldrick. "We've found someone to take care of her while you're gone."

"Who?" asked Omar.

Neelu gave her friend a knowing smile. "Only the best," she replied, repeating the words she had used to describe that 1965 Greg Noll Slot Bottom hanging on her father's wall.

During the past twenty-four hours, many of Omar's visions had been fulfilled, and he wondered if another dream had finally come true.

But, for now, a little uncertainty was more than enough. "A real legend, huh?" he said.

Neelu nodded.

Omar turned toward the door of the helicopter and gazed outside. The crimson sun began to set on the horizon, but for one SoCal skater — and the rest of the world — a Revolution was rising.

The Beginning.

OMAR GREBES_
CODE NAME: **STALEFISH**

AGE: 15

HOMETOWN: Imperial Beach, California

SPORT: Skateboarding

INTERESTS: Punk, Food, and Girls

BIO: An active fifteen-year-old boy, Omar Grebes never slows down. When he's not shredding concrete at Ocean Beach Skatepark, he's kicking through surf at Imperial Beach or scarfing down fish tacos from the nearest roadside shop. His wiry, six-foot frame can't hide his live-or-die lifestyle — scars on his elbows, fresh road rash on his knees, and a first-degree sunburn on his nose. However, Omar's not afraid to show off these "battle scars" — often wearing little more than a t-shirt, board shorts, and a pair of black skate shoes. The Bones Brigade and the SoCal surf culture have heavily influenced his personal and skating style. At the park or on the street, Omar is as clean, creative, and inventive as they come.

STORY SETTING: West Coast

ABOUT TONY HAWK

TONY HAWK is the most famous and influential skateboarder of all time. In the 1980s and 1990s, he was instrumental in skateboarding's transformation from fringe pursuit to respected sport. After retiring from competitions in 2000, Tony continues to skate demos and tour all over the world.

He is the founder, President, and CEO of Tony Hawk Inc., which he continues to develop and grow. He is also the founder of the Tony Hawk Foundation, which works to create skateparks and empower youth in low income communities.

TONY HAWK WAS THE FIRST SKATEBOARDER TO LAND THE 900 TRICK, A 2.5 REVOLUTION (900 DEGREES) AERIAL SPIN, PERFORMED ON A SKATEBOARD RAMP.

ABOUT THE AUTHOR_

DONNIE LEMKE works as a children's book editor and writer in Minneapolis, Minnesota. He has written dozens of graphic novels, including the Zinc Alloy series and the adventures of Bike Rider. He also wrote *Captured Off Guard*, a World War II story, and a graphic novelization of *Gulliver's Travels*, both selected by the Junior Library Guild. Most recently, Lemke has written several chapter books for DC Comics.

AUTHOR Q & A_

Q: HAVE YOU PARTICIPATED IN ANY ACTION SPORTS? HOW HAVE THEY INFLUENCED YOU?

A: As a teenager, I skateboarded a little and probably got good enough to pop a decent ollie. But growing up on dirt roads in rural Minnesota didn't give me a whole lot of opportunity to practice outdoors. Instead, I spent A LOT of time honing my skills with a controller — playing *Skate or Die!* (talk about old-school) on Nintendo or *Tony Hawk's Pro Skater* for PS one.

Q: COULD YOU DESCRIBE YOUR APPROACH TO THE TONY HAWK'S 900 REVOLUTION SERIES?

A: When developing the idea for Tony Hawk's 900 Revolution, I was definitely influenced by books, video games, and movies I've watched. Specifically, manga, such as *Dragon Ball* and *Scott Pilgrim*, heavily influenced the quest aspect of TH900 Revolution. In *Dragon Ball*, a child named Goku searches for seven mystical objects. In *Scott Pilgrim*, the main character must destroy his girlfriend's seven evil exes. Like video games, both these books have strong objectives, which keep the reader engrossed until the very end. I'm hoping this series is just as addictive.

TONY HAWK'S 900 revolution

TONY HAWK'S 900 REVOLUTION, VOL. 1: DROP IN

Omar Grebes never slows down. When he's not shredding concrete at Ocean Beach Skatepark, he's kicking through surf or scarfing down fish tacos from the nearest roadside shop. Soon, his live-or-die lifestyle catches the attention of big-name sponsors. But one of them offers Omar more than he bargained for . . . a chance to become the first member of the mysterious 900 Revolution team and claim his place of history.

TONY HAWK'S 900 REVOLUTION VOL. 2: IMPULSE

When you skate in New York, it's about getting creative, and fourteen year-old Dylan Crow consider himself a street artist. You wo catch him tagging alley wa Instead, he paints the streets with board. He wants to be seen grind rails in Brooklyn and popping oll at the Chelsea Piers. But when Dy starts running with the wrong crow his future becomes a lot less cert . . . until he discovers the Revoluti

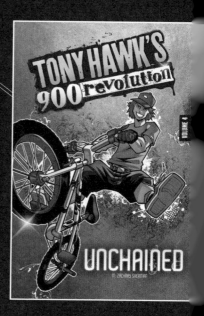

TONY HAWK'S 900 REVOLUTION, VOL. 3: FALL LINE

Amy Kestrel is a powder pig. Often hidden beneath five layers of hoodies, this bleach-blonde, CO ski bum is tough to spot on the street. However, get her on the slopes, and she's hard to miss. Amy always has the latest and greatest gear. But when a group of masked men threaten her mountain, she'll need every ounce of the one thing she lacks — confidence — and only the Revolution can help her find it.

TONY HAWK'S 900 REVOLUTION, VOL. 4: UNCHAINED

Joey Rail learned to ride before could walk. He's tried every wheeled sport imaginable, but always comes back to BMX frees The skills required for this da sport suit his personality. Joey i outdoor enthusiast and loves ta risks. But when he's approac by the first three members the Revolution, Joey must n a decision . . . follow the same path or take the road less trave

IMPULSE

. . . Nestled inside the wooden container, on top of several strips of newspaper insulation, sat the broken tail of an old skateboard. Splintered and frayed, the wooden kicktail still had part of its grip tape intact on top. However, the graphic on the bottom was almost scraped off from overuse. The Artifact measured three inches wide and six inches long.

"A broken skateboard deck! Really? Seriously? This is so stupid!" Dylan Crow pulled the Artifact out of the box and waved it in the air, upset and confused.

Detective Case gazed at Dylan's hand gripping the board piece and shaking it violently.

"Kid, look — look at your hand!" he said.

Dylan's face suddenly changed from anger to shock at what he saw.

A stream of electricity flowed over his hand. The strange energy enveloped it, making a slight crackling sound. It trickled out of the board and onto Dylan's fingers and palm.

"What is this?" asked Dylan.

The teen started to get scared.

He'd never seen anything or heard of anything like this before. The blue bolts leaped from fingertip to fingertip as he wiggled the broken board in his hands.

Smiling from ear to ear, Case tried to calm him.

"Kid, that's the Artifact!" he explained.

"What?" Dylan squeaked out.

"It likes you," said the detective. "I don't know why, but man does it like you!"

"That's great," said Dylan. "But what is it?"

Case shook his head and shrugged. "Seriously, we don't really know. I mean that? That's a kicktail from a broken skateboard. But the energy —? Some people think it's a key. One that, when assembled with all its other parts, will unlock some kind of power . . . . If those guys were to get their hands on it, who knows where it could end up. We can't let that happen!"

Quickly, Dylan placed the tailfin back in the box. He slammed the lid, locking the latch back in place.

The electricity promptly stopped.

"I don't care," he said and quickly handed the box to Detective Case.

Read more about Dylan Crow in the next adventure of . . .

Tony Hawk's 900 Revolution